A Midwest Horror

A Midwest Horror

By

Kristoffer Ryan

This novel is just a work of fiction—relax. Any resemblances would be not only coincidental but pretty scary.

First Edition

Cover art by Norbert Yates

ISBN: 979-8-9909594-3-9

Chapter 1

The whirring of the mosquitos was enough to drive him mad any other time, but today, he could barely hear them. In fact, he didn't even notice them. His mind was too busy buzzing around itself, trying to make sense of the worst day he had ever had. The stick he had been using to push the cat turds around the disused sandbox became a fly swatter. His arm reflexively flailed in the air in front of his face, trying to drive the buzzing horde away as they were becoming impossible to ignore.

Maybe it was time to go inside?

"SHE NEVER EVEN TOLD ME I WAS WORKING THE GODDAMN MORNING SHIFT," came a shout from somewhere inside the house.

That was all the motivation he needed to plunge the stick back into the sand and continue shifting it around to see if the cats hadn't buried something more interesting than what he had been finding. He looked at the rest of the sandbox fort and remembered the summer his dad had built it for him and his brother. Back before he knew how bad dad's drinking could make life for everyone.

Now, the fort stood as a monument to a better time and was mostly used as the neighborhood litter box.

One of the mosquitos landed on his cheek and as he slapped at it, his finger bumped into his swollen and bandaged ear.

"Crap," he said to the mosquitos.

His eyes darted around the yard in a panic, and he prayed to God that nobody had heard him swear.

He was safe.

No one else was dumb enough to be outside after the sun started to set and the swarm of bugs emerged. This summer had been particularly wet and all Northern North Dakota was infested with bugs or flooded out as Devils Lake continued to grow with each rainy day. That didn't matter much to him. All he cared about were the frogs and garter snakes that had shown up to eat all the bugs. He and his little brother, Chris, had spent the last few months catching as many as they could. There was no real point to it as they inevitably let them go, but it had become a competition, one that kept them outside and away from the chaos inside.

However, despite what the adults were calling an Indian Summer and it still feeling hot out during the day, the snakes and most of the frogs had retreated to their burrows. All that was left was falling leaves and bugs, mainly mosquitos. The adults were all waiting for the first good freeze to relieve them of their nuisance, but he had been hoping that it would stay nice, at least until Halloween.

The last few years of trick or treating (and really the only ones his eight-year-old mind could remember), they had spent more work than it was worth digging a tunnel through the snow to get to the neighbor's house to trick or treat…to then get turned away because the owner hadn't even left home to buy candy. He remembered last year, he only got a Mary Jane or two from another neighbor across the street. It just never felt worth the effort and the cold to venture out.

This year, though, all his wishes had been answered. Tomorrow was Halloween. It was still nice out and surely, all that candy would be enough to wash the taste of the worst day of his life out of his mouth.

He could feel a bead of sweat running down his cheek where he had slapped the mosquito a minute ago, and he wiped the bead away. He looked at his hand after catching the drip and saw that it was blood. Instinctively, his fingers reached back up and traced the source to his ear, which was still throbbing. He knew it was an accident, but it didn't help assuage his anger toward his dad as he thought back on the start of his horrible day.

***

Breakfast was ready to go by the time he reached the bottom of the steps that morning. His mom was waddling her way out of the kitchen carefully holding the pot in front of her. His eyes searched the table, as it looked fuller than usual, and he was trying to figure out what was different.

"Crap," he thought.

As soon as he thought the swear, mom interrupted his train of thought. It was like she knew what he was thinking.

"Drew, go get your brother. Your dad is home, and he is not in a good mood," she said in her quietest but most serious tone.

"Ok," Drew said and nodded as he turned quietly and made his way back upstairs.

Drew knew his dad was going to be in a bad mood today, but he hadn't expected him to be home for breakfast. Dad was usually out the door and at work before Drew even got out of bed. His heart picked up speed as he got to the bedroom he shared with his brother, and his anxiety grew thinking about dad being home for breakfast.

"Chris, get up." He shook his brother's foot from the end of his bed.

"SHUT UP!" Chris yelled and kicked the air where Drew's hand had been.

"You shut up; dad is home," Drew responded in a tone similar to what his mom had just used on him.

Chris shot up in bed.

"Crap."

He jumped down and raced around the room, grabbed his pants from the floor, then started trying to dig through the mess in the dresser to find a shirt. Drew saw him struggling and grabbed a clean shirt from the pile of folded laundry that sat on top of the desk. The dresser was there, but putting stuff in there took too much time. The pile was more efficient.

"Here, hurry up," Drew said and turned to hurry back downstairs. If Chris got in trouble now, it was going to be his own fault.

When Drew got back downstairs, mom was in the living room with two babies in car seats who just arrived. It was the first of the babysitting kids. The babysitting kids was what he and his brother had called the group of strange kids for as long as mom had been using their house as a daycare facility. There were only two babies right now, but after school, there would be another ten kids digging through his stuff and making a mess that he was going to have to pick up.

Drew hated them.

Chris joined him at the table, and both were now sitting quietly, waiting for dad to emerge. Drew hoped dad wouldn't be as mad as mom figured he would be. Mom made her way back to the table after propping the bottles for the babies and was in the middle of putting the pale, soggy oats into the bowls when dad opened the door to his bedroom. The look on his face said it all. Unfortunately, he looked as angry as Drew hoped he wouldn't be.

The silence around the table was painful as they waited for him to dictate the morning.

He sat in front of his bowl of oatmeal and ignored it, instead choosing the newspaper.

"I can't believe we pay for this garbage; I should be getting the damn thing for free since I'm the one pushing all the paper. You think that bitch would even consider it?" It was a question no one could answer without drawing his anger, so everyone stayed quiet.

Drew knew his dad hated his boss, some lady named Linda, but he didn't know why. What he did know was that his dad left to "push paper" at the newspaper printer and he was usually gone by now. Then he would get home, eat dinner, start drinking, and wait for someone to slip up.

Right now, all Drew wanted was to finish this oatmeal and get out of the house. He knew the school wasn't open yet, but he could take his foam football and play catch with Chris until the other kids started showing up. He shoveled another spoonful of the mush into his mouth, trying to swallow it before he started gagging. Oatmeal was the bog-standard breakfast at his house and despite him not hating the taste, the consistency made him a gagging nightmare.

His dad rattled his paper and Drew's watery eyes met his. There was a flash of anger and Drew knew immediately that he better swallow or he was going to hear it. As he pushed the lump of mush toward the back of his throat, there was an all-too-familiar resistance. His fingers flew to his mouth and began to pull.

Part of the hair had already made its way to his throat. Drew could feel it pull past his gag reflex as he lost it and gave an audible, "HURRR."

"Oh, Jesus Christ, here we go. WHAT?" his dad yelled as he threw the paper into his own bowl of oatmeal.

Drew, who was still fishing the last couple of inches of the stray hair out between his lips, looked at his mom, whose hair was billowing about her nightgown in an "I don't give a shit" fashion.

"There was another hai…HURRR," Drew tried to explain through a gag. The tears were flowing now and not just from the gagging.

"Just pull the damn thing out," dad said daringly. He was as familiar with this fight as any, and his tone implied he wasn't in the mood.

"No, it's ok, Steven. I'll just toss it," mom said as she reached over Drew to grab the bowl.

Suddenly, there was a flicker of movement and the familiar jingling of a belt buckle. In one not-so-swift motion, his dad had pulled his belt out of its loops and let it fly. Only, he let go of the wrong end. The buckle made a resounding crack as it hit the side of Drew's head. Drew's arms grabbed out for the table and tipped the mostly full bowl of oatmeal onto the floor. He instinctively tucked his head down below the edge of the table for safety in case of a second incoming blow. When his eyes would focus again, he could see blood dripping into the oatmeal, which only made his stomach turn again.

"HURRR."

Without a word, Steven stood up, backed away from the table, and walked into the bathroom. When he came back, he had a roll of toilet paper, which he tossed to his wife.

"Put this on it…How bad is it?" he said with his head already turned toward the door.

"It's bad. His ear is split at the top." Her hands were busy investigating and applying the toilet paper.

Drew was trying his best not to cry despite the free-flowing tears. The ringing in his ears was only intensifying and the side of his head was throbbing. He was mostly scared his dad was going to get mad again, but part of him was grateful that the hair-enriched mush had ended up on the floor. At least he didn't have to finish eating it.

Through all of this, Chris had silently finished his oatmeal and was now racing to the opposite door that dad was eyeballing. He was trying to get his shoes and his backpack on before he drew fire as well.

"Chris, before you go, grab me that white tape in the bathroom drawer," Mom said, cutting off his escape.

With his shoes untied and his backpack struggling to keep up, Chris shrank past dad on the way to the bathroom. There was a commotion in the bathroom as, for the second time today, Chris rummaged through a messy drawer.

Dad decided he had had enough of being a family man for the day. He made his way to the kitchen and back door.

Before he left, he yelled back, "Sorry I got so mad, Coyote; I'll take you for a drive when you get home from school."

Drew's ears perked up at the word *coyote*. His dad always pronounced it Ky-oat. It was a nickname he gave him on one of their drives. The drives were always a good time. Dad would take him out on some back roads and crack a few beers or have

Drew mix him some rum and Cokes. Then they would just drive. Sometimes, they'd even stop to fish while dad took a piss. The drives had always been Drew's favorite thing to do. Only lately, the drives had soured a bit. They had gone from being lighthearted day trips to dad bringing his gun and talking about killing himself.

Although recently, dad had been letting Drew drive. He was small and could barely reach the pedals on his dad's Travelall, but he had gotten the hang of it. Last time they went out, dad had told him he was glad he was getting so good at driving, so that after he killed himself, Drew could drive the car home because mom was going to need it. At first, his dad talking about killing himself made Drew cry himself to sleep. But, over time, the repeated threats had lost all meaning and suicide drives were just another normal day, only with something fun to do.

"It's ok. Sorry about the oatmeal." Drew smiled through the tears as his dad turned his back and walked out the door.

Part of him felt bad for his dad despite the ringing in his ears, and he was excited about the drive after school. But there was an angry part of him that wanted to yell "Don't forget to load your gun!" It was small but over time, he could feel that part of him, the resentment, growing.

With Drew's ear clumsily bandaged, the boys made their way to school on the abnormally warm October day. Drew got more nervous the closer they got. He knew kids were going to ask about his ear and all he could come up with was to tell Chris that, if anyone asked, that they were playing catch and he caught it with his ear. Everyone could get a good laugh at his expense, but at least it wouldn't embarrass the family or dad.

After the bandaging of toilet paper and white tape by his mom (who never apologized for getting her hair in his food again), they were running late. They barely made it up the steps to the school when the late bell rang the first time.

"Later…and remember we were just playing catch, OK?" Drew said to his brother and pointed to his ear. Chris, who was racing off down the hallway already, yelled back.

"OK."

Drew knew he was going to be late if he didn't run, too, but there was an issue his bladder needed to take care of immediately that kept him from pumping his legs. As he rounded the corner near the bathroom and his classroom, his teacher, Mrs. Rockow, was in the hallway lurking, waiting for kids to be tardy.

"You'd better hurry, Drew. There will be no compromises," the too old to be a teacher yelled at him.

There was no way he could explain a late slip to his dad, so despite his better judgment, he made his way to class.

His bladder did not approve of this choice.

The classroom was already full of nervous kids as he made his way to the only vacancy, which was his seat. The kids sat absolutely silent, petrified of the decrepit old woman as she shuffled back into the classroom and slammed the door shut behind her.

Drew chalked it up to his kind of old-fashioned good luck that he had managed to have Mrs. Rockow as both a kindergarten and now a second-grade teacher when the school had shifted teachers around last summer. Drew's Grandpa would have probably explained that Drew only hated her because she was a good teacher, holding him accountable.

Grandpa probably would have been right, but it didn't stop the fact that she was scary.

"Will everyone stand for the Pledge of Allegiance," she said, staring at the flag, hand over heart.

The kids obeyed and chairs squeaked on the linoleum as they stood and placed their hands on their hearts as well.

"I pledge allegiance to the flag of the United States of America…"

Drew's mind couldn't focus past his ringing ear and bursting bladder, so he half-hearted the rest of the pledge and bounced in place.

After the pledge, he noticed Mrs. Rockow giving him the eye.

He didn't know if it was the bouncing or the ear, so he tried to relax and not think about taking a piss. He tried that throughout the uncomfortable math lesson, where her eyes constantly met his and he tried to keep his legs from bouncing. But as the social studies lesson got started, he knew he was in a losing fight. He had seen other kids get bathroom passes and run the gantlet of Mrs. Rockow's questions about what they were going to do in there, but he couldn't bring himself to interrupt class and ask for himself. He could feel a fluttering in his chest just thinking about stopping her and telling the entire class he had to pee. His cheeks flushed with shame just imagining it. Making the other kids not hate him seemed to be the hardest thing to do, and giving them ammunition like this was playground suicide.

Forty-five minutes until gym…He could go then when they went to the cafegymatorium. The gym teacher always seemed nice, and Drew knew he would let him go relieve himself without making a big deal over it.

Social studies was a distant memory as the urge to pee consumed him. Maybe he could just raise his hand and ask, he thought, trying to build up the nerve.

Then he remembered her big speech a month ago about telling on bullies and doing the right thing. Just an hour after her big speech, during playtime, he had seen a bully he hated breaking a girl's LEGO castle. Well, after raising his hand that time and trying to do the right thing, his teacher decided he was a tattletale. She proceeded to put a troll doll down the back of his pants, so the tattler had a tail. That recess with bright orange hair sprouting from his backside was miserable, and if he could just hold it for…he looked up at the clock.

Forty-four more minutes.

He could avoid whatever creative punishment she had in store for a kid who had to pee during her lesson.

Drew bounced in his chair for a minute as the lesson ended. He couldn't wait for gym class. Just as he was about to raise his hand, Mrs. Rockow stood up and said she had to go to the office.

On her way out the door, she made direct eye contact with Drew again and gave him a once-over, which made him feel even more uncomfortable. Now with the teacher gone, he was stuck—no one to ask permission, no one to punish him. Just him, his desperation, and a classroom full of kids waiting to laugh at him when he pissed his pants.

The kids all stayed quiet while working on their handouts. The only noise was coming from Drew's chair as his body bounced to fight back the urge from his bladder. He looked at the clock.

Twenty minutes to go…It was too far away. Drew knew at that moment that he wasn't going to make it.

A bit of pee started to flow and once it started, he couldn't get it to stop. However, the bouncing stopped. Drew froze in his seat, waiting for who was going to notice his shame first.

Then, right at the peak of his panic, when the drips began to hit the floor and echoed artificially in his mind like a telltale heart, the gym teacher walked into the classroom. He explained to the class that Mrs. Rockow was busy in the office so they could start PE a little early. Normally, this would have excited Drew. But, with his pants soaked in pee, it just seemed like another obstacle he would have to deal with.

His mind raced for a way out of this situation as they marched "right side of the hall, eliminate the fall" down the hallway.

There was none.

The only grace he could find was that the pee had completely soaked his shorts. At least they were all the same color and there was no obvious pee spot.

Once in the gym, the teacher sat them all down to explain how the rest of the day was going to go. They were going to play pumpkin tag and then afterward, they were all going to get changed into their Halloween costumes to get ready to go to the State School. Once they were all dressed up, they were going to go to a haunted house the residents had set up and trick or treat at the rooms of the old people.

He had reservations about going to the State School due to him recently having been attacked by monsters there. However, his mom had convinced him that the field trip was going to be at a different part of the facility where there were no people with "severe disabilities" as she phrased it. She explained, "Going trick or treating there is just a bunch of free candy from people's grandparents who don't have a place to live." Drew was still resistant to the idea, but all that free candy was impossible to resist. Plus, his entire class and teachers would be there, so they could protect him and would probably keep the monsters away, since it was such a huge group.

Lost in thought, Drew suddenly remembered something.

"Crap," he whispered to himself, then quickly checked the gym to make sure nobody heard him.

All of that stupid stuff with dad and the oatmeal made him forget his costume on the desk up in his bedroom. His mind began to race again, knowing that he was going to get in trouble with Mrs. Rockow for not bringing a costume. For just a moment, he forgot his wet pants and was panicking about his costume and the fact he hated field trips because it was always something: no lunch got packed, someone stole his dad's gloves on the sledding trip and now he was worried all day about telling dad he had lost his gloves, no money for the restaurant they stopped at, the kids were teasing him all day unsupervised, one thing after another. Field trips were just a bigger hassle than they were worth.

Lately, he had been "forgetting" his permission slips, and opting to stay behind and watch movies with a substitute teacher or sitting in a classroom that didn't go on the field trip. There was no getting out of this trip, however. Since it was in town and was only going to take a couple of hours, no permission slip was needed.

As the kids in the gym all got up from the semicircle around the gym teacher, one of them noticed the wet spot that had formed under Drew.

"Eww, what is that?" they yelled so everyone would notice.

Suddenly, the semicircle became a full circle, with Drew at its center. Now in a full panic, he searched for a way out and saw his gym teacher making his way to the middle and looking directly at the wet mark. Then, for some reason, the teacher looked straight up at the ceiling.

This was Drew's chance.

"I don't know." Drew looked around and gauged their response quickly. He saw they were still confused and not yet accusatory. "When we sat down, I didn't notice, but there was a puddle on the floor and now I'm soaking wet."

The kids all looked at Drew like they were all about to laugh. Then the gym teacher interrupted.

"Well, why didn't you tell me? That ceiling has been leaking all summer, and with that wind last night, we probably gotta get the maintenance man back up there."

Drew couldn't believe his luck. It worked. Now there was just the matter of his wet pants and his forgotten costume. As the rest of the kids started playing pumpkin tag, his heart was still in his throat, but he pretended to be involved, running when he felt like it was appropriate. From the sideline, he could see the teacher, just like Mrs. Rockow, was giving him a side-eye and before long, Drew knew something was up. As if to confirm this, the gym teacher beckoned with an outstretched hand.

"Drew, c'mon over here," he said in a friendly tone. It was not a tone many adults usually used with him, and it generally meant bad news, or that they wanted something.

Drew hurried over. The drying pee was starting to itch and burn, so he had to keep his legs apart, which altered his gait slightly. He ran up to where the gym teacher was and waited for the bad news.

Instead, the teacher had Drew follow him with another motion from his free hand as he made his way to the other side of the gym, where his office was.

Once inside, he walked over to a big box in the corner and began digging around. After a few seconds, he stood up and with a smile, he handed Drew a pack of tighty-whities still in the plastic and what looked to be a pair of used jogging pants.

"Here, sorry you got all wet from that leaky roof," he said as he gave Drew a warm smile.

Something in it told him he knew he had pissed his pants, but Drew found it hard to believe an adult would be that forgiving or nice.

"Why don't you go shower off really fast in the locker room and meet us back out here to put on costumes?"

This got Drew even more upset than he was before because he could tell the teacher was being nice and now, he had to make him mad and tell him he forgot his costume on his desk at home. The tears started again before the explanation, but Drew got it out anyway.

"Well, my mom had to fix my ear cos we were playing catch, and it got super crazy and then when I got to school and went to PE and I remembered I left my costume on my desk and now Mrs. Rockow is going to be even more mad cos she's already at the office…I'm sorry." Drew stood, not wanting to look at another disappointed adult, so he chose to eyeball the floor instead.

"Hey, no biggie, man. You go take a shower and when you get done, we will figure something out for a costume. It probably won't be as good as the one you made but at least Mrs. Rockow won't know the difference." He paused, then added, "Don't worry about Mrs. Rockow being in the office. I know why she's there and I can assure you you're not in trouble."

Drew couldn't believe what he was hearing. It sounded too good to be true. But as he looked at the teacher's face, he could tell he was being genuine.

"Ok, I'm sorry."

"Shut up with your sorry and go take a shower," the gym teacher laughed.

Five minutes later, Drew was clean, was wearing fresh clothes, and his anxiety had abated. He was now sitting in the gym teacher's office while the teacher tightened the strings for the paper plate mask that he had helped him make. The teacher had even changed the bandage on his ear, so it didn't look so stupid. Drew was starting to think maybe this day was going to turn around after all. Hell, he was on his way to go get free candy and had made his way through the mess that was this morning unscathed by his peers.

Then through his cut-out-paper-plate-eyeholes, he could see Mrs. Rockow, the principal, and a woman Drew didn't recognize marching toward the gym teacher's office, parting the pumpkin tag kids like the Red Sea.

Drew's heart sank.

Chapter 2

Drew used his stick and poked at the sand in his corner of the box, but the kitty repository had been exhausted. The mosquitos were eating him alive, so he abandoned the stick and prepared for hand-to-hand combat.

The swatting began. And judging from the yelling still echoing in the yard, he wasn't going inside quite yet. He still had some of his worst day ever to ruminate on anyway. It happened to be the worst part, and just thinking about it brought goosebumps to his flailing forearms.

There was no safety net offered by a nice gym teacher on the field trip to the State School.

***

Drew had developed a fear of the State School earlier that summer. He and his friend Jeremy had been riding their bikes on the sidewalk between the cemetery and the row of buildings that comprised the institution for the elderly, severely handicapped, and insane.

Usually, the ride past that area to the park was scary because the cemetery was adjacent to the sidewalk. The tombstones felt like a reminder that it was only a brief passing and eventually, he'd be in there with them permanently.

That day, however, there was a scene that caught his eye just as they rounded the corner.

There were a couple of ladies in outfits like what nurses wore. Drew was sure they had a title for what that job was but he couldn't recall it. He didn't have time to think that deeply on it, either, because the next thing he saw was the monsters in the wheelchairs that the nurse ladies were pushing around.

The one nearest him had a gigantic misshapen head that was almost perfectly round. A scraggly mound of hair that perched directly on top of its head was blowing in the breeze. There was a noise emanating from just behind this terrifying visage, a gurgling mixed with what sounded like laughter.

Drew's eyes momentarily left the person in the first wheelchair to see what was making the sounds behind it.

To his horror, the thing in the other wheelchair was making the sounds. Its head was also deformed, but unlike its companion, it was anything but symmetrical. Its forehead sprouted from the monster's face at an upward angle and as the wheelchair bounced on the uneven concrete, the mass jiggled. The chin on the monster's face had taken the opposite approach as its forehead and sagged away from her face in a lazy downward trajectory.

To Drew's young mind, their faces resembled a full moon and a banana, monikers that stuck as he regaled people with his tale of surviving the monster attack.

By the time he realized that he was on a collision course with the monsters, it was too late.

Jeremy had taken the high road up through the cemetery with his skills, which had been honed by three extra years on his BMX. Drew, unskilled and terrified, tried to turn off the sidewalk, but the edging was fresh, and the rut was deep. Just deep enough to trap his front tire and topple him when he over-corrected. As his body flew over the handlebars of his bike, he could already hear the giggles and gurgles of glee coming from the wheelchair-bound monsters. Their hands were all over him now, pulling at his clothes and his hair.

"HELLLPPP!" Drew screamed at the top of his lungs. This part was omitted in his retellings and since Jeremy was already long gone and not coming back, there was no one (outside of the nurse ladies) to say otherwise.

Drew could hear the nurse ladies trying to calm down both the monsters and him, but it was no use. They were fixated on the young boy lying bleeding on the sidewalk.

Panic set in, and Drew started to kick his legs and flail about helplessly in the monsters' grasps. The pulling stopped and when he opened his eyes, Drew could see only their huge misshapen faces filling his field of view. Suddenly, their grips were ripped free, and the nurses were pulling them by their shoulders back into a seated position in their respective chairs.

The moment the monsters released their grips, Drew scurried the few feet to where his cheap BMX lay, wheels still spinning. He grabbed it and in a moment of skill outside of his ability; he wheeled it around and began pedaling for his life. The only thing he could hear besides his own heart was the apologies coming from the nurse ladies.

Normally, he would have stopped and apologized right back, but not that day.

When Drew got home, he was still shaking, bleeding, and crying. He was near hysterics and by some blessing, his dad wasn't home, so mom could act more mom-like and less like a doormat.

Drew cried and tried to explain the story of how he was attacked by monsters and his mom, while bandaging his knee and wrist, tried to explain to him that they were just disabled people with deformities. She went on to explain hydrocephalus in her best layman's terms, but the explanation fell on deaf ears.

Drew couldn't possibly explain to her that monsters were real because he barely believed it himself.

***

Now fighting the tornado of mosquitos in the sandbox, Drew regretted not taking his own advice and skipping the field trip. He wondered what movie the kids who got to stay behind for bad grades got to watch. It could have been anything, and it would have been better than the morning he spent lying to the prying hens in the cafegymatorium and the afternoon at the State School.

***

The group of hens had made their way across the gym and through the awkward group of ogling second graders who had stopped playing pumpkin tag when the group of women marched through the crowd. They cut a beeline toward the gym teacher's office and him.

Drew sat and nervously wondered what was going on, but more importantly, he was worried if his dad knew what was going on and what his punishment would be later.

It didn't take long to find out.

"Drew, just make sure you tell the truth, OK?" the gym teacher said as the older women got closer to the door.

Suddenly, Drew realized the gym teacher's compassion and kindness had just been a ruse. The gym teacher was in on it, whatever it was.

Now feeling betrayed and vulnerable in borrowed underwear and jogging pants, his heart sped up and he could feel an acid taste at the back of his throat. A precursor he was used to since puking from nerves had become a regular thing. His mom had told him that "the butterflies are just kickin' your ass again," usually followed by a laugh. Drew swallowed the bile past his beating heart and steeled himself for the onslaught.

Letting them see he was nervous was a sure indication of guilt.

"Hello, Drew, I'm Mrs. Powers. You know Mrs. Rockow and Mrs. Thompson," she said before even closing the door behind her, giddy with excitement from getting to poke her nose around. She paused, waiting for a reply, but the shy and terrified Drew said or did nothing, so she continued. "We have become aware of a certain situation Mrs. Rockow has brought to our attention." She motioned at the hag next to her, who grinned and met Drew's gaze. "We are just concerned about your wellbeing. Also, we want you to know that anything said in this office will not be repeated and nobody has to know what we talk about, ok?"

Now confused, Drew nodded, almost hypnotized by her speech. Her tone didn't match his expectations of trouble, and this opening dialogue made it sound like maybe he wasn't in trouble after all. His guard lowered a bit, but his heart pounded away.

"We are worrying about how many injuries you seem to get. Last week, you had bruises up and down your arm."

Without warning, her claw-like hand reached out and grabbed his arm hard enough to leave a fresh set of bruises herself. She then waved his arm in front of the other hens. It looked like her hypnosis was working on them as well, as their eyes followed her finger up and down his arm, highlighting the yellowing bruises his dad had left when he was fighting with Chris last week.

Drew was now aware of what was happening, and he was defensive and pissed off. He had seen enough movies and after-school specials to realize what they were doing. His dad had a short fuse, but he was a good dad. He always took him on drives and took him to garage sales. Sometimes, they even got pancakes on the days when dad's stomach didn't hurt from the hangover, except dad always called the pancakes "panny wannies." Hell, they even had a camping trip planned for the dam outside of town if the weather stayed nice. "One more fishing trip before it freezes solid," dad had promised.

There was no way he would betray his dad to this group of busybodies. Drew's defenses went up, and he resigned himself to his usual tactic with adults.

Just don't talk to them.

"Now this week, it's your ear," she continued her examination and removed the fresh not-toilet paper bandage. "Is there anything you would like to tell us about? Maybe something going on at home?"

Drew faked his best confused look and pushed his shoulders up slightly. His head shook a vigorous no.

"Are you sure, Drew? It's safe here," she asked, almost pleaded. She needed something to talk about at coffee that evening.

Again, Drew shook his head.

"Well, would you like to tell us what did happen?" she pried.

Drew shook his head one more time, but this time added a bit of exasperation to settle the point. It didn't work.

Mrs. Powers stood arms crossed, now obviously getting irritated. He knew he would have to say something, and he just hoped Chris remembered to keep his end of the story straight.

"Well, me and Chris were..."

"Chris and I," Mrs. Rockow chimed in, never late to pile on.

"Yeah, well, Chris and I..." Drew looked for her approval. "Well, we were just playing baseball and he wanted to see how high up he could chuck it and if I could still catch it." He surveyed their reactions. "Well, just as it got really high, I lost it in the sun, and I turned my head just in time so it didn't hit me in the face."

The hen party looked at each other in disbelief as if they knew Drew had just lied, but his story was solid enough to sow doubt.

"Are you sure about that, Drew? This is the place and time if you have something to say where it can't come back to hurt you." Mrs. Powers attempted her last-ditch effort.

Again, the confusion sat on Drew's face and his shoulders shrugged. Though he stayed quiet this time. He was done with this conversation.

"Ok, well, if you don't want to ask for help, you're not gonna get it." Her facade fell completely now and the angry old bitch she really was, returned with a vengeance.

Sensing the shift toward anger, the gym teacher stepped in.

"Well, just remember, Drew, if you ever need help or need to talk to anyone, all of us are always ready to listen and my office is always open to you, especially if you need help making more costumes." His motives were nice enough from what Drew could tell, but if he was on the same side as the hens trying to get his dad in trouble, he was an enemy now.

Drew nodded in acknowledgement and waited for more questions. None came. Just one last snotty retort from Mrs. Powers.

"Well, I hope you know we are going to be asking your brother about this game of catch as well." She sneered, and the hens followed her out the door past his gawking peers.

It was out of Drew's hands now. All he could hope was Chris wasn't an idiot.

"All right, buddy, why don't you join the rest of the guys for some pumpkin tag and get ready for tricker treating at the State School." The gym teacher offered this with a smile that seemed sheepish as he rubbed his hands together in front of his chest.

"Ok, thanks for the clothes and the mask. I'll have my mom wash it and I'll bring it back on Monday." Drew bolted for the door, desperate to be anywhere but around the accusatory adult.

"Just keep it, buddy," the gym teacher called after him.

Drew heard him but already knew he would never take his sympathy. He didn't care if he had to sneak into the office and risk getting into trouble. These underpants and jogging pants were going back into that box one way or another.

Pumpkin tag made no sense. He must have missed the rules, or these kids were just ok with running around with no purpose yelling about rules at each other. Either way, Drew didn't feel like participating. His nerves were a wreck, and they still had the field trip to get over with. His sense of dread was building with every minute and the closer it got, the less enticing the free candy sounded. Today didn't feel like the day to test the waters at the State School where the monsters lived. But he didn't have a choice. No adult was going to listen to him.

There was no missing permission slip, no excuses that would work. Just a trip to a place he didn't want to go to with people he generally didn't like or trust.

"Ok, kids, time to go. Get your Halloween pails or pillowcases, make sure you got your costumes..." The gym teacher paused and winked at Drew, who thought, *Thanks, idiot, now everyone knows I forgot.* "...line up two by two and partner off. It's time to get on the bus and get spooky." He tried a fake movie-style monster laugh, which got all the kids going, except for Drew.

They paired off and Drew got stuck with the ginger kid, Devin, who acted like he was crazy. He could never shut up and was always bouncing off the walls. The exact opposite of Drew, who hardly ever talked and sure as hell wouldn't be bouncing off the walls with adults around. Devin didn't care about adults and seemed like he did whatever came to mind. Drew thought about his great luck again. Not only was he having to go to the monsters' house, but he was going to have to babysit this insane kid and get in trouble whenever he got in trouble.

As the bus bounded to life, the tacky fake spiders and spiderwebs swung around, tangling in the madness that was thirty or so kids and all their homemade costumes. The smell of Halloween paint, colored hair spray, and wax lips was intoxicating.

Halloween was usually Drew's favorite holiday and for a moment, he was lost in listening to the other kids talk about candy and their plans for tomorrow, as long as it stayed nice.

But, as the sprawling complex that was the State School grew and filled the windows on the bus, his heart filled with dread. The bile taste once again was the most prominent taste in his mouth.

"HURR."

Drew tried to gag quietly, but some kids heard and looked. Drew faked a laugh and tried to smile through his now watery eyes and added another more fake-sounding gag, pretending he was being gross for Halloween. His stomach rolled around violently. Something shifted and he felt like he had to pee again…at Moonface and Bananahead's house.

This was going to be a long afternoon.

Chapter 3

A neighborhood cat lurking in the bushes behind Drew startled him as it crunched through the leaves gathering in the bushes. Drew almost let out a squeal because his nerves were so shot, but he held it back. He was worried the sudden sharp sound in the evening's silence would draw some unwanted attention. His social battery was on E.

The yelling from inside had stopped and Drew knew it was only a matter of time before mom or dad got bored and came looking for him. He picked up a handful of what he hoped was sand and tossed it on the leaves to scare the cat away without hurting it.

The company the cat was offering was just as unwanted as everyone else's. As the stray bounced away into the gathering darkness, Drew's mind did the same and he drifted back to the worst time in history to take a bathroom break.

***

"Get out of the way, buttface!" Devin yelled at a boy twice his size. The half-pint ginger knew he was off limits for a beating because the teachers had explained that Devin just had more energy because he was special. Special was the code word for pain in the ass as far as Drew was concerned.

The larger boy rolled his eyes and put his arm up to let Devin and Drew get past.

"Sorry," Drew whispered as he passed the kid Devin had slighted.

He was desperate to keep up with his obnoxious partner. The last thing he needed was more trouble for letting Devin out of his sight.

"Shut up, pecker-head," one of the boys said to Drew loudly as he passed under his arm. The adults had already left the bus, so he was free to call Drew whatever he wanted without getting in trouble.

"Yeah, Stickboy, get out of the way," another boy shot the familiar insult at Drew.

Drew flinched, expecting a punch to the back of his head.

"Sorry," Drew echoed himself and scooted out the door to the bus.

The pecker-head insult stung Drew doubly. Not only was it a name he was too chicken shit to say at school, or anywhere he wasn't alone. It was also unwarranted because he had already apologized for something he didn't do.

Drew felt like a coward and hated it.

Mrs. Rockow lined them up and counted them off, all while explaining the expectations of the day…none of which Drew heard a single word of. His bladder was once again consuming most of his rational thought. The part of his mental capacity that was left was busy keeping an eye on Devin, hoping against hope that he wasn't going to get him into trouble with teachers or the other kids again.

But what the hell was he supposed to do? The adults couldn't even control this kid, but Drew could surely expect to get yelled at when Devin inevitably colored outside the lines.

However, all that fell to the side when Mrs. Rockow interrupted his misery with a final announcement.

"OK, CHILDREN." She clapped twice. "Let us continue into the building. And remember these people are being very nice to us, so we need to use our best manners—no staring, no pointing, no laughing. UNDERSTOOD?" She eyeballed the crowd menacingly.

More code words.

Drew knew this meant they were about to see some stuff that they would normally stare, point, and laugh at.

Drew got the feeling Mom had lied to him. How could she know where the monsters lived at the State School? She didn't even believe they were real. Everything she said was just more lies to get him to do what "the adults" wanted him to do.

By the time the train-like group of children entered the building, his bladder had made standing still nearly impossible. His hands were sweaty while they clutched the pumpkin-shaped pail, and the thin plastic strap was digging into his palm.

The half-hearted attempt at a mask from a paper plate was unsurprisingly falling apart, so he had to try to keep adjusting the string, so it stayed on his face. Ultimately, he ended up walking the first part of the tour with his head tilted back to aid in keeping the plate perched on his nose.

Panic was setting in as they moved into the building, away from the pristine lobby area staffed by humans. He could only assume most of the tunnels and closed doors housed unimaginable monsters waiting for an opportunity.

Drew's eyes were darting around, looking through any and every window, and he was praying he would not see Bananahead grinning back at him.

Every time he turned his head, he swore Moonface would be right behind him, reaching for his clothing again.

"First stop is the costume contest," Mrs. Rockow called out from ahead. Devin and Drew had been placed at the end of the line. More than likely, the positioning was strategic so the two moms who were chaperoning (and busy chatting currently) could keep a closer eye on the "special" kid.

Drew nearly laughed out loud at the mention of the costume contest and the thought of what he imagined he looked like with his head tilted back and a paper plate perched on his nose. However, he was in too dire a situation with his need to pee to risk a laugh and possibly piss himself the second time in a day.

His nerves were frayed, but he knew he better build the nerve to ask to use the bathroom soon. The adults would undoubtedly be annoyed by having to help him search for one. But as they rounded a corner, he spotted some relief. The all-too-familiar blue sign with a woman in a dress and a guy in a hat.

BATHROOM

Written in bold letters confirmed what he already knew.

There was no good reason not to ask, right now. His bladder wasn't going to wait much longer, and they weren't going to get any closer to relief.

"Excuse me, ma'am." Drew stopped in his tracks and turned. The panic was obvious, even under the ridiculous mask.

"Go ahead but hurry up…Devin, wait here for him. We will be up at the auditorium at the end of the hall." They continued their chit chat and walked toward the end of the hall, and all too quickly, they were again lost in their chit chat.

"Yeah, hurry up, pecker-head," Devin taunted, using the fresh insult he had just learned on the bus.

The insult carried none of the weight it had coming from the kids he wouldn't mind being friends with.

Drew ran to the urinal, but it was too tall, so he ran into the open stall next to it.

Pure bliss radiated upward from his groin. There were some footsteps in the bathroom with him and he wanted to turn and look, but he was boxed in by the pale blue stall divider.

The water turned on at the sink and Drew was partly relieved, as he doubted monsters would wash their hands.

The stream continued to flow from his bladder, and now he just wished it was over so he could fall back in line and be secure in the comfort of the herd.

"AGGHHHH." The scream left Drew's throat before he knew what was happening.

A torrent of cold water came down over the pale blue divider along with the pumpkin pail used to hold it. Drew was soaked with cold water and the screaming made him piss on the floor.

The dousing of water was followed by a maniacal laughter he knew belonged to Devin, and then the sounds of running footsteps. Devin's laughter got louder with every step he took, but Drew could hear it fade down the hallway.

The voices of the chaperones were obviously in hot pursuit.

That meant Drew was now alone and dripping wet.

He knew nobody in the class saw him leave the herd except the two ladies and Devin. The water dripped from his clothing and strands of hair were interrupting his vision. His paper plate mask and the nice not-toilet paper bandage were lying on the floor in a puddle.

Not sure what to do, Drew picked up the mask and tried to put the string back through, but the holes were deteriorating as the paper lost its fight with the water. Now pissed off, Drew took it and tossed it in the toilet, followed by the nice bandage, and for good measure, he threw his own stupid pumpkin pail at the bowl. It didn't fit, but it perched there anyway, smiling at him on the bowl.

With his heart racing, Drew ran into the hall, splashing as he went. The only information he could remember was that the kids were all going to a costume contest at the end of the hall. *How hard could it be to find a group of kids in this place?* Drew asked himself to assuage his fears. Then, he reached the end of the hallway, only to be confronted by two options looking like mirror images of each other. Neither gave any indication that it contained either a large group of kids or a Halloween party. He tried to hold his breath so he could listen better, but his heart was pounding too hard to make that possible. He contemplated shouting out but knew asking for help rarely worked and most of the time ended up in trouble.

One thing Drew knew was that he was fast. The monsters he had seen were mostly wheelchair-bound, it seemed. It was the only idea he had. At a full sprint, Drew chose left. Not for any reason other than it was on the same side of the hall as him. He tried to keep calm and look in every window, tried to hear every sound, but the panic was blinding him. At the end of the hall, impossibly, there were two more mirror-image choices.

Without breaking his stride, he chose the right side this time.

Then, up ahead, Drew could swear he heard kids laughing. He stopped and briefly felt relief, as he could most definitely hear laughter now. His feet took over again and he got closer to where it sounded like the noises were coming from.

Except it seemed weird. The closest he could get to the sound of his classmates seemed to come from an empty, dark, gym-sized room.

As Drew peered through the darkened window, he could make out Halloween decorations and orange lights, but some sort of decorations blocked the other side and his view. Drew saw movement in the darkness and was sure it had to be the other kids on the far side, probably being judged for their costumes.

Tentatively, Drew cracked the door to get a better listen.

Confirmed.

It was definitely his class, or at least part of it. He could recognize the voice of a bratty girl saying her too-often-used catchphrase.

"Bitchin'."

Followed by:

"Kathy, watch your mouth."

Despite the foreboding look of the gym, he walked in. He hoped he could just melt into the group and take his lumps from separating from Devin. The water had soaked him completely and as he took his first steps on the linoleum, his feet gave audible squeaks that echoed across the gym.

"They're here. They snuck up on us," he could hear a slow-sounding adult male say from somewhere in the darkness.

"Where, Where…Jimmy? Where are they?" a female voice called back.

"Over here at the other doors, they are tricking us…GET HIM!" the monster screamed out.

Drew could barely process what was happening. The scream ringing out through his open mouth didn't ask permission. Neither did his feet as he fled in blindness toward where he thought the rest of his class was.

Maybe it was a trick the monsters had planned to trap him and lure him into the gym by mimicking his classmates. The decorations seemed to come to life and suddenly, there were monsters surrounding him. Some were witches, and there were werewolves, vampires, zombies, ghouls, dead doctors.

It was everything Drew had ever been afraid of.

Somehow, they had all gathered in one place to attack him. Maybe Moonface and Bananahead had spread the word about him coming to their house.

None of it made sense. The hands were on him now and the shouts of "Get him" had turned into a Romero-esque cacophony of moaning. Drew kept screaming, but the fight was out of him, so he assumed the fetal position and waited for his flesh to tear from his bones.

Out of nowhere, the lights turned on overhead.

"Relax, HEY, EVERYBODY, RELAX." The panic in the stranger's voice was palpable.

Then a soft humming tone started making a BOOP BOOP BOOP noise over an intercom.

"Gymnasium, building C, response team please," a voice said calmly. Drew couldn't tell if it was a human or a robot speaking.

BOOP BOOP BOOP

There were more voices now, and the moaning was subsiding from the crowd. However, the hands were still all over his body. Drew briefly peeked out of squinted eyelids and could see it was two of the witches who were still groping him.

Hands appeared from behind the monsters and yanked them away. The next moment, the same hands returned and lifted Drew straight off the ground and into the air above the crowd.

From his new vantage point, Drew could tell he was in a world of trouble.

The people surrounding him were (in the fluorescent lights) not monsters. They were old people and handicapped people in costumes. Some of the costumes were even worse than the one he had deposited in the toilet.

Confusion was clearing itself naturally and making way for shame. He saw the rest of his class enter from the opposite side of the gym and his eyes locked with Mrs. Rockow's.

Drew was sobbing, without a costume, soaking wet, and had just been attacked by a group of senile dementia patients and handicapped adults.

The first thing Mrs. Rockow had to say was...

"Where's Devin?"

Drew didn't answer her.

The laughter and shouts of "Stickboy is crying" coming from the other kids would have drowned him out anyway.

Instead, he tried to hide his shame the best he could while perched on the shoulder of some strange guy, who in a minute, was going to wonder if the kid he helped had pissed on him because his shoulder was all wet.

The only saving grace was the same lady who let him go to the bathroom must have had some sense of responsibility for creating the chaos, as she offered to drive Devin and him back to school and home, respectively.

Mrs. Rockow didn't object.

Drew felt like he was dreaming as he directed the somewhat nice-looking mom to his house. It was hard to make conversation or entertain her questions, but he did his best. Mostly, he just apologized for getting her car wet and assured her it was just water from when Devin splashed him. She said she believed him and said how she would have screamed and cried if she got stuck in that haunted house with those patients, too. She wondered aloud who thought that going to the State School was a good idea for a bunch of kids.

Thankfully, she seemed to understand how to hold a conversation with herself, and the only expectation of Drew was to point out the correct turns to get him home.

As she pulled up in front of his house, Drew saw his dad's Travelall sitting in the driveway in the back yard.

That wasn't good.

He shouldn't have been home until late, especially since he didn't work that morning. Drew rubbed his ear in remembrance of his dad's appearance at breakfast.

"Thank you for the ride. Sorry about your seats." He tried to offer her a smile, but they were in short supply.

However, hers were not.

"Don't even worry about it. I'll blast the heater and it'll be dry by the time I'm home." Her big pretty smile full of lipstick and white teeth made him feel so good for some reasons that he wouldn't understand for a couple of years yet. But aside from being pretty, she was the rare kind of adult, the nice kind.

Her own smile was enough to get a smile out of Drew now.

He found one for her easily this time.

"Have a good night, thanks for the ride." He shut the door gently, so it didn't slam, and watched the pretty blonde disappear down the road. Part of him wanted to chase her down and ask what she was making for dinner.

"The hell are you doing home?" Dad shattered that dream from the window near the TV.

"I could ask you the same thing," is what Drew wanted to say.

"I uhh got wet at the apple bob at school, so they sent me home."

Drew was pleased with his agility. He hadn't even considered coming up with an excuse. The shock of being attacked by monsters and then humiliated was still wearing off. If anything, he had only expected mom to be at home. If dad had been at work, Drew would have been able to just tell her about his shitty day, and possibly, she would make him something hair-free to eat to make him feel better. He was already mad about missing out on all the candy at the State School and was starving since he missed breakfast.

For now, he was just glad he was cleverer than his dad.

"Ok, well shit, get in here and you can come on a drive with me, Ky-oat," he called out, only slightly slurred.

Drew couldn't believe his ears. Dad had actually remembered that he said he'd take him for a drive. Drew didn't even care if dad whined and was mad the whole time if he let him drive on the back roads. Hell, he'd even grab his gun for him.

"Ok, I'll get changed really fast." Drew was excited now and the trauma of the day melted away at the prospect of some one-on-one man time with dad.

"Well, put on some work clothes," he yelled into the mudroom, where Drew was stripping off his wet clothes at lightning speed.

Ugh, Drew thought. That meant they were getting wood or pickin' spuds (an activity Drew wasn't aware of the fact was stealing until years later). Well, either way, he was out of school early and there was no way his day could get worse.

Drew joined his dad in the Travelall a couple of minutes later after briefly talking to mom at the back door.

"Dad got fired, so just be good, ok? Do what he says cos he's probably in a bad mood." Mom breezed through the multiple warning signs like it was no big deal.

For her, it wouldn't be. She was going to be at home for a couple of hours until the babysitting kids showed up, and she would be watching soaps, and eating stuff she shouldn't be eating since dad said she was getting fat.

"Uhhh, OK," was Drew's only response as his nerves once again started to build tension, and he sprinted even faster toward the already running truck.

The drive to their first stop was in total silence.

Dad seemed sheepish, and Drew's ringing ear was probably the cause. Drew wished he could just say, "It's ok, dad, I know you didn't mean to hit me with the buckle" but somehow, he thought it would only make dad even more mad.

Dad parked at the gas station and left the truck running. A clear indication that Drew was meant to wait there. Drew watched him make his way past the cold case to the bottles. Then on dad's way back past the cold case, he reached in and grabbed two Pepsis.

Sweet.

Drew knew he was going to get more than "Make some room."

Just as he predicted, when dad got back in the truck, he tossed the two Pepsis toward Drew.

"Make some room for me and the other one is for you," Dad said without missing a beat.

Drew unscrewed the cap on one of the Pepsis and took a healthy chug. The sugar hit his empty stomach and for a minute, it threatened to roll over. Drew held it back. He thought about all the candy he missed out on by being a baby again and wondered how his classmates made out at the State School when they got done laughing at him.

Tomorrow was going to be his time, though. Nobody could stop him from filling his pillowcase (his pumpkin pail was probably still sitting on the toilet), as long as it stayed nice out.

As he pulled the Pepsi away from his lips, dad was already handing him the bottle of rum. Drew topped it off for him, put the lid on, gave it a gentle swirl, took the lid off carefully, and handed it back.

They were a well-oiled machine.

Dad grabbed his mixed drink and tossed a pepperoni stick at Drew's head.

"Here, I grabbed you one, too," Dad said as he took a bite of his own pepperoni stick and chased it with his rum and Coke. Drew could never figure out why he didn't call it a rum and Pepsi.

Starving, Drew snatched the pepperoni from the seat where it landed and he started munching away, copying his dad by chasing it with his own "Coke."

"Hey, I'm gonna need your help tonight, but also in the next few weeks." Dad took another bite and chased it; Drew did the same. "I uhh made some changes at work and while I find something else, you guys are gonna really have to help cut corners and not complain about stuff, ok?"

Drew noticed the lack of a gun in the car, so he listened carefully, as it wasn't his dad's standard pity parade.

Besides, he didn't know what else he could cut out of his life—so many corners were cut already that most days felt like circles. So, all Drew offered was an ear and the occasional nod as his dad muttered on.

The mixed drink was doing its job well, lubricating his jaw.

A few miles down the road and a list of reasons about why dad was frustrated with his life later, Drew realized why he was wearing work clothes.

"Are we going to see Grandpa?" Drew asked, trying his best to seem excited or at a minimum, not aggravated. He loved Grandpa but he and dad always got in a big fight.

"Yep, he needs help stacking wood in the basement…Why?" dad asked.

"No reason, just wondering," Drew lied.

Drew's worst day ever wasn't over yet.

Chapter 4

The mosquitos were draining Drew alive. The night air was muggy and thick with decay. Mom and dad's fighting was still echoing around the yard, but Drew had a smile on his face anyway as he recalled the visit to Grandpa's house. It managed to be the best part of his day despite there being a bit of work involved. Grandpa always had a good story and a soda or two for the road.

***

The ruts in the driveway at Grandpa's house were deep. They twisted the chassis of the Travelall as it lumbered its way to the end of the driveway and the beginning of the chore to come.

By now, dad was incapable of avoiding the gouges in the road. The wheel twisted in his hands like a ghost was in control and dad didn't seem to mind because it seemed to know where it was going, and he was too drunk to fight with it anyway.

The truck momentarily left the road as the ruts ran shallow at the end of the driveway near the parking lot by Grandpa's house. Dad resumed control of the vehicle and swerved into the empty spot beside Grandpa's own disused truck. Dad swished the rest of the rum and Coke around in the bottle, tipping it up to finish what was left. Drew eyed his own drink and wasn't about to finish it off because he wanted to save it for watching scary movies later if he ever got time tonight.

"You ready? Did you bring your gloves?" Dad asked as he swung his door open.

"Crap," Drew said and immediately regretted it.

Dad gave him the side eye, then took his own gloves and smacked Drew in the chest with them, hard enough to make him gasp, but soft enough to make him laugh.

"Watch your mouth, kid."

As the gloves fell into Drew's lap, he shifted his pop out of the way, grabbed them, and swung his own door open.

It was the best he had felt all day. He didn't care if the gloves smelled horrible and felt slimy on the inside. He was just glad dad was in a good mood.

The doors to the Travelall slammed in tandem. Then almost instantly from the porch came a booming voice.

"Jesus, Stevie, you almost hit my damn truck. You already at the bottom of another bottle or what?" Grandpa's thick old voice yelled.

"Hell, no, it's your damn driveway, you old coot. You better get somebody out here to blade it." Dad tried to laugh the insult off, but the older man wasn't having it.

"Well, maybe if you could show up and help without me having to call you a dozen times, it wouldn't get so damn bad," Grandpa huffed. He was nearly ninety, but he was still imposing. "You keep it up and you're gonna be the next one to make my shit list."

Grandpa was referring to a list of names he kept updated of all the people who had pissed him off. The list itself was located on the lid of his toilet seat. He would plug in his soldering iron and burn the offending family member's name into the wooden lid for all to see and contemplate while they did their business.

"Just like your dad, lost in the bottle and lazy." Grandpa was nearly yelling at this point.

Drew could tell the last bit had stung his dad. Dad lowered his head and marched up the steps to the porch, where Grandpa was waiting with the door open and said nothing.

Drew's real grandpa had died when Drew was only two, so he didn't have any actual memories of him. Dad liked to talk him up when his jaw was properly lubricated, but other than that, never really talked about him. A few times, Grandma had tried to "set the record straight" about how his real grandpa wasn't a saint. Drew never wanted to listen to too much of it because it made him feel guilty talking about a guy he never really knew. Great Grandpa just became Grandpa for both dad and Drew.

"Oh, jeez, I see you brought some help. Which one is this?" Grandpa joked. That was his standard greeting for any of the many grandkids he had.

"Hi, Grandpa," Drew said, keeping it short. He had never drawn the ire of his grandpa and sure as heck wasn't going to end up on his crap list.

"Stevie, don't even bother going inside. Head out back and take the window off cos I already got the split stuff on the trailer next to it," Grandpa barked.

Dad flung his gloveless hand up in agreement and marched, head down, around the back of the house. Drew followed his grandpa into the house as the old man held the door for him.

Before he got too close to the open door, Drew pulled in one last breath of fresh night air and prepared himself for the onslaught.

Drew only managed to hold his breath a few seconds and when he took his first breath from the inside of Grandpa's house, he nearly gagged. His stomach was aching from all the false alarm gags and lack of anything to eat but a pepperoni stick. The smell of raw garlic and onions was overwhelming. It was so thick, he could hardly take a second breath. His eyes watered as he made his way through the kitchen toward the steps leading to the basement, where the smell was only horrible, not impossible. Drew had wondered many times on his visits how his grandpa could stand to live with the smell.

One time, when he was younger (and dumber), Drew had just outright asked Grandpa about the smell. His grandpa had first offered him an eagle's claw, which was when he took one of his six nubs he called fingers (He lost the fingers to bandsaws and table saws with increasing velocity as he grew older. He kept the fingers in the freezer in case they could figure out how to put them back on someday.) and poked you as hard as he could on the top of the head. Then he offered Drew the simple explanation that the reason he outlived everyone in his family, including four wives, was that the majority of what he ate was raw garlic and onions. The answer seemed reasonable to Drew, so he never asked again, although he wasn't about to emulate the practice.

The basement offered some relief, just as he had expected, and Drew sucked in a breath of fresher basement air. When dad finally got the storm window off the outside of the house, the fresh blast of cooling night air was more than welcome. As soon as the board on the window slid out of the way, chunks of split firewood started flying in, nearly hitting Drew in the legs. He stepped back and let his dad get a head start on him.

"Let him make a pile before you get started or he'll take your damn head off," came a voice from behind Drew in the basement.

For some reason, Drew thought of Bananahead and let out a squeal. He spun, nearly tripping on a log.

"Jeezaloo, you're a jumpy little fella…why don't you go grab a beer and calm your nerves." Grandpa smiled and rubbed his nubby hand through Drew's hair, sparing him an eagle's claw.

Drew wriggled away and gave him a giggle.

"Ok, Grandpa, you want one too?"

"You bet your buns I do."

Drew ran back up the steps, holding his breath, and flung open the fridge at the top. There were a couple of silver bullets and some PBR, but Drew knew better and grabbed two A&Ws. Then before he was out of breath, he ran back to the tumbling chunks of wood and Grandpa, who was now sitting in his chair by the police scanner and a small black-and-white TV, which seemed to have sprouted wire hangers in every direction. He handed Grandpa one of the pops after he cracked the top for him.

Grandpa eyed the root beer quizzically for a second and gave Drew a wink.

"Good choice."

Then Grandpa noticed Drew's ear. Drew had re-bandaged it and his clumsy work was an eyesore. He was surprised it had taken Grandpa this long to see it.

"What'd you do to your ear?"

Drew tried to be quick on his feet because he knew Grandpa could smell a lie a mile away.

"Nothing, just being stupid." Drew hoped the double talk would help Grandpa imagine it was him being stupid, playing too hard, rather than being stupid and not just eating his hairy oatmeal.

As the wood continued to tumble in, the awkwardness grew. The double talk seemed to work as there was no follow-up about his ear. But the silence was painful. Drew never knew what to say to adults.

Thankfully, Grandpa didn't care much what anyone thought and just let his mouth do its thing.

"You remember what I told you about life and how, if you let it take control, it acts like those damned ruts in the driveway?" Grandpa was looking out the window at his drunk and muttering grandson clumsily tossing the split wood through the window. "Well, the quickest way to find yourself in one of those ruts is to follow your old man into a bottle. Stick to these." Grandpa smiled a weary, tired smile and shook the A&W in his hand.

Drew thought back to the many warnings about ruts and taking life by the horns and avoiding the ruts or risking ending up a lonely old man begging for help from a drunken grandson. Those adult worries seemed a lifetime away, but the warnings never landed on deaf ears. Drew knew he would never get in a bottle like dad.

"So, Drew…or Chris?" Grandpa smiled. "You got your Halloween tomorrow."

"Yeah, hopefully it stays nice out," Drew said.

"Well, I got a feeling it's gonna stay nice for a coupla more weeks. At least that's what the almanac says and I ain't about to argue with it. You gonna hit the whole town twice and fill your pockets with candy?"

"I hope so. I had to go home early from school cos I got wet at the apple bob today, so I missed out on all the candy from the old people at the State School." Drew winced at the lie and inadvertent insult that just came out of his mouth.

Grandpa gave him the same side eye he had given dad when he lied about not already being in a bottle.

"Well, that ain't no good. Nobody's got as much money to waste buying candy to give away to kids as us old people do. Too bad you got wet at an apple bob…" he said sarcastically and gave another side eye to Drew. "Well, I didn't get you any treats except that sody-pop and I'm too old for tricks. How about I give you a scary story instead…a real one from when I was about your age." Grandpa was sly. He knew Drew was a sucker for anything scary.

Despite being terrified most of the time, Drew still got a bang out of anything horror-related and, just like Grandpa figured, he was already hooked.

"Sure."

"I bet your old man never even bothered to warn you about the Sidehill Gouger, did he?"

"Uhh, nope." Drew had no idea what he was talking about.

As Grandpa began his story, the sound of the wood being tossed in the window and dad's muttering faded, and even the sound of his grandpa's voice seemed to match the cadence of Drew's imagination.

Drew was immersed.

***

The Sidehill Gougers were ferocious beasts that used to live exclusively in Northern Europe, where our families were from originally. Only trappers and mountaineers ever saw them because the monsters' range was limited by the hills and mountains. Their bodies resembled a stout goat or a thick elk, depending on its age. But instead of fur, they were covered head to toe with green and yellow scales, which helped them blend into the gentle rolling hills of the lowlands. Their tongues were forked, and the Gougers spat them from their maws constantly, tasting the air for something to eat. And as for what they ate, it was nothing but fresh meat. If the heart wasn't still beating in its victim's chest, racing with fear, the meat wasn't fresh enough. Their hooves were cloven like a goat's, but on each toe was a claw it could use to grasp and rip flesh. At night, its eyes burned yellow, and it was the last thing many men had ever seen.

However scary as that might sound, the most identifying feature of this creature was its legs. One set of legs, could be left or right, was longer than the other. The offset legs made them well-adapted to running around mountains carving spiraling trails as they went with their sharp hooves. But when and if they tried to turn around, the long legs being on the short side would force them to tumble from the mountains to their death. Also, if they ended up on flat terrain, the unbalanced legs would force them to spin in circles until they starved to death.

This evolutionary development meant they were trapped in the lowland hills and mountains of Northern Europe. That was until I made a horrible mistake.

You see, Gougers are born either clockwise or counterclockwise. If the left legs were longer when they were born, they were clockwise, as they could only navigate the hills in that direction. Same goes for the counterclockwise Gougers, except in reverse.

Typically, when an counterclockwise Gouger meets a clockwise Gouger, their only option is to fight to the death as turning around is death for both.

Or that's what we all had thought growing up.

People would often hear strange noises in the mountains and more often than not, they would chalk it up to mortal combat between opposing Gougers. This kept most kids and unexperienced people out of the danger the hills and mountains offered.

Until one fall, when a blight hit the crops and unrest hit the governments, and starvation became a real possibility. The danger of the high grounds and the Gougers paled in comparison to starving to death or watching your family do the same.

So, the braver, younger, stupider kid I was back then had to do something. I got it in my head that I was going to go on a trek up in the woods and hills, and I wasn't coming home until I had something to eat for everyone.

I set out early before anyone in the family could ask any questions and object. By the time I was too far up in the hills for anyone to come for help, I started to feel like I had made a terrible decision. Not only were there Gougers to be afraid of, but the ground was wet and steep. I nearly fell a dozen times, and my damp cheap clothes weren't doing much to keep the cold out. After hours of feeling out of my element and at my physical limitations, I decided to turn around. I thought I was lost for a moment, then I came across a path in the woods cleanly cut into the hill. I traced the path with my eyes and saw it corkscrewed its way up to the top of the hill.

Since the going was easier on the trail, I carried on and tried to at least make it to the top. I thought maybe, with the higher vantage point, I could see something that would lead to a meal and a more unobstructed route home.

The path was so cleanly cut, it almost seemed manmade, except for the many cloven footprints that lined it and lack of any evidence of human footprints. Clearly, something was using it often.

By the time I reached the summit, I was exhausted and had resigned myself to making it straight back home after I took a cursory look around. Well, to my surprise, perched right there at the top near the end of the trail was a nest made of rocks. In the center of the bowl-shaped mound were six yellow and green eggs the size of cantaloupes. I had no idea what kind of bird had laid the eggs, but I wasn't going to look a gift horse in the mouth, either. There were six of us at home and it seemed like a blessing from God or fate that I was to find that path and those eggs.

I took my hessian sack from my bag and wrapped the eggs in my bedding and extra clothes to ensure they made it back down the mountain in one piece. There was a storm growing to the west, and it was headed my way, so I planned on running flat out down the trail and home with my bounty. I spotted a route that led just to the edge of the clearing where town started a few miles below me on the horizon. I noted some landmarks on the route, big trees and rocks, that I could use to make my way when I was buried in the woods, and just as I loaded up the last egg....

***

"All right, what the hell? Am I gonna be out here all night or what? DREW, STACK THE DAMNED WOOD," Dad yelled from the window.

Drew jumped like the Travelall as he left his own mental rut and returned from Northern Europe to land back in North Dakota.

His dad's voice had broken both his and Grandpa's immersion and Drew could've sworn that he saw Grandpa jump, too. If it was scaring him just retelling it, maybe it was a true story and not just a tall tale. Grandpa wasn't a liar, but he did like to tell a good story.

The lines of reality blurred in Drew's mind as he pulled on dad's stinking slimy gloves and got to work stacking the tossed-in pile of split wood up against the back wall. He was flying through the familiar chore, eager to get back to the story of the Sidehill Gouger.

The front door opened upstairs, and Drew could hear his dad cough and mutter under his breath about the smell. Drew noticed as he tested the air that he couldn't even smell the onions and garlic anymore. Maybe Grandpa was onto something after all?

The sound of the fridge opening came from the top of the steps, followed by the crack of a can. Drew could almost tell by the sound that it was a silver bullet. The look Grandpa gave Drew about the sound agreed with him.

"Can you stack and listen? I think your old man wants to get going." The sound of the front door slamming upstairs seemed to highlight this.

"Sure... Sorry," Drew said and continued to stack while he waited to be transported back to the top of the mountain in Northern Europe.

It was easy. Grandpa was great at this.

***

Ok, well, I was standing there looking at the storm and loading them eggs up when I could hear a scratching, clawing sound coming up the path I had just taken.

Scraaape...THUMP...Scrape...THUMP...

Through the clearing at the top of the mountain, I could see an animal I thought was a large deer making its way up the path. Except it was lumbering in a fashion that looked strange to me. It leaned over far on one side...Scraaape...then as it dragged a longer set of legs from behind it...THUMP. Then the monster locked its burning yellow eyes on me.

Well, I would love to tell you the story of how I fought the Gouger, and we ate Gouger meat for dinner, but that would be a lie.

What really happened was those burning yellow eyes went straight through my soul. My body chose flight, not fight. Before I even knew what was happening, I was running and tripping and slipping down that hill at top speed. I didn't care how dumb I looked or how wet I got. All I knew was that Gougers couldn't run in a straight line downhill—it had to take its own corkscrewed path down the mountain or risk tumbling to its death.

So, that's what I did, I ran in a perfectly straight line back home. If a tree was in my way, I ran into it. If a boulder blocked my path, I tripped on it. Nothing was going to make me break my straight line. My landmarks were completely forgotten.

Then a roar behind me almost made me freeze solid. It was guttural and full of bass. It echoed off every tree in the forest. Looking back now after seeing movies and the sounds monsters make in them...that's what it sounded like. How Hollywood makes monsters sound. Then it was joined by another, only this one was a slightly deeper octave and came from the opposite direction.

"OAAAAAAAAR."

The roaring and the running continued as the rain and thunder joined them. By the time I hit the flatland and the clearing outside of town, my lungs felt like they were full of hot lead. The rain was really pouring by the time I hit town, and the thunder was drowning out what was left of the roars of the Gougers back up the hill. I was too close to the comfort of home to stop running, so I sprinted with whatever energy was left in me. Right until I ran my straight line right through my own front door.

When the door flew open with wind and rain blowing in, mom objected, until she saw the look on my face.

She could tell I was terrified.

While I was telling my mom what had happened, my dad stumbled through the door. He caught the tail end of what I was saying and chalked it up to a wild imagination and a storm that had caught me off-guard.

That was until I went to my hessian sack.

It was still heavy, and I was praying to God there was enough left of the eggs as evidence to make my parents believe that at a minimum, I had found them. My hands went into the bag, and to my surprise, returned with a perfectly intact egg. I had no idea at first how the yellow/green eggs made it back with me tumbling down the mountain, but they had.

My dad gasped at the sight of them.

More than one belly from my brothers and sisters let out a roar, as they had sat listening to the story, when the eggs and the promise of a meal were revealed.

I tried to tell them we needed to take them back, that I had made a mistake. But dad, wanting to comfort the growling bellies of his kids, had all the excuses. Gougers weren't real, it's just eagle eggs cos they built their nests in rocks, could be some kind of lizard eggs or something. And, even if the Gouger was real, it was stuck in the hills and since we lived on the plains, we were safe.

The best excuse he had, though, was that everyone was starving.

I knew there was no reasoning with starving people and my stomach was just as empty. So, with a minimum of objections, Mom took the eggs (with much effort put into cracking the leather-like shells, which explained their survival on the panicked trip down the mountain), onions, garlic, whatever was left of the sad vegetables in the bin and made the most delicious egg hash any of us had ever tasted. The yolks of the eggs had a flavor like how a spice market smelled and the whites were as meaty as a steak.

There were no regrets as we went to bed with full bellies that night. As everyone snored and farted in their sleep, I lay awake for a bit thinking about my adventure and wondering if I was the first person ever who had bested a Gouger.

Scrape…thump…scrape...thump...scrape...thump.

I froze in my bed. It was the recently familiar sound of the Gouger. But the rhythm was much, much faster this time, double at least.

I rolled over in the bed I shared with my siblings and tried to get a look out the small upstairs window.

It was too dark.

FLASH…BANG

The lightning-thunder combo illuminated the yard and made my ears ring. But, in the flash of lightning, I saw them.

It was two Gougers.

They were leaning on each other with their longer set of legs on the outside supporting their weight and their shorter legs held between them, interlaced, dangling above the ground, and flailing in anger.

I couldn't believe my eyes. They were no longer trapped in the hills. They were at my front door. They were using each other's strong legs to overcome their genetic limitations. Holding each other with their weak legs and supporting their bodies with the muscular long legs had doubled their speed and their power.

I lost sight of them in the darkness, but a crash from downstairs let me know where they were. The next thing I heard was mom's screaming. Then it stopped abruptly. That's when the gurgling started. Not knowing what else to do, I reached from the end of my bed to the ladder that led up to our kids' loft and pulled it up.

A roar came from below us, and my younger siblings were crying and hiding under the blankets and me.

I told them to keep quiet. But the roars continued as I could hear the Gougers kicking everything in the house. Glass was breaking, wood was splintering, but all I could hear was the fading of my mom's gurgles for help.

Then there was a gunshot in the darkness, followed by a tremendous crash as I felt our entire house shake.

The roaring was back outside and receding to the hills. The calls for help, though, were growing as neighbors were responding to the attack. Someone called out from downstairs to the loft and told me to lower the ladder so they could get us out of there. I obeyed on instinct from the authority the adults represented — I lowered the ladder despite my reservations.

In shock, I assisted the other kids down one at a time, where they were being hurried away to a safe, dry, warm place to figure out what to do next.

Just as I lowered myself on the ladder, I could hear dad yelling from somewhere at the back of the crowd. My dad had been at the public house and when he saw the condition of his house, he flew into a fit of rage. He wrestled the rifle from our neighbor and took off into the dark through a giant hole the beast had torn through the back wall of our house in its escape.

Lightning flashed again and I could see my mom lying in a pool of her blood. Her face was twisted with fear and shock.

***

"DREW, are you about done down there? We gotta get goin' cos mom's gonna have dinner ready and I'm starving to death up here." Dad again broke their immersion.

"Jesus, Stevie, shut the fuck up for a minute," Grandpa snapped back.

Drew could have choked his father at that moment. All he wanted was to finish the story. But Grandpa yelling at dad brought a smile to his face.

"Well? What happened next?" Drew's eagerness earned him a smile from Grandpa.

"Well, maybe we ought to do the rest on another day. You can come stay over Christmas break if you want to and help me with some chores." The older man seemed to know that any frustration he earned would surely be put back on Drew on the drive home with his dad.

Grandpa's smile faded from his dry lips and he got serious again.

"Let's just say I never saw my dad again, and after we buried mom, they sent us to live with her brother who had moved to this godforsaken wasteland in this beautiful country. Every so often, though, I think I catch sight of the Sidehill Gougers passing between hills on the edge of my property, waiting for me to not be paying attention or to be too drunk to fight them off. And every so often, I curse myself for pissing off a mating pair of Gougers. See, near as I can figure was that counterclockwise Gouger and a clockwise Gouger had fallen in love rather than fight to the death. Then I came along and took their eggs. So, now maybe they owe me one and are coming after my 'eggs' …them eggs being you and your cousins and anyone else important to me." Grandpa didn't finish this story with his usual flourish and fun way. He was dead serious.

"LET'S GO…NOW!" Dad yelled from upstairs.

"You better get going, kiddo," Grandpa said, softening slightly from the story. "I'll put the window back on myself. Grab yourself another beer for later when you're watchin' movies on your way out," he said with another wink.

"Ok. Thanks for the story, and the sody-pop. I'll tell dad I'm staying over Christmas and I'll help with chores if you finish the story the right way. Wait, is the Gouger really here now…how?" Drew said, trying on the name Grandpa used for pop. He was unsure of how he felt about the story.

"Well, sounds like a plan to me. You better run, kiddo…love ya." Grandpa waved him away and clicked the TV full of hangers on.

"Love you, too. Bye." Drew sprinted up the stairs feeling scared, anxious, and entertained.

Right now, the Sidehill Gouger was just another thing to worry about. But he loved being scared. It added some excitement to the cut-corner circular days.

The drive home was quiet. At the end of Grandpa's driveway, and the ruts that reminded Drew of Grandpa's warnings about life and addiction, dad stopped.

Drew knew what that meant.

His door was open before dad's, and he was sliding into the driver's seat. By now, Drew knew all the dirt roads to take to get them at least to the bridge outside of town, which was on their street. Then it was just a matter of taking the alley to the garage.

Dad situated himself, then held up the Pepsi he bought earlier for Drew, who was saving it for scary movies that night.

Not that Drew needed another scare.

As he drove, Drew's eyes were locked on every hill, looking for those telltale corkscrew paths leading up to the rock nest full of green eggs.

"Mind if I finish this off, coyote?" Dad asked while he filled the void in the bottle with rum.

"Nope." Drew paused. "Hey, dad, why didn't you warn me about the Gougers?"

"The what?" dad asked, clearly puzzled.

Drew had never considered the fact that maybe Grandpa didn't share that story with dad because he didn't trust him or like him.

"Oh, never mind," Drew said and refocused his eyes on the road.

A few minutes, and the rest of his rum and Coke later, dad was sleeping in the passenger seat. Drew, however, was lost in thought about the worst day ever and the Sidehill Gougers. The lines from the plowed-under fields looked like long legs chasing their car down the road, like some kind of zoetrope monster.

Another slight bump on the horizon caught his eye, but to him, more closely resembled Mt. Everest. Drew could swear he could see the telltale spiral path leading up and up and…

The wheels of the truck left the road, and the ditch gave a sudden bump, which stirred his dad.

"Crap."

"You got it?" Dad asked, half-interested.

"Yep, sorry." Drew was already back on the road. His hands tightened on the wheel. He waited for dad to smack him for the swear, but it never came. Instead, the slow, heavy breathing of his sleeping returned.

The rest of the drive home was uneventful, although less fun than usual, as he was now searching everywhere for the Gougers and hills. By the time they pulled into the driveway, dad was back awake and trying to pretend he hadn't slept half the ride home.

"Ok, get inside and get some dinner."

Dad was going out to the shop. Which meant he wasn't done drinking. All Drew hoped was that dad would get drunk enough in the shop to stay out there and not interrupt the scary movies.

The back door offered only more misery on top of an already miserable day. He could smell what mom was making before he had even gotten inside. Spanish rice…the worst day ever wasn't over yet.

But at least he had the sody-pop from Grandpa for later on.

Then Drew saw the look on mom's face…it was going to be an even longer night than he had imagined.

Drew decided to quietly sneak back outside to stew on his day and to hide in the sandbox fort until he was forced to go in.

Dad went in a few minutes later, beer in hand, walking right past Drew without seeing him hiding in the sandbox pushing cat turds around with a stick.

The yelling started shortly after.

Chapter 5

Drew sat in his sandbox, done reflecting on his worst day ever up to that point. The cat turd supply had been exhausted. The moon was lighting up what the sun left behind. There was a swarm of mosquitos that would suck every drop of his blood if he dared sit still, and yet he still wasn't ready to go in. Drew couldn't decide what was worse—letting the mosquitos suck him dry or going inside with a freshly pissed-off dad.

Drew decided to let the mosquitos have their way. He wasn't going inside yet, not until he had to.

Mom's mood was still all over her face when he finally walked in the back door after she called him to come inside an hour later.

The first thing she did was eyeball the soda in his hands.

"Oh, no, you're not gonna suck down another soda and sit there looking at your dinner with a belly full of sugar. How many did your dad and Grandpa already let you have? And where did your dad go again? I just saw him. Back out in the shop or did he go to blow his last paycheck at the .45 Club?" Mom's questions came in a flurry. She hated the gun/drinking club his dad "belonged to." They mostly just drank and tried to win on the pull tabs at their favorite bar (unless someone had kicked them out for fighting again).

Drew took just a second to assess the situation. He pondered the list of questions and chose to answer the one that wouldn't get him in trouble while simultaneously putting her fears of soda to rest by putting it in the fridge. He was saving it for scary movies anyway, not chasing down crappy Spanish rice.

"Well, I saw dad a few minutes ago and he went back out to the shop; but I don't think he wants to go anywhere." He hoped the soda being shut safely inside the fridge and knowing dad was staying in for the night would put her in a better mood.

"Ugh, well, why the hell didn't he come back in and get some dinner?" She waited for a response, but when Drew's shoulders shrugged, she went into action.

The clinking on the plate was furious as she dumped a mound of the pinkish rice creation onto a plate. Then she grabbed two slices of bread and smeared them with a thick layer of margarine and tossed them on top of the rice.

"Here, take this out to him. Maybe he'll just sleep out there tonight and leave me alone." She hesitated. "Don't tell him I said that." She flashed a warning sign that Drew understood clearly.

Dad could be a jerk, but his anger was so sudden and sharp that it always caught Drew off-guard. As unpredictable as it was, the punishment happened right away when he got caught being stupid, so where the beating came from always made sense.

Mom, on the other hand, was sneaky. She would get mad and then let you think everything was ok. Sometimes, a whole day would pass. Then…SMASH…she would sneak up behind you while you were watching TV or eating or anything and smack you with her favorite instrument of fear. A gigantic plastic green ladle. Drew feared that ladle more than dad's belt, or fist, or whatever he could get his hands on.

"I wouldn't tell him that. I'm not crazy," Drew answered. It wasn't a lie. There was no sense in rocking the boat. He just wanted to watch *USA Up All Night*, or *Monstervision*.

Just as Drew was about to take the plate out to dad, the back door opened and he walked in.

The arguing started again almost instantly.

Drew didn't want to hang out and listen and catch flak. Eventually, when they got bored with yelling at each other, they'd look at him and more than likely, it would escalate to more than yelling. So, quietly, he slunk into the dining room and waited for his last hurdle of the day. The Spanish rice.

Dad left the kitchen in a huff, slamming the back door behind him and a few kitchen cabinets swung open quietly. Mom let out a startled squeak at the mysteriously swinging doors, then started more clanking in the kitchen. Drew smiled about the mysterious swinging doors. He knew why they swung open but nobody else did, and it scared them. Drew loved that he was the one doing the scaring.

After reflecting on the day, the State School, and the Sidehill Gouger story, his ear and the interrogation from the witches at school, Drew's nerves were shot. He searched around the yard outside the window while he washed his hands in the bathroom sink.

Drew knew there were no hills or mountains, but he still feared he would see the mating pair of Gougers standing there, leaning on each other, their short inside legs kicking around wildly, their burning yellow eyes watching him from across the yard.

The coast was clear of monsters, but there was another horror on the horizon—the smell of onions, tomato soup, and burnt rice filled his nostrils, making his eyes water.

Bailey was in the kitchen following Drew around, wagging his tail like a madman, hoping some food would end up on the floor for him. Or maybe he could smell the rice and knew his favorite kid was going to end up feeding most of it to him at some point?

Drew noticed the lack of his brother, Chris, who never seemed to get in trouble, and always had a friend's house to escape to for the weekend.

"Where's Chris? Lemme guess, a friend's house?" Drew yelled into the kitchen, snottier than he intended.

Mom flashed him a look of annoyance over her shoulder.

"Seems like you know already," she barely responded.

Drew wasn't jealous of Chris or his friends or the kids at school who had everything they wanted. He was jealous Chris was never around to get in trouble, or if he was, he had a "headache" and since he was younger by less than a year, his parents babied him. More than anything, Drew was jealous of how Chris and everyone else at school just seemed to get along and make friends so easily. It wasn't as if Chris or the kids at school were smarter or better than Drew at sports. Chris, in fact, was a dumbass, and so were most of the kids at school. But those dumbasses didn't want anything to do with Drew. So, Drew was stuck at home most of the time waiting to get in trouble, wishing he were anywhere else, with anyone else.

Drew had a friend or two. The better of the two only talked to him on summer break when the cliques from school took time off. The other friend was a babysitting kid who was two years older. The two of them had spent most days together the last couple of years, but a few weeks ago, Jeremy's mom had decided he was old enough to watch himself and save her the cost of daycare at Drew's house.

Since then, Drew had seen Jeremy at school, but their recesses didn't match up. Plus, Jeremy had friends who were his own age to hang out with and didn't seem to have much time for Stickboy.

"You already washed your hands?" mom asked as Drew waved his dry hands at her. "Ok, grab this plate before it gets any colder," she warned him.

The plate was a heaping helping. Drew didn't know why she gave him so much, but part of it had to be malicious joy. She loved to watch him squirm, especially on the days when she was mad at dad.

Drew tested the pile of rice with his fork, and it barely moved. He picked out a piece that was mostly rice and not just giant chunks of hamburger and tomato. The bland, slightly sour rice didn't immediately make him gag, so the first bite was ok. He took a piece of bread but scraped the sour margarine off it. He thought if he could just pile the rice between the bread and eat it hot dog style, maybe all he would get was the taste of bread since flavor wasn't on the ingredients list for his mom's Spanish rice.

"No more bread after that or you'll get full of that and not eat the rice." His mother's frustration at the all-too-familiar fight was already clear in her voice.

Drew didn't need a reminder of that morning; his ear was still throbbing with every heartbeat.

"I won't. I promise I'll eat it," Drew offered with a weak grin.

"Sure." Mom rolled her eyes.

Halfway through the sandwich, though, Drew feared his mom was right. His stomach could barely hold a whole sandwich, let alone a sandwich and a pile of rice. But he wasn't about to miss his movies.

Drew held his breath, pinched his nose, and took a huge bite of the Spanish rice sandwich. If he ate fast enough, he wouldn't get full and probably would barely even taste it.

Then it happened.

A sickeningly familiar feeling in his mouth, like how a fish must feel when the line goes taut.

A gag rose in his throat and his fingers began fishing the hair from his mouth…again. He had barely pulled out an inch when the gag hit full force.

"HURRRR…BLECH…"

Drew spat the huge mouthful of half-chewed-hair-infused Spanish rice onto his plate. The hair stuck in his front teeth and a couple of pieces of rice clung to it. He pulled it and it snapped. Now he had to find the other end quickly before he gagged again and really lost his stomach full of soda.

Thankfully, after some frantic searching, Drew found that the other end wasn't still in his mouth.

He hoped he hadn't swallowed it. The thought made his eyes water.

"HURRRR…"

"Oh, my God. SEE…that's what happens when you take such huge bites. You're gonna choke," Mom said, letting herself off the hook for the hair dangling from Drew's fingers. "I don't care if you sit here all night; you're not getting up from the table until that plate is clean." She got up from the table in a huff and went to her bedroom.

Drew was pretty used to sitting at the table and falling asleep, so this didn't bother him. But missing his monster movies did.

There was a brief negotiation attempt as Drew called after her in the bedroom. Drew knew it was a losing battle when something else came back out of her room.

The monster was wearing the most terrifying mask Drew had ever seen, and he let out a shriek.

"MOMMM, NOOO."

"Shut up and finish your dinner," his momster said in a whispered gravelly voice that really sold the outfit, and she swirled the black cape behind her back. "If I see you get up from that table before you're done, I'm sleeping under your bed tonight," it warned.

The momster was a favorite of hers. She liked to use it to get some quiet time during the day when her soaps were on. She would go to her room and put on the mask with a long black cape, then run around the house growling until Drew, Chris, and the babysitting kids were sufficiently terrified.

Then she would plant herself on the couch and watch her shows while the kids either hid outside, or huddled in a group behind the couch she was sitting on if they were too young to go outside alone.

No matter how many times she put it on, it still terrified Drew.

Drew looked from the momster to the piles of Spanish rice on his plate. Upon second examination of the half-eaten sandwich portion, he saw the other half of the missing hair poking out streaking across the plate.

Well, at least he hadn't swallowed it.

There was no way (momster or not) that he was going to eat another bite.

Momster's cape swirled again as she left the room. Drew sat wide-eyed, terrified that if he moved, it would come growling back to scare him even more.

The TV clicked on from the living room and for a moment; Drew heard the familiar theme music playing for *Monstervision*. The TV clicked away quickly, dashing any hopes that he might at least get to listen to a spooky movie. Drew thought he heard the momster giggle as she flipped away from his favorite show, knowing it was pissing him off.

Then she watched the news for a bit, then some boring love story movie…Drew's mind drifted at the table… then some thinking about peeing his pants at school…then some thinking about the State School and where Moonface and Bananahead had been during the attack in the gymnasium…then thinking about the Gougers and wondering how Grandpa's story en…....

Drew woke up with a jump, like he was falling from his bed. His knees hit the table and made the plate that was still sitting on it jump and clank. His eyes wouldn't focus, so he blinked until they started to adjust.

It was dark.

The house was completely quiet except for the crackling of the unnecessary wood burner behind him. A noise from mom and dad's room made him look, and he saw the door was shut. Momster must have just gone to bed. The plate of half-chewed Spanish rice sandwich and its brother, the untouched pile, stared back at him in the dark.

His stomach growled in protest; he was starving. If he kept this up, he was going to end up back on the BRAT diet with the chalky shakes for old people.

Last summer, Drew had to get a toenail pulled and while he was at the doctor's office, they weighed him. They told mom he was underweight; she avoided culpability by explaining that Drew was a picky eater with a weak gag reflex. The doctor's suggestion was banana, rice, applesauce, and toast, the BRAT diet. Also, he suggested weight gain shakes they used for nursing home patients who had problems keeping weight on. It was the worst couple of weeks because rice and bananas with their hair-like strings were a no-go for Drew. So that left apple sauce and toast, both of which he liked, but he could eat only so much of it. Then there were the shakes. Heavy, too sweet, and chalky, they had always left him feeling sick, like he just ate a huge Thanksgiving dinner. Thankfully, the cost of the diet ended up changing his parents' minds. Before long, he was back to eating whatever she had mixed with her hair that day.

Right now, in the kitchen's darkness, Drew was so hungry, he'd even drink one of those shakes. He decided to go check if there was anything in the fridge that mom wouldn't notice was missing.

His chair made a little sound as he pushed back from the table, so he tried harder to be quiet. He was scared momster was waiting to come out in its mask and make him scream again. He made his way around the table fumbling in the darkness as his eyes adjusted.

Suddenly, his feet were on fire.

"Owwww ouch…crap." Drew did his best to keep the cries of pain quiet.

He forgot dad had hung up a bunch of tinfoil behind the wood burner, and it made the tiles in front of it feel like lava. Drew had carelessly stepped on them and now his feet felt burnt. Drew could tell as he made his way to the back porch to cool them off that he was going to get a blister, as the skin on his heel already felt puffy.

The night air was cool, but warm for the season. Definitely too cold for mosquitos now, though. His mind and his feet enjoyed the moment of bliss in the back yard. Being outside had always made him feel his best, and the cool night air was relaxing.

Then his bliss was interrupted by some giggling coming from the shop.

Now that he was tuning into the night's sounds around him, Drew could hear music coming from dad's shop, and some more giggling.

Drew's heart sank a bit.

Dad had a bad habit of having his friend, a pretty Indian lady who lived two houses over, come over for drinks when mom went to bed. Drew knew it was wrong and if mom found out, again, it was going to be another miserable few months.

Drew's ears perked up, trying to pick out some details of what they were saying, but it was just bad country music and feminine sounds of joy.

A growl from his stomach threatened to betray his stealth, and his burnt feet were getting cold. He took one last cursory glance around the yard to see if maybe the Gouger was standing by, waiting to kill another member of his family for revenge on Grandpa.

Nothing.

No yellow eyes burning in the darkness.

The humming of the fridge seemed to increase by a magnitude of ten when Drew opened the door to look for a munchie of some sort. He worried that it would wake momster up, so he hurried through the contents of the fridge.

Nothing.

Just a pot of Spanish rice, some condiments, dad's beers, and HIS SODA. Drew had never been so thankful to see a root beer in his whole life. It wasn't his favorite flavor soda, but right now, it may as well have been ambrosia. He snagged the can and went back to the mudroom to crack it so mom wouldn't hear.

Now slightly chilly, soda in hand, he went to warm up by the wood burner and drink his soda. He avoided the lava by hopping over the chair he had sat in for dinner and vaulted to the other side, where the floor wouldn't be so hot. The old wood burner that wasn't hooked up to the chimney anymore sat in the corner and made a convenient seat. He took a drink of his soda and listened hard for dad.

If Drew heard the back door, he would bail upstairs before dad saw him. But, judging from the sounds in the shop, it was going to be a while.

Drew's fingers fidgeted around the edges of the stove while he sat there wondering what Chris was up to with his friend. The busy little fingers found something in the cavity at the top of the stove. Drew's memory fired up, and with more than a little joy, his fingers pulled the plastic package out of the hole. It was his brownie; he had totally forgotten about it. They got them as treats from Mrs. Rockow for Halloween earlier in the week. Mom stopped him from eating it before dinner and fearing for its safety when dad got home, Drew had tucked it away in his hiding spot in the old wood burner.

The first thought he had was to tear off a piece of the tinfoil dad had stapled to the wall and wrap his brownie in it so he could warm it up on the top of the hot floor. Quietly, Drew took the plastic off and encased the brownie in the slightly dirty but cleaner-than-the-floor tinfoil.

While he waited for the floor to heat it up, he turned it every few seconds and sucked on the chocolate-flavored plastic it had been wrapped in. When it was ready, Drew resumed his perch on the old wood burner, warm brownie in one hand, root beer in the other. He had to make sure to hide the evidence before he snuck up to bed, but for right now, he was anxiety-free and enjoying himself for the first time that day, outside of Grandpa's story.

He looked at the clock on the microwave in the kitchen.

12:34.

It was tomorrow, Halloween.

Drew had survived the worst day of his life. And today already had a good start. It was Halloween, he was full, and he was going to get so much candy tonight.

Drew fell asleep in the corner by the wood burner. Bailey was at his feet, the soda can was still in his hand, his head was full of thoughts of trick or treating, costumes, kids he might see and need to avoid, State School monsters, and Sidehill Gougers.

Chapter 6

"Drew, WAKE UP!" Mom yelled as she shook him awake from the corner he had fallen asleep in. Bailey was gone, but the plastic brownie wrapper and the soda were still there, divulging his secret late-night binge to mom.

She eyed his surroundings and furrowed her brow.

"Thought I said no soda until you finished your dinner." Her tone was pretty angry for so early in the morning.

"Sorry, I got thirsty last night, and I couldn't sleep," Drew said, trying to come up with a better explanation, but she had caught him off-guard.

"Well, it's ok cos I warmed it up for you."

Drew's olfactory senses woke up now and the familiar smell of the dreaded Spanish rice was hanging in the air. His guts reflexively turned over and his eyes watered.

Mom was already on the way back to the kitchen as Drew stood up.

His eyes looked at the table in watery shock.

There sat his plate of dinner from the previous night, the untouched pile and the chewed-up sandwich he had spat out. He refused to look more closely, as the sight of the half-eaten hair would make him lose his brownie for sure.

The only difference in the meal from last night was now the piles of mush were steaming. Mom had gone through the trouble of warming it up for him before she caught him red-handed in the corner by the wood burner.

Drew stood there, astonished. Even for momster, this was savage. He looked toward the kitchen, half expecting her to emerge in the mask he knew was fake. He waited to scream in terror.

Nothing.

With no fight left in him and feeling slightly lightheaded from being so hungry, Drew marched to the table.

The first step on his burnt foot reminded him of the lava, and he jumped past it to the safety of his chair. He perched on his chair with his feet under him and his knees tucked to his chest, staring at the plate but not seeing the food.

"Hurry up—we've got stuff to do before the babysitting kids start to show up," Mom called from the kitchen.

Drew picked up his fork and poked the pile reluctantly. He wondered where dad was because his parents' bedroom door was open, meaning it was vacant.

He looked around for signs of what was going on but his nose, which had woken up before his other senses, picked up a smell that wasn't Spanish rice with hair.

This actually smelled good.

BURRRGGLLE.

Drew's stomach agreed loudly. He was starving despite the unwanted leftovers, looking back at him like a pair of crazy cartoon eyeballs from the plate. The fork grabbed a bit of rice with no chunks of tomato, and no hair, and slowly moved it toward his lips.

Just as the fork touched his lips and his stomach rolled over in protest...

"ST...OP." Mom's laughter interrupted her warning. "Don't eat that."

Drew's mind swirled in confusion. He didn't know what the joke was or if she was even talking to him. Nobody else was home. Chris was going to be gone until Sunday night and dad was MIA.

"Happy Halloween. You got your first trick." Mom was still laughing but looking directly at him. "I made you biscuits and gravy. Your dad got up early and wanted breakfast before he and your uncle went out. I saw your plate and knew you'd be hungry, so I figured I'd make your favorite." Mom looked almost pleasant, almost pretty, when she laughed.

Drew's heart nearly leaped from his chest. He loved biscuits and gravy and hardly ever found hairs in it.

The memory of momster yesterday was already fading away.

Drew snatched the plate he feared a few seconds earlier and ran to the trash can in the kitchen. The lid to the can smacked the wall with a thump as Drew stomped on the pedal that opened it. He scraped the piles off the plate with gusto.

"Peckerhead!," he yelled at the wonky piles of Spanish mush in his mind as they tumbled into the trash. He wasn't quite foolish enough to test those waters with mom yet, even if she was in a good mood. So, he kept the insult between him and the rice.

After Drew wolfed down the biscuits and gravy, Mom had him busy getting stuff ready for the babysitting kids, which meant cleaning up the house and hiding any evidence of their private lives. Today was slightly different, though. Mom also had him go out to dad's shop and find the card tables and a few lawn chairs.

The excitement was in his feet as Drew skipped to the shop with a full belly. He knew he'd get crap if anyone saw him skipping, but his neighborhood wasn't too full of kids, and it was early. Plus, he thought it was fun.

The shop door squeaked a bit as he swung it open. The first thing he did was reach into the black void and feel for the light switch. First, he found a spider web. He retracted his hand and tried to shake the webbing off. After a few unsuccessful attempts, he wiped his hand on the wet grass. It worked, but his hand was now soaked, so he dried it on his pants.

More carefully this time, Drew found the switch, and the shop light flickered on.

Instantly, Drew saw a pair of women's underwear lying on the floor by where dad sat and drank.

Drew felt a burst of anger for his mom, who had just made him biscuits and gravy. Drew was under no illusions of what the underwear meant, and with a field goal kick, he booted them under the workbench. He hoped the mice would find them and make a nest.

Mom could never see them.

A dark cloud grew in his head, but the sight of the lawn chairs and the card table reminded him of why he was out there.

It was almost time to carve pumpkins. So, with the panties taken care of and forgotten by everyone but the mice, and maybe the pretty Indian lady, Drew made a couple of trips to get the table and chairs inside.

Mom had a few newspapers that dad had stacked next to the wood burner, and she handed them to Drew along with a roll of tape. Drew knew what to do, and he laid the vain attempt at protecting the table down and taped the corners.

By the time Drew had all the chairs set up and newspapers taped down, there were already three of the five babysitting kids at the house. Apparently, they hadn't eaten breakfast. So, with a small amount of displeasure, Drew watched them eat the leftover biscuits and gravy he planned on saving for at least the next three dinners.

Mom didn't care if he ate leftovers from the fridge instead of what she made for dinner, because then, she didn't have to throw it away.

Drew was finishing up the babysitting kids' dishes, muttering to himself about his biscuits and gravy getting eaten, and mom was putting on Halloween cartoons. The other two kids had shown up, and they were all lined up in lawn chairs watching the familiar re-runs. Drew had one more task before he joined them.

The Halloween box.

The giant box that used to hold cases of adult diapers had been the family's off-season storage for everything Halloween-related for as long as Drew could remember. He always knew it was getting close to his favorite season when mom would tell him to go out to the shop and grab the Halloween box. The whole family, except dad, who probably watched TV, would dig through the box and spend a whole day decorating their bedrooms and the out-of-the-way corners of the house. Pumpkin carving and costumes were left until Halloween day but the season lasted all month.

By the end of the day on October first, the entire house was a madhouse of fake spiderwebs, orange lights, and Beistle cardboard cutouts of witches, pumpkins, cats, and ghosts. The bendy arm skeleton was Drew's favorite, and each day until he took it down, he would readjust the cardboard limbs into some sort of new contortion.

This year, he and Chris even took a bunch of dad's rum bottles, since they were clear, and filled them up with food coloring and water so it looked like a mad scientist's laboratory, like the movies.

The last dive of the season into the Halloween box was to find costumes to wear the day of and to get the pumpkin painting and carving tools out. With Chris being gone, that meant Drew got first dibs on whatever he wanted to wear before mom let the babysitting kids dig through and play dress-up.

Drew already knew what he wanted.

The green ghoul mask, the purple cape/sheet, the face paint that wasn't mixed up and full of faux fur, and the black curly-haired wig. He had already painted an old pair of gloves with a can of green spray paint so his exposed fingers wouldn't ruin his disguise.

It was too early for all that, though, so Drew picked out his choice pieces. He stopped and reminisced on a costume that had gotten him onto the cover of the newspaper, with no help from his dad working there, he was sure.

It was a giant Pink Panther his dad had won for him at the state fair. They had unstuffed it on Halloween last year after realizing Drew was about the same size. They added a zipper and stuffed the tail and nose with newspapers. He spent the night feeling like a movie star as everyone who saw him had something nice to say and the newspaper van stopped him at the library for a picture.

Drew was sure at the time that it was going to make him famous.

Still smiling, Drew wondered if dad was going to be back before he left for trick or treating. He hoped so. Drew wanted him to see the costume he was going to wear at least.

Now he took the enormous box out to the living room. Minus his stuff and Pink Panther. He wasn't sharing that with these kids. He watched as they dug through the remnants and he grew impatient.

Halloween is Grinch Night was blaring on the TV and it drew him in. He was lost in the show, and the time the kids took to get dressed seemed to fly by.

When the movie was over, mom called Drew back to the kitchen, where she was sitting and doing a crossword puzzle. She asked him to take the pumpkins out and get them all started.

Without hesitation, Drew grabbed the smallest five first, making sure they were distributed to the babysitting kids. Then he grabbed the massive one he had talked mom into grabbing last week when they were grocery shopping. It was no minor effort to convince her, but it was going to be so worth it.

Halfway through *The Halloween That Almost Wasn't*, a cheesy movie but a staple of his Halloween, Drew was barely making a dent in the massive pumpkin's guts. He regretted his choice already.

The slimy guts were burning the skin on his forearms and each time he plunged his bent spoon back in for another scoop of guts, it felt like the rash got worse. His wrist was already cramping up. The soggy newspaper was shredding and mixing with the guts to create a paper mâché-like substance that was sticking to his pumpkin. It left behind backward headlines and tidbits of local news from the ink on the pumpkin's skin.

It was a mess.

An hour later and part of the way through *Ichabod and Mr. Toad*, he was finally done.

The babysitting kids had long since finished carving their basic toothy smiles on their much simpler to gut pumpkins and were now sitting on the couches watching the movie.

Drew had a plan for his now-hollow pumpkin. He had been planning it for months. The exhausted fingers on his hand tried to grip the slippery knife, but it kept making mistakes. He wanted to go an inch, but the clumsy knife plunged too far and went six. By the time he was finished, the pumpkin looked nothing like it did in his imagination. In fact, it didn't look like anything except someone attacked this poor pumpkin with reckless abandon.

Deflated, Drew spun the pumpkin around to the non-nice side. The brown warts were thick on this side and there wasn't a nice flat surface to try again on.

The clock and his abilities were working against him. He decided to carve a stupid basic triangle face pumpkin like the cardboard ones on the wall. With the Beistle cutout as a template, Drew was more easily able to emulate it, and before long had a fairly good resemblance carved into the unpleasant side of his pumpkin.

There was only one thing left to do. He held the candle out for mom as she flicked the lighter. Drew carefully tilted it sideways, putting a few drops of wax onto an old mason jar lid. Then he poked the candle into the cooling wax and blew it out. Mom assisted him with the other five, and before long, their assembly line had cranked out all six smiling pumpkins complete with candles.

A late lunch was on the stove, mac and cheese, so Drew hurried with the help of a couple of the bigger kids and set the pumpkins on the front porch. When they were done, lunch was on the table.

Mom had made Halloween mac and cheese as a surprise. It tasted the same. The only difference was she boiled half the noodles in purple-dyed water and half regular. Then she mixed them with cheese sauce and voila, Halloween mac and cheese. Drew only wished she would have added hot dogs, but he still appreciated the effort. Plus, it was hair-free.

Aware of his limitations earlier, when trying to make his imagination come to life with his hands, Drew knew he would need help with getting his face painted.

"Hey, mom, if I do all the lunch dishes, will you paint my face? Kinda like a ghoul, but if it was a demon, too. So, green with black eyes, red lips, and painted wrinkles…or something like that." Drew waited impatiently while mom eyed her crossword again.

"Well, you were gonna wash the dishes anyway, but I suppose since you've been a good helper today, I can do that…I don't know about painting wrinkles, though." She smiled and immediately had a flash of knowing and pushed her pen back to the crossword to see if it fit.

Just a couple of hours later, Drew was standing in front of the mirror. He couldn't believe his eyes. From his vague instructions, mom seemed to know exactly what he wanted.

The newspaper van was definitely going to find him again. Even if they had just fired dad, his costume was so good, they'd have to put him on the front page.

Full of pride, pillowcase in hand, and an extra big hug for mom, and Drew was out of the house. It was early still, but he wanted to walk around for a bit and let people get a good look at him. But to complete the costume, he had to wear the mask first. Then, when people saw him and the boring mask, he could pull it up and show off his mom's masterpiece, scaring them in the process.

Quickly, Drew realized one of the errors in his plan. The stupid mask was mixing with the chilly evening air directly on his glasses. Every time he took a breath, the fog on his lenses grew. Before long, the fog was droplets that were dripping into the mask, making it feel slimy and awful.

Then Drew realized his other error.

He was a chicken.

There was no way he was ever going to go up to anyone, stranger or not, and then have the courage to play a gag like taking off his mask to shock them. It was a stupid and short-sighted plan.

Drew was glad dad never showed up to see this disappointing costume.

The only saving grace was mom's face painting.

Drew ripped the mask from his face and suddenly, the third error was obvious. The cheap paint that had been masterfully applied to his face was now a brown smear on the inside of the cheap mask.

His heart sank in his chest as he stuffed the mask into the pillowcase. A reflection on the Ben Franklin store's window caught his eye and confirmed his suspicions.

It was ruined.

Now it was just a mix of face paint on a sad clown.

Drew was mad at himself as he leaned in to the reflection to try to salvage what was left, smearing the paint with his fingers in vain.

Over his shoulder, he caught sight of something that made his hair stand up. It was someone in a wheelchair being pushed around by someone in a tuxedo.

It reminded Drew of how much there was to be afraid of, outside of the fake ghost and goblins running around the streets.

Moonface and Bananahead.

The muscles in his neck resisted the rapid whipping motion as Drew flung his head around to see which monster it was being pushed toward him. Unfortunately, the alien mask was preventing him from discerning which monster this was, but he wasn't about to stick around and find out.

His feet slapped the pavement as he ran, headed to the safest place he could think of.

The park was always safe at this time of year. The migrants had followed the field work away from town to greener pastures farther south. This meant the temporary encampment in the park was gone, at least until next spring, and he could go hang out there again without getting in trouble.

On his run, he was sure to avoid anything resembling a hill, making a mental note of any inclines. The Gouger monsters from the story were still fresh in his mind.

He passed Jeremy's house and didn't see his bike. This meant he was out with his other friends from school. Part of Drew hoped he would run into him, and they would take him around with them, but he knew it was a pipedream.

By the time he was at the park, the sun was setting, and more and more kids were lining the streets as the porch lights clicked on, signaling it was time.

The door knocking had begun.

Drew wanted to avoid the initial rush of toddlers and parents, but also didn't want to wait too long until the candy was down to bare bones and the adults got stingy. Also, he didn't want to wait until the herd of kids thinned out too much because he was depending on them for safety. He didn't mind going alone, but he hated the thought of being out alone at night with the monsters from the State School and the Sidehill Gougers. His hair stood up again as he looked at the ever-thinning tree line, hoping not to see the giant beasts pressed together, looking for vengeance with their burning yellow eyes.

The neighborhood, although dark, was welcoming and there was an atmosphere of fun in the air. The littler kids were finishing up their rounds, so they still had time for baths and stories before bed (but not too much time to get a sugar high.) Their parents were waiting in tight-knit little cliques at the ends of blocks chatting, letting the kids do the collecting of candy (all of which would be "inspected").

Pumpkins, all better than Drew's pathetic attempt, lined the porches and yards. Fake spiderwebs and black lights were ubiquitous. There was more than one old man sitting in a rocking chair dressed as a scarecrow, waiting to stop the heart of any unsuspecting kid.

Drew knew this trick.

Some people really went all out and had boom boxes with cassettes playing spooky noises and Halloween atmosphere. One guy on the rich side of town even had a fog machine and some crazy lights flashing around his decked-out yard.

A few of the costumes were amazing. The wearers of these were sure to be future local celebrities once the newspaper van found them. But most were just homemade. More sheet than cape. He suddenly felt less insecure about his own conglomeration, and whether it was going to make him famous.

A group of kids walked past him, and Drew decided it was now or never. He slunk in behind them, hoping they wouldn't notice. He made sure to keep a distance that would let strangers know they weren't together.

Drew followed them most of the night, listening to them knock and repeat the line, "Trick or treat." It saved him the trouble of talking to adults most of the time as he came up behind the other kids and held out his pillowcase. There was the occasional smartass who looked at the group of kids with their store-bought costumes and did a double-take on him, always saying the same stupid thing—"And what are you supposed to be?"

Drew's unwavering answer was a shrug of his shoulders and an outstretched pillowcase.

He lost the safety of the group as they went closer to the side of town that had what Drew considered to be hills…mountains tonight, though, full of Gougers.

Drew saw his brother, Chris, was up ahead with a few of his buddies. For a second, Drew thought they made eye contact, but a split second later, Chris grabbed one of his friends and ran across the street. The group followed along. Drew hoped it wasn't intentional but felt lonely because of it anyway.

Instead of continuing, he hefted the bag in his hands, trying to decide if he had enough candy. Then he remembered the mask at the bottom, taking up space. He could put it on and take off his cape and gloves and just re-hit all the houses he just visited. It was safe, after all. And it was late enough that it wasn't like he was taking candy from little kids, just teenagers and overweight housewives hoping for leftovers (though those porch lights likely went out long ago).

So, that's what he did.

Drew simply retraced his steps. With one minor hiccup. Early in his turnaround, one of the smartass old men had again asked him what he was. Drew, like an idiot, offered the same answer as before, shoulders and pillowcase. It must have felt too familiar to the old man, who retracted the piece of candy and gave him a suspicious look.

"You been here already tonight?" the old man asked. Drew knew better than to lie to old men. Grandpa could sniff out a lie before you even told it.

"Yes, sir. I lost my group and just wanted a little more candy before I have to go back home...sorry," Drew apologized and backed away from the steps.

"Aww, hell, I can't punish a kid who's gonna tell the truth." The old man laughed and held out a whole handful of candy this time.

Drew hesitated. He never trusted adults.

"Are you sure?" he asked, waiting for a catch.

The old man grabbed his pillowcase and stuffed the candy in with a wink. Without waiting for any further interaction, Drew hollered back a "Thanks...sorry" as he moved on to the next house. Now Drew just had to remember not to give himself away again.

The rest of the haul went well enough. There were no more people suspicious of his trick, just double the candy. Though the atmosphere was shifting. The welcoming nature of the once-busy neighborhood was fading into something darker, more sinister, a place that harbored monsters. There was starting to be more and more signs that the darkness was growing, as he hurried through his second trip, but he still felt safe.

The smiles on the pumpkins had faded as the candles burned out, leaving behind eerie skull-like orange faces watching him from the dark porches as the porch lights clicked off around him, indicating the candy was out or they were sick of kids (or they wanted leftovers). The safety the porch lights offered was slipping away with the end of Halloween.

Some of the bulbous orange skulls had already ended up like the millions before them, smashed to bits on the sidewalks and roads. The melted wax pooled around their skulls like blood in the growing moonlight.

It was the teenagers' turn to have fun. Any kids Drew's age better be at home working on a belly ache or risk losing their haul to the stronger, more mature teenagers. Drew wasn't too worried about them. He was small, but he was fast and doubted any of them would have enough resolve to actually run him down and fight him for his candy.

He just had to stay on his toes and not get snuck up on.

At the end of the second circuit, he ended up right back at the park where he had started. The same bench he sat on a little bit ago would offer some safe harbor while he pre-went-through his candy as the lemon light from the park kept the monsters away.

That was one of mom's rules. You couldn't eat any candy until she looked at it to make sure it hadn't been poisoned. What this really meant was that she was going to cherry-pick his bag and leave him with whatever she didn't like. Drew even heard some warnings on the news about checking candy, which only confirmed his suspicions that adults were working together to get candy from their kids…and who knew what else?

There was a noise behind Drew, who was now putting his choice pieces of candy into the sheet/cape to hide it from his mom, careful to look for needle pokes on each one because everyone knew that was how they poisoned it.

Drew knew well the sound coming from behind him.

It was the sound of a bike on cement and clanking beer cans.

It was another one of the town's monsters.

Can Man.

All the kids talked about him and his huge knife, which he used to open trash bags, and little kids. At first, Drew didn't believe it. He asked his dad about him after he was going through the dumpsters out back one night. Dad said he was a harmless mute who worked harder than anyone in town, and people should just leave him alone.

Then one night, he had heard Can Man rifling through the trash cans in the alley, then there was a loud yelping. Drew had looked out his window to see the Can Man pedaling away furiously into the night.

The next morning, their neighbor's dog was found dead in their yard…right by the alley. Drew tried to tell his parents, but they said the dog had just got hit by a car and limped home to die. Adults never believed in monsters. Drew knew better.

Now the Can Man was rapidly approaching and as Drew gauged the distance between them, trying to decide what to say or do…

They made eye contact.

That was all the motivation Drew needed and he repeated the run he had made earlier in the night.

Drew could hear the Can Man pick up speed to match his pace, so Drew cut through some back yards and weaved his way between houses. He was out of breath but suddenly realized he was in the high grounds. The hilliest part of town. Which in reality was as flat as paper, with the occasional ten-foot rise and gentle fall. To Drew, in the dark, it may as well have been the Alps.

He was too far into the neighborhood to turn around and face Can Man, and now his only way out was to run past the cemetery and the State School. He knew either Moonface or Bananahead was out and about, or at least he thought it had been one of them in the alien mask being pushed around. But that meant at least one monster was unaccounted for.

Drew stuck to the streetlights as by now, the porch lights had all been shut off and the once-kid-lined streets were all but abandoned. His eyes darted around, and his heart raced. Every noise was a clawed and cloven hoof. Every breeze was the wind of a wheelchair racing toward him. The bag of loot was heavy in his hand as the monument of shame grew on the street ahead of him.

The buildings of the State School suddenly reminded him of the castles in hammer horror movies. All it was missing was the lightning, but the nearly full moon assured him that wasn't a possibility tonight.

Industrial noises came from the property on his right, full of monsters. Ghostly noises came from his left in the cemetery full of ghosts. The Can Man's cans were rattling in the cage on the back of his oversized tricycle. Fear kept Drew on a straight path, just like Grandpa's story, avoiding any obstacles that might trip him up like on the day of the monster attack, when he wrecked his BMX. His heartbeat matched his footsteps and still he pounded his feet harder. The bag of candy swung wildly, and he heard more than one wrapper hit the ground. Despite his panic, he readjusted his grip to save what was left.

Finally, his house came into view. Lined with goofy smiling pumpkins and his monstrosity, which was shining light out of every facet he had carved. He slowed to a walk and tried to calm his nerves by eating a Twix.

One fewer for mom.

He snuck into the back porch mudroom and stashed his lucre behind the shoe box so it would be left out of his mom's well-intentioned thievery.

Then he snuck back around front and blew out the candles on the pumpkins that still had them burning. There was no one left to impress on the streets except Can Man, and Drew's pumpkin was embarrassing his whole family at this point.

By the time mom went through his candy and took her fill, dad was home. Drunk. But happy. He also helped himself to a good-sized chunk of Drew's haul, and while admiring Drew's hard work, gave him a noogie. They sucked, but it felt better than the belt and even if it hurt, dad's playfulness was always welcome.

Drew was exhausted, but the scary movies were just starting. As he settled in and started in on the candy, mom let him know she saved him some biscuits and gravy from this morning. She even offered to warm it up for him.

By the time the microwave beeped a few minutes later, Drew was already stuffed from candy, but aside from it being his favorite food, mom's kindness couldn't be wasted.

He ate every bite.

As the movie switched to one about some psycho family who thought their chainsaw was family , Drew sleepily connected with the idea. He always thought dad's chainsaw was awesome and someday, he would be the one running the chainsaw while someone else stacked the wood. The sounds of the saw cutting something or someone apart rang out from the TV and brought with it the thoughts of stacking wood at Grandpa's and the Gouger.

A few minutes later, dad went to bed. Before he did, he shut off all the lights in the living room so they wouldn't keep him awake. The TV (whose auto-dimming light sensor had failed years ago) went to black and white and the details of the movie were barely visible on the screen.

"Drew" was all it took for mom to get Drew to grab the flashlight and hold it up to the sensor. The image on the screen brightened, and the color returned to the pallid faces of the psycho family. His arm was still tired from the pumpkin carving and the pillowcase full of candy he saved from the Can Man, so he propped it up with the pillow he had been lying on.

His eyes felt so heavy and with little effort, his mind returned to Grandpa and stacking wood and Gougers and his candy on the porch that he had to remember to get once mom went to bed and take it to his room….

Instead, he fell asleep, flashlight still pressed up against the sensor.

Mom must have covered him up and put the flashlight away because when Drew heard the crash of cans in the alley, he was too tangled up in a blanket to react.

Chapter 7

Drew's knees still hurt from biffing it last night when he jumped awake from the crash outside. Mom's job of tucking him in on the floor had done its job. His feet tangled in his blanket as he ran for cover, and he tumbled forward onto his hands and knees. He was glad he was on the carpet instead of the lava floor, but now he would have rug burn for a week.

The crash in the alley was so loud that Drew figured dad must have heard it, and he had expected him to make his own crash when he came out of his bedroom, suicide-drive-pistol at the ready. Then Drew could have sneaked up to the relative safety of the upstairs while dad protected the house.

Instead, there had been nothing except mom's snoring.

Drew thought last night that the Can Man must have followed the trail of candy that had been jettisoned from his pillowcase candy bag on his panicked run home. He imagined Can Man lurking in the alley tripping over garbage cans, ready to kidnap him and do whatever monsters did to kids when they were alone.

The darkness of the room slowly revealed itself in gray tones as his eyes adjusted. The green light from the microwave clock helped. He remembered peering into the blackness on the other side of the house through the kitchen. The door to the mudroom was dimly lit by the moonlight filtering in through the dirty browned screens enclosing it.

Then there was a flash of movement and what had sounded like hooves stomping in the back yard, loud enough for him to feel it through the floor.

WOOOFFFF

"AAAAAGGHH"

The beagle's tail gained momentum, but his ears lowered at the sound of fear coming from Drew's mouth. The presence of his loyal friend gave Drew the courage to at least make it to the landing of the stairs, which was only a quick sprint up to his room. He could skip three steps at a time and make it in four giant leaps. He had done it before running from ghosts.

"Let's go to bed," Drew said to Bailey, not caring if he woke anyone up at that moment. All he could think of was Grandpa's story and him sitting upstairs in the loft, safe from the Gougers. Sure, he used a ladder, and Drew had stairs, but maybe it was enough to stop them in their unbalanced tracks.

Drew's feet barely touched the ground as the pair raced up the steps. Bailey's excitement was obvious and by the time they both leaped from the doorway of his bedroom to the bed, he was wagging his tail so hard, the bed vibrated.

Drew lay awake most of the night listening for more signs of the Gouger.

But now, in the bright, warm morning (still nice out like Grandpa had promised), Drew rubbed his quickly scabbing rug-burned knees and felt like a baby for hiding under his covers all night.

The branch in the back yard was lying almost directly in front of the back door and last night's events replayed with clarity now that the fear of the dark and Grandpa's damn story had faded. One good thing was that nobody woke up and Chris wasn't home to give him crap about staying up all night being scared of the dark.

The dying old tree in the back yard had played one last Halloween trick on Drew and a limb had snapped, crashing in the back yard, where he had imagined the Can Man was lurking in wait for him in the darkness with the Gouger.

The brightness of the morning was making his sleep-deprived eyes feel like someone had rubbed them with rock salt. At least there was no school today. Drew planned on securing his stash of candy in the hole in his floor from the old chimney. It was one thing Chris feared that didn't bother Drew at all since he was the one who had helped dad make the hole in the first place. Then, after stashing and eating a bit of candy, he would take a nap until someone bugged him for something.

However, right now, he had to deal with this branch.

The branch outweighed Drew by at least a hundred pounds. There was no way he was going to be able to drag it to the spot behind the shed where all the dead branches went. Not in one piece. Too bad football was on, and dad made it clear when he had given him the task of cleaning the yard up that he "was busy." It would have only taken both of them a couple of minutes to drag it back to the branch pile together.

An exasperated sigh left Drew's lips as he made his way to the shop, hoping he didn't find any more panties. The saw was right by the door, so he didn't have to go in too far. His forearms were still tired from the pumpkin carving the night before, so the chore of sawing the branch into three sections took twice as long.

Once he was finally done with the branch and back inside, Drew saw mom was busy making chili for Indian tacos later. Another favorite of Drew's, but prone to hair depending on how the Cowboys played and how pissed dad was afterward. But even if there was a hair in the chili, the Indian fry bread was delicious with butter and cinnamon sugar.

"Oh, C'MON, REFS!" Dad yelled from the living room. That was followed by a crisp crack from a fresh beer and a pause long enough for a drink. "That's bullshit," he followed, sounding better after some beer.

"Hey, mom?" Drew waited the mandatory three seconds for a response before he rattled on. "I'm pretty tired from yesterday and staying up late holding the flashlight." He paused again as mom only contemplated the crossword she was back in front of while the chili simmered. "Can I just hang out upstairs for the rest of the day?" Drew hoped for some reward at the mention of the favor he had done for her.

Without a pause, like she had just been waiting for bait, mom responded.

"Well, you didn't do that great of a job holding the flashlight, since I had to shut the movie off when you fell asleep holding it and the screen went gray…But I suppose if you finish the dishes, you can go upstairs for a bit." She waited a second. "Until I call you or need you for something…and I better not get any lip."

Drew looked at the mountain of dishes and started boiling on the inside. He wasn't sure how mom managed it, but every single pan was always burnt to a crisp. His general tactic was to "soak" them and hope it either landed on Chris's or mom's shoulders later. But with Chris enjoying yet another fabulous weekend getaway and with mom having the upper hand, he resigned himself to at least half the day washing dishes.

A half-hour later, Drew was upstairs opening candy wrappers with pruned fingers and itchy skin on the underside of his arms. The soapy, greasy, dish water had mixed with his mild skin irritation from the pumpkin guts to form a full-blown rash.

The Twix was helping, though.

After eating too many choice pieces of candy, Drew found himself with a choice sugar high. He tried to take a nap, but his feet were bouncing, and his mind was racing. The arguing from downstairs had gotten louder for a bit after some terrible kicker missed a field goal and lost the game. But now it was quiet. That was the worst. He knew dad would be bored and on the pick. The best thing Drew could do was stay quiet and upstairs; fingers crossed they'd just forget he was home.

The rest of the day was mundane, thankfully.

Drew read a few old books he had already been through about a dozen times. There was intermittent fighting from downstairs, but once the afternoon game came on, dad settled down and watched quietly unless he needed another beer. Drew preferred the games where dad didn't have a dog in the fight cos it just distracted him and didn't piss him off half the time.

"Hey, Barbara, put that chili in the fridge and let's get some pizzas!" Dad yelled across the house downstairs. Drew's ears perked up; Pizza Hut was always hair-free.

"No, we can't afford that, and I already fried the Indian bread." A rare act of defiance from mom the buzzkill.

"HEY, DREW, YOU WANT PIZZA OR INDIAN TACOS?" Dad inserted Drew into the argument, knowing he would be hanging on every word.

Drew felt slimy.

He could feel dad using him…but it was Pizza Hut. And he knew it was what dad wanted.

"PIZZZAAA."

Now Drew felt hungry.

"Come on, Barb, one more time before we can't afford it for a while…at least until I find something," Dad said, using his last tactic on mom.

Mom had lost the argument when dad saw the pizza commercial five minutes ago.

Dad had probably sat there deciding how to tell her without being a jerk, though he would be if he had to. Mom slammed the chili into the fridge loudly enough to let everyone know she disagreed, but she would oblige.

When the knock on the door came twenty or so minutes later, Drew ran to the front door, money in hand, ready to be the hero returning with pizza. Instead, he found Chris.

Just in time for pizza.

"Yo," Chris said as he brushed past. "What's everyone doing?" Drew knew what he was really asking.

"Football, and now we are getting pizza. Dad seems ok, though. What'd you do over at Tony's?" Drew asked, only to be polite because he could really not care less.

"Just trick or treating…God, get a life." There was a tinge of guilt in the reply. "Plus, they took me out to eat at Ginny's," Chris said, referring to the nice restaurant on the golf course side of town where his friend Tony lived.

Not a place Drew would be eating at any time soon. Drew thought of his own friends. He doubted Bailey could afford to take him there, no matter how hard he wagged his tail.

Out of jealousy, Drew slugged Chris in the arm. Chris was younger, but slightly bigger. However, Drew was always stacking wood and doing chores with dad while Chris was at sleepovers or having another "headache." Chris looked at him like he wanted to do something.

Part of Drew wished he would.

Even if getting in a fight meant another beating from dad. Because despite being a scared little baby most of the time, Drew never shied away from a brawl. And if it meant a spanking, so be it. As far as Drew was concerned, it was worth it to not stack another scoop of cowardice on his already full plate. He didn't have much pride, but he tried to save what he could for himself.

Just as Drew could feel himself getting ready to lash out and throw the first punch, a knock on the door behind him made him jump. The shocked response induced chaotic laughter from Chris, who went into the living room from the front porch where Drew now stood red-faced paying the pizza delivery guy.

"Thanks," Drew said and put the money on top of the pizza boxes so the two could swap roles.

"No problem…later." The teenage boy snatched the money and ran back to his little red car with a…red hat? Drew wasn't sure what the logo was, but it was easily recognizable as his favorite, even if it was the only pizza place in town.

The pizza was as good as expected but mom put a damper on the mood by not eating any. Which pissed dad off.

As the arguing started, Drew and Chris took their cue and got showers out of the way. An early bedtime was better than what they were working up to.

That night before bed, and after Chris ate way more than his share of pizza even though he already got to eat at a fancy restaurant, Drew had a plan to get even with Chris for laughing at him earlier.

He talked Chris into trading candy, while keeping his best stuff hidden in the hole in the floor.

The boys both dumped out their bags and made piles for traders, keepers, and maybes. Chris's pile was larger, of course, but the haggling was epic. By the end of it, Drew figured he had come out way on top. Drew gave up the bigger pieces of candies he wasn't so fond of for little stuff like Mary Janes and Tootsie Rolls to fill his bag back up to the brim. With his hidden stash, minus what he had already eaten, Drew figured that now he had enough candy to last until Christmas.

Luckily, dad drank too many beers and fell asleep early. That made it easier to relax. Drew didn't have to bother lying awake waiting for him to come up the stairs because dad got bored fighting with mom.

School the next day was more of the same.

More teasing by the kids at recess about getting scared at the State School. More Mrs. Rockow being a bitch. More fake-nice gym teacher trying to be his buddy. More calls of Stickboy, a moniker given to him by his classmates, similar to the ones Drew had given Moonface and Bananahead: descriptive and appropriate. The nickname followed him around the hallways while he kept his head down. Somehow, the name had even followed him home recently and on more than one occasion, dad had called him Stickboy while he gave him a much-deserved smack with the belt. Even Chris had jumped on the bandwagon and used the name more and more freely. Mom was the last holdout.

The only bright spot of the day was the weekly trip to the library. Drew brought the books he had almost memorized over the past week to return for five more. He couldn't keep the smile off his face on the walk past the full classrooms "right side of the hall, eliminate the fall" to his favorite room in the building.

As soon as the class filed in and the librarian saw him, she smiled and waved him over. She knew what he liked and usually had choice books set aside just for him. Always scary, or as scary as an elementary school library would let her get.

"I got a new book for you that I think you're going to love," Mrs. Hill said, beaming. She handed Drew a purple-tinged book with an ominous-looking house on the cover. The title of the book was written in a font with an unmistakable texture, something he experienced and saw very often...GOOSEBUMPS...the title warned in its prickly-fleshed font.

"Goosebumps," Drew said out loud with equal parts amazement and wonder.

The smile on the librarian's face grew; clearly, she'd been expecting his reaction.

"Well, that's the name of the series, the actual book is called *Welcome to Dead House*." She emphasized the title with a spooky cadence, which Drew appreciated. "It seems like if these books end up selling well, there may be more, and if you like it, I'll be sure to get them for you."

"Thanks, Mrs. Hill." Drew couldn't believe his luck. This was an actual book. Not something he could fly through in five minutes and written for babies. The act of kindness wasn't lost on him, and Drew didn't believe Mrs. Hill was like the gym teacher with his ulterior motives. She genuinely liked him.

Drew figured she just liked him because he liked books as much as she did. She was the one teacher who went up to bat for him last year when they tried to put him in special-ed. The teachers seemed to be convinced that his lack of talking to them was because of a developmental issue and not the fact that adults were not to be trusted. Drew knew if he messed up with one of the two-faced adults at school and dad heard about it, well, it wouldn't be a good night at home. So, he figured it was better to just stay quiet. However, when he heard about special-ed and the meeting he had to go to, he knew he would have to stand up for himself and prove he didn't belong in that class. He spent all afternoon in the bathroom being sick to his stomach at the prospect. But, at the last minute, the meeting was canceled. Only later did Drew hear from eavesdropping on his parents that Mrs. Hill had stepped in and explained that "Drew was just shy, but very bright and reading books that were way above his grade level."

There was a follow-up meeting a week later where Drew had to do some testing. After that, there was no mention of special-ed. Although there were talks of skipping him ahead a few grades, his size was going to make that difficult with some of the older kids, so it was best to keep him where he was. Now, Drew considered Mrs. Hill a friend and someone he could talk to at school.

Mrs. Hill and Drew made some small talk about the books he was returning today, but Drew was too distracted by the textured letters his fingers were treating like braille. The new book was burning a hole in his concentration. He walked around the library with the other kids, mindlessly poking at various titles and eventually finding one that might actually be helpful. It was full of monster hunting tips and tricks. The part that caught his eye was the bigfoot section. They advised putting flour on the ground so you could see if there were footprints being left behind. This trick was also useful for ghosts, the book said, because if you thought you saw a ghost but there were footprints left behind, you were being tricked because everyone knew ghosts floated and didn't make footprints. Good advice. Drew logged it in his memory bank; sure, the tips and tricks would help with the Gouger and other monsters. He slid the monster hunting book into his hand behind the Goosebumps book.

"Whatcha got there, teacher's pet?" One of the jerks from Drew's class snatched the book he saw Mrs. Hill give him. The jerk clumsily flipped the cover and pages, threatening to crease them.

"Stop!" Drew reached for the book, but the jerk pulled it away. The jerk had thirty pounds on him, but Drew could feel a familiar burning in his stomach. It was the same way he felt when he was fighting with Chris before the pizza guy scared him. The feeling was getting harder to fight back lately. He was sick of the other kids. He didn't even want to be friends with those idiots; he just wanted them to ignore him like he did them.

"If you don't give it back, I'm gonna…" Drew started.

"Gonna what, Stickboy?" he growled under his breath at the threat, careful to keep the tone hidden behind the bookshelf with them.

For a split second, the feeling in Drew's stomach was in his clenched fist. He almost let loose. Then the smiling face of Mrs. Hill and her kindness was front and center. Drew didn't want to make her mad or get her book torn up by this kid because he couldn't control himself. Plus, the beating from dad would be legendary.

"I'll tell Mrs. Hill." The response slid out of Drew's mouth like crude oil. Drew hated the feeling of cowardice more than the boiling in his stomach, but he really liked Mrs. Hill and really hated that snapping belt.

"Oooh," the jerk teased, "not your girlfriend."

Drew's face flushed with embarrassment. He did think she was really pretty, and it was all over his face now.

Thankfully, the bully lost interest when he heard another argument across the library and dropped Drew's book in the aisle. His attention span was as small as his IQ. When the jerk made his way to the picture-book section with his friends, Drew retrieved his own book from the floor and went up front to wait and check out his other monster hunting book. He thumbed through the first two or three pages of the *Goosebumps* book and couldn't help himself as he started reading. He was hooked.

Then the "special" ginger kid Devin started throwing a tantrum shortly after; apparently his argument had escalated. He tore through the library, yelling insults and tearing books from the shelves. That was the end of the class's library visit.

Drew spent the rest of school distracted. He found himself rushing through every printout to give himself a few extra minutes of reading between lessons. This got him in trouble with Mrs. Rockow, so he had to put the book away in his desk, where it sat taunting him until the bell rang. Even on the walk home, he stumbled and tripped on familiar cracks in the sidewalk while he flipped pages. By the time he got home, he was a quarter of the way through. His chores dragged on but were finished before too long and after begging mom to let him get away from the babysitting kids and go up to his room before 5 o'clock, he found himself on his bed tearing through chapters.

When Drew realized he was halfway through the book, he stopped himself. He wanted to draw the pleasure out just a little longer. He didn't want it to end. Every chapter was a cliffhanger, and the terror was top-notch. Despite wondering what was going to happen next, he tore himself away. After the marathon reading session, he needed some candy.

While the pile dwindled in front of him, Drew flipped through the monster hunting book and by the time he was a few pages in, he had started formulating a plan of his own.

With all these new tips and tricks, he could catch the Sidehill Gouger or at least get proof of it. Dad had promised to take him camping, if it stayed nice, and that would be the perfect opportunity. Drew had all the supplies the book suggested he might need for a bigfoot (though it should work for a Gouger): rope, flour, flashlight, camera…everything an amateur monster hunter might need.

This was it; this would be the plan that could get rid of Stickboy, his way of proving to people that he wasn't just a scared baby. He was tired of feeling like a scared pee-pants baby, and a dork, and a coward, and Stickboy. If he could catch a Gouger, they would all see at least part of who he really was. With dad's help, of course. But they would all still see how brave he could be even if his dad was with him. Hell, the newspaper van would probably even come back to take a picture of him with the captured beast.

***

After dinner, Drew couldn't get the dishes done fast enough. Dad and Chris were watching TV and grabbing beers, respectively. Mom was "cleaning," which meant she was making piles of stuff Drew would have to put away later, when she got sick of looking at them. He rushed back up to his research and planning. His army surplus gear, which dad took him to spend his birthday and Christmas money on last spring, was perpetually packed. Always ready for any whim dad might get to take him camping. The monster hunting supplies, on the other hand, were going to take some sneaking around. It wasn't as if mom was going to give him her bag of flour, or dad was going to give him a coil of rope from the shop. Nothing they would miss, but nothing they couldn't part with either. The hardest part would be applying some gentle pressure to dad without pissing him off, to actually take him camping. But first things first, he needed the supplies.

Drew would have to wait until everyone was asleep to do his sneaking around in the dark, gathering monster hunting gear. As he lay there waiting for the sounds of sleep to start coming from his family, he was lost in thought about the Gouger and hoping his rope was going to be strong enough, and that he would be brave enough.

Then a sudden lack of noise smacked him like thunder. All the humming and whirring white noise coming from freezers, fridges, floor heaters, and whatever else was electric shut off all at once. The lack of input left his ears sounding like he was listening to a seashell. Sounds of imaginary rushing water were all that was left.

The only real sound was from Chris's gentle breathing and moths hitting the screen outside the window, though they would be gone soon with no light to chase. Drew's ears slowly adjusted to the lack of stimulation, and he knew what happened. The power got shut off again. It wasn't the first time. Sometimes, it even happened for reasons other than delinquent bills, like lightning. But this wasn't one of those times. The pizza leftovers from the day before gurgled in his stomach, echoing off the walls. Mom was right—they should've just eaten Indian tacos. Now they were all going to have to deal with dad getting mad about the electric bill not getting paid.

Well, at least Drew didn't have to worry about someone turning the lights on while he snuck around, just dad's bad mood until mom figured out a way to pay the bill. Drew swung his legs into the blackness and made his way to his camping bag for the flashlight. He was excited to feel like a spy on a mission. A shiver ran up his spine from the adrenaline rush. He just hoped he didn't run into the Gouger or Moonface or Bananahead or Can Man. The night was full of danger, and he wasn't ready yet, not without the monster hunting supplies.

Chapter 8

Every creak in the floorboards was a gunshot in the darkness and crystal-clear silence provided by the lack of electronics. If he got caught now, he was going to get in big trouble. The bathroom, his best excuse, was behind him now. Drew tried to walk without lifting his feet, to convince the floorboards not to betray him. The shuffle was effective. He was a pretty good sneak. The doorknob on the back mudroom off the kitchen was cold in his hand as he slowly twisted it, knowing there would be a loud click when it released. He held his breath.

CLICK

Even Drew, who was expecting the sound, jumped. He held his breath, listening for any disturbance in mom's snoring or dad's own *click* as he chambered a round in the suicide pistol. Nothing. The door swung open easily after that. Drew had seen to the squeaky hinge problem a few months ago. Another great plan that almost backfired big time. But now the plan gave him a good secret laugh at least once a week.

When Drew had started sneaking out a few months ago to light off leftover 4th of July smoke bombs, he got caught by the hinges. Luckily, at the time, he played it off as having to take Bailey out to poop. But he wouldn't make that mistake twice. The next day, Drew had snuck around the house with a stick of butter, applying it to every hinge in the house. In fact, it seemed to work so well on the doors that Drew decided all the hinges in the house needed the same treatment. After an afternoon of sneaking and un-squeaking every hinge on every door, cabinet, and storage bin, the hinges were slathered in butter and swinging like a dream. Drew was proud of himself…until dad got home. Dad seemed to notice something was up the second he walked in the door. He had walked in, paused, held the door for a second, and then swung it back and forth a couple of times. Then he looked directly into Drew's eyes.

Somehow ,Drew avoided a direct accusation, probably because dad was a few rum and Cokes into his evening, but the look implied dad thought something was up and Drew was involved. Throughout the night, dad had curiously swung a few cabinets and doors in the house, but seemed to forget about it when the TV turned on. Then when an argument started a little bit later and dad stormed into his room, Drew assumed he was going to bed…but he returned a second later with his jacket and slammed the door to his bedroom, hard.

The vibration from the slam reverberated through the house and the old, uneven wooden structure resonated with it. Half of the doors and all the cabinets in the kitchen swung open silently, in unison. Dad spun around like a poltergeist was terrorizing him in a moment of panic.

"WHAT THE HELL?" he yelled, eyeing the still swinging doors.

Chris had let out a squeal of his own and even mom jumped. Drew knew that having no reaction to the swinging doors was going to implicate him, so he stifled his laugh and dropped his jaw in faux surprise. Dad tried to act like he was still mad and continued stomping toward the back door, which was waiting eagerly for him, already open. He slammed it behind him and a couple more doors inside swung open to join the rest of them.

Even now in the dark mudroom thinking about that night when the buttered hinges scared dad, Drew laughed to himself. He looked down at Bailey, who was patiently waiting to go outside with him, tail wagging, wondering what Drew was laughing about. Dad had investigated the buttered hinges a few times after that, but had never figured out why the doors suddenly became possessed. Drew, on the other hand, would laugh wildly when anyone stomped too hard or shut a door too hard and a few of the buttered hinges went to work.

The outside door opened quietly, of course, and Bailey bumped past him, too excited for the tedious task of sneaking. His nails clicked on the wooden steps down to the yard. Drew, still in sneak mode, shuffled down the steps, knowing they would groan from his weight if he went too fast. It was cold outside, but it was warmer than it should be. Too cold for mosquitos anyway. As he made his way across the back yard, Drew had two realizations. First, mom didn't pay the electric bill and it wasn't some freak power accident. Their porch light was the only one on the block that was out. At least it was late, and the obvious sign of being white trash was obvious only to him. Second, dad was gone. The Travelall was missing. Drew wasn't sure how dad left without him knowing. Drew wondered if mom even knew he was gone. The pretty Indian lady and her missing underpants came to mind.

"Bailey, come back here," Drew called as his buddy was wandering toward the alley. It was the same alley the Can Man killed his neighbor's dog in, and he wasn't about to let that happen to Bailey.

The thoughts of the Can Man started the panicky feeling in his stomach. He tried to settle himself back into sneak mode but found his eyes wandering to the trees, looking for Gougers, too. His ears were on high alert for the sound of empty beer cans bouncing on the back of the oversized tricycle. Bailey was done with his business and now stood next to Drew, who clicked on his flashlight, not wanting to go into the black void of dad's shop without it. The beam broke the darkness but only added new a layer of shadows for monsters to hide in. All the rope was on the far side of the shop and as Drew and Bailey made their way over to it, the flashlight beam danced around the blackness, Drew didn't want to let it settle long enough to let the monsters get comfortable in the shadows.

The rope was up too high to reach, so Drew pulled a wooden crate full of scrap metal and junk closer to stand on. He stood on the solid edge of the crate and reached as tall as he could get. His fingers laced around the bottom of the coil, and he tried to pull, but the nail it was hanging on held on tightly. Drew shook the coil, hoping to get it to jump over the lip of the nail, but as he shook, there was a noise behind him.

It was dad's Travelall lumbering its way up the alley toward the parking spot outside the shop. Now in a panic, Drew shook the rope violently and it let loose. The sudden shift of the weight brought the rope down on top of him and the crate tilted backward. It came up hard as his toes rolled off the back and the front of the crate smashed into his shins, spraying rusty screws, scrap metal, old spark plugs, and other random junk all across the floor of the shop.

Drew landed hard on his butt, but his hands flew to the blinding pain in his shins. Both were numb from the point of impact down. His hands could feel the broken skin and slippery feeling of blood on his naked legs. Drew regretted not putting on blue jeans for this mission. The sound of dad's motor didn't care if his legs hurt as it growled closer to its parking place in front of the shop. There was only one way out, and in a few seconds, it was going to be cut off by dad, who was in an unknown condition of sobriety.

A screw dug into Drew's palm as he tried to get himself to his feet. He pulled it out quickly and tried his weight on his shaking legs. They worked, but they hurt badly. He sprayed the floor with his flashlight in a panic, looking at the mess he made and the drops of blood spattered on the concrete. The monsters were forgotten. Dad was home.

There was no time now to clean up the mess he'd made. He would rather catch a beating later under suspicion than now, red-handed, with a more than likely drunk and pissed off dad. Dad didn't even know the power was out yet and that would only exacerbate the situation.

"Crap." Drew flipped the flashlight off, hoping he hadn't already given himself away with it. Luckily, the headlights washed out whatever may have been visible as they pulled in just feet away.

"Bailey," Drew whisper-yelled.

His buddy seemed to sense something was up and played along. The two of them slid out the door and closed it at the same time dad closed the door on his Travelall.

They couldn't make it back across the yard or dad was going to see them, so the only choice was to circle around the shop the opposite way dad was now walking. To the alley, right where the neighbor's dog was killed. Drew was trying to watch the trees, the alley, and the yard at the same time, trying to anticipate where the attack would come from first. He took the rope, which he had somehow hung onto, and tied it around Bailey's neck, not wanting him to run up to dad and give them both away. Slowly, they both crept around the shop. Drew was going to have to wait until dad was inside and then wait until he fell asleep hard enough for Drew to sneak back in.

Then the light to the shop clicked and there was no response from the bulb it was connected to.

"What the fuck?" dad said from inside the shop, followed by some rummaging on the tool bench.

Then a pale-yellow beam of light illuminated the alley from the shop window. Drew instantly recognized it as the ancient flashlight dad had swiped from Grandpa. Dad was now aware the power was out.

"OH, WHAT THE FUCK." Dad was also now aware that Drew had made a mess.

Drew's heart sank. He didn't expect dad to be out, let alone go back into the shop instead of inside. The rope in his hand felt hot and accusatory in his hands. He had to get back inside fast. If dad decided he wanted justice now and went up to Drew's room to dole it out, and he wasn't there... The only thing Drew could do was run down the alley, around the block, through the front yard and into the only unlocked door on the house, the one he'd just snuck out.

With Bailey in tow, the two sprinted the short distance. Bailey gave him some courage and the streetlights (the city always paid the power bill) lit the way. There were no monsters fast enough to catch the pair of sneaks and they were around the block and already slinking back inside through the mudroom. The buttered hinge swung closed silently behind them as they made their way through the house, less worried now that they were inside but still in a hurry in case dad came in looking for the culprit who wrecked his shop. Maybe Dad would just think it was the poltergeist that opened all the doors? Drew couldn't help himself and laughed out loud on the way up the steps to his room. He was scared, but now the adrenaline was wearing off and the shaking legs settled. He rubbed the gashes from the crate and felt them scabbing over already. Despite making a mess in the shop, he felt good about the mission. There was a spanking coming his way, mess in the shop or not, so he wasn't too worried about that.

Drew untied Bailey, who was worn out from the adventure and late-night run. He was licking his paws at the foot of the bed, not worried one bit about the consequences. The rope was wet from the grass, so Drew hung it on his bedpost and took his wet socks off. With the rope secure, he needed only a couple more things for the monster hunting kit. He could get the flour from mom's pantry in the mudroom tomorrow when the babysitting kids had her distracted. The lighter would be trickier, but he knew she kept it in her crossword drawer next to the sink. He could just linger on dishes until she left the room and grab it quickly. No sense in risking any more sneaking tonight.

Drew fell asleep waiting for the sounds of dad coming back inside for the night. Waiting to see how mad dad was going to get about the mess and the electric bill. His eyes grew heavy, waiting for the punishment that didn't come. Not that night at least.

SNAP…SNAP…SNAP.

Dad waited until the morning.

Drew's eyes flew open. The panic in his stomach had been waiting all night for this, and it tensed up. He was scared…but less scared than he was of Moonface, Bananahead, the Can

Man, and Gougers. Those were the actual monsters. Another spanking from dad was going to hurt, but he knew what to expect so the fear of that had worn down to a nub. It was still not going to be very fun. Drew held the thick edge of his blanket up to his chin and waited.

SNAP

That was one of dad's favorite tricks. He could increase fear by increasing anticipation. The leather belt was doubled over and grasped at both ends. Then he would pull the ends apart rapidly, forcing the loose part of the middle of the belt to SNAP together. Just the sound of that used to make Drew cry when he was younger. Now dad would get three or four good smacks in before the tears started.

Dad was in the hallway upstairs now. There were only three SNAPs left until he was standing there looking at him.

"I'm not even going to fucking ask why you messed up my shop," he said before he even got to the doorway. "Because nobody else would have done it, and honestly, I don't even care why."

SNAP

One final vigorous snap as he entered Drew's room. He looked in Drew's direction, not even glancing at Chris, who was tucked under his covers pretending this wasn't happening. Before dad's eyes even got to Drew, they landed on the coil of rope drying on the bedpost.

"What is my rope doing up here?" Dad asked, not wanting a response. His eyes burned into Drew's own now after finding the stolen rope.

"I was just putting a kit together for when we go camping," Drew offered, not wanting to lie, but knowing it didn't matter.

Drew's knees were pulled up to his chest now, and he was pushed up as close as he could be to the headboard on his bed. His answer only infuriated dad further.

"IN CASE YOU DIDN'T NOTICE, YOUR MOM CAN'T EVEN PAY THE FUCKING ELECTRIC BILL AND YOU THINK I'M TAKING YOU CAMPING?" Dad yelled.

The loudness of it made Drew recoil further, his face now twisted in a grimace, fearing the oncoming assault. Then dad lowered his voice to a threatening growl and leaned in.

"If you think I'm going to take someone camping who destroys my shop and steals my rope, you got more than this spanking coming your way and I ain't gonna be there to help with that." The rum was still thick on his breath.

"Sorry. I won't bug you about camping, I promise," Drew pleaded. "I'll pick up the shop, too. I forgot I spilled the junk bo..."

"STAND up," Dad ordered, no room for arguments in his voice.

"PLEEASE, nooo," Drew begged as his dad grabbed his ankle and slid him off the edge of the bed. Drew's butt hit the floor hard, knocking the wind out of him, preventing further pleading.

"Take your pants off," Dad ordered coldly. The anger was still there, but it was ebbing.

The air was being forcefully sucked back into Drew's lungs and gave him another opportunity to beg for mercy.

"No...please just a regular spanking," Drew said, crying already.

He didn't make it three smacks this time. The tears rolled freely. Having to take his pants off for a spanking didn't just make it hurt way worse. It was humiliating, and Chris would be making fun of him for it all week.

There was no room for mercy from dad. He had a lesson to teach. Dad grabbed Drew's shorts and in one motion, pulled not just them but his tighty whities down too. Now, bare-assed, Drew attempted to hide his shame and cover his wiener with his hands, which gave dad the opportunity to grab him unobstructed. Drew was forced over dad's lap and his legs, now twisted in underwear and PJs, flailed in the air behind him as he tried desperately to avoid the oncoming lesson.

It came anyway.

***

Breakfast didn't see his day getting any better.

After a toilet paper-tape bandage was slapped onto his shins, without question of how they got like that, breakfast was served. Mom was out of oatmeal, patience, and electricity. She attempted a Dutch-oven sized omelet on the top of the woodstove. What she produced was questionable vegetables with even more questionable cheese she found in the fridge, mixed with runny, uncooked eggs. The wood stove was only simmering because anything more would cook everyone in the house alive. Dad's habit of having it burning from late September until mid-May didn't care if it was an Indian summer or not. As mom plopped the mush into his bowl, the first thing Drew did was search through it for a hair. The runny consistency made this relatively easy. No hair, but the deeper he dug, the more he didn't want to put it in his mouth. All he could think of was Grandpa's story about the Gouger eggs with garlic and onions. Drew shifted on his sore ass and contemplated how much worse it would get if he didn't finish his breakfast.

He forced it down somehow. But not for long. After Chris teased him about his bare-assed spanking on the way to school, he ditched him for his friends. This gave Drew the perfect opportunity to puke behind a garbage can. His stomach had spent all night being upset and the morning punishment, from both parents, was too much. He watched the half-cooked eggs and half-rotten bell pepper splash onto the side of someone's trash can and felt bad. After a cursory search for a garden hose to spray it off came up empty, he simply left it for the Can Man. The thought of the man gave Drew the shivers, and he looked up and down the alley to make sure he wasn't going to be bumping into him or getting bumped into by him.

School sucked. More teasing, more Mrs. Rockow being a bitch, more Drew wishing he were anywhere else. The only bright spot was Mrs. Hill stopping him in the hallway and asking about *Goosebumps*. Drew had finished it that morning in class and had already started it over. When Drew told her how much he loved it, the pretty smile on her face nearly doubled in size. She told him that in fact it was a series, the next one was already out, she had already ordered it, and it should be there by library day for him.

Drew tripped over himself, thanking her, then spent the rest of the day wondering how some people ended up like Mrs. Rockow and mom and dad, but some people ended up like Mrs. Hill or the gym teacher. Drew made a promise to himself that when he had kids, he was going to be like the gym teacher and marry a girl like Mrs. Hill. His face turned red thinking about it while he ate his tots alone at lunch.

After school, Drew ran into Jeremy. They talked about Halloween and their hauls of candy and eventually got to talking baseball cards. It was deadly serious business between them. They had both been collecting for as long as they knew each other and had an agreement not to screw each other over like they would other kids in trades. Instead, they would help each other fill out their rosters. Up to this point, Drew had full rosters for Topps and Fleer from 1983 (the year his dad started a modest collection, which Drew inherited) until 1991. Jeremy was slightly behind but with all of Drew's doubles had almost caught up. This current year, though, Jeremy was pulling ahead. He had a lawn mowing job and more money, so he could buy all the new packs of cards while Drew fell behind, looking for change in dad's truck and in the couch.

They went to Jeremy's house and traded cards for a while so Jeremy could fill in some blanks and Drew could get his doubles from this year. While the Beckett pages turned furiously, and deals were made, the boys talked about camping and fishing. Drew was still pretty upset from that morning. His hot ass had cooled off, but the heat from dad canceling his camping trip with him only increased. The one chance he would have had to catch a Gouger and prove he was brave was slipping away.

Then Drew had a great idea. He and Jeremy could go camping themselves at the park. The migrants were gone. It was still nice out (like Grandpa had said it would be), and most importantly of all, Drew was on a mission.

After a brief discussion and only a little convincing, they both came up with alibis to get them out of the house on Saturday. Jeremy was always ready to go fishing, so Drew leaned into that, omitting the monster hunting portion because he knew Jeremy and knew if he told him too soon, he wouldn't go. Jeremy wasn't the horror aficionado that Drew was and had a yellow streak when it came to anything scary.

With camping and sneaking out plans made, the rest of the week flew by. The only time it slowed down was late Friday during the library visit, when Mrs. Hill handed him the second in the *Goosebumps* series. Other than that, the rest of the week was gray. Drew barely heard any of the teasing the kids gave him, barely felt the spanking dad gave him for not picking the shop up fast enough after school, barely felt mom crack a ladle on his skull while he was watching *The Gate* (he forgot to wash a pan he left to soak). He barely even thought of monsters…which may have been a mistake.

By the time Saturday morning rolled around, and Drew was making his way out of the house with his gear (including monster hunting supplies minus a nice rope, which dad made him put back, although Drew had replaced it with a clothesline), he already felt braver. Mom bought the excuse Drew had sold her. All he said was he was staying the night at Jeremy's. She seemed so happy that Drew had been invited somewhere that she forgot to ask any questions. But Drew knew the alibi was foolproof because Jeremy's mom had stiffed mom on a babysitting bill. There was no chance mom would call her and check in even if she did care enough to do so.

With the whole day freed up, he and Jeremy would have a few hours to set up camp and fish before he would have to start setting up his trap. A tingling started in his spine from excitement, momentarily relieving the cramps in his stomach. Drew just hoped the only monster that would show up would be the Gouger. He wasn't prepared to trap Moonface, Bananahead, or the Can Man…not yet.

Chapter 9

Drew's bag bounced on his spine. It was full to bursting. He could hear the weight gain shakes mom had gotten at the store the other day, now sloshing around in there. She had reminded him while they were shopping of how expensive the shakes were and how broke they were, so not to waste them.

While they were shopping, she had picked through sales and coupons, trying to make her list feed everyone until dad got work. Her face was still red from the fight that morning about going on food stamps. Dad was too proud for them, and mom said that was stupid because the government money was meant for "situations like these.: Mom lost and Drew felt proud of dad's pride. Until they were in the checkout lane. The woman next to them had a cart full of all kinds of treats and snacks and good food like Red Baron pizza. Drew wished he could turn the Hamburger Helper and oatmeal filling their own cart into something more similar to hers. When it came time to pay, the woman pulled out these little pieces of paper that looked like foreign money.

"You can't use food stamps for dog food, ma'am," the cashier said to Drew's surprise — not surprise at the dog food, but that the food stamps could buy you the kinds of food in her cart.

"Jeremiah, put this back and grab the dog a few pounds of burger. He likes that better anyway," the woman with the food stamps said to her son as she handed him the enormous bag of kibble to put back on the shelf.

Simultaneously, the clerk's, mom's, and Drew's mouths had fallen open. Drew processed the layers of this conversation in complete shock and came up with two conclusions. Dad's "pride" was costing him top-tier munchies. And he would never waste the weight gain shakes that mom bought him again…plus he would do his best to eat all his dinners. Mom was making ends meet that weren't even in the same neighborhood and Drew felt proud of her.

Tonight, while camping, he would be sure to finish the shakes she bought him, no matter how full they made him feel, along with the Doritos and Slim Jims he grabbed at Ben Franklin's. He dug all week for change, coming up empty, but ended up finding a five-dollar bill in the locker room at school. The baseball cards on the rack near the register took what was left of his good fortune while he was checking out after grabbing the snacks.

Jeremy was a block down from his house, waiting for him on his bike. Drew felt stupid for not bringing his own bike, but he doubted he could have pedaled with all his gear anyway.

"Where's your bike?" Jeremy called out.

"Flat tire." Drew didn't feel like explaining.

Jeremy hopped off his bike. Drew held out a handful of cards for him. They were doubles or cards he knew Jeremy needed. It didn't hurt to build some goodwill with a guy who had a reliable way of earning money.

"What's that?" Jeremy asked.

"I got some packs at Franklin's, and these were doubles. Do you want to take your bike back home first?"

"Nah, I'll walk it." The gears on Jeremy's bike clicked as they walked.

As the boys walked to the park, their poles poked out of their bags. Both instinctively picked up their pace and didn't mention the attack from Moonface and Bananahead as they passed between the State School and the cemetery along the way. They knew better than to spook themselves this early, before they were going camping. The small talk was all about fishing, camping, and (from Jeremy's end) girls. By the time their pace slowed and they entered the park, they were already both snapping their poles back together, fidgeting with their packs while they walked, so they didn't miss out on a single cast.

Surprisingly, the small campground at the front of the park had a few fancy campers and at least three other sites with tents. This late in the season, the small crowd seemed like a rush. The Indian summer had everyone out squeezing the last bits of freedom out before the snow put them all in an icy prison for the winter. The boys laughed to themselves at the manicured sites with water spigots. That wasn't camping. Camping involved being in the woods and not being able to see concrete. The jokes faded as they entered the woods. It seemed disrespectful to shamble into the wilderness and its serenity with giggles. The crunching of the drying leaves echoed around them as they adjusted to the change in the environment.

Drew's ears were keen to listen for hooves, but he doubted the Gougers were dumb enough to come out in the daylight. The path the boys were following was also too uneven for wheelchairs and tricycles with giant bins full of cans. It was the perfect spot to catch a Gouger and not be bothered by the other monsters.

The bags hit the ground on the spot the boys agreed on earlier in the week. It was a spot most adults were too lazy to walk to, far enough out so they could have a fire, and no one would see the smoke. Plus, it was right next to the river so they could fish even when it got dark…although Drew had other plans.

"Do you think Mrs. Hill is pretty?" Drew asked the older boy, testing the waters, unsure if the way he felt about her was normal.

"Hell, yeah, she is. About the only teacher worth a damn at the whole school, really." Jeremy smiled at Drew. "And you are her little pet," he teased.

It didn't hurt coming from Jeremy like it did the other boys.

"No, I'm not. Who even said that?" Drew objected, but his red face told the truth.

"Everyone knows that. She always has books set aside and comes up to you at lunch and rubs your shoulders." Jeremy made a motion with his neck and head wobbling around as if Mrs. Hill were there rubbing them.

"Well…at least it ain't Mrs. Rockow," Drew teased.

Both boys forgot the sanctity of the woods and laughed wildly. The boys left their bags at the spot they would camp later, but now it was time to fish. They made their way to the river and tossed in their lines without much talk. As soon as the lines settled in the water, Drew regretted not grabbing drinks before they left their bags.

"Hey, you want a sody-pop?" Drew asked, using Grandpa's lingo.

"Sure…nerd."

They both laughed again like maniacs.

Drew ran back to their bags and shuffled through his pack, fishing out a Pepsi he snagged from dad's stack of soda in the mudroom. The cold weight gain shake pressed against the back of his hand while he dug, and a pit formed in his stomach. His hand turned and grabbed the pink bottle for himself. There was a crunching of leaves that made him freeze in place for a second and scan his surroundings. The river protected him to the rear, but in front of him was nothing but thinning trees. The bare lower sticks had lost most of their leaves while the canopy stayed as full as possible, soaking up the last rays of summer. Something about the naked branches was skeletal. Looking through them creeped him out, but he scanned the woods anyway. Seeing nothing, Drew realized how glad he was that Jeremy was with him. He ran back to the river, a little freaked out, drinks in hand.

"Jesus, shake it up, why dontcha," Jeremy said as Drew sprinted back to the river.

"Sorry, I left my pole in the water," he lied and handed the older, braver boy the shaken soda.

"What's that?" Jeremy asked, eyeing the shake.

"Well. Last time I went to the doctor, he said I was under-weight, so I had to drink these sometimes. They are pretty good, though."

Drew held the bottle out. Jeremy grabbed it and took a drink.

"UGH, tastes like chalk and strawberry milk." He handed the bottle back and cracked the Pepsi Drew had brought for him. It sprayed both of them with sticky sugar water.

"Ahhh, it's not so bad." Drew grabbed the bottle and chugged it in one huge drink. His stomach felt like it might pop, but he smiled. It went down so fast, he didn't even taste it, which was good because he didn't waste it. Mom cut corners for him to get it.

More laughter as the mood lightened, and the boys swished their sticky hands in the river.

The jokes and talk of baseball returned as they continued fishing. They spent most of the day like that. Taking turns grabbing sodas and pissing in the river, giving ever-increasingly stupid advice on why they weren't catching fish, and soon enough talk of starting a fire. They knew it was forbidden for kids, but it just wasn't camping without one. Since they had spent more than a couple of hours casting into the river with no fish, they split up and collected some sticks for the fire.

Jeremy stowed his gear, Drew collected his, then they went in opposite directions. One upstream, one down. Drew was glad he got the path back along where they had already walked. He was familiar with it, and it would give him some time to prepare the place that looked like a natural chokepoint for the Gouger trap. As he walked, he picked up some dead branches that seemed thick enough to be worth grabbing. Though his mind was on the Gougers, his eyes were on the skeletons swaying in the breeze, pretending to be trees.

Drew put the sticks on the ground near the natural chokepoint and surveyed the area. It was a perfect spot for a monster trap. First things first. He grabbed a branch from a small evergreen that most resembled a broom, and he began sweeping the area where the small clearing narrowed between two trees. He stayed alert as he worked, making sure he wasn't being snuck up on. The sun was racing him now. He didn't bring his flashlight with him because he didn't anticipate the modest canopy to block so much light. With the speed at which the early fall sun was setting, he had only about ten minutes before it was "dark."

There were a few branches on the narrow chokepoint that Drew thought might snag his rope, so he snapped them off. The last thing he had time for was placing a thick branch into the forks of the two trees at the narrow gap. The branch was thick enough to hold strong once his rope was tied off.

"What are you doing, playing house?" a voice rang out in the silence behind him.

"AAAAAGHHHH!" Drew screamed and wheeled.

"WHAT?" Jeremy said, bug-eyed and scared.

"Jeez, man, don't sneak up on me like that." Drew's heart was racing. He would have felt more stupid if Jeremy hadn't been scared, too.

"Sorry. But really, what is that?" Jeremy motioned to the stick Drew had just finished placing.

"Uhh nothing…well, something for later." Drew tried to cover his tracks, but the older boy's curiosity wasn't going to let him off the hook.

"What?"

"I'll just show you. Come help me grab my bag." Drew walked back toward the campsite, planning how to tell Jeremy along the way.

It was mostly quiet between them as they retrieved their packs and got close to the chokepoint again.

"Well, last week, my grandpa told me a story about a monster called a Sidehill Gouger." He hoped the hook was enough for the boy to let him start his rendition of the story without getting spooked off immediately, and would keep him quiet while Drew told it.

"What's a Sidehill Crouger?" Jeremy asked.

"Gouger...Guh, Guh," Drew corrected. His hook had worked.

Drew spent the better part of the next five minutes trying his best to do his grandpa's story justice. As the darkness grew around them, so did Jeremy's eyes. The only interruptions were the occasional, "Unh uh no way" from Jeremy while Drew simply kept talking.

By the time Drew had finished, both boys were spooked and standing about six feet closer together than they had been at the onset.

"There's no way that's true," Jeremy contested at the end, trying to convince himself.

"Well, that's what Grandpa said, and he never lies. Plus, afterward, I swear it chased me through the hills by the houses near the cemetery after trick or treating," Drew embellished a little.

"Well, even if it is, what the hell does that have to do with this?" Jeremy motioned to the area Drew had prepared.

Drew slammed his hand into his bag and fished around for a minute and grabbed what he was looking for, dragging the coil of used clothesline along with it. It was his monster hunting book from the library. He had checked it out again on Friday so he could show the parts of the trap he wanted to make to Jeremy, assuming he got that far.

"This book tells you everything you need to know about how to catch monsters, especially big ones in the woods. It even has some stuff about ghosts at the back." Drew was anxiously watching Jeremy flip the pages now, hoping he didn't tease him about believing in monsters.

"No way. This book is about bigfoot, not a Sidehill Couger," Jeremy argued.

"Gow-jer," Drew said slowly, feeling annoyed, "and yeah, it's mostly like that, but we can use it for Gougers cos I bet a bigfoot is probably even stronger than one of them, so if it works on him, it will work on the Gougers," Drew said convincingly.

"Dude, we were supposed to camp and make a fire. I don't want to hunt monsters." Jeremy was clearly spooked.

"Ok, ok, you don't have to do anything. Just wait for a minute for me, please," Drew pleaded, not wanting the hunt to be over. "Plus, it will trap it and keep us safe tonight…don't be chicken," Drew taunted now.

"I'm not chicken, but I'm not stupid either," Jeremy said with his feathers ruffled.

"Ok, sorry, just wait for one second," Drew said, not leaving room for an objection.

He hurriedly took the plastic rope and tied it around the base of the thicker of the two trees, at the narrow place where he placed the stick in the forks. Then he tossed the slack over the bridge he had made between the two trees.

"Do you know how to make a lasso…no, a noose?" he asked Jeremy, realizing the stupid book never covered that part.

"No…I'm leaving," Jeremy said, obviously wanting to get out of the darkness of the woods. His eyes were playing the darting game like Drew's had done since he first heard Grandpa's story. He edged away from the steep bank of the river where the Gougers might be able to run with their offset legs.

"Just wait five more seconds," Drew begged again.

His hands tried their best to make a knot that resembled a noose. He grabbed the baggie of flour from his backpack and started sifting it around the chokepoint, being careful not to step on it. Now, for the bait. He pulled a pair of underwear he saved from getting washed out from another sandwich bag in his backpack.

"What the heck is that?" Jeremy asked in the fading light.

Drew reached back into his backpack and tossed the flashlight to Jeremy.

"Here, hold this for me." Drew waited, realizing the next thing he was about to say sounded crazy, so he would have to lighten it up. "And those are my dirty underwear. I figure the bastards must hunt by smell, so get a whiff, baby." Drew feigned a laugh and flapped his underwear in the air in front of him.

"Oh, man, our sodas were in there." Jeremy tried to laugh as well.

The joke worked to lighten the mood and the beam from the flashlight Jeremy was holding relaxed enough for Drew to secure the tighty whities to a branch just above the noose, careful not to disturb the flour with his own footprints.

"What's the flour for?"

"So, if someone is tricking us, we can see the human footprints and not hooves with claws," Drew said simply.

"Who is gonna trick us, dude? You're crazy." Jeremy was over it. "I'm leaving now and I'm taking the flashlight."

"Ok, it's ok, I already got it mostly ready. We can take a picture of it later if the trap works." Drew shook his Polaroid in the beam of light.

The walk back to the campsite was awkward but the fire they started was crackling and warm. However, as the sun finished setting, both boys started shivering. The conversation was suddenly lacking, and Drew could tell Jeremy's mood had changed after the Gouger story. Drew felt bad for scaring him but as they finished setting up their tents and got ready to eat, the mood eased a bit.

Jeremy was busy cooking hot dogs, and Drew was getting out the chips when they both heard the footsteps in the woods. They tried to convince themselves that it was just a curious deer, but the story was too fresh in both of their minds to let that be real.

"Hey, man...you can have the hot dogs...I think I gotta go home," Jeremy blurted out, already grabbing his bag.

"What, why?" Drew said unbelievingly. "Dude, don't be scared. I'm sorry, it was just a story...please, don't go."

"I'm not scared. I just never told my dad I was going to stay overnight. I think my mom might know, but I gotta make sure or I'm gonna get in trouble...like how your dad gets," Jeremy protested with the insinuation.

"Well, can I come to your house?" Drew asked, realizing the camping trip was over.

"No way, dude. My mom hates your mom cos she told everyone at the bar she was a thief," Jeremy said, obviously masking his fear with anger.

"Well, she is. My mom babysat you guys for like that whole summer and your mom never even paid her for it." Drew was pissed off now, too. Mom might be mean to him sometimes, but she always helped people and didn't deserve to get treated badly.

"Whatever...STICKBOY!" Jeremy yelled back as he pedaled away as fast as he could. His loose backpack was the last thing Drew saw as it bounced away in the darkness.

The insult stung that time.

Now left in the growing darkness alone, Drew didn't know what to do. The hot dogs were burning. His pup tent was set up. His trap was already set. All he had was a long walk home in the dark to a beating. Through the woods, past the cemetery and the State School, the Can man was probably already out prowling through alleyways. Plus, if he went home, he would get in trouble for lying about his alibi because mom would be sure to check a story out like Jeremy's parents sending him home in the dark alone. Or he could stay and tough it out and not be a pee pants baby about it.

The sounds of the woods turned sinister. Every noise became a pair of Gougers prowling. The footsteps he tricked himself into thinking had belonged to fawns earlier became heavy and seemed to circle the bubble of light created by the modest fire. Drew tossed what was left of the sticks onto the fire and watched the embers dance into the darkness. He made sure none landed, so they didn't start a fire. The hot dogs were all but burned to a crisp at this point, so Drew just let the coals eat them. He wasn't hungry after that shake anyway.

There was a giant cracking of a branch somewhere in the forest behind him where Jeremy had gone looking for sticks. Another flaw in Drew's plan—he should have made two traps, one on each side of the trail. For a second, Drew tried to convince himself it was just a falling branch like the one in the back yard the other night.

THUMP…SCRAAAAAPE

The sound was unmistakable, just like Grandpa had described it.

Drew grabbed his flashlight and pointed it toward the sound and froze. The sounds stopped as well, knowing better than to attack in the light. Drew's free hand, which was not busy shaking the flashlight, started pushing the pup tent down and stuffing it, along with his sleeping bag, back into his backpack. The camping trip was really over now. Drew wished he could put the fire out, but it was the only thing that was going to slow the Gougers down as he made a run for it.

There was a part of Drew that was screaming to stay. Get out the Polaroid and sit tight…this is it. This was Drew's opportunity to prove he was as brave as dad and the other adults. Bravery seemed to be the only difference between kids and adults, as Drew never felt intellectually challenged by them and they were always messing stuff up just as badly as he did. He never didn't pay the power bill; he just made a mess in the shop.

The yellow, scared side of Drew won, with a little more motivation from the Gougers.

THUMP…SCRAAAAAPE.

Closer this time.

Drew was already running. The Polaroid bounced against his spine in the backpack, which was only half as full as it had been a couple of hours ago. The flashlight swept from the trail ahead of him to the path behind him.

THUMP…SCRAPE…THUMP..SCRAPE..THUMP.SCRAPE.

They were gaining on him now.

The flashlight stayed pointing forward, shaking in his hand as he tried to illuminate the path ahead. Drew didn't want to turn around. He didn't want to see them or their burning yellow eyes or their glowing green scales. His eyes were trained on the ground directly in front of his feet. He couldn't afford to trip on a root like some bimbo in a horror movie, so he kept his eyes locked on the ground ahead of him.

SMACK

Something grabbed Drew around his neck from behind and slammed him into the ground, sending up a giant cloud of white dust. The flashlight was suddenly obstructing his view rather than helping, like high beams in a fog. The sound of his own terrified breathing filled his ears, and he could taste blood in his mouth. He coughed and spat, feeling his neck for blood from the attack while he tried to suck air past the pain.

The white dust billowed around him while he stumbled back to his feet, feeling dizzy. He panned the light around, looking for the Gougers, but saw nothing. Then, when he pointed it back down the trail in front of him, something swung into his face.

"AAAAAAGGHHHHH."

It took Drew only a split-second to realize what it was. It was his clothesline noose. The noose had held tight, but the cheap plastic rope had snapped when it caught him under his chin. He spat out a mouthful of blood and licked the cut on the inside of his lip. The flour he sprinkled on the ground earlier was still thick in the air from his tumble.

The only thing his monster trap had caught was an idiot who was bad at making plans.

Still terrified but now feeling stupid, Drew grabbed his bag, leaving the monster hunting supplies behind. They were useless. He ran the rest of the way to where the woods opened to the safe harbor of the manicured campsites and their concrete pads. He couldn't go home, but maybe he could spend the night surrounded by happy families who were gathered around fires roasting marshmallows and playing board games. Maybe he could have fun by osmosis.

Feeling more stupid than scared, he made his way to a spot in between two of the fancy campers. He got a funny look from one of the wives, but her husband took her by the sleeve and led her away. Drew didn't know that you had to pay for spots and that he was now setting up his tent right in the middle of two people who had paid. All he knew was that he was safe for now.

As he re-staked his tent and realized he had left his sleeping bag in the panic, something tapped his shoulder.

"AAAAGHHH…sorry," Drew said almost in the same breath as he looked up and saw the husband who had dragged his wife away.

"It's ok," the guy said with a smile and a light chuckle. "We wanted to know if you wanted a burger or some marshmallows or anything. We've got too much to take home with us in the morning."

The offer was welcome but maybe Drew was more like dad than he knew as his pride had him politely reject the offer. He flashed the Doritos and Slim Jims from his bag for proof that he had dinner. He almost showed the nice guy the shake, but didn't feel like answering questions about that. Before he left, the guy said if Drew needed anything, he could knock on the camper any time of night. Drew couldn't believe the disparity in how adults acted. Some were more like his monsters, some were more like, well, adults. He knew he would rather let the Gougers eat him than ask for help, but he wished he could get in the camper and go home with them in the morning, too.

***

There were no more Gougers that night, no scales, no burning yellow eyes.

Drew woke up feeling better than he had, maybe ever. Sure, he had failed in his hunt, but he was thinking most of it might just be in his head and maybe monsters weren't as real as they seemed. His solo night of camping proved to him at least that he wasn't a chicken who ran home like a baby, like Jeremy, who was older than him. The swelling in his throat seemed to feel better as he chugged the last shake from mom. It had never tasted better. He quickly packed up what was left of his gear and gave a nod to the guy who had been nice for no reason last night. The guy was packing the fancy camper, ready to go back to their probably even fancier house. Drew started whistling while he walked back to the campsite in the woods that he had run from the night before. He felt pretty good, considering.

As Drew passed the idiot trap, headed back to the campsite for his sleeping bag, he took the clothesline out of the tree and kicked the flour into the dirt. "Leave it better than you found it," the mantra from scouts rang in his memory. The bright morning washed away his nerves and Drew was convinced the chase last night was ninety percent imagination...that was until he saw his campsite.

His sleeping bag had been stomped, by something, into a muddy mess. It was ripped apart and the ground around the campsite was devoid of grass. Instead, it was muddy and wet, like the fairgrounds after a rodeo. There were coals and ash stomped into the mixture, and the rocks that had lined the fire had been strewn about.

The Gougers were real.

The sprint back out of the forest was much easier than it had been in the dark. And he didn't fall into any of his traps. He just kept on running. Past Jeremy's house with his bike in the front yard, past the cemetery and State School, past the alleyways the Can Man hunted in, and well away from anything that resembled a hill. He was getting familiar with the flattest path through town.

The red door on the front of his house had never looked so welcoming, but its red paled in comparison to the color of mom's face when Drew walked in the door.

Chapter 10

It stayed nice out for the two weeks like Grandpa had said it would, but he didn't get to enjoy all of it. His coffee buddy Harold showed up to take him out for breakfast and found his body in his yard. He was dead.

When Drew walked in the front door from the night of monster hunting, the smell of candle smoke was thick in the air. Drew was busy picking cockleburs out of every exposed piece of fabric. His fingers pulled at them at them while his red-faced mom explained to Drew that Grandpa was gone. The good mood from surviving the camping trip was all but forgotten. A lump grew in Drew's throat. He tried to fight back the tears, but mom's own didn't make it any easier. Before long, they were crying together in the candlelit room. Chris, who had never been close to Grandpa (mostly because he was lazy and Grandpa hated that), was busy coloring by the window where there was enough light. He didn't seem bothered at all.

Drew's fingers found a stubborn cocklebur stuck behind his ear and his fingers worked at it while he started asking the hundred questions he had. But he knew mom wouldn't have the answers. Even if she knew the answers, Drew doubted she would share them with him.

"But...what happened to him...he looked good at Halloween." Drew hitched as he talked.

"He was just old, sweety. Think about it, almost a hundred. He had a pretty good run." Mom tried to comfort him, but it didn't help.

"No, it wasn't a good run. The Gougers ate his mom, and he had to move away from his home and his friends, and his own kid was a drunk who died, and he was alone in that stinky house." Drew was pissed now. "The only time he wasn't alone at home is when me and dad went over to help with chores and dad doesn't even like to go over anymore because Grandpa is the only one who ever would tell him the truth."

Suddenly, very aware of what was coming out of his mouth, Drew darted his eyes around the house, praying dad wasn't just lurking somewhere absorbing the insults, ready to snap the air with his belt.

Mom confirmed his absence. "He's gone with your uncle."

Drew's fingers finally got a good grip on the stubborn cocklebur behind his ear and gave it a good tug. There was a pinching feeling that was all too familiar. Drew looked at his fingers and the little legs of the tick were crab-walking in his pinched fingers, trying to escape. Its body was only slightly swollen and still brown. It hadn't filled itself enough with his blood to swell and discolor to that sickly white resembling the top of a Q-Tip.

"TICK!" Drew screamed, forgetting for a minute that Grandpa had just died.

"AAAAAGHHHHHHHH" The box of crayons Chris was using tipped over and a rainbow of crayons spilled over the edge of the card table. Chris took off running to the bathroom.

Drew's pants were already on the floor, followed quickly by his tighty whities and his shirt. His pride was of no concern as he stood naked and panicking in the living room. His arms were out to his sides as he spun wildly in circles. Mom was doing her best to give him a once-over. But he was spinning too fast for her to be effective at the search.

"Drew, stop, I can't see anything." Mom grabbed him by the shoulders and stopped his momentum.

His hands flew to his privates and started feeling around as he prayed to God he didn't find some unknown nodule on his bits. Then he saw the look on mom's face. It wasn't good.

"Let's go to the bathroom." Her face had gone from a deep red to a pale white.

"AAAAGHHHHH. WHY!" Drew was freaking out.

"We have to smear them in Vaseline. If we just yank them out, their heads will get stuck in your body and get you sick," Mom said, trying to stay calm.

Drew knew she hated ticks just as much as he did. Mom didn't even go camping anymore after her own panicked strip session when she found a tick the last time she went. She was probably responsible for the panic that set in both boys at the mere mention of a tick. The fear of ticks seemed to be contagious.

"THEM…how many are there?" Drew felt dizzy.

"Just go. Where were you at that you got so many?" The reasonable question hung in the air for a minute.

"Me and Jeremy were just down by the river, and I forgot the OFF." It was mostly true. He was by the river with Jeremy, and he had forgotten the Deep Woods Off. Usually, mom would bathe him in it before he left if she knew he was going to be fishing or playing in the woods. All the monster hunting had distracted Drew from the real threat.

Chris was perched on the toilet in his underwear, scratching his scalp when mom dragged Drew through the open bathroom door. The bathroom candle that was the size of a coffee can was burning brightly enough to illuminate the faker. The closest Chris had gotten to the outside was when dad opened the door to leave earlier that morning. Watching him pretend to be scared and looking for imaginary ticks only pissed Drew off.

"Get him out of here," Drew said, holding his privates.

"Go upstairs," Mom barked at Chris.

"NO way! It's dark up there," Chris argued.

"Then go in the living room," Mom offered the alternative.

"NO! Drew dropped ticks in there," Chris argued again, now holding his legs to his chest on his perch.

"GET OUT!" Drew yelled, sick of the argument. He needed these parasites off his body now.

At this, Chris's attitude returned. He jumped down from the toilet and marched out of the bathroom.

"Have fun with your ticks, Stickboy." He scooted quickly past Drew, who tried to throw a punch but only left his privates exposed, so his hands clapped back into position.

Mom smacked Drew on the back of his head hard enough to ring his bell. Then the slathering started. She smeared Vaseline through his hair and then searched his body for more stowaways. Each time she found one, she would put a dab of Vaseline on it. Each dab increased Drew's anxiety. He stood there naked while mom continued dabbing.

"What were you doing at the river?" mom asked, seeming to make small talk. Drew knew better. She was trying to catch him in a lie.

"Nothing, just fishing."

Weaving the web took all Drew's attention and he was distracted from the slowly suffocating ticks. He could feel them trying to wriggle their way out of his body if he thought about it too much.

"Oh, yeah? What'd you catch?" mom asked with zero skill.

"Nothing much except for some moss."

"So, if I call Jeremy's mom, she's gonna say you boys were fishing?"

Mom offered the idle threat, but Drew knew there was no way in hell she was going to call Jeremy's mom. Not unless it was to fight with her about the unpaid babysitter debt.

"Sure, I don't care." Drew knew he had won.

"Well, what happened to your shins?" Mom pointed to the scabs from his night of sneaking and stealing rope from dad's shop.

"Mom, ticks PLEASE." Drew couldn't take lying anymore.

"Chris, bring in the hot water pot from the wood stove," Mom relented, seeming to want the situation to just be resolved.

There was no answer.

"CHRISSS!" Mom yelled again and waited. "Jesus...don't move. I'll be right back."

Leaving Drew alone with the ticks and thoughts of his dead grandpa, mom went to grab the pot of water that perpetually sat on the stove. The wriggling ticks were itching as they vacated their feeding holes. Drew watched carefully for them to make an escape. The last thing he wanted was for the little bastards to get loose in the house.

Mom was back with the pot of water, which was sending up warnings of steam that it was too hot for his skin. She grabbed the other bucket of water, which they used to flush the toilet, and added the pot of near-boiling water to it, making a lukewarm mixture. Then she grabbed a pair of tweezers and the candle by the sink.

"Don't move." Mom began the extraction.

Each tick popped and burned with the aid of the Vaseline as mom held them to the flame. Each pop released a bit of tension until the only thing left was the thoughts of Grandpa. All said and done, mom pulled thirteen ticks off his body. When they finished, his skin was shining from the Vaseline and his hair resembled a greaser from the '50s. Mom tried her best with the bucket of quickly cooling water to get the Vaseline off, but it didn't work very well. She slicked his hair back with dad's plastic comb instead.

"Hey, that looks pretty good on ya." Mom was obviously trying her best to lighten the mood.

"Thanks…and thanks for getting the ticks off of me." Drew was freezing. "Can I go get dressed?"

"Yes, please." Mom laughed. "And when you get warmed up, take that bug-infested bag outside and shake out all your gear…and refill the flush bucket, please."

"Ok." Drew was glad she wasn't going to pry any further about his night out.

As he hung the clothes on the line and shook out his tent, Drew thought of the sleeping bag he had left behind. The Gougers had stomped it into oblivion, but Drew wished he had tried to salvage it. Now he was going to be left without one next time dad wanted to go camping…if there was a next time. Dad always broke his promises, and Drew didn't think he would be going solo camping again anytime soon.

The hand pump in the yard sloshed as he filled the flush bucket and his fingers slid through the oil slick on his head, searching for any stragglers. The first thing he was going to do after he shook out his gear was put a bottle of OFF in his camping bag. It was an easy way to avoid at least one of the monsters and easier to carry than another idiot trap.

Dad got home a few hours later, drunk, and letting everyone know how close he was to Grandpa. The lion's share of the pity should be his. Everyone in the house seemed to know this as the attention was all on him and how the death would affect his mood. They were all on their best behavior.

Without the TV for a distraction, dad's mouth served as entertainment. He told tall tales about all the stuff he imagined he had done with Grandpa. Drew could sort most of the BS from the truth because, out of anyone in the house, he had spent the most time with Grandpa. But he listened anyway, pretending to be interested. Then the tall tales turned to anger about how Grandpa never had anything nice to say to anyone. Which wasn't true. He just hated liars and lazy people. Dad checked both boxes. Drew tuned dad out and let his mind wander, only paying attention when dad asked for him to grab him another Pepsi from the mudroom.

"Make some room for me, too." Dad smiled drunkenly.

"Ok." Drew took a big chug of the soda, and judging by the smile, thought it was safe to ask a question that had been burning in his mind. "What happened to Grandpa?"

The smile disappeared.

"What happened? The stubborn son of a bitch wouldn't just call and ask for help." Dad took a drink of his rum and Coke. "He thought he could move that pile of split wood by himself and got crushed in the process. I told him not to make you stack it so high on that hill…I knew this would happen," Dad said almost proudly, like Grandpa died from not taking his advice. As if he deserved the punishment of death for ignoring advice coming from someone as clever as dad was.

Drew thought back to the pile of wood dad was talking about. Grandpa had paid him a few sodas to stack it early last summer. Grandpa kept telling him higher, so that's what Drew had done, trying his best to impress him. It was green split stuff, chunks of elm that he wanted to dry in the sun for the summer. The warning from dad about stacking so high was somewhere in the memory and Drew suddenly felt guilty. Was he responsible for killing Grandpa with a poorly stacked pile of wood?

"They found him in the middle of the yard halfway between the house and the pile of wood…" Dad was cut off.

"Steven, stop. They don't need to hear this," Mom said.

"Shut up, Barb. It was his own damned fault, stupid old codger. All he had to do was listen to me and he'd still be alive instead of beaten to a pulp by his own pride." He flashed anger at mom and continued unobstructed. "They found him bleeding from every hole in his body, his hands full of grass. He was clawing at it, trying to crawl back to the house to call for help…is that how you want them to end up?" He took another drink, looked angrily at mom, and used a spinning finger to point at Drew. "Looking like they were trampled to death in a stampede because they were too smart to listen to me?"

The last words sent a chill up Drew's spine.

"Boys, time for bed." Mom had had enough.

"But mo'om, it's not even 10 o'clock," Chris complained, obviously enjoying the drunk talk. He was never at risk of being the one to draw dad's ire, so it was only ever entertaining to him, not intimidating.

"Come on, Chris," Drew said in his best big brother tone.

"Trampled to death" echoed in his mind. Drew didn't want to hear one more word slandering Grandpa and about the way he died.

"NOW!" Mom insisted.

The boys marched upstairs by candlelight; Drew was the oldest, so he got to hold the candle.

"Trampled to death."

They both changed into PJs and avoided talking as the rift between them grew by the day and idle chit chat was becoming a thing of the past. Drew ran his fingers over every inch of his body and again through his greasy hair. Nothing.

"Trampled to death."

Drew tried to read his new *Goosebumps* by sliding the candle to the edge of the dresser next to his bed, but he couldn't focus on the words.

"Trampled to death."

The camping trip flashed through his imagination. There were the fun parts before the sun went down. Then there was preparing the trap, telling the story to Jeremy, and then building the trap itself. Maybe the Gougers had been watching, listening…maybe the Gougers were mad. Drew remembered the walk back and his sleeping bag the morning after…

"Trampled to death."

Drew was now convinced he was responsible for Grandpa's death. Not because of the precariously stacked pile of wood…but maybe. But more likely, it was because he had pissed the Gougers off by warning people about them and trying to trap them. Then in an act of anger or revenge, they had stomped his sleeping bag and his grandpa. They had been hunting Grandpa for years anyway. Maybe the sleeping bag was the missing link. Maybe they could smell Grandpa's house from when Drew used the sleeping bag there when he was stacking wood. The onion and garlic had infused itself into the bag and once the Gougers got a good whiff of it, all they had to do was follow their nose like that toucan from the cereal commercial.

The words on the *Goosebumps* page blurred as tears of guilt filled his eyes. He tried not to think of Grandpa all punched full of holes from the flailing legs of the Gougers. The two beasts clinging together over his lifeless body, their short legs in the middle flailing at him with their clawed toes making hole after hole.

"Are you crying?" Chris asked from the other side of the room.

"NO," Drew objected, but the sniffing back of some snot betrayed him.

Drew sat up in bed and slammed the *Goosebumps* on the dresser, blowing out the candle by accident.

"Great, now it's dark, idiot," Chris complained.

Drew knew the problem wasn't going to go away, so tears or not, he got out of bed and went to the pants he had taken off and left on the floor with his other dirty stuff. He rummaged through the pockets and found the lighter he had taken camping. The flick of the flint illuminated the room like lightning while the candle took its time to come alive and wash the room in a dim yellow.

"Is that mom's lighter? She was looking for it... I'm gonna tell," Chris said, ever helpful.

Drew blew out the candle.

"Ok, fine, sleep in the dark with the Gougers," Drew threatened.

"NOO, stop." The squeal threatened to bring a drunken dad upstairs, and Chris knew it.

"Ok, ok, I'll light it if you keep your mouth shut. I'll put the lighter back in the morning. I just needed it earlier and forgot." Drew re-lit the candle, which took much less time to brighten now that it was warm.

"Maybe you should keep it in case the candle goes out again." The fear of the dark was contagious, too. "And what's a Gouger?" Chris wondered aloud.

"Nothing…maybe I'll tell you someday, but it's too scary for a baby."

It felt good to have the upper hand for a change. But he would never share Grandpa's story with Chris. It was Drew's from Grandpa, and he wasn't sharing it.

The arguing downstairs started shortly after that. The boys knew better than to make waves, so with the white trash lullaby, they fell asleep. Both were dreaming of Gougers but in very different ways.

***

The funeral was six days later. After a week of having greaser hair and getting teased at school for it, still not having electricity, and dad being perpetually drunk and crabby, the funeral was almost a bright spot at that point. When they went into the church, Drew didn't know what to expect. He had been to Sunday school before it got embarrassing because all the other kids had nice clean clothes. Mom and dad stopped going a couple of years before he and Chris stopped. Drew thought it was mainly just a nice way to send them out of the house for some kid-free time on Sunday mornings. Then when mom found out that he and Chris had stopped going and instead had been playing at the elementary school playground, they kind of just stopped going and talking about church altogether.

Now walking through the pews, he felt like a parasite, like one of the ticks. Taking the comfort of the church during a hard time like a funeral but ignoring it any other time. It felt bad. The nice words from the priest about Grandpa, though Drew wondered if he even knew who Grandpa was, only increased the guilty feeling. They all had lined up to "pay respects." Drew had no idea this meant he was going to come face to face with his dead Grandpa. But that's where the line led. By the time it was his turn, he was already quietly panicking. His sweaty fingers were raw from playing with the edge of the huge suit jacket he had borrowed from dad. The coffin loomed up ahead and Drew could see the familiar outline of the top of Grandpa's face. The tip of his nose and his round cheeks were all he could make out, but it was enough to be recognizable.

Then it was his turn. He walked to the coffin and took a deep breath, trying to build his nerve. But Drew noticed something with that deep breath. The garlic and onion smells were gone. This wasn't Grandpa. Not anymore. The grayish lump of flesh in the cheap wooden box resembled him, but it wasn't. Drew was fascinated. The fear of the body was gone, and he looked it over, trying to find the holes from the Gougers. The fancy suit was hiding them. Part of him wanted to undo the buttons and see for himself, but he knew that was wrong.

"Sorry," Drew whispered. "I know you're not in there, but maybe you're close." Drew looked around for any signs of ghosts. "I should have had a better rope, and I should have been braver. If I could have caught the Gougers that night, you'd still be stacking wood."

Drew turned and finished making peace, hoping no one had heard him confess. They were all too busy with their own emotions to care about a kid. There was a seat for him next to Chris where he sat, feeling better about telling Grandpa's body the truth. While the rest of the funeral goers paid their respects, Drew wondered about Grandpa's Gouger story and the cliffhanger ending. Was there more to it? Had he left out some important details that would keep Drew safe? How had the Gougers followed him all the way to North Dakota?

The buffet started after they lowered Grandpa into the ground. As the cheap tables filled with food and cups filled with booze, the crying slowed to a crawl. Soon enough, the stories started, along with jokes and laughter. The adults were first through the line of card tables filled with questionable pasta salads and room-temperature casseroles. Drew watched in horror as they plowed their dirty fingers into serving trays. Spit flew from the well-lubricated lips while they stacked their flimsy paper plates. Drew watched the spit land in the troughs of slop like a soft rain. The fat late-season flies were searching for a safe, warm harbor from the approaching winter. They filled the banquet hall, swarming the sweets, landing, and regurgitating on every treat.

Drew watched the buffet in horror, sidestepping slowly toward the inevitable…then it was his turn. Drew took one pleading look over his shoulder, but the expectation on mom's face meant he had to eat something. This wasn't the time to have a fight over him getting too skinny. Drew looked through the remnants in the troughs. It all looked the same, inedible. He poked the German potato salad, trying to get to the bottom where it might be clean, and spooned a little onto his paper plate. The Kraut Bierock seemed safe enough because they were in a basket, so he fished one out from the depths. The only thing that was left that seemed edible were the hot dogs, which were still on the grill.

"No bun?" someone Drew should probably know asked, holding out a slightly burnt hotdog with his pincers.

"No, thanks," Drew said, trying to be polite but praying the guy didn't insist.

"Okay," the stranger said and dropped the naked dog onto the plate, which promptly folded in Drew's hands.

Drew found a chair and sat there, trying his best not to gag. He got the hot dog down first and fast, before the flies landed on it or some drunk came to offer sympathy and spat on it. The Bierock was more difficult because he started to feel full, but he got it down. Drew eyed the potato salad. Eating it was not going to happen, so Drew started poking it around his plate, hoping the paper plate was thirsty enough to absorb the potatoes.

The sad faces around him were slowly turning red from the booze. Looking at them made him feel angry. The last thing Grandpa would have wanted was a bunch of people sitting around wasting daylight and getting drunk. Drew stood up and stomped over to the garbage can and tossed what was left of his "food." Then he went outside and found the swings in the modest playground, where he sat and thought about Grandpa and all the chores he helped him with. He thought about the last time he saw him and his cliffhanger.

Was this going to be the end of Grandpa's Gouger story, a sad funeral with terrible food?

Somehow, Drew knew better.

Chapter 11

The rest of the funeral was as depressing as Grandpa's actual death. The gossip started early. Dad's whining about the power bill and his own dad's death was unending, and there were a couple of mouth fights followed by a fist fight between his cousins. If there was a heaven, Drew thought Grandpa was looking down and updating his shit list by the minute. The only good thing that came from the evening was the fact that dad's whining seemed to pay off. He ended up getting enough sympathy to pay the electric bill with a "little bit" leftover for Christmas. But dad explained he'd "have a job by then," which meant he planned on drinking it away long before the holidays started.

When the power came back on Monday, it was a relief and a curse. Drew was finally going to be able to take a hot shower and finally wash the remnants of the Vaseline out of his hair. Despite his best efforts with his rag shower from the wood burner bucket, he could never get the slippery feeling out of his hair, and it showed to everyone in his class, all of whom were relentless about letting him know how it looked. Plus, he would finally not be stuck in the dark all night and could get back to reading the nights away. He was currently in hot anticipation of the next *Goosebumps*, which Mrs. Hill had assured him every time he saw her, was on the way. On the other hand, the power getting turned back on meant chores, and lots of them.

It seemed dad knew this too because as soon as the lights were on, he was in the shower. Then, as soon as he could find his wallet, he was out the back door. He had to make sure he took enough sympathy with him to buy rounds for his buddies at the .45 Club. The Christmas fund was going to be smaller by closing time, Drew thought.

"Ok, boys, time to get life back to normal," Mom said almost cheerfully.

"Yep," Drew said, trying to match her excitement despite his feelings on the matter.

"But mo'om, my head still hurts," Chris whined expectedly.

He knew the power was going to be back on today, so he woke up with a headache in anticipation of the chores. It was always a surefire way out of helping with anything.

"Chris, are you kidding me? Take an aspirin. We gotta get this place cleaned up before your dad gets back." Mom's cheerful mood was fading fast.

"It's ok, mom, we got this. I'll help." Drew would rather do Chris's share of the work than risk getting mom in a bad mood and getting another ladle smack to the back of his head while he was watching movies later.

"Fine, but if your head hurts too bad to help, it hurts too bad to watch TV, so you can go lie down in a dark room until it's better," Mom scolded him.

It was obvious that she was aware of his little trick, which was more effective on dad. Drew couldn't even remember the last time Chris had gone with them to get wood or spuds or corn.

"But mo'om," Chris whined.

"GET UPSTAIRS…" Mom lowered her voice. "…and out of the way."

Drew knew better than to stick around and see this play out as he ended up being the target for mom's anger once Chris won. It was better to get started on the chores anyway. The buckets of water littering the house were the first things he saw that needed to be taken care of, so he started there. The only one he left was the hot water pot on the wood burner because they had had the power come on before, only to lose it a few hours later and then have to wait forever for the water to warm back up on the wood stove. By the time he was done with the buckets, mom was done with Chris. Her mood was only slightly dampened. She directed the chores now, and the two of them worked together.

They did the obvious stuff first. Sweep, mop, dishes, scrub the corners that the candlelight didn't illuminate. Then the bigger stuff. Mom started with the fridge and told Drew to go look at the freezer in the mudroom. The old chest freezer's humming lulled Drew into a sense of ease as he approached. As soon as Drew lifted the lid, he was assaulted. The smell hit him like a fist. The rotten venison and stolen produce had congealed into a rotting mass at the bottom of the freezer and a haze escaped the open lid.

"RUUUHHHH," Drew half gagged and screamed as he slammed the lid.

He ran from the smell out the back door, leaving the buttered hinges swinging silently behind him. The inside door swung open silently and a silhouette of mom filled the space.

"Jesus, Drew, what is that?" Mom said as she looked toward the freezer. "Oh, my God, we shouldn't have opened it." She slammed the inside door to the mudroom hard in an attempt to seal the house off from the stench.

"AAAAAGHHHH," mom screamed from behind the closed door.

Drew ran back up the steps to the door and swung it open, then closed it behind him quickly to keep the funk out.

"What happened?" Drew asked, looking at his mom, who was staring into the kitchen.

He followed her gaze and saw all the doors on the cabinets swinging wildly and understood instantly. It was the poltergeist she thought she was afraid of…the buttered hinges all swung silently. It was a monster Drew had created for her.

"These fucking doors." Mom was clearly afraid, and Drew felt bad for ruining her good mood.

Drew, unafraid of the poltergeist, ran around and shut all the doors, including his parents' room.

"Sorry," Drew offered absentmindedly as he got back into the kitchen.

"Sorry for what?" mom said, suddenly suspicious.

"For the freezer," Drew lied.

"How about we don't open it again until it freezes solid? Then you can chip it out with a chisel from dad's shop. Until then, let's get back to work." Mom was over it.

They worked quietly for a little while longer until mom disappeared. Drew was busy picking up the rest of the candles and putting them away when suddenly the door to his parents' room opened silently behind him. Drew couldn't hear the hinges, but he could hear an all-too-familiar muffled breathing.
It was momster.

For a second, he froze in fear. But as quickly as it came, it was gone. This wasn't a real monster. This was just mom wanting to take a break from life and kids and watch TV without anyone bugging her before dad got home. It was a monster she had created for him.
Drew played along.

"Aaaagghhh," he squealed lightly and ran for the back door, knowing she would make a beeline to the couch. Sure enough, by the time he was sitting on the steps, the static click of the TV coming to life came from inside.

Drew sat outside for a few minutes, letting the momster think she had won. Then he remembered he had to get his stuff ready for school tomorrow. He sucked a huge breath of chilly night air into his lungs and rushed into the mudroom to get his backpack. The hook held him up for a second, but he shook the bag loose and made it back inside the kitchen. After the towel under the door was stomped back into position to seal out the funk, Drew dumped the contents of his bag onto the table. A few gnawed-on pencils rolled away, and his thermos almost hit the floor. He grabbed it just in time, and the weight of it reminded him of its contents. It was the worst, wild rice chicken soup. It was Chris's favorite, but one of the worst for Drew, second only to Spanish rice with hair. Mom made it all the time.

Drew was glad mom never found the uneaten meal, or he would have gotten a ladle. Quietly, before momster found out, Drew snuck to the sink to wash the thermos's contents down the drain. As soon as he wrapped his fingers around the lid and twisted...

BOOOOM.

The thermos exploded in Drew's hand. The lid smacked him in his split ear, which rang from the impact. Rotten wild rice chicken soup was dripping from his face. Drew looked around in shock and realized that what was left of the soup was now covering every surface in the moments-ago spotless kitchen.

"WHAT WAS THAT?" momster yelled as it appeared in the kitchen's doorway.

Drew was stunned and unable to speak at first.

"It was my thermos…it exploded," was all he could manage.

Momster surveyed the kitchen and smelled the air through her mask.

"Why the hell did you throw up in your thermos?" Momster said, still muffled by the rubber mask.

Drew was confused by this question. Until he started to breathe again. She was right. It smelled and looked just like puke.

"Ruuuhhhh," Drew gagged. "I didn't. It was wild rice soup I forgot to eat at school."

"What was that sound?" Chris yelled from the top of the stairway.

"Shut up, go back to bed," Momster said, not turning around.

Chris's feet didn't argue as they pounded their way back to their bedroom.

"Oh, my God. It must have started to ferment, and it built up pressure until you messed with the lid." Momster looked at Drew and the scene in the kitchen. "We better get this cleaned up before dad gets home."

She grabbed Drew's head and stuffed it into the kitchen sink, where she sprayed him off. She took care around his split ear, which was turning purple again in a hurry. Momster was still unaware she was wearing the mask. Drew didn't mind. After his head was clean, they both took rags and scrubbed the mess away in silence.

"Look at that," Momster broke the silence, pointing to a mark left in the now-cleaned ceiling from the lid of the thermos. "You're lucky it only glanced off your ear or you'd be unconscious."

"Holy crap," Drew said, amazed at the mark that left a perfect impression of the thermos lid in the sheetrock ceiling.

"Ok, go take a shower before dad gets home," Momster said, trying to hurry back to her show. "And watch your damn mouth, kiddo."

Drew could almost see her smiling behind the mask. He knew he had to come clean before he could feel clean.

"Mom, don't be scared of the doors anymore." The weight lifted off his chest a bit.

"What doors?" Momster asked, breathing hard through the mask.

"Whenever someone slams a door or stomps, and they all swing open…that was me." Drew gauged her response, but she was only grinning that ghoulish green smile of the rubber mask. "I tried to fix the squeaky one on the back door with WD-40 but it stunk so I tried butter and it worked. But it worked so good, I did it to all the doors and now they won't stay shut." Drew didn't care what the outcome was; he just didn't want mom to be scared of his monster anymore.

"But…don't tell dad, please," Drew pleaded. Not just because he didn't want to get in trouble, but he kind of liked that it scared him.

"You did that?" Momster asked.

"Yeah, sorry." Drew waited for the ladle and the attack from momster.

Instead, momster started laughing.

She laughed so hard, she had to sit down on the kitchen chair. When she lost her breath, she ripped the mask off her head in a sudden realization. She looked at the rubber mask in her hand and her laughing only increased. Drew joined her.

After they both calmed down, mom promised Drew she wouldn't tell dad about the hinges if he wouldn't tell Chris about the monster mask. They agreed. It was the last time Drew ever saw that mask and the last time mom ever made wild rice and chicken soup. Drew read a book one time that called this a win-win scenario.

That shower was the best shower Drew had ever taken. He washed the whole last month off his body and out of his mind, at least until the hot water ran out. Then it was back to reality. But at least he was clean, and the power was back on, and he was no longer a greaser.

***

Life got back into its comfortable rut. Snow blanketed the spaces between the houses and the dead crops. The fan was back in the cellar door opening in the kitchen to keep the pipes from freezing while making the rest of the house unbearably cold. Dad's sympathy from the funeral was running out, so the threat of the power getting shut off loomed again. They all knew if the power went out now, it also meant no water since the hand pump was now frozen solid. Christmas was getting close. Drew knew this because the Toys "R" Us catalog had shown up. The imaginary shopping started, and he and Chris had been fighting over toys they would never get. The fishing shows on public access taunted him of the spring that was too far away. And the ever-present isolation of a Midwestern winter began.

The monotony of it all was broken for the first time in weeks when it was time to go get a Christmas tree. They always went out to Grandpa's to get a tree, and this year wouldn't be any different. Dad promised. He said he didn't care who had paid the back taxes on Grandpa's property. Drew didn't know what that meant. All he knew was he was glad to be going back to Grandpa's, even if he would not be there.

The excitement faded quickly as they entered the driveway. It was all different. The trees Grandpa wanted help trimming back were gone from alongside the road. The ditches had been mown even though they were filling with snow. Somehow, worst of all, the ruts in the driveway were gone. They had been replaced with a fresh blading and a fresh load of gravel. Drew thought of the rut Grandpa always talked about being stuck in in life—the warnings he gave Drew every time he visited about the ruts in life. Grandpa's rut ended with his death, and now, even the ruts in his road were gone. The sadness grew in Drew's heart. Grandpa was really gone, and so was anything that resembled him. The sadness seemed contagious because by the time they reached the end of the driveway, and they all saw the construction site set up halfway through the demolition of Grandpa's house; they knew they were buying a tree this year. Dad spun out and threw fresh gravel in the new owner's driveway before speeding out the rut-less road and back onto the highway.

***

A couple of weeks before Christmas and a week after they decorated the store-bought tree, the cabin fever was at a high pitch. Everyone in the house was on each other's nerves and the arguments were never-ending. That was when dad broke the fever with what he said would be good news. While Chris and Drew (mostly Drew) cleaned up, Mom was so excited that she made pork chops for him and spaghetti for the rest of them. This was so dad felt nice and special while he made his big announcement that night at dinner.

"Well, don't worry, everyone, Christmas is saved." He was referring to the fact he had spent the rest of the sympathy, and they all knew it. "I finally found a job." Dad took a bite of his chop.

Drew instantly wanted to run and grab the Toys "R" Us catalog and show him all the stuff he had circled in anticipation of this moment.

"It's gonna mean I'll be home less during the days and weekends cos I start on overnights and my days off are Mondays and Tuesdays."

Drew was ok with this.

"And it's gonna mean we won't be able to do a lot of camping and fishing until I build up some leave after I'm off probation." Dad looked at Drew and scrunched his face up in an apologetic manner.

Drew was ok with this, too. He had already gone camping alone and when he improved his Gouger trap, he wouldn't even be scared anymore. If not, he'd just camp next to another nice family at the campground. They didn't seem to mind too much. Plus, he didn't have to deal with dad being a jerk the whole week leading up to a camping trip if he went alone.

Drew nodded in solidarity, scrunching up his own face.

"Well, where is it? Where'd you get a job?" mom asked, clearly excited to be over the "hump."

"The State School," dad said proudly.

Drew's heart sank. Dad was going to be working with the monsters. He got mad at his dad once in a while, but he knew what the monsters were capable of, and he didn't want to lose him. The monsters were dangerous, and adults didn't believe in them.

"NOOOO!" Drew yelled.

Chapter 12

Drew heard the door to the Travelall slam, and the powerful engine turned over. The tears on his cheeks felt cold in the small cubby that formed the window in his bedroom. Even though there was lath and plastic stapled to the outside to keep the cold out and he couldn't see through it very well, he wanted one last look at dad before he left. He had tried to explain to dad how scary the State School really was and that it was full of monsters. But all that had done was piss him off during his big announcement at dinner and it got Drew a spanking at the table (it was pants-on so Drew barely noticed, and he was more worried about the Bananahead and Moonface getting dad). Dad pushed away from his mostly eaten pork chop and went to the shop for the rest of the night, leaving Drew with a pissed-off mom.

She got even with her ladle after dishes were done while Drew was watching TV Land.

Now with Chris snoring away in his bed, Drew rubbed the goose egg on his head as dad's lights came alive and glowed on the snow around the truck. The lights lit up like halos through the plastic on the window and Drew watched them disappear down the alley. Drew stayed perched on the dresser for another minute, waiting to see the same lights round the corner around the block. He cried a little harder once they appeared and disappeared right where he expected them to. Dad was gone. His first night shift at the monsters' house.

Drew repeated the act of crawling up on the dresser and crying every night when dad left around midnight. He didn't want to miss his last look at dad. But now, school was suffering. The monotone voice of Mrs. Rockow got into his head and the burning in his eyes started a blinking. The blinking got harder and harder until Drew found it almost impossible to keep his eyes open and before long, he was sleeping at his desk. Mrs. Rockow wasn't impressed. She would sneak up on him and slam a book onto his desk, invariably making him scream like a girl in front of the entire class. Just more ammo for them to use against him. Drew didn't care; he was watching dad leave and never come back on a nightly basis. The warning letter mailed out with his mid-quarter grades, Drew *did* care about. Mom had intercepted it and promised not to show dad if Drew promised to "pull his head out of his ass." Drew tried his best.

Christmas was just around the corner and although dad had promised he had saved it by getting a job, he wasn't getting his first paycheck until after the first of the year. Everyone understood this meant most of the gifts were going to be from extended family and/or mostly clothes. Drew chucked his Toys "R" Us magazine that night, knowing it was just going to be a painful reminder from that point on. They still hung lights, mom still made Christmas cookies and Chex Mix, and the store-bought tree glistened with tinsel. Tinsel that found its way onto every sweater, every inch of carpet, and even in every pile of Bailey's poop. Drew thought tinsel was the perfect decoration for a holiday he felt the same about. It was pretty, but it always got messy.

All said and done, it was fine. The boys each got some much-needed clothes and a couple of Ninja Turtles action figures, so it wasn't a total loss. Drew was happiest for the blue jeans as his had lost their knees already, and the iron-on patches itched like crazy.

Mom found out about Drew's crying at the window at night because Chris had tattled on him after he woke up and saw him one time. Mom kept Drew up that night to say goodbye to dad in person before he left, thinking it would help.

Dad was puttering his lips while he got ready. He would take a deep breath and let it out slowly, letting his lips flap and make a slapping sound. It was something he would only do if he was really mad or really nervous. Drew wanted no part of either.

"Steven, will you talk to him before you go? He just wants to say goodbye...he worries about you at work." Mom gave Drew the oops face where she pulled the corners of her lips toward the floor, realizing she almost broke her promise not to tell dad that he cried.

"Why? What's he scared of? I'm gonna get hep-C from wiping butts?" Dad shot back coldly as he grabbed a giant piece of wood from the stack on the wall, needing to feed the wood burner for the night before he left.

Drew didn't understand the reference, but he would once his class went to the library tomorrow.

"Steve, stop, he just wants to say goodbye." Mom tried to buffer the anger.

"I don't got time for a lecture...Goodnight, coyote...OK?" Dad said to the door on the wood stove.

He slammed the giant piece of wood down, and the doors to the bathroom and his bedroom swung open silently on their buttered hinges. The only sound they made was when the knobs reached the walls.

"AAAAGH…" dad chirped, quickly cutting it off mid-scream.

The doors really did scare him.

Drew looked at mom and she tried her best, but the corners of her lips rose just the littlest bit. It was all Drew could handle, and he burst out laughing. Mom couldn't help herself either, because as soon as Drew started, she joined in.

"I'm gonna nail those fucking things shut and everyone can just climb through a window." Dad slammed the chunk of wood into the wood burner and slammed the door. "I'm glad you both find it so goddamn funny."

Drew tried to stop the laugh, but he couldn't. Dad stomped away from the wood burner toward the kitchen. Drew knew better and tried to shrink away at the last second, but he was too busy laughing. Dad lunged across the corner of the table and snatched Drew's arm. He pulled him across the table and stopped halfway, where he gave three resounding thuds on Drew's butt. The cabinets in the kitchen swung open.

Dad let him go and pounded his feet through the kitchen and out the back door.

"Now I get to wipe asses all night so you idiots can sit around and laugh about it all you want." One last door slam accentuated his exit.

Drew looked at mom in shocked disbelief.

"I told you talking to him was a bad idea." Drew ran upstairs without waiting for a reply, holding his burning cheeks as he ran up the steps.

That night, he didn't bother waiting and crying like a baby while dad pulled out. He lay in bed burning with anger and fell asleep with a belly full of it. That night, he dreamed of Moonface and Bananahead. The Can Man was their contact on the outside world and was feeding them information about Drew's whereabouts. The Gougers in his dream were pets of sorts for the Can Man, kind of like hunting dogs. They chased him all over town and eventually trapped him in the same gymnasium he had been attacked in at the State School on Halloween.

Drew woke up in a puddle of his own piss.

He snuck around the house, trying to hide the evidence. He tucked the wet Ninja Turtle underwear into the bottom of the hamper so they might dry before mom got around to washing them. While Drew stood in the bathroom giving himself a rag shower in the sink before the quickly drying pee started to itch, he looked at his reflection. The bruises on his hips and back weren't as bad as usual. Dad had been busy with work, so they were fading. He looked at his butt and his left cheek was still dark red. Then he turned and looked at his ribs poking through his skin and his sunken cheeks with his hollow, tired eyes looking back at him.

"Stupid Stickboy," Drew said out loud.

He hated what he saw and flipped the lights off, finishing the rag shower in the dark. He was mad at himself for being skinny, for being a baby, for caring about dad, for worrying about monsters, for not hurting the kids at school who teased him, for not hating Chris, for forgiving mom sometimes and trusting her. While he waited for the sun to come up, Drew thought of all the things he hated.

The fog of the nightmare, pissing his pants like a baby, and the belly full of hate stayed with Drew and ruined his entire day. Even the new *Goosebumps* from Mrs. Hill at the library barely helped. Especially after Drew looked up hepatitis C while he was in there and had a new monster to worry about.

When Drew got home from school, dad was still awake. Something Drew was getting used to not happening. With the night shifts, he hardly saw him anymore.

"Drew, come here a minute." Dad was clearly drunk but seemed softer than the booze usually made him.

"Why are you sitting up crying all night? And be honest with me," dad said.

Drew was perched on the edge of the couch, unsure whether to be honest with him.

"Well…" Drew had to be brave at some point. "I hate that you work at that place. Those people in there aren't people; they are monsters. I've seen them. They tried to attack me one time and these nurses barely stopped them." Drew tried his best to sound reasonable.

"*They* who?" dad wondered.

"Moonface and Bananahead." Drew told the truth.

"Are those the water heads your mom was talking about?" dad asked.

"Hydrocephalus, but yes, that's what mom said." Drew was glad he remembered the word and dad was obviously shocked by its usage.

"Ok, hydrocephalus, then…well if you know a big word like that, how can you still believe they are monsters?" Dad posed.

The fuzzy logic made little sense to Drew, but he could see he made little sense to dad either. So, he just shrugged.

"So, you what, sit at your window and watch me leave every night…ugh…cos you don't think I'm coming back?" Dad asked softly, barely a whisper. He seemed to clear something from his throat while he talked.

Drew thought he saw dad's eyes getting wet, and his face was redder than usual.

"Kinda…I guess so," Drew said, unable to look away from dad's wet eyes.

"Ok, go get some chores done," Dad finished the conversation in a hurry.

Drew did his chores, puzzled by his dad's words. Dad kept drinking. Within an hour or so, when the arguing started, Drew went upstairs to be out of the line of fire. Even though he was upstairs, the argument was clear. Dad hated his new job and was blaming everyone for it.

"I spend eight hours just chasing them around, wiping asses, and changing diapers. And let me tell you, they don't even seem like they want the help. They are biting and hitting and screaming, and it's all I can do sometimes to not punch them. Fucking Randy tricked me into this damn job cos he couldn't find anyone else to work for him in that nuthouse. I'm telling you, Barb, every time I go in for a shift, I feel like one of my rum and Cokes; each shift takes another sip and pretty soon, all that's gonna be left inside me is a bunch of ice cubes rattling around." Dad finished the sentence by shaking his empty drink and clinking the cubes in now-empty rum and Coke.

The thought sent shivers down Drew's spine. How much colder could dad get?

***

Early the next week when Drew got home from school, dad let him know he had a surprise for him. Drew could hardly focus while he did his chores. What could it be? A fishing trip? No, still too frozen solid. Maybe a road trip to see his uncle? Nope, too broke still until dad got paid. The questions became more outrageous as Drew fathomed the possibilities while he worked.

Then at dinner, dad surprised him...

"Hey, Drew, you might want to get some sleep this afternoon," Dad said and took a sip from his virgin Pepsi.

"Oh, yeah, why?" Drew said, giddy with anticipation.

"I'm gonna take you to work with me and show you there are no monsters there; you can help me wipe some butts." Dad was obviously joking about the butts, but he was deadly serious about taking Drew to work with him.

Drew swallowed hard.

It was going to be a long night.

Chapter 13

The door to the Travelall slammed harder than Drew intended. He was mad dad was making him go to the State School, so giving the door a little extra effort seemed appropriate. Dad smacked him in the chest with the back of his hand.

"Don't slam the door."

"Sorry," Drew said under his breath.

The engine roared to life, and the truck bounced as dad slid it into R and started backing out of the parking spot outside the shop.

"You ready? Don't be scared," was dad's advice as he started puttering his lips.

Dad didn't seem angry, so the show of nervousness wasn't comforting in the slightest. Drew had tried to take a nap during the day, but was afraid he would fall into the same nightmare with the Can Man and the Gougers herding him into the trap they set for him in the gymnasium. Instead, he tried to read. Eventually, he gave up when he couldn't focus and had to keep rereading pages. He ended up waiting at the top of the steps with Bailey bouncing his feet after mom and Chris had fallen asleep. Then he heard dad start to move around in his bedroom. After a rum and Coke and a quick tooth brushing, it was time to go.

Drew was already exhausted.

***

Dad turned into the gas station, which was probably the only thing still open this late, and Drew figured dad was going in for a refill of rum and Coke before work. Instead, he looked at Drew.

"Come on." Dad opened his door and hopped out, but left it open as a signal for Drew to follow.

Drew bounced across the bench seat and slid out dad's door. He took extra caution to not slam it behind him and trotted to catch up with dad, who was now holding the door to the store open for him. It was a pretty rare occasion dad took him into the store. He always said it was because the boys always begged him for shit, but that wasn't true. Well, at least not for Drew. He followed dad to the cooler section and watched him grab an orange juice. Drew was shocked. He never saw dad drink anything but soda (mostly with rum) and beer. Dad's hand went back into the cooler and grabbed a store brand strawberry milk, then tossed it at Drew.

"Here, go grab a snack or something to eat before we hit the mill."

Drew suddenly forgot about monsters and work. The possibilities in the aisles surrounding him seemed endless. But he had to hurry, and not get greedy. He didn't want to piss dad off right before they had to hit the mill. Drew wasn't sure what the expression meant, but it sounded cool to him, so he logged it for later use. He flew through the aisles; his eyes were looking at every package and every price tag. Instinctively, he went for the candy first, but that was a rookie mistake. He saw the chip aisle and the Cool Ranch Doritos and decided to test his luck.

Dad was up at the hot case looking through sandwiches and pasties when Drew caught up with him.

"Whaddya like — bacon, sausage, just egg..." Dad asked, leaving the question open-ended for Drew.

"Umm, how about the beef stew pasty?" Drew rolled the dice again.

"You want beef stew and..." Dad looked at the bag of Doritos. "...chips for breakfast."

"And strawberry milk." Drew hoped the healthy choice balanced the others out. "And technically, I never went to bed, so it could be dinner, or a midnight snack." Drew looked up at the clock, which was at ten till.

"You never went to bed? You nut." Dad smiled. "Well, if the workin' man wants beef stew, chips, and strawberry milk for his pre-work meal, that's what he gets."

Drew couldn't believe his luck. The rest of the way to the State School, the two ate mostly in silence because dad warned him to eat fast before they had to clock in. About halfway into the pasty, Drew realized it was too huge, so he wrapped it up and chugged his strawberry milk. He would save the chips and the rest of the pasty for after work.

The parking lot was almost empty when they pulled in. Dad parked under a light next to the building and hopped out. This time, he closed the door behind him. This signaled to Drew that they had to be serious now and use their own doors. The night air was cool, and dad puttered his lips while they made their way to the back of the castle-like building. In the distance, the sound of a man screaming at the top of his lungs, followed by the yelling of half a dozen others, rang out across the parking lot. The screams rebounded off the wall of the castle so Drew could hear it twice.

"Don't worry, that's Wiley hole. We won't be going in that building tonight…or at least you won't be," dad said to Drew, who was staring up at him wide eyed and terrified.

"What's that? What's Wiley hole." Drew wanted to reach over and grab dad's hand, but it was time to be serious.

Dad had warned him at dinner that he better not embarrass him, and he better take this job seriously. Plus, Drew knew he was too old for that.

"Wiley HALL," dad emphasized, laughing to himself. "It's where they put the, uhh, difficult residents. They can be dangerous, but mostly to themselves, so we will keep you out of there for tonight. Maybe on your next shift."

The building was deserted inside after dad let them in through the huge wooden doors. There wasn't anyone in sight. Their footsteps echoed down the halls like thunder. Drew's palms started sweating and the nails from his clenched fists were digging into his skin. He tried to relax his breathing; dad was right here with him. But every door was a threat. A black void housing some unknown bizarre creature waiting to get the jump on them. They rounded another corner and finally saw some life.

"Morning, Steve," a lady behind a desk said. Her cup of coffee was so hot, it had steamed up her glasses. She pulled them off and flapped them around, trying to chase the condensation away.

"Good morning, Louise," Dad said in a voice Drew didn't recognize. It sounded friendly and softer than usual.

"And who do we have here — a new resident…or another runaway?" Louise asked, glaring at Drew.

The question sent shivers down his spine. Drew never realized they had escapees.

"Well, actually, we had to hire some new muscle for Wiley Hole." Dad smiled slyly.

"Wiley HOLE? I love that." She laughed hysterically for a second before collecting herself. "Well, if they are gonna send you over there, maybe we can finally get some order in that place." she joked, sizing Drew up. "You on rounds tonight?" She now directed her attention back to dad.

"Ugh, yep. Why, what do you got for me...us already?" Dad looked at Drew and winked.

Drew wasn't in the mood for jokes but winked back and feigned a smile anyway.

"You better get to Ward B. Nobody from the afternoon rounds went over there. They've been quiet since curfew, but I bet it's a mess in there." Louise looked apologetic.

"Ok, no worries, I'm gonna go grab a cart and head that way. Better get him some gloves too." Dad chuckled.

The two of them then continued down the long halls. The signs in these hallways all had doctors' names on them, so it felt less dangerous. There was a stairway they finally reached that stretched down into a labyrinth of tunnels. The tunnels were full of twists and turns and signs pointing in so many directions that Drew quickly became lost and felt dizzy.

"Ok, buddy, now we are going into the resident's wards. This is where we keep the people who need help and can't live on their own, but you need to remember that you are a guest in their home because this is where they live. Got it?" Dad was dead-serious.

"Got it," Drew tried to whisper, but the halls amplified it.

"They are all going to be sleeping, hopefully, so just stay quiet and stay out of the way."

Dad grabbed a metal cart loaded with cleaning supplies. He also stopped at an enormous row of boxes of adult and children's diapers. He stuffed some of each into the lower part of the cart. Drew looked at the enormous boxes full of Depends and wondered if that was how the Halloween Box had started its life.

"Hopefully, we won't need these." Dad shook a fistful of diapers in the air.

The cart squeaked down the hallway until they finally reached an elevator and took a quick ride up. When the doors swung open, it hit Drew like a punch to the gut. The smell of human feces and urine was overwhelming. It was also mixed with a sweet, overpowering smell, which was like maple syrup. Drew's eyes watered and the pasty in his stomach flipped around violently, threatening to crawl back up his throat if he took another breath.

"Ok, here's the deal. I'm gonna go into the ward and take care of whatever nightmare is waiting for me in there. You are going to sit here and wait for me and if you hear anyone, just stay out of sight." Dad's warning hung in the air.

"Hear who?" was the only question Drew could muster while thinking about the endless possibilities.

"Mostly staff. This is the children's ward, so if you see any adults, it will be someone else working, so stay out of sight." Dad looked hesitant. "You won't get in trouble, but I don't feel like answering questions."

Drew suddenly got the impression he wasn't supposed to be here.

"O K..." Now Drew not only had monsters to worry about but adults as well.

"You'll be fine. Just stay quiet. They have some books and toys over there, I think, but be careful; don't put anything in your mouth."

With the last ominous warning, Drew could only assume it was related to the hepatitis C. Dad disappeared through a door that he had to use a key to get into. Now, alone in the dayroom, Drew surveyed his surroundings. Dad had said this was a children's ward. The box of broken toys and crayon marks on the wall seemed to be proof. Drew couldn't believe kids actually lived here. He thought it was only adults who got locked up in this place. The smell was thick, and the concrete bricks were filthy. It was the most unwelcoming building he had ever been in. It was like a filthy prison from a horror movie. The fear in his mind subsided and was slowly being replaced with pity.

Curiosity got the better of him and he snuck around with the skills he had perfected at home. The hallway closest to him had two closed doors and an open area at the end. Drew made his way to the opening and when he poked his head cautiously around the corner, he realized it was a bathroom. Against the wall, with no dividers or a curtain or anything, were perched five porcelain toilets connected to the wall with thick shiny pipes. Against the far wall was a single enormous bathtub. Everywhere there were remnants of feces and used toilet paper. Drew was shocked not only at the state of the filth, but at the complete lack of privacy the children had. He imagined himself sitting on the edge of one of the massive toilets trying to relieve himself while a crowd of other "residents" watched him or joined in. In the corner of his imagination, a madman was splashing around in the bathtub, but it was filled with an unknown brown liquid.

"But I still have to go. PLEASE don't make me wait until wake-up," a whiny voice called from behind him where dad had disappeared behind the locked door.

"Shut up." The irritation in dad's voice was all too familiar. "I'm gonna let you out. Just let me get my key." There was a jingling.

"I REALLY HAVE TO GO TO THE bathroom." The last word came out in a hollow whisper.

"I'm serious. If you wake them up, we are gonna have a problem come wake-up call. GOT IT?" Dad's last words weren't a whisper at all.

The jingling got more vigorous, and Drew sprinted back to the dayroom to hide. The door swung open just as Drew dodged behind a pillar next to the TV. He tried to keep his pounding chest from betraying him and forced himself to breathe quietly. There were footsteps just a few feet away from him as he hugged the pillar. As they passed him, Drew couldn't help himself. He had to get a look at one of the "monsters."

A boy, maybe ten years old, scooted past Drew's hiding place. Drew couldn't see his face. All he could see was his mostly naked body and a diaper that was bursting with feces. The white t-shirt he was wearing looked dirty even in the dimly lit hallway. A smear of brown was spreading between his thighs as he duck-walked to the bathroom. The sounds of him relieving himself followed and Drew plugged his ears, trying to give him some privacy. Soon enough, he reappeared in the hallway with no diaper, just the dirty t-shirt. Now Drew could see his face. He looked like him. Brown hair, big blue eyes, way too skinny. He wasn't a monster; he was just a Stickboy like Drew.

As the boy got a little closer, Drew forgot all about hiding. He could see the boy's face now. It was beet-red, and tears were drying on his cheeks. How long had he waited for someone to come and let him use the bathroom before he lost control? The question erased the smell from his sinuses and a lump in his throat replaced it.

"Who are you?" The half-naked boy suddenly made eye contact with Drew, who was standing out in the open.

"Drew... Who are you?" The question was innocent.

"Bob," the boy said, smiling despite standing there half-naked, covered in shit.

He held his hand out with his grin growing by the minute. Drew hesitated, thinking about not having heard any water running for Bob to have washed his hands with. When he saw Bob pull his hand back reflexively, like he knew he was contagious with a deadly virus, Drew took a step out and snatched it before it returned to his hip, then shook it violently.

"Why aren't you in bed?" Bob asked, still holding his hand.

He had taken control of the shaking and didn't seem like he ever wanted to stop.

"I'm, uhh, just working with my dad, I guess. I don't live here," Drew explained as he was feeling a bit awkward with the handshake.

"You don't? Where do you live?" Bob stopped for just a second before cutting Drew off and continuing, "We get to go to the garden in the mornings on Tuesday and Thursday, but in the winter, there is no going outside unless it is on a day trip with staff, mostly for sledding. Can your dad take us both outside in the morning? I can show you the garden we are going to make in the spring for beans. That was what my dad grew at home when I could live there." The excitement in Bob's voice grew with every word.

In just a couple of minutes, this monster had shown him more kindness than all the kids at school put together. The lump in Drew's throat grew even larger, but there was also an anger coming from somewhere he didn't understand.

"Umm, sure, I bet my dad will let us. He has to work until eight, but we don't have anything to do at home anyway."

Drew wasn't sure the details of that statement were true, but he wouldn't mind seeing Bob's garden and hanging out outside for a while. It would be better than sitting at home.

"BOB." It was dad. "What are you doing? Get back in here and get to bed. I'M SERIOUS."

Dad had latex gloves on and was holding a spray bottle. He flashed Drew a look that said he wasn't happy with him.

"OK, but can you take me and Drew outside in the morning?" Bob was almost yelling again, clearly excited.

"Yeah, now get in here and get back to bed," Dad said in a voice that said he was losing his patience.

"Ok, bye, Drew. See you in the morning." Bob duck-walked back to the doors with the lock where dad was waiting.

"Bye, Bob," Drew said and caught a look at a clearly unimpressed dad.

Drew tucked himself back behind the pillar.

"Ok, let's wipe you off, get a fresh diaper on ya, and get you back in bed," Dad said, softer now.

Drew looked around at the bars on the windows surrounding him and the locks on all the doors. Why were they locking Bob up like this? He didn't seem to be dangerous or even that handicapped. The anger and sadness brought a thousand questions to his confused mind while he waited for dad.

After what felt like hours, dad reappeared looking more worn out than he did when he went into the ward.

"Ok, one down, too many to go." Dad pushed the cart back to the elevator and Drew followed.

They were back in the maze of tunnels again. This time, they went down a section that had cloth shackles affixed to the wall, with small metal benches beneath them.

"Must have been a quiet day. Most of the time, there are two or three nuts down here being punished for fighting with staff or trying to hurt themselves," dad said flippantly.

Drew tried to imagine a bad day with the wall full of shackled men, women, or children. Their able muscular bodies fighting against the restraints. Victims of both their minds and the State. He imagined them having just enough sense to realize how awful their lives were and all they could do was lash out violently as all other recourse eluded them.

They rounded another corner now, and the sign at the end was brighter than the rest.

Palliative Care, it read in fluorescent backed letters. Drew would have to look up what that meant later. Dad had grown quiet on the walk down the tunnel, like he was expecting something that he was hiding from Drew. *Maybe this is where they keep the monsters*, Drew thought suddenly, feeling terrified again.

"Last stop for you, Coyote," dad said and looked down at Drew with a look Drew couldn't quite interpret. Something like sympathy maybe?

"Ok," Drew said, feeling the anticipation.

He braced himself for whatever a Palliative was, hoping dad could protect him from it. His dad's hand had never looked so inviting as Drew's own were slimy with sweat.

There, lying on two separate beds, were Amy and Cynthia.

A nurse looked up from the foot of the farthest bed and smiled. The smile was so burned into Drew's memory from replaying the attack on his bike in his mind that he felt like they were old friends.

"Hello, I'm Susan." The nurse smiled like she knew something. "And this is Amy." She pointed to a bedridden woman whose forehead and chin were so swollen that they protruded from her face, leaving her resembling a banana; Amy smiled at Drew. "And this is Cynthia." She pointed to the other woman, whose face was so swollen all over, it pulled her features tight like a full moon. She tried her best to smile through her already stretched-out lips. "They have a disease called hydrocephalus, and it makes their brains hold too much water, which causes severe swelling and pain." Just like mom thought, Drew remembered. She was pretty smart sometimes.

Drew looked at the "monsters" from his nightmares. He had never felt smaller. The two bedridden women looked miserable, and they were trapped in this place just like Bob, maybe even worse, depending on what palliative was. All the fear and awful thoughts he'd had of these two didn't disappear completely, but they turned into something even worse. Guilt.

Then Drew received his biggest shock of the night, maybe of his life.

"I'm sorry we scared you so bad when you fell on your bike that day, but me and Cynthia don't get out much." Amy motioned to Cynthia, who tried again to smile and jiggled her head in agreement.

Amy could talk.

Drew's mouth fell open in disbelief. Somehow, he had imagined they were so handicapped that anything outside of eating children and suffering was impossible. The monikers he created for them echoed in his mind and felt like poison.

Bananahead…Moonface.

"We were going to try to help you up, but by the time we saw how scared you were, you were already back on your bike doing about eighty miles an hour." She smiled wildly and her chin lifted with her smile.

Not only was Amy not mentally retarded, but she was lucid and spoke as well as mom. It was a moment of pure horror and shame. How could someone with a perfectly fine brain be trapped in a body like that, in a place like this? He tried to blink away the tears forming in his eyes.

"I'm…uhh, uhh… I'm sorry. I was a stupid baby last year and I'm not gonna be like that anymore." Drew didn't know what else to say. He was at a loss. There was no cleverness to get him off the hook this time.

Amy laughed, and Cynthia chortled.

"I sure as heck don't think you were a stupid baby. If I were a kid, riding my bike and I saw two monsters like me and ol' Cynthia here, I don't think I would have been brave enough to shake them off and ride my bike away like a bolt of lightning. I prolly would've lain there and cried…prolly would've peed myself." Amy eyed Drew quizzically. "How long did it take you to get home? Just a few seconds, I bet."

The whole room laughed now, and Amy's sense of humor lightened the mood. Drew had never felt smaller or let off the hook so kindly in his whole life. Not only was Amy just as smart as mom, but she was also intuitive and kind. Qualities

Drew didn't find usually came all together in adults, yet this one had them. Some sick twist of fate had trapped her with her own flesh and now the state had locked her away in a labyrinth.

Drew stayed in the room talking to Amy for as long as dad was talking to the cute nurse, Susan. Cynthia was a veritable encyclopedia on dinosaurs and board games, so they lost themselves in talking about the two. Before long, Amy was back to talking about the bike Drew was riding, and Drew could hear the longing in her voice. So, he told her all about it. The pegs for tricks or to hold friends if he had any, the beads on his spokes that spun in when you slowed down, its solid chrome frame. He even told her about the jumps he could do and riding with no hands. Amy hung on every word. By the time he got ready to explain his plans for building a dirt BMX track in the woods, dad was grabbing him by the shoulders and telling him it was time to go.

Amy looked disappointed that the conversation was over but put on a smile. Cynthia jiggled and chortled, also looking quite pleased with the break in their monotony. Amy made Drew promise to come back and tell her all about the BMX track in the woods, and Drew said he would.

"I work here now, so I'll get time to come back sometime." Drew wasn't sure how true this was.

Amy gave him a wink.

Susan gave dad an extra-long goodbye and a flirty look she thought Drew wouldn't notice. It didn't bug Drew as much as the panties in the shop, but it still made him feel bad. He would give dad a pass today, though. He had helped Drew beat two monsters. The lesson hadn't gone unlearned.

Dad said it was time to take Drew home after the visit to Palliative Care. Drew was disappointed, but he was exhausted, so he didn't complain. His head was swirling with emotions as dad led them out of the maze beneath the State School. He was relieved the monsters were gone. Also, he was proud of dad for working such a hard job. He felt embarrassed about being a stupid baby when dad would leave for work at night. But most of all, he felt angry. He couldn't pin the emotion down, but he knew the way they were treating the residents wasn't great. It seemed like the staff cared, but the system was broken.

Dad told Louise at the front desk he was going to take an off-campus lunch to run Drew home fast. He finished a beer along the way, and they made small talk about the tour. Drew was too preoccupied with his own thoughts to listen very closely. When they pulled up in front of home and dad didn't even put the gear shifter in P, Drew knew it was time to go but he had one more burning question.

"Dad…are we going to take Bob outside?"

Chapter 14

The snow receded briefly in April.

It was just a tease.

It came back with a vengeance and the snow stayed deep until late May. Drew knew it was spring, not because the snow was gone, but because his pants with no knees had all become cutoff shorts. Except the pair from Christmas, which kids were now teasing him about because he wore them almost every day.

Just more ammunition for the kids at school.

Thankfully, that was ending as well. Drew had been dreaming all winter about camping and fishing. He tried not to worry about monsters as much anymore after the trip to the State School. Except for the Can Man, who still prowled the neighborhood, collecting cans and vulnerable kids. Hills were still best avoided as well since, as much as Drew tried to tell himself monsters weren't real, he knew for a fact his sleeping bag had been stomped into the mud. And, in all likelihood, the same culprits had killed Grandpa later that night. What else could it be if not for the Sidehill Gougers?

As much as Drew was getting itchy feet to go camping, dad was right. Since he'd started the overnights at the State School, dad didn't have any time for that, or much else. Now, dad was either working, sleeping, or "relaxing" with a rum and Coke. It seemed no matter how many drinks he had, he never "relaxed" and most of the time, he just got more pissed off.

One benefit of all the work was dad didn't have as much time to sit around and stew, just waiting for something to irritate him. That meant fewer spankings.

Drew wished all the monsters were gone, not just Cynthia and Amy, so he could just go back to his spot at the park and camp. The memory of the night Jeremy bailed on him was still fresh and woke him up in sweats a couple of nights a week. He was braver now, but still not brave enough to go camping alone again, not yet.

School finally got out and as the long days of summer dragged on, the boredom grew. All the dreams of camping and fishing, riding his bike, making a dirt BMX trail in the woods, hanging out with Chris and Jeremy, none of them happened. Chris had left Drew's bike out in the driveway one night and now dad had it hanging upside-down from the tallest rafter in his shop as punishment. Drew would rather have taken a spanking, but dad didn't have time for that. Drew wanted to ask for it back but that was risking lighting dad's shorter-than-usual fuse. Jeremy was a ghost all summer. He had made new friends his own age and since mom wasn't babysitting him anymore, there was nothing forcing him to hang out with Drew, so he didn't.

Worst of all, his dad had got Chris a Nintendo for his birthday, after his paychecks finally started rolling in. Drew was insanely jealous, thinking back on his own lean birthday with pizza and a couple of fishing lures. Not only that, but Chris didn't have to share it because it was a birthday present. Drew got to play sometimes if Chris was gone or if he wanted to play a two-player game, but outside of that, Chris liked to hold it over his head. Now Chris hardly even came out of the playroom upstairs with the tiny TV, his beanbag, and the NES.

This left Drew flying solo for the summer, just like he had all year in school.

One bright spot of the summer was that since dad slept all day, he never felt like mowing the lawn. Dad had taken a Sunday morning off from sleeping and taught Drew how to use the lawn mower. The hardest part was pulling the cord fast enough to turn the engine over. Drew learned to start it on the sidewalk, where the blade didn't drag on the grass, to make it easier. Also to not take too big of a bite of lush grass so it didn't slow the blades down and make the engine die.

It was scary at first because his dad propped the little door on the lawn mower (meant for a bag to catch clippings) open with a stick so it didn't bog down trying to mulch it. As a result, rocks, dog poop, sticks and grass constantly pummeled his shins. To avoid this, Drew would spend extra time removing all the debris from the yard, especially Bailey's piles.

It was hard work, but the more times he mowed the yard, the easier it got. By the time July rolled around, his rows were straight, the grass was all the same height, and even pulling the cord was easier.

Drew loved it.

Dad even paid him for it. Now Drew's arms were looking less like sticks and more like branches. The racoon-mask tan on his face from his glasses was dark and his hair was bleaching in the sun. It kept him busy and out of the house a couple of days a week. And the pocket full of cash didn't hurt either.

Drew saved most of the cash, but he couldn't help raiding the penny candy rack at Ben Franklin's once or twice a week. Most of it didn't cost a penny, but he could leave the store with enough candy for a few days for less than a buck. He also spent a few bucks on improving his monster hunting trap. Just in case.

At the end of July, mom was the one who made a surprise announcement for a change. She and dad wanted to go to August the Deuce, and they were going to leave the boys with Gramma Bean for a week afterward. So, the boys had a "little vacation" before summer was over, she explained.

Her "little vacation" was hell on Earth, based on Drew's experiences. Gramma Bean was almost a hundred years old. Her real name was Bjornsdottir, but neither of the boys had been able to pronounce it as little kids. Mom suggested Gramma B as an alternative. Drew heard bean, repeated it at a barbeque to thunderous laughs, and the name stuck. Drew thought it stuck partly because Gramma Bean was very skinny. But also, it was partly because it made people laugh at someone who generally roused feelings of terror.

Not only was Gramma bean a nasty mean old woman. She had a disease called porphyria. It wasn't bad when she was young, but after she went through the change women get in their fifties, it got terrible. She had to stay in darkened rooms because the sun would make her skin blister and any time she ate, it caused her incredible pain. Drew figured this was why she was so mad all the time, and he tried to understand. But after he found out they also called it the vampire disease, he couldn't help shake the notion that she might be a bloodsucker.

August the Deuce was a festival for Icelandic heritage that was held in the town of Mountain. It was usually home to around a hundred people, but during the festival, it swelled to a thousand or more from the second to the fourth of August. There were food stalls set up, live music, and sometimes people were doing talent shows or hawking crafts. Mostly, it was just a bunch of drunken adults having a good time while the kids played hide and seek. It was fun, but it sometimes ended with the dreaded week at Gramma Bean's, so a cloud hung over it.

Drew could have argued with mom about the trip while dad was at work, but after he heard dad was taking time off, there was no hope. Instead, Drew got ready. He packed his fishing gear. Changed the line in his reels. Double-checked his monster trap supplies, finding them lacking. He also made a stop at Ben Franklin's to stock up on munchies. Then Drew spent a week getting the yard ready, so it still looked good by the time he got back.

The morning they were leaving for Mountain, they were all sitting around waiting for breakfast, when dad yelled out in surprise.

"What the hell is that?" He was pointing at Drew, who was sitting on his chair with his knees pulled up to his chest and his shirt pulled over his knees.

Drew looked behind him and was shocked to see a Gouger egg.

The yellowish spotted egg was much larger than a chicken's egg and it rolled off his chair when he turned to look at it. It hit the ground with a heavy thump and continued rolling to the wall.

"AAAAGGHHHHH!" Drew screamed.

Drew jumped off his chair in shock and ran to the other side of the table, putting as much space between him and the Gouger egg as possible.

"Drew laid an egg." Dad laughed. He looked surprised at Drew's reaction.

Suddenly, a remnant of a memory came flying to the front of his thoughts. He remembered when he and Chris would sit by the wood burner after taking a bath with their towels wrapped around them, waiting to dry off. Dad loved to sneak up behind them and put an egg under the towel. Then he would say, "The boys laid eggs," leaving both boys in shock as they had felt nothing. But the existence of the egg had been proof enough for the boys at the time. So, they would all laugh about it while mom scrambled them for breakfast.

Drew felt embarrassed.

It wasn't a Gouger egg, just a porcelain egg from the decorative bowl in his parents' bedroom. Dad was just trying to be funny.

Drew had to mask his embarrassment with anger or risk letting them know how dumb he felt.

"Jeez, dad, that is so STUPID." Drew knew it was a line crossed as soon as he opened his mouth. He darted for the back door before dad could get hold of him.

After waiting outside for five minutes, Drew was shocked dad hadn't chased him down and beat him. Maybe he wasn't even mad? Drew gave it another five minutes, but finally worked up the nerve and cautiously made his way back inside.

Everyone was busy putting things away and stacking bags by the door, so they were ready for dad to load them into the back of the Travelall.

Dad came out of his bedroom carrying his suicide pistol.

"Here, put this out in the truck for me. Sorry about the egg. I should've known you've outgrown that kind of stuff." Dad's feelings looked hurt.

It stung Drew worse than a punch to the gut would have.

But maybe dad was right a little bit? Maybe Drew was getting too old for that kind of baby stuff.

"It's ok. Sorry I was a jerk. I just never even expected that egg to be there." Drew smiled sincerely.

The suicide pistol wasn't an odd addition to the travel supplies. Dad took it anywhere there was going to be over five people. Drew happily loaded it up in the glove box and looked at the pile of bags sitting by the back door, ready for the trip.

If he was getting to be too old to do baby stuff, maybe Drew needed to do man stuff.

Before dad was back out with his own duffel bag a few minutes later, Drew had all the gear loaded up, including his own. The fishing poles weren't going to get all tangled up because Drew had all the lines taut and straight. The dirty tackle boxes were at the back and away from the luggage.

Drew had been paying attention.

Dad looked at the vacant space and went out the back door with his duffel. He came back in a few minutes later, lips puttering away, and busied himself checking freezers and fridges and stoves and locks on windows and the wood burner ash can.

"Drew, grab Bailey's food so we can take it over and leave it with your uncle while he's watching him for us," Dad said from the mudroom.

Drew sprang to life from the living room and sprinted for the kitchen, where the huge bag of food was waiting. Dad must have been impressed with his packing job if he wanted him to grab the big bag. The bag felt light compared to the lawn mower and Drew lifted it easily. He realized how much stronger he was getting and smiled to himself.

***

Dad stopped at the gas station on the way out of town for a refill. As he opened his door, Drew knew he had to test the waters of manhood.

"Hey, dad, can I come in?" Drew asked, trying not to sound nervous.

"You got your own money?" Dad asked, waiting outside his door.

"Yep." Drew patted his pocket proudly.

"Ok, I don't give a shit." Dad left the door open and walked away.

Drew started bouncing across the bench seat to follow.

"Dad, me too, right?" Chris said expectantly from the back seat.

"You got your own money?" Dad repeated with a sly smile.

"Uhh, no…" Chris said, now less boldly.

"Nope… Come on, Drew," Dad said, looking cool as hell to Drew.

Drew finished bouncing out of the seat and only paused for a second while he swung the door closed to give Chris a snotty look.

"Mo'om," Chris whined.

Drew slammed the door and made his way inside with dad, smiling like crazy.

Dad went straight to the liquor rack and Drew hit the cold case. With a Pepsi and Powerade in hand, he then found the candy/snack section that he was starting to get familiar with. He grabbed a few goofy candies like Baby Bottle Pop and slide whistle suckers. Then he got the important stuff. Slim Jims and Cool Ranch Doritos. He hurried to the counter to get in line behind dad, so he didn't piss him off.

"You sure you want to spend your money on all that?" Dad asked, eyeing the pile of junk food in Drew's arms.

"Well…yeah, I saved some of my money back and I'm saving some of it for Gramma Bean's." Drew felt stupid now.

"Oh, good plan," Dad said. "They got that little general store, too, by Aunt Scrooge's house." The name grated on Drew's nerves.

He knew the general store was there, but he hated going near Scrooge's house. She sat on her porch just waiting for kids to harass.

"Oh, yeah, duh," Drew said, pretending.

They got back in the car, and Drew reached into his bag. He grabbed the Pepsi first. The bottle hissed as he opened it and he took a huge swig.

"Here, I made room." Drew held the soda out to dad.

"Did you get that one for me?" Dad looked at the Pepsi he had grabbed for himself.

"Yeah, now you can have two rum and Cokes." Drew was so happy with his surprise.

"Well, shit, here, fill 'er up, bartender," Dad said in a Southern twang and passed the bottle of rum.

He slipped the truck in R and then D and got back on the road.

Drew poured carefully, spilling a little bit of rum on the back of his hand. He passed the drink to dad and licked it off.

It tasted like it smelled, but Drew liked it.

"I saw that." Dad looked at Drew. "Here, you better check if you put enough in." He handed the recently mixed drink back to Drew.

Drew was unsure if it was a chokepoint, a trap, but dad's mood gave him confidence. He took the bottle back and took a drink of the Pepsi, which now had an almost coconut flavor from the rum.

It was good. Drew could see why dad liked it so much.

"Perfect." Drew had no idea how well the drink was mixed, but he passed it back to dad.

Mom started laughing on the far side of the bench seat.

"Like father, like son," she said, still laughing.

"And for you, cos I know you don't want to get fat from all the sugar in soda." Drew handed mom the Powerade proudly. "And for you so you don't cry all the way to Gramma Bean's." He handed the goofy Baby Bottle Pop and slide whistle sucker to Chris.

Mom and dad looked at each other, the Baby Bottle Pop, and Chris's now-red face.

"Thanks, Drew, you picked perfect snacks for everyone," Dad said, still looking at the baby bottle-shaped candy.

The whole car erupted in laughter, including Chris.

The rest of the short trip was fun. All the mustard and bean fields were at peak growth. They looked like a sea of yellow and green on either side of the road. Drew laughed at the illusion of the running man made from the rows in the field flying by the window like some weird animation. It was cartoonish and funny during the day. Drew was hypnotized by him making his long strides through the fields. He thought of the same rows last fall when they were rotting into the fields for the winter.

The last time he saw Grandpa. The day he told the Gouger story.

Drew could see the eponymous hill that the town of Mountain was named after growing in the windshield now. The mood was so good a few minutes ago, but the closer they got to the isolated Icelandic town, the more dread Drew could feel building inside him.

Chapter 15

August the Deuce was actually a good time. They set up a tent in the front yard of Gramma Bean's daughter/caretaker, Scrooge. The festival had her too busy with gossip to be too much of a hassle, though, so staying in her yard wasn't so bad.

The festival itself was busy this year. There were more food stands than last time and more kids to play with who didn't know Drew was Stickboy, so he was safe to play with.

Once the streetlights came on and the parents made their way to the kegs, the kids started their game of hide and seek. There were two teams picked at random; one hid and one sought. The only rule was you had to stay on the eight blocks that lined either side of the four-block-long main street. Drew was on the hiding team first and earlier in the day, he had spotted a giant rhubarb plant near the alley that was a perfect spot.

Drew sat under the canopy of the rhubarb, motionless, for almost an hour before the other team got too mad about seeking for so long and gave up. Drew was careful to sneak away from his spot so nobody found it, and he made his way back to the calls of "NO FAIR."

After being accused of cheating, the hiders had to submit. Just to keep the game going, the hiders became the seekers. Drew didn't get another opportunity to hide because after the next round of hiding and seeking, the kids got distracted by a ball and ended up kicking it in the street until the parents came staggering away from the block party to take them to bed.

The day after was full of music in the streets and some games the adults were playing, though there was less drinking that day. Most of the adults were hungover and already dreading the drive home the next day.

What was left of the kids played more street kickball, but some cliques started forming, so Drew spent the day trying to make a fire with sticks behind Scrooge's house. The library was running out of scary books, so in an effort to broaden his horizons, Drew had checked out survival craft books. The method of fire starting that he'd read about and was trying now involved some old rope and a couple of sticks. He thought he saw smoke once, but his hands were too raw to give it another shot.

Later that night, mom brought back pylsur with lefse and pickled pike, all stuff that Drew liked and seemed to be safe enough to eat. He looked at the food stalls carefully and thought they all looked clean, and the people who were making the food weren't gross, plus they all wore hats, so no hair.

That night was uneventful and now early the next morning, Drew was watching mom and dad pull away for the week. Drew felt the all-too-familiar lump in his throat as he flapped his hand in the wind as dad's Travelall disappeared down the road. The festival was fun, but now Mountain was going to be returning to the isolated creepy little town that it was the rest of the year.

Chris hadn't even bothered coming out to say goodbye to mom and dad. He had already set up his Nintendo in the spare room Gramma had with a TV, and had made it very clear to mom before she left that he wasn't going outside. Chris rented a few games before leaving town, knowing he wouldn't be home to return them. Late fees were a worry for the next person. This meant he had plenty to do besides say goodbye or hang out with Drew.

Drew was glad Chris wasn't here, so he couldn't see him getting ready to cry.

To stop the tears, Drew ran behind Gramma's house toward the barn. He had seen a ton of stuff in there the other day when dad sent him in there to get a cooler for his drinks. Some of the old stuff in the barn might make good camping gear or even upgrades to his lackluster monster hunting pack.

On his way to the barn, Drew saw Gramma's vast garden and took a detour. Everything was huge and full, and most of the plants were almost as tall as he was. It was probably about an acre, but once you were in the middle of it, it felt like a different world.

The trellises of beans towered above him, with their fingerlike fruits hanging everywhere. Drew plucked one off and took a nibble from the flesh-colored pod. It was crisp and sweet. Drew grabbed a handful to munch on while he was rummaging through the barn. Who knew what Scrooge was going to make for dinner, but based on experience, he better fill up now in the garden.

He took another bite of the bean while admiring the curling tendrils that grabbed the wires, keeping it glued to the trellis.

The bite of the wax bean stuck in his throat as another lump appeared.

The bean had rattled a memory loose in his mind.

He forgot to go back and take Bob outside with dad. In fact, he had forgotten all about Bob the day after the visit to the State School. Drew had a dark thought. Maybe that was why the

State School was in the middle of nowhere in his little corner of the world. If no one saw the residents, they never thought of them. And, if someone did see them, like Drew, by the time they got back to their regular life, they instantly forgot about them.

Drew tossed the handful of beans on the ground. The guilt was overwhelming, but there was nothing he could do about it. But if he forgot about the beans, he could forget about Bob.

The barn was full of stuff, but most of it was just old farm junk, although he did find a better rope that he set by the door so he could sneak it off later and trade it out with his old clothesline. There were also a few old rat traps. The huge snapping kind. He practiced setting them a few times, and the reports of failure echoed like gunshots in the huge barn. They gave Drew a good idea, and he set them by the rope to grab it all later when the coast was clear.

Scrooge was inside cooking by the time Drew got done poking through all the stuff in the barn. She was stirring something furiously with her hair swinging around in giant arcs, and immediately had orders for Drew when he appeared.

"You go get yourself cleaned up and get back here to warsh some dishes and take out a few things for me." Her odd accent made no attempt at hiding itself.

"Ok, I'll grab Chris, too." Drew didn't give Scrooge time to object as he ran away to "warsh" up and get Chris, hoping to halve the workload.

Drew slowed down as he went past the dark room where Gramma was. He hadn't seen her yet, and he wasn't sure she even noticed the boys were visiting. She was much worse than last time they were here. Drew gathered this from what mom and dad had been talking about, that Gramma Bean was less

"less lucid." Drew was going to have to remember to look that up later.

There was no overwhelming smell of garlic in Gramma's room, like there had been at Grandpa's. Drew thought it was more evidence that she was actually a vampire. She couldn't have used garlic to stay alive like Grandpa because it would have killed her like any other vampire, so the only other thing that could explain her unnaturally long life was bloodsucking.

There was ragged breathing and the smell of sick coming from the room as he passed. The faint glow of her ancient TV was pouring across the dark hall. Drew walked as silently as he could, fearing she would call out to any noise for help.

Now that he was past the danger area where he thought Gramma could hear him, there was one more hurdle, and then he could wash his hands and grab Chris.

The steps to the upstairs.

The steps led up to Alvin.

Alvin was an uncle who at one time, was "the cool kid in town," according to mom. But after a heavy night of drinking when a girlfriend left him, he had parked his car on the railroad tracks. Drew's family liked to say he just drunkenly passed out and ended up there. The rumor everyone else heard was that it was a suicide attempt. Either way, he survived a head-on collision with the train.

It left him crippled and angry at the world.

Now Alvin was hiding in the top floor of Gramma's house. Mom said he was a hermit who had the largest comic book and baseball card collection she had ever seen. Dad said he was crazy and waiting for Gramma to die to get her money. Both agreed that Drew and Chris should avoid him at all costs.

The bathroom faucet was either all cold or all hot water and both were on the extreme ends. Drew chose hot to wash, cold to stop the blistering.

Chris was in the room next to the bathroom, so Drew poked his head in after he was done washing up.

"Hey, Scrooge wants you to take the trash out," Drew half-lied.

"NO, she doesn't. That's your job," Chris yelled, but stopped when he heard footsteps above them.

Alvin must be awake.

"Well, you better go tell her no, then. I'm gonna wash dishes." Drew ran away back to the kitchen. If he was fast enough, Gramma would trap Chris as he waddled by.

"YOU JUST DON'T WANT TO TAKE IT OUT COS YOU'RE SCARED OF THE GOUGERS," Chris screamed behind him. Drew regretted ever telling him about them in the first place. He would never share the story with anyone again. It was his.

"WHAT…? Who said that?" A weak voice tried to get Drew's attention from inside the dark bedroom.

Drew looked back. There were still Nintendo beep boop beep sounds coming from the room Chris was in.

He had never even given chase.

Dad was right, the video games were changing him. And because of his big mouth, Drew was the one stuck going in to see Gramma. At least she was trapped in her bed now. Before, when she still walked around, her skeletal figure would pace around all hours of the night and appear out of nowhere. It was terrifying.

Drew held his breath as he entered the room.

"Hi, Gramma Bean, sorry Chris was yelling." Drew tried to get his eyes to adjust to the dark by squinting.

"Who is that…which one are you?" Gramma's sheets moved when she talked, exposing her almost-glowing white skin.

Drew could see her now. Her bones poked the fabric that still covered her, her exposed ankles were bruised, and her skin looked so thin, it looked like it might fall apart just by looking at it. The look of confusion on her hollow sickly face let him know she wasn't joking when she was asking who he was like Grandpa always had.

She had lost even more weight than the last time Drew had seen her. Her eyelids hung open even when she blinked, and the whites of her eyes were red. Even in the darkness of the room, he could see every bone and vein through her translucent flesh.

There was a huge selection of salves and balms on a shelf next to her, trying their best to mask her smell of decay. Her mouth hung open, exposing her pearly teeth. Her face contorted permanently looking like she might start screaming at any second.

"I'm Drew, Steven and Barbara's kid." Drew knew the appropriate response despite feeling like he should run away.

"Why the hell were you yelling about Gougers?" Gramma didn't care who he was.

"It was Chris." Drew tried to shift the focus.

"The hell you know about Gougers anyway?" Gramma seemed angry on top of the confusion.

"Just what Grandpa told me about why they were after him." Drew wanted this to be over already.

"Your Grandpa Gunnar never messed with no Gougers. Why are they after him? Go get him for me." Gramma was getting mad at her husband, who had been dead for years.

"No, not Grandpa Gunnar, my other Grandpa Gordon...well Great Grandpa Gordon really." Drew didn't have the heart to tell her about either grandpa being dead.

"Oh. Well in that case, you better tell your other Grandpa Gordon that you love him because there ain't nothing as vengeful as a pissed-off Gouger and if he's got one after him, best he can do is move to the plains and hope it turns in circles till it dies." Gramma advised.

Drew was shocked that she seemed to know about the Gougers and seemed to think they were as real as he and Grandpa did.

"Well, I think the Gougers got him already. They said he got crushed by a pile of wood that I stacked too high, but I think the Gougers stomped him. And guess what, even living on the plains won't help you cos Grandpa stole the eggs from a mating pair of Gougers—one anti-clockwise, one clockwise. They use each other to lean on for strength so they can even run on the prairie too." Drew was so full of questions. Maybe Gramma had the end of Grandpa's story.

"I told you Gunnar never messed with a Gouger. Where is he?" Gramma looked lost.

"He's dead, mom. Dad died years ago." Scrooge had snuck up on their conversation and let herself in.

Drew was relieved but frustrated. He wanted to get more information.

"Ahh, bullshit, you said that about my sister, Margret. You said she died, but she was here last night. We talked almost until that damned blistering sun started coming up. She was so mad about the state of her room, she nearly pulled me out of bed by my ankles to get me to clean it up for her." Gramma was motioning to her leg with a knobby finger.

"Mom, Margret died before dad did. Her room's been full of crap for as long as I can remember now." Scrooge was putting the bacon fat sandwich on the table for Gramma.

Gramma said bacon fat sandwiches were the only food that didn't hurt to eat... *except blood*, Drew thought.

"Sure, sure, then who was in here last night? I pulled myself out of bed?" Gramma's eyelids, which didn't close all the way, blinked in frustration and she wiggled a bony finger at the light switch furiously. Her focus was back for a moment and the imposing figure she once was returned. "Turn the lights on, damn it."

Scrooge complied and flipped the switch, flooding the room with light. They all winced and squinted. When their focus returned, Gramma was now using her bony finger to point at her leg. It was covered in bruises, roughly in the shape of how fingers and a thumb might look if they held a particularly tight grip on someone.

Scrooge's eyes got big, and she stared at Drew.

"I didn't do it." Drew mistook the look as an accusation.

"I know that, you dolt. But those were not there last night when I left because I gave her a head-to-toe sponge bath and was looking for sores." Scrooge's usually stern face looked sullen and scared.

"Maybe Alvin?" Drew offered.

SMACK

"HE WOULD NEVER." Scrooge's anger returned and fired a shot across his right cheek.

She didn't hit as hard as mom could.

"Sorry." Drew didn't even bother rubbing his cheek.

"Well, you should know better. He's a gentle soul who wouldn't hurt anyone, especially his own mom." Scrooge softened a bit. "Go get the dishes done and eat something. I'll get that brother of yours to take the trash out."

"Ok, but what about Gramma?" Drew asked, genuinely freaked out. Now there was a possible vampire, a hermit, and a ghost all in one house.

"Get Gunnar. Tell him if he don't pick those beans, those bastard birds will get them," Gramma argued with someone neither of them could see. "And somebody find Arvid—I need a drink like you wouldn't believe."

"Gramma will be ok. She is just not very lucid at the moment." The definition of the word Drew was wondering about revealed itself in context.

"Ok." Drew left and washed dishes, lost in thought about ghosts and Gougers and vampires and hermits.

Chris never showed up to take the trash out, so Drew did it himself. He stopped and scanned the hills around the house first, though. Maybe Chris had been right, maybe he was still a little scared of the Gougers.

But even if he was scared, he still did it. The trash still got to the can.

On his way back inside, Scrooge was leaving for the night, in a hurry, looking over her shoulder at the empty windows on the huge house as her ankles strained and wobbled under her weight to get her down the steps.

She was quick to leave Drew and Chris with the house full of monsters and ghosts.

"She's ok for the evening. You boys know how to call me and I'm right across the street. If there is something really bad…call for Alvin…OK?" Scrooge asked, already walking away. "Put the leftovers away when you're done and don't leave a mess for the field mice."

"Ok," Drew said, already knowing all the food she cooked would end up in the fridge.

He wasn't hungry and couldn't imagine getting one of her hairs in his mouth.

Then she was gone, and Drew was back inside, standing in the kitchen alone. Every corner of the old homestead seemed to hold a threat, so his eyes darted around non-stop. He hurried through the rest of the kitchen clean-up, feeling like he was being watched, checking over his shoulders constantly.

Then, not wanting to be alone, and with nothing else to do, he snuck back to his room, past Gramma, and watched Chris play Nintendo.

"Wanna play a two-player game?" Drew asked after watching for a while.

"Nope," Chris barely offered.

"Fine…peckerhead." Drew finally used the insult out loud. Mom and dad were nowhere around and there was barely an adult around either unless you counted Gramma or the hermit.

"Uhhh, I'm telling," Chris warned.

"Go ahead, tell Gramma," Drew countered.

Chris just went back to his game.

Drew grabbed his bag and pulled out his snacks, along with a survival craft book. He unwrapped a root beer barrel and popped it in his mouth. Drew crinkled the wrapper extra hard.

It worked.

"Can I have one?" The only thing Chris liked more than Nintendo was candy.

"You play two player with me and I'll let you pick three pieces." Drew had the upper hand now.

"Five pieces" Chris tried to negotiate from a losing position.

"Four but no big ones, just the small stuff."

Chris popped the game out of its slot in the Nintendo.

"Ok, but I get to pick the game." Chris tried to reclaim some ground and Drew let him.

He didn't care what they played; he just wanted to play.

The two of them ate candy and played games until almost when the sun came up. They would stop to get a soda or see if there were chips in the kitchen a couple of times, but the rest of the house felt too imposing to linger outside their room for long.

Alvin paced from two to four in the morning, leading the boys to question each other about what he did up there all the time.

Drew woke up before Chris, and after realizing how much candy they had eaten, walked to the general store to see what they had to stock back up on. He spent a couple of bucks but didn't want to spend it all, so it was just little stuff.

On the way back to Gramma's, Drew was feeling too good out in the fresh air to want to go back into the possibly haunted house full of monsters. The rhubarb plant he hid under during hide and seek was right around the corner and with Scrooge over at Gramma's, he could sneak across her yard to get there.

Drew sat under the giant plant five minutes later, sucking on a ribbon candy, and fell asleep. When he woke up, the sun was still bright in the sky, but he still wasn't ready to go back to Gramma's. He decided to practice his friction fire skills again, under the cover of the rhubarb canopy, where no one could see him and laugh at him.

He pulled off a piece of the rhubarb leaf above his head to give himself a bit more light to work with while he made his spindle and prepared some tinder, just in case he got an ember.

Drew rubbed the sweat from his lip and got a taste of the rhubarb sap that was on his finger. It had a bitter but pleasant feeling on his tongue. He ripped off a tiny piece of leaf and chewed on it, getting more of the numbing sensation. The leaf made his mouth water, and he spat the green juice onto the ground, laughing to himself about the color.

Then he got back to work and started to spin the spindle on the block of wood he found and was using as his fireboard. Amazingly, after not too long or much effort, a tiny plume of smoke appeared. Shocked, Drew pushed harder, rotated the spindle faster, and blew on it. This produced a nice little plume, but his arms were getting tired now. He was forced to slow his pace to a crawl from exhaustion and he eyed his progress approvingly.

He was close.

Absentmindedly, he grabbed another piece of the rhubarb leaf and chewed it.

"OH, MY GOD, HE'S GONNA KILL HIMSELF," a familiar angry voice screamed from the yard behind Drew.

Chapter 16

Scrooge ripped Drew out from under the rhubarb and pushed her fingers into Drew's mouth. She fished around in Drew's mouth and pulled out the chunk of leaf he was chewing on. As soon as she pulled the leaf from his mouth, she started ripping the rhubarb plant up by the roots.

"Eating poison and trying to burn down my garage…WHAT IS WRONG WITH YOU?" Scrooge's red face highlighted her anger.

Her feet were stamping the ground where Drew had been trying to make a fire and her free, left hand was smacking Drew over and over. Some smacks landed on his face like she intended, but most were clumsy and landed everywhere else.

Drew had no idea the rhubarb leaves were poisonous. He ate pies made from the stalks all the time and a jam that had rhubarb in it as well (he liked the rhubarb, but he loved the jam for the little orange slice candies mom put in it as it cooled).

Scrooge, however, knew the leaves of rhubarb were toxic, and after she yelled about the attempted arson and suicide all the way to Gramma's house, the whole town of Mountain did as well.

Now Scrooge had him pinned on the kitchen counter and was trying to force some witch's brew she called Ipecac down his throat.

"No, please don't. I can't drink that. I didn't even swallow any of it. I was spitting it out, and it was just a tiny little bit,"

Drew pleaded with his knees pinned down by Scrooge's huge belly.

Scrooge's hands were at his neck, forcing his head back, restraining his breathing.

"You swallowed more than you could even know, even if you were spitting like a little demon. Now open that damn gob." Scrooge was prying her finger into his cheek, forcing the flesh between his teeth.

Drew could either start bleeding or open his mouth.

His mouth opened reluctantly, and Scrooge upended the questionable bottle that looked like it came from a pharmacy out of a Western movie.

The bitter liquid made the socket of his jaw ache as it touched his tongue. It was viscous and as he swallowed the first bit, he choked and sputtered. A brown bubble formed on his lips and popped. A droplet of the liquid landed on his pupil and momentarily changed the hue of the kitchen.

Everything was blood-red.

Scrooge's pleasure from the situation was obvious on her smiling face, which, with the blood-red color shift, made her look like a demon. This made Drew scream and blink until she returned to her normal angry-colored self.

Her face was still pretty red, though not from the poison in his eyes.

"Hahahaha!" Chris was laughing wickedly from the corner of the kitchen.

His hands were pulled up to his face in excitement similar to Scrooge's. It was the first time he had left his video games in two days.

"SHUT UP, Chris!" Drew yelled as the brown liquid ran down the corners of his mouth.

He had swallowed most of the bitter substance and already he felt like he was going to regret not letting Scrooge just gouge his cheek out and risk dying from the rhubarb leaf.

The Ipecac burned all the way down his throat, and his stomach was already rolling around.

"You better have swallowed it all or I'll go get another bottle." Scrooge lifted his chin and looked into his mouth. "Fine. Now you go get a bucket or set up shop in the bathroom while you get rid of the poison."

Drew knew what that meant.

He chose the bathroom next to the room he and Chris were sharing since it was the farthest from any of the monsters in the rest of the house. Drew sat there waiting on the cool tiles of the bathroom floor, knowing from the boiling in his guts that this was going to be a very long night.

Scrooge was busy, back in the kitchen now, making a bacon fat sandwich for Gramma, muttering to herself about how much she hated kids. Chris was in the room next to him. The beep boop beep of the video game was back on.

The video game sounds were making the spinning room even more nauseating. Sweat was beading up all over his body. His socks felt wet, so he slid them off and leaned back against the porcelain tub, which felt nice and cool and eased his fluttering stomach. He pressed his back against it as hard as he could.

Maybe if he just relaxed and breathed, he wouldn't feel like puking, and he could just sleep it off next to the tub.

"Hurr Hurr HURRR…" The gagging started as soon as the thought finished.

His heart was racing in his chest, and the sweat was dripping from his nose.

He wasn't going to make it.

His stomach lurched violently, and his mouth filled with spit. Drew crawled the couple of feet to the toilet and a torrent of brown liquid poured from his mouth with hardly any effort. A few more streams and heaves later, Drew thought he was in the clear because there was no way there was anything left in his guts after that.

He was wrong.

The rest of the night was a haze.

He could barely hold his body up while he continued to puke. His face almost touched the seat more than once, but the sheer terror of letting that happen seemed to give him enough strength to finish puking and crawl back to the cool tub each time. The cramps in his stomach made it hard to move from the fetal position. Even while sitting upright, he had to keep his knees pulled tight to his chest. At some point during the night, Drew felt like it was hard to get a deep breath, and his lips started to tingle. The world started to turn gray around him.

It was getting hard to keep his eyes open.

"Are you ok?" It was a man's voice Drew didn't recognize.

Was it Grandpa Gunnar? Drew was confused, but too weak to roll over and see if it was his ghost. He was in no shape for a fight or even a scream, so he stayed motionless, waiting for the ghost to do whatever it was going to do.

"I heard Scrooge caught you." The voice was closer now.

It moved something behind Drew and Drew could feel a breeze blow across his cool but now dry skin, leaving goosebumps in its wake. The sweating had stopped, and his lips and tongue were dry. Two firm hands lifted Drew and placed him back down on a nice, dry, fluffy towel.

"Light as a bird," Grandpa Gunnar's ghost said.

It laid another towel over him and tucked in the edges. The dry fabric felt nice on his cold skin. Drew's head lifted and something soft was put under it. Then the feeling of a cup touched Drew's lips.

"Easy, not a lot, it prolly won't stay down for long."

"Thanks, Grandpa." Drew was falling asleep listening to the voice take a leak and flush the toilet a couple of times.

Drew realized Grandpa's ghost was now probably cleaning up his puke mess.

"Sorry I made a mess. I'll clean it up in the morning," Drew offered, his cold, pale face hot from embarrassment.

"Save your energy. You're not done," the voice said and walked away.

Drew fell asleep hard and never heard the voice walk quietly back upstairs. There was only one more bout of puking that night, but by that point, his stomach was so empty, there was nothing left but bile.

***

That whole next day, Drew spent in a fog.

His heart continued to race, and the sweat continued to pour after he drank some water. Eventually, he found enough strength to climb into the bed next to where Chris was still playing his video game. The beep boop beep no longer made him want to puke, so Drew could tell he was getting better.

Drew stayed in bed until the next morning, hating Scrooge's guts the whole time. Chris never offered to let Drew play, but he didn't mind, as his head was still spinning.

The strength returned to his body after he ate some toast with butter almost forty-eight hours after eating the rhubarb leaf. Drew avoided Scrooge and made it himself before she showed up to make Gramma a bacon fat sandwich. While he was sick/poisoned, Drew had come up with a plan.

He was going camping.

There was no way he was staying in this house full of monsters until mom and dad came back. Chris was too busy with his game to notice him missing, Gramma wasn't lucid, Scrooge didn't care as long as he wasn't in her hair, and Alvin...Drew had a fuzzy flash of puking and thinking Grandpa was with him... well, Alvin didn't matter either.

Drew grabbed his bag of gear from the porch and made his way out back to the barn, where he had stashed the rope and the rat traps. He stayed sneaky, even though the sun was barely up.

Sneaking made it more fun.

After grabbing the stash, he hit Gramma's garden. He grabbed a cucumber and a handful of the wax beans. They were so good, the guilt from not taking Bob outside couldn't keep him away. Plus, he would remember to ask dad if they could go visit Bob before the end of summer so he could show Drew his garden. Drew snagged a few raspberries and strawberries and put them in the side pouch with the veggies.

Luckily, the general store was open early. The coffee crowd of old men was all gathered at a wooden table, already busy gossiping. They didn't even notice Drew as he walked around the modest selection and spent the last of his cash. It was worth it if it kept him out of the house until mom and dad came to save him. On his way out of town, to where Drew knew the woods and river met the "mountain," there was a creepy road called "beer can alley." Hundreds of empty beer cans had been threaded onto the branches of the trees that lined the road, most of them from the recent Deuce of August festival. The early morning breeze rattled them in the trees and brought to mind one thing: Can Man. Drew shuddered and looked around in every direction, wondering if the psycho could have pedaled that huge tricycle all the way to Mountain to collect these cans as well.

Drew sprinted the rest of the way down beer can alley and as soon as he had a chance to leave the road and the possibility of running into people, he cut into the woods.

The closeness of the trees and brush was instantly comforting. He always felt best out in the woods, fishing and goofing around. The buckbrush was waist-high, and Drew remembered the last time he went stomping through the woods and all the ticks he had accumulated. He high-stepped to a small clear spot and fished around his bag.

After a liberal dousing of OFF, Drew felt better and continued to the river. An animal trail led the way and Drew took mental notes, not only so he wouldn't get lost, but he was habitually looking for chokepoints on the trail that would work for a Gouger trap.

The canopy of the deciduous forest was thick and blocked out most of the sun except for a perfect flat spot near the river. It seemed like it was custom-made for his pup tent.

Before long, Drew was all set up. He took the sleeping bag out of his bag and fluffed it by shaking it in the fresh air. Hopefully, this would also knock loose any debris or bugs that had been hiding out. Then, after a liberal dousing of OFF, he laid the sleeping bag neatly in his tent. His snack and food bags were hanging on a branch next to the tent, so it was off the ground and away from bugs. And now, splayed out in front of him was Drew's new and improved monster hunting gear.

Drew knew he was in prime territory for a Gouger and since Gramma knew about them too, it meant they could be close. One thing was for certain. Drew was tired of feeling like a baby and letting the adults make him feel scared. This new trap could help him beat the Gougers and he could stop being scared of camping. That way, if the adults were being awful, he could escape to the woods whenever he wanted.

His excitement grew as he looked over the gear. The rope he swiped from Gramma that he had actually learned to tie a noose in this time; talcum powder, not flour, for footprints this time; a trip wire rig for his camera in case he froze again so it would take a picture on its own; dirty socks he found in his locker at the end of school for bait; the flashlight they used to keep the color on the TV when the lights got turned off (he wondered if mom was watching movies in black and white cussing him out, waiting with her ladle in hand waiting for her own chokepoint); and three huge rat traps from Gramma's barn.

Drew was certain that this trap was flawless this time. He smiled to himself while he made his way back to a chokepoint on the trail not too far away from where he had set up camp.

He hung the noose first, this time higher than his neck, just in case (he didn't need to build a second idiot trap). Then he used the eye bolts and strings, which comprised the trip wire portion of his kit, to set up the Polaroid part of the trap. He placed the camera pointing down on the trail from up a branch and jumped down to the ground beside his bag.

The rat traps were a bit scarier. The triggers were rusty and didn't want to hold. More than once, he thought he was going to lose a finger, but after what must have sounded like someone target practicing with a rifle in the woods, the traps were set.

Drew hid the traps under a thin layer of leaves and pine needles and then he dusted the entire area with talcum so there was evidence of the clawed hooves, or people's feet.

Last but not least were the socks that were wrapped up in a bread bag to keep the funk off his other stuff, especially his food. Drew held his breath, not sure of what the contents would smell like while he tore the bag open.

He couldn't help himself and took a whiff, anyway.

"Oh, jeez, if that does lure them in, it might kill them," Drew said out loud and laughed to himself all the way back to his campsite after baiting the trap.

The rest of the day, Drew spent fishing.

It was unbelievable.

The bluegills were practically jumping out of the river and hooking themselves. Drew threw them all back. He could eat them, but he wanted a catfish. He caught five trout but couldn't stand the chalky taste of them, so tossed them back as well. The river was small, so Drew had to move locations frequently to keep from scaring the fish too much. After a few more bluegills, Drew finally caught a catfish. It was a keeper, so without hesitating, he took his scout knife from his pocket and cut the spine behind its head. Then he flipped it over and cut from the poop chute to its chin, spilling the guts in the process. Drew fished the guts out with his fingers and tossed them into the river. He didn't care if the other fish got full off their buddy's guts now. This fish was more than enough for him to eat, and any more fishing would be just for fun.

By the time the catfish was sizzling on the small grill that he propped up on the rocks surrounding his fire, the sun was dipping. Drew had lost all sense of time and had hardly spent any time thinking about adults or monsters. As he dug into the

white flesh of the catfish and munched on some wax beans, Drew wondered if maybe he shouldn't just tuck tail and hike back to Gramma's before it got too dark to find his way.
The thought of Scrooge's blood-red smiling face and beer can alley being harvested by Can Man convinced him to stay.

The comfort that came from this reasoning waned as the darkness grew.

One nice thing about Mountain was that there didn't seem to be as many mosquitos as there were at home. Dad said it was because all the water around here was moving, and the mosquitos couldn't lay their eggs in it. It must be true because even with OFF, you would still be getting swarmed at home, but here, there wasn't even a buzz. Drew tossed another couple of sticks onto the fire and watched the embers float around. One of them drifted into the grass.

"Crap." Drew got up and chased it, not wanting to start a forest fire.

He stomped in the area where he thought it had landed, probably looking like Scrooge fighting the imaginary rhubarb blaze.

"OOOAAAAHHHH…"

A roar erupted from the woods between him and town.

The bass from the vocalization shook the trees around him and the wildlife all went quiet.

Drew froze.

It sounded like the noise demons made in scary movies.

His brain scoured every corner for an explanation. There was none. No animal he could think of made a sound like that, not outside of the Discovery Channel. Drew's mind created a scenario of Gramma Bean wandering around senile and half naked with the Gouger on a leash out in the woods, hunting him down. Ready to punish him for leaving without telling anyone.

Drew rushed back to the campfire and tripped on the stake line from his tent. His hands reached forward to protect him and in the process knocked his soda off its rock perch, directly into the fire.

The syrup sizzled on the coals, and the light from the fire flickered out for the most part. The last bits of its light illuminated only the branches closest to him. They looked like skeletal arms reaching out from the blackness. Drew scrambled over and started blowing furiously on the coals, trying to save the fire, pulling at the dry grass next to the tent and piling it onto the embers.

"OOOOAAAAHHHHRRR!"

The roar was closer now and had changed in tone as if it was excited…or onto his trail.

Drew's lips were stuck in a kissy face near the fire pit. He forgot to keep blowing while he was frozen. The embers smelled like burnt sugar and the fire was completely dead.

Now in total darkness, Drew scrambled back to his tent, feeling the ground to guide his way. His hand found the stake line he had tripped on, and he traced it to his bag next to the tent. Clumsily, he searched for the TV flashlight. His panicky hands quickly found it and clicked it on.

The beam raced around the woods in the general direction of the roar. Drew noticed the beam was weak and brown. He thought back to all his late-night monster movies holding the flashlight to the light sensor so he could see the picture, and he now regretted every second of wasted batteries. He should have planned better and got new batteries at the general store in Mountain before he left today instead of more candy.

How long would the brown beam keep the blackness at bay?

Then his heart sank even further. What if the light was just directing the Gouger straight to him like a lighthouse in a storm?

Drew clicked it off, now conserving batteries and his location. The scared baby part of Drew wanted to climb into the tent and pull the sleeping bag over his head and just pretend this wasn't happening. The part of him that wanted to survive knew that was a death sentence — he remembered the stomped sleeping bag the last time he camped. There was nowhere to run in a tent. He would just stand his ground and wait until the last second before he shined the weak beam in the monster's eyes, hopefully buying him enough time to bury the scout knife in its chest. The small knife was already in his hand, clenched so tight it was hurting.

Drew stood there frozen in the dark, waiting to see if his flight or fight response would kick in when the time came. Anything besides just standing there and letting it trample him to death like Grandpa.

"OOOOAAAAHHHHRRR!!"

The sound was right on top of him now. He could hear grass crunching under rhythmic footsteps just in front of where he was standing.

Thump…Thump…Scrape…Thump…Thump…Scrape.

Flight won.

Drew ran through the blackness. Every skeletal branch reached out to grab him. Every handlike root tripped his feet. Progress was slow, but he had to keep moving, in a straight line, just like Grandpa in his story.

He tried to listen for the monster chasing him, but his own clumsiness in the dark was preventing him from hearing anything but the sounds of his escape through the dense undergrowth. The brush opened up suddenly and Drew's speed increased. Only now, there was nothing under his feet and Drew could feel himself falling.

SPLASH!

The cold water splashed up around him as Drew somehow landed on his feet. He was knee-deep in the river.

He stopped long enough to listen to the woods around him. His eyes and ears were desperate for anything. Any indication of where to run for help or where to run from danger.

Nothing.

He tried to quietly make his way up the bank, but the splashing wasn't concealing anything. The mud made him slip backward a few times, forcing him to land loudly back into the river. After one last tremendous effort, he was standing back up on the bank, looking around. He wished there were a moon out tonight so he could see anything. His eyes strained and Drew prayed silently for them to adjust to the blackness like a cat's. His heart was racing like it had from the Ipecac and the sweat was also back. The river trickled behind him, and Drew suddenly had a realization.

He was lost.

The blackness had swallowed him up and now he didn't know which direction was toward town or toward the cemetery farther down the river. Or if he was even still on the right side of the river. Or how far he had run in his flight of fear.

Panic started to set in.

The last option he had was to start screaming. He knew it was useless, something a pee pants baby would do, but there was nothing else he could think to do.

Drew sucked in a huge breath of air, preparing his lungs to let out a scream that would save his life.

"AA…" Just as the scream started…

FLASH!

A bolt of lightning hit the woods to his left, where his eyes were focused.

At the moment of the flash, Drew could see something.

It was huge.

At least as tall as dad's Travelall and just about as long. He swore he could see legs beneath its belly swinging wildly and just as the image faded into the void; the beast turned two heads to look in Drew's direction. The flash had illuminated four burning yellow eyes that were staring right at him.

Drew waited for thunder that never came.

It wasn't lightning; it was his Polaroid.

Drew felt a sense of pride despite his fear. At least that part of the trap worked.

Drew knew the Gougers were imposing monsters based on Grandpa's account, but he never expected them to be so huge. The flight response was gone. All that was left in Drew was fight. If he turned and ran, he would be even more lost, and the monster would still be on his trail. There was no way he could hope to outrun it, but maybe he could surprise it.

Water dripped from his pants, and the little splashes landing in the mud were all that Drew could hear. He held the knife and flashlight tightly. His last lines of defense. He thought of the scary movies where they wasted their flashlights until they were dead, and he steadied his thumb on the sliding button.

Not yet.

Not until it was right on top of him.

Thump…Scrape…Thump…Scrape…

They were moving now. Closer through the void separating him from them.

Thump…Scrape…Thump…

BANG!

"OOOOAAAAAAAAAAA!"

The demonic-sounding howl didn't sound as excited this time.

It sounded scared.

The ground rumbled as a series of footsteps thundered through the woods. They were moving away from him.

Drew took a breath, realizing he had been holding it longer than a pearl diver from the Discovery Channel. The footsteps were so faint that now, Drew wondered if he was imagining them. He stood there like a statue, thumb on his flashlight button, knife still digging into his palm. Listening, hoping, praying. Drew was fairly sure something had scared them off. Judging by the gunshot, it was probably a hunter or a local who heard the attack going on. Maybe it was Scrooge out looking for him? He wanted to call out to the rescuer, but the fear of drawing the Gougers back to his location kept him quiet. Drew's eyes were locked on the area where he had made eye contact with the Gougers. It was where he last saw the beast and as long as he kept his eyes locked on that spot, he wasn't lost, he was looking at where he had set his trap.

Drew stayed that way until morning.

***

As soon as the sun was bright enough to erase any shadows and threat of getting even more lost, Drew cautiously made his way to where the camera had flashed in the night.

He was right; it was his trap that had been sprung in the night. Drew looked at the noose hanging limply on one side of the chokepoint. It had obviously fallen when the beasts ran into it and had been useless. Even more so than the last trap—at least that one had caught an idiot.

Drew hardly noticed the failed noose, though. He was looking for the Polaroid. The camera was still holding onto it above him on the branch where he had secured it. The already developed photo was waiting to be snatched. Drew shimmied up the tree and popped the photo out of the mouth of the camera. He unwound the trip wire and put the camera's free strap over his shoulder. Then, like a monkey, he grabbed the branch and dropped. He let his feet dangle for a moment before letting go of the branch so he would land lighter and not hurt the camera.

He looked at the picture and was shocked.

It worked.

He had a picture of one Gouger's huge yellow burning eye filling the frame and burning into his own. Even in the daylight, the eye scared him. Drew looked around the empty woods, scanning the trees for the beast.

Now he would have proof to show everyone the Gougers were real and tell them the story of how he beat Grandpa's monsters.

BANG!

Drew barely flinched.

He had moved a stick with his foot and set off one of the forgotten rat traps. Drew looked at the ground. The white powder was useless for footprints. It was just a mess of leaves and talcum now. Nothing discernable as a print. The second trap let out another loud snap as he set it off too, and he was now looking for the third. He found it after a quick search of the area where he had left them. The third trap was now a good distance away from the others, lying upside-down. Drew turned it over with the stick, half expecting it to snap in his face.

Sandwiched between the board and the metal killing part of the trap was a shiny black claw.

It was as long as his middle finger and razor-sharp.

Drew pried the jaw of the trap open and let the claw fall into his hand. Bits of yellow flesh were still clinging to the edges of the non-sharp end. Drew turned it in his hand, amazed. That was what had scared the Gougers away. The BANG he heard was his trap taking one of their clawed toes off.

Now he had physical proof to go with his picture. He looked at the flashlight still in his other hand and pushed the switch into the on position. It still had juice. If he were a movie character, it would have died in the darkness just like him. Drew had never been prouder of himself. He finished picking up the monster trap, noticing the disgusting socks were completely absent. That was fine. The Gougers could have them. Drew fingered the claw in his pocket carefully. He would keep this in return.

A part of Drew hoped the Gougers were scared now. Of him. Scared the way Drew had been scared for so long. Drew didn't feel that way anymore. It was someone or something else's turn.

He had beaten Grandpa's monsters on his own.

Drew was swimming in confidence on the way home. There was no pressing need to look over his shoulders. Beer can alley no longer drew visions of Can Man in his imagination. By the time he got back to Gramma's house, he was feeling better about himself than he ever had.

No one even knew Drew had been gone.

Chris was still in his room. Gramma was still in hers. Scrooge was nowhere to be seen. Drew wanted to brag but thought better of it. This victory was his. Adults never listened anyway, and Chris would just call him a liar. He would keep the picture and the claw a secret, one that he could share with himself anytime he felt like a baby again.

Drew ate some toast and heard the familiar pacing coming from upstairs. By the time he thought about what he was doing, he was already at the top of the steps and knocking.

KNOCK KNOCK KNOCK…

The pacing behind the door stopped, then approached the other side. The knob twisted slowly, and the door opened.

"Hi, uncle Alvin, uhh, thanks for covering me up in the bathroom the other night."

Drew smiled at the man peering through the cracked door. His hair was long and black. He was holding a black cane with a white tip that reminded Drew of a magician's wand. A scar ran across his face, from his neck to the opposite ear.

"Well, you looked like hell. I couldn't let you freeze to death on the bathroom floor and Scrooge wasn't about to give a damn." Alvin smiled at Drew.

"You want a soda?" Drew held out the ice-cold Pepsi.

"Sure…You want to look at some comic books?" Alvin looked confused.

"Yeah," Drew said excitedly.

Why had he waited so long to come up and say hi?

Alvin and Drew spent the next two days reading comics, talking baseball cards, and playing Alvin's own Nintendo…two player. Drew had no idea why everyone in the family treated Alvin like a curse. He was the coolest adult in the family. Surely the only adult who had comics and video games. He even had a huge collection of movies, most of which were horror.

Unfortunately, mom and dad came to get them early. To Drew's surprise, he didn't want to leave. He had been helping with Gramma Bean and she wasn't scary anymore, even if she wasn't lucid and now had no recollection of Gougers. Now Drew just felt awful for ever thinking Gramma was a bloodsucker. Scrooge had even lightened up after the newness of the boys had worn off and they were just part of the routine.

While they were saying goodbyes, Alvin made an appearance to everyone's surprise but Drew's. They gave each other high-fives, and Alvin handed Drew a bag and shot him a wink.

"I bet Chris shares now," Alvin said with a smirk.

Drew looked in the bag. It was loaded with comic books from the series he had gotten into about a swamp man. Also, a ton of Nintendo games. Alvin must have raided his stash and picked out some choice games for him.

"You sure?" Drew asked Alvin with a grin he couldn't control.

"Yep, and next time you visit, you can swap them out with some fresh ones." Alvin was grinning, too.

***

The drive home was quiet. Dad was puttering his lips, nervous about work again. Chris had taken one look in the bag Alvin had given him and given mom a "mo'om" in frustration.

He knew the days of hoarding the console were over if he wanted to play any of the new games.

While the Travelall bounced along down the highway, Drew fell asleep, Gouger claw gripped tightly in his hand, deep in his pocket.

Drew never saw Gramma Bean again, and they never stayed at her farm again. She died that winter and there was a messy fight about property and money that drove a wedge into the family. Drew never heard a conclusion, but he hoped Alvin got the lion's share. Sometimes on dark scary nights or days when he was feeling scared of dad, Drew would pull out the Polaroid and look the Gouger right in the eye.

He had beaten a monster and thought he could do it again if he had to.

Drew often wondered if that was how Grandpa's story would end. If he had written the final chapter of the Gougers himself.

Part of him, the part that liked to be scared, hoped not.

Chapter 17

The streetlight at the junction up ahead was the only light aside from Drew's headlights in the moonless black night. The junction took Drew off the straight flat highway on the prairie and up through the twisting, turning highway that led home through the hills. The Nova kicked into a lower gear as Drew slowed to take the turn. His car felt like it was riding funny, but Drew hardly noticed. His heart was still racing from the fight he just got into with his friends on Battle Mountain. The crack running down the center of his windshield was evidence of how intense it had been.

He had replayed the fight and the events leading up to it over and over in his mind during the first half of the thirty-mile drive home, and after taking the turn at the junction, he planned on doing more of the same until he pulled into his spot in the driveway.

The Nova roared as Drew stomped the accelerator to the floor. He was already doing almost twenty, but the tires chirped in excitement anyway. It was "too much power for a kid," his dad had bothered saying after only talking Drew into buying it. Probably because dad was slightly jealous of the muscle car since Drew had put so much work into it. Drew thought dad never believed he would get it running and if he did, not like this.

For almost two years, every penny Drew had made, outside of gas money and lunch money, had gone into restoring the old muscle car. Two years of every free minute not spent in school, mowing lawns, or at work making tacos at the local Tex-Mex restaurant was spent in his friend Joe's garage with a Chilton's manual.

Then, after endless long nights and even longer days, the Nova was running. It wasn't perfect at first, but after a long eighth-grade summer, Drew had it ready to drive for his first day of high school. He was the first kid in his class with a car and though he had trouble getting people to like him when they first moved to the Black Hills, the Nova cemented him as part of the cool kid group—at least if they wanted to go to lunch off campus or wanted a ride to a party.

Drew made improvements to the 1974 Chevy Nova Custom SS constantly. Chrome block hugger headers, he had stroked the 350 small block to a 383, added an 850 cfm 4-barrel Edelbrock carb, had it balanced and blueprinted, camel hump heads...just about any part that could be upgraded was. The paint came last, but now even that looked good.

Drew was lost in thought about his restoration. It was a momentary reprieve from the stress of the fight he'd had at Battle Mountain. He was too lost in thought to remember the recent addition of a DIP in the road where the newly resurfaced portion met the old.

His wandering mind missed the yellow DIP sign desperately telling him to SLOW.

BANG!

Drew bounced so hard in his bucket-seat that his head hit the roof of the car. The wheel tried to twist in his hand, but he held tightly. Just when Drew thought he had the situation under control, the car tilted and lurched to the right. A metallic scream rang through the night. Sparks lit up his passenger side rearview mirror. He pressed on the brake and pulled to the right. The shifting weight of the vehicle and the tilt made the correction too easy and instead of hitting the shoulder, Drew bounced into the ditch.

The dust swirled around him as the car skidded to a stop.

"Holy crap," Drew yelled to himself.

His heart was racing in his chest again. It hadn't had any time off in a couple of hours. Drew sat in the car for a moment, catching his breath, wondering what the hell had just happened. The engine was still roaring, so Drew backed the key off but left the lights on and the hazards blinking.

He was halfway between town and home. About fifteen miles either way. It was late on a Friday, but any traffic showing up on this back highway after midnight was next to none. If there was to be any traffic, it was probably someone stinking drunk, trying to make their way back home after the bar ran them out.

Drew did the math in his head, trying to figure how fast he thought he could walk the fifteen miles to home. Maybe two hours if he hustled, three at the most. The car door creaked as it swung open, sounding like a hinge from a haunted house movie. It could use some butter. Drew laughed to himself as he exited the car, thinking back on the house with the butter hinges his family moved away from when he was a kid. Dry grass crunched under his feet as he made his way around to the back tire, where the weight of the car seemed to lean toward. Maybe he could fix it? It was too dark to see anything very well. The only lights were from the junction about half a mile behind him and the intermittent blinking from his hazards.

Drew wished he still had his camping gear with his flashlight in the trunk. He had opted for a bandpass speaker box for his two 12″ Kickers instead.

Looking at the tire in red hazard light flashes, Drew could tell he was screwed. He lay on the ground and looked under the back bumper. Something swung against his face, tickling his cheek. Thinking it was a spider, Drew flapped at it blindly but quickly realized it was the line connecting to the air shocks. It was dangling away from the hydraulic shocks that usually held the frame up.

The loose air line meant the car had lowered onto its rusty old leaf springs and when Drew hit the DIP in the road, something broke. The air line had probably pulled loose when he turned around in the field of brush up on Battle Mountain, trying to escape the trap he had found himself in. Drew just prayed the damage wasn't to the axle itself.

It was too dark to see or do anything about it now.

Drew looked at the road ahead and behind. It wasn't too bad; it was really dark, but he could still make out the white line in the road. He thought for a moment about sleeping in his car and waiting until morning. But he had a ton of stuff to do tomorrow outside of going to the Halloween party.

The chill of the night air made him zip his hoodie as his feet slapped the pavement. He wasn't walking, but he wasn't jogging either. He would just be happy if he made it home before 2 a.m.

The blackness that the Black Hills were named for was even more pronounced in only starlight. The gentle rises and slopes of black cut the gray of the night sky in a stark contrast.

Drew remembered the little town of Mountain and what they had called a "mountain." These were the Himalayas comparatively. The night air was crisp, but with Halloween two days away, this was a tropical heat wave. Old timers, including his boss/friend Joe, had all started calling it an Indian summer again.

Joe was a salty old WW2 vet full of good advice. For some reason, he had taken Drew in as a grandson-like figure. It started the summer dad made him start mowing Joe's lawn for free. Dad had been working for Social Services helping elderly people at the time. He had mostly used the position to meet old vulnerable people and find creative ways to help them part with stuff he wanted for himself.

Drew was one of those creative ways.

Having your twelve-year-old son mow, trim, and weed their yards was a great way to curry favor. Drew didn't mind the volunteer work at first because dad let him use his lawn mower. After he finished mowing the free yards, Drew eventually found some pay yards. Some neighbors and old-timers had caught wind of the hard-working kid who would mow any yard for five bucks. The word spread like Devils Lake every summer in North Dakota.

Pretty soon, Drew had to start to refuse paying jobs because there wasn't enough light in the day to mow them and the free jobs dad was offering all over town. Drew started to resent the volunteer work. After a particularly bad fight with dad wherein dad took his lawn mower and locked it up because Drew didn't mow one of his bilkees' lawns, Drew used his savings and bought his own lawn mower at a garage sale. After that, Drew just stopped doing the free jobs. All except for Joe, who always had a Root Beer for Drew and sympathized with him mowing his yard for free, but he also reminded Drew that he "wasn't going to look a gift horse in the mouth."

Joe's garage was where Drew found the Nova. It sat there for almost two years waiting for Drew to buy it. Drew never spent a dime of his lawn mowing money outside of refilling his gas can and buying trimmer string. He had shown dad the Nova one time while he randomly showed up at Joe's while Drew was mowing. Probably trying to bilk something else off him, but Joe wasn't dumb.

Drew took dad into the garage with Joe, who had already agreed to a $4,000 price tag and showed him the car. Dad loved it, like Drew knew he would, and after Drew had explained how he was saving up to buy it, Dad had wholeheartedly agreed after shooting Joe a wink and a smile. Drew knew the smile meant dad had no faith in his ability to buy it, but Drew knew better and so did Joe (who instantly shot the same wink back at Drew when dad wasn't looking).

Joe knew who dad was and what he was up to. He didn't like him very much and wasn't shy about letting Drew know it. To be fair, most of the town knew dad by then and what he was up to. The town they worked and went to school in now was too "hoity toity" as dad liked to say. The people in town weren't amused by dad's drunken antics. Then, after dad hurt his back lifting an old person at work and got onto the pills, people really started to not like him.

Drew couldn't blame them.

During his eighth-grade summer, Drew finally saved enough lawn mowing money to buy the Nova. Drew took a wad of hundred-dollar bills to Joe's house with a huge smile plastered on his face. Joe, with a smile on his face, handed Drew the keys and the title. They were sealed in an envelope that had

"FOR DREW" scrawled onto the flap. Drew wondered how long the envelope had been sealed, waiting for him to buy it.

After two weeks spent in Joe's garage with Joe looking over his shoulder, giving advice but not telling him what to do, Drew had the Nova running.

"Runs good enough to get you back and forth from Point of Rocks to here. So, you can get yourself a real job now," Joe said after the engine came to life.

"Yeah, but I doubt anyone wants to hire a thirteen-year-old, but at least I can drive myself to town now and I don't have to wait for a ride, so I can get started and finished mowing way earlier," Drew said, giddy with excitement.

"Well, what if I said you're done with lawns cos I got you a real job? You gotta be there I 'spose bout eight or nine tomorrow, though, so she can train you. But hell, a trained monkey could sling tacos, you'll be fine," Joe had explained cryptically.

"What job?" Drew's excitement grew by the second with the prospect of not only starting high school with a car, but an actual job as well.

"Well, you know my daughter Tina owns Taco John's, and I told her you were gonna be needing some money for gas and car parts. Told her you were a damned hard worker with a good head on his shoulders, too, so don't be going there and making me look like an asshole. You better work your butt off and show up on time." Joe stopped and looked Drew in the eyes. "And if you think this means you're off the hook for mowing my yard, you got another thing coming cos I kept a damned key for that thing for myself." Joe jingled his pocket.

Drew just laughed, and Joe joined him.

Shortly after it was running, Drew was cruising town on his maiden voyage and finding things he already needed to fix. Just as he was getting ready to get on the highway and head home, he saw his friends Nick and Jay walking through town. Drew pulled over after they saw who was driving the cool new muscle car and eagerly waved Drew down with shocked looks on their faces.

"Where the hell did you steal this?" Nick had said, not joking.

"I didn't have to steal it, numbnuts. I bought it." Drew said, feeling cooler than the other side of the pillow.

"You're gonna get pulled over, though—you don't even have a license," Jay argued.

"Yes, I do. Well, not a full one. I got my learner's permit on my birthday and last week, I made my mom take me in for a driving test. Since I live out of town, I get an Ag permit, but I'm only supposed to drive from work or school to home," Drew said, feeling like an adult. "You guys wanna go to Point of Rocks with me?"

"I'd rather go cruising for chicks or find a bowl somewhere," Nick suggested.

"No way. I just took one lap through town. I'm not gonna risk it again. But I got like half a joint at my house, and I can bring you guys back into town in the morning cos I gotta go to work anyway," Drew suggested, remembering the joint in his closet that was waiting for someone to finish it with. He hated smoking alone.

Nick and Jay exchanged glances and shrugged. A few minutes later, they were on the road to Drew's house in Point of Rocks.

Dad had moved them from North Dakota after the State School made some changes on account of the abysmal treatment of the patients. They downsized, and the town he grew up in dried up. Instead of moving to the new town where dad found a new job and that had a school, dad picked a town about thirty miles away, with a population of ninety-six, and no school or jobs. It made having a social life hard because he was stuck at home thirty miles away all the time.

But the Nova had changed all of that.

Freshman year started and the kids he was friendly with became good friends because now Drew could hang out in town and drive himself home whenever he wanted. Also, if mom and dad didn't feel like driving him to town, he didn't have to miss a party or football game or whatever was going on.

Girls had started coming around, too. The years of manual, mostly voluntary, labor had given him the body of a gym rat that didn't go unnoticed by them. By the end of sophomore year, it was Drew and his close group of friends who were planning the parties and setting the tone for the rest of the kids in class.

There were a couple of kids, though, who seemed to resent Drew's rise in popularity over the last three years of high school, and Drew had had no idea until tonight how much they hated him.

Nick and Jay, his "best friends." The monsters he had just gotten in a fight with on Battle Mountain.

The names made Drew shudder as he looked back at the blinking hazard lights from the Nova and the junction's light in the distance. The safety net of their light was an illusion, and every step he took farther away was a step into the void. Drew hesitated for a moment and considered turning around and sleeping in the cockeyed Nova. Then he remembered he wasn't a pee pants baby anymore and quickened his step.

Drew tried not to think about monsters, two of which he had made friends with.

It was too dark.

Instead, Drew tried to think back on the summer when they left North Dakota.

***

He remembered saying goodbye to Jeremy and his secret camping spot at the river. Selling all his toys at the garage sale so they had enough gas money to make it to their new home. Drew remembered his last walk past the State School and how it looked small and unimportant after it had shuttered its doors. It no longer resembled a castle in a Hammer horror movie.

The last impression Drew had of the town he grew up in was of the Can Man.

On their way out of town, they saw him pedaling furiously, also headed out of town, probably to the small trailer court on the outskirts to dig through garbage cans to find his returnables.

Drew remembered locking eyes with him as dad got stuck behind someone turning off the main road. The pace of dad's Travelall slowed to match the Can Man's for a moment. In that moment, Drew got a good look at him and felt silly for being scared of him the whole time he was a baby. Drew was growing up after beating the Gougers in Mountain and now could see that the Can Man was just a dirty old man trying to make a living.

Drew, out of guilt or feeling stupid, had shot his hand up and waved, offering a smile as well. The Can Man had obliged and returned the smile and wave. Then, just as dad was picking up speed and pulling away, the Can Man had one more surprise for Drew. He pulled his Bowie knife out of his waistband and flashed it in front of him, waving it a couple of times before running it across his throat and tucking it back into his filthy pants. Drew looked from the blade to his face and the Can Man raised both eyebrows quickly in a "come get some" fashion.

Drew tried to explain to dad what happened, but adults never listened; they were too busy worrying about the drive ahead and the trailer they were towing that didn't feel quite right. Chris didn't care, as he was busy playing his Tiger racing game.

That was when Drew realized some of the monsters he created for himself might be real. And, although he had beaten a few of them, it might be best to keep his eyes open for chokepoints.

***

"Crap." Drew was mad at himself for doing nothing but think about monsters while he was stuck walking home in the dark.

He quickened his pace to what had to be a jog, not wanting to be out here for any longer than he had to be.

Thump…scrape…thump…scrape…

Something in the ditch was keeping pace with him.

Drew froze and listened.

Thump…Scr…

The footsteps continued slightly longer than his and then halted. Now standing in the pitch-black, Drew felt vulnerable, scared of the dark and what it was hiding. Even if he wanted to turn back and run to the safety of the Nova, he was going to have to cross paths with whatever he had just heard walking in the ditch behind him. The footsteps were familiar and unmistakable, but Drew was trying to convince himself it couldn't be real.

It was the second time tonight he had heard what he thought he remembered the Gougers sounding like, from the times he heard them when he was camping in North Dakota. Drew hadn't even thought about the Gougers in a few years until today. Maybe it was the Halloween season? Maybe it was the fact his friends had revealed themselves as monsters, and monsters liked company?

Whatever it was, it seemed like something was inviting monsters into his life again. Drew didn't know whether what was in the ditch beside him was monsters, but he did know better than to run from a real predator like a mountain lion.

He started walking again, hoping the raccoon, or mountain lion, or whatever it was, got bored and decided to wander off. For good measure, Drew switched sides of the road and kept his pace slow, being extra careful not to appear like scared prey.

Now, with monsters on his mind and his senses on high alert, Drew followed the white line on the oncoming traffic side of the road. He had to be a couple of miles away from his car by now. He looked back as he crested his first of many hills to come.

The last light of the junction and his Nova's hazard lights dipped below the summit as he continued walking in complete blackness.

How did he get here, in the dark, running from monsters? Drew knew the answer to that was complicated, but it all started with a stupid night of drinking just before school started.

***

Drew, Nick, Jay, and another friend, Josh, had gotten hold of a handle of vodka somehow. The details of that were lost to Drew now. They had all camped out in the clearing behind Nick's house and gotten drunk. Nick was having Jay stay the night and Josh and Drew snuck out later to join them. The night started slow with screwdrivers, but before long, they were doing straight shots and found themselves walking around town feeling drunk and stupid.

At some point, they had gotten the attention of the overnight cop, who chased them through the neighborhoods, splitting the group up as they scrambled from his car.

It was fun at first, running and hiding, trying to make their way back to Nick's house. But when Drew found himself alone sneaking his way back, he got an eerie feeling, like he was being followed. Drew had plenty of practice sneaking and hiding, so he dodged from shadow to shadow, now hiding from the fear of being stalked rather than a cop who was too fat to give chase on foot. After finally making his way back to the tent, Drew found Jay passed out in the tent, but he was alone.

Nick was nowhere to be seen.

The back door to Nick's house swung open outside the tent and Drew saw a flashlight break the darkness.

Thinking fast, Drew slid into Nick's sleeping bag and buried his face under the covers.

It had to be Nick's dad checking on the boys.

Nick's dad was almost as big of a jerk as Drew's. In fact, the last spanking Drew ever got was from Nick's dad. They had been playing upstairs in his house and Nick pointed down through a vent in the floor above the kitchen table. Drew saw that he was pointing at a coffee cup and when he looked back at Nick, a huge loogie was dropping from his lips. It landed right in the cup of coffee, to the surprise of all the adults at the table. It splashed hot brown liquid and thick spit everywhere. Nick's dad had marched upstairs and after all the boys refused to narc on their friend/host, Nick's dad just spanked them all. It was the last time Drew went to Nick's house when his dad was home, and the last time he ever got a spanking.

The tent door suddenly unzipped, and a beam of light filled the cramped space.

Drew was frozen with fear, wondering what Nick's dad would do to him if he found him in the sleeping bag instead of Nick. He could hear Nick's dad take a drag from his cigarette and then zip the tent back up. Drew let out his breath slowly and listened to him finish his smoke on the steps, then go back inside.

The ruse had worked.

A while later, Nick showed up, alone.

"Dude, where were you? Your dad was just out here checking on you and I had to pretend I was you sleeping," Drew said, slightly pissed off.

"I was looking for Josh. I think the cops got him," Nick said, wide eyed, seeming like he was hiding something. A sly grin was plastered on his drunken face.

"Oh, crap," Drew offered, his standard response to anything surprising.

"What?" a too-drunk Jay said, sitting up and swaying in his bag.

"Josh got caught, I think," Nick explained again.

Drew moved over to make room for Nick to get into the tent. Drew moved Nick's backpack to make a place for him to sit and a spiral notebook sat there looking at him in the dim streetlight filtering through the screen window. On the cover, there were drawings of decapitated heads with Xs on their eyes and a rough drawing of a Volkswagen Bug.

"What the hell is this?" Drew asked, picking the notebook up and flipping it open. A crude map was drawn on the first page with another X marking a spot labeled "bury body and car here."

Drew looked at Nick, with a smile on his face, not sure what he was looking at.

Nick and Jay shot each other a nervous, drunken glance. Nick reached out and grabbed the notebook like a child snatching back a stolen toy.

"Nothing. You don't want to know about this," Nick said in a daring manner.

"What? Why? What body are you burying?" Drew sensed the mood shifting around him. His stomach fluttered a bit, but maybe it was from the Vodka and OJ.

"Should we tell him?" Nick asked Jay, clearly wanting to relieve himself of his big secret.

"Fuck, I don't care. The more the merrier." Jay lay back down, too drunk to participate any longer.

Drew looked at Nick, who had a look on his face that he had never seen in all their years being friends.

"We are going to rape Stephanie and then kill her," Nick said, his face twisted into a smirk.

***

OOOOOAAAAHHHHHRRRRRR!!

The roar emptied the night of silence and shook Drew out of the memory of when he learned his friends were monsters.

Drew skidded to a halt in the loose grit on the surface of the road. His hand flew into his pocket reflexively, looking for something to defend himself with. It came back out with the only thing that was in there.

His mechanical pencil.

He clenched it in his fist, straining his ears against his better judgment, listening for another howl.

The howl.

It was unmistakable.

One of the Gougers was definitely back.

Drew started to jog again, but as soon as his feet started moving, he heard a familiar sound in the ditch next to him…

Thump…Scrape…Thump…Scrape…

The Gouger was matching his pace perfectly in the ditch beside him. Drew had to try to keep it off-balance. He had to put the short legs on the other side of the road so the incline would put the Gouger's short legs on the downhill side, tipping it over.

At a dead sprint, Drew switched sides of the road. The mechanical pencil started to hurt his palm and reminded him of the scout knife he had held much the same way the last time he confronted the Gougers while camping out in Mountain.

With no hesitation, the footsteps were back on his side of the road, crunching the grass. The increased pace made the

Thump…Scrapes land more heavily. He could feel them shake the ground when his own feet made contact. Then Drew noticed something in his panic. There were still footsteps coming from the other side of the road.

It was both of them.

The mating pair of Gougers that had followed Grandpa and killed him for revenge over their stolen eggs. With no other choice, Drew ran to the center of the road. The dashes of the yellow passing lines flashed beneath him. He tried to run harder, but he knew if he kept it up, he would be gassed before too long and the Gougers would be able to trample his exhausted body easily.

As if sensing his plan, the footsteps raced ahead of him. The Gougers thundered in the tall grass of the ditch, leaving him behind. Then in the road in front of him, Drew could hear their thunderous footsteps leaving the dry grass and starting to hammer on the pavement.

The footsteps stopped for a moment, just a few feet ahead of him.

Drew used his imagination to paint a picture of what he couldn't see. Their tiny inside legs wrapping together to join their bodies into one hulk, now able to run on any terrain, level or not.

They had cut him off and set up a chokepoint, a trap. Right now, they were probably rearing up, ready to stomp him into mush.

Suddenly, their fiery yellow eyes lit up not more than ten yards ahead of him. All four of their burning yellow eyes bored into Drew from either lane.

OOOOAAAAHHHHRRRR!!!

They let out another howl of triumph.

A sudden sharp sound broke the stalemate in the middle of the road, fighting for Drew's attention from behind. Drew took his eyes off the pair of revenge-driven Gougers and turned, just briefly, to see what was making this new sharp sound.

He saw another pair of burning yellow eyes cresting the hill he had just sprinted over.

The new, third Gouger, was barreling toward him, letting out a continuous sharp howl as it rushed closer.

Drew was surrounded.

Chapter 18

The new set of eyes from behind him were moving at a speed that was too fast, even for a monster. The howl it was making was familiar and didn't bring any emotions of fear. It was a noise Drew recognized.

The car that was racing down the highway toward Drew slammed on its brakes. It skidded to a stop just before it was too late, stopping about ten feet short of where Drew was flapping his arms wildly. The honking stopped as soon as the car did.

Drew didn't bother looking over his shoulders or asking permission to enter the vehicle. He sprinted to the safety of the stranger's car. The door wasn't locked and without waiting, Drew jumped in, slamming and locking the door behind him.

"DRIVE!" Drew yelled, scanning the area around the car outside his window, expecting the Gougers to be staring him in the eyes.

"I knew that was your car," a familiar voice said behind Drew.

Drew spun his head in shock.

It was Chris.

"What the hell are you doing?" Drew suddenly realized he was in his mom's car and the shock made him forget the Gougers for a moment. "You gotta get out of here." The urgency of escape beat out the question of why his brother wasn't locked in his room playing games or whatever he did in there all the time.

"Was that a moose?" Chris asked, slowly accelerating.

"YOU SAW IT? ...Faster," Drew said, stunned, pointing the way home with his finger.

"Well, I saw something in the road ahead of you...why? What was it?" Chris seemed interested.

This might have been the most the two of them had said to each other in six months.

Drew thought about explaining the Gouger again and trying to convince him it was real, like he had when they were kids. But Chris didn't have much of an imagination. Chris also never had the benefit of Grandpa's stories or the experience of coming face to face with a monster alone in the woods.

"I guess it must have been a moose," Drew said, knowing there were no moose in the Black Hills.

Drew's eyes were watering, and his legs were shaking now that the adrenaline was wearing off.

"Are you crying?" Chris said, smirking.

"Fuck you, my eyes are cold. I been running for like an hour," Drew said and cranked the heater. "You got a smoke?" Drew didn't smoke often, but he could use one now.

Chris pulled out the pack he kept on him. It was the one thing that got Chris to go outside since dad wouldn't let him smoke in the house.

"You're lucky dad wanted me to grab pizza. You would have either gotten eaten by a moose or had to run the rest of the way home. So, now you owe me a smoke and a ride to town whenever I want," Chris said, still smirking.

Drew didn't care; he had to give Chris rides to town whenever he whined to mom anyway, but remembered why the two didn't hang out. Chris always kept tabs on debts owed to him, but if he owed you something, he was the first to forget. Any time the two of them hung out, Chris would end up starting a fight over some imagined debt owed to him. One cigarette borrowed a week ago became a carton last month.

"Yeah, sure." Drew didn't feel like talking to him anymore, so he cranked up the radio in mom's car.

The speakers cracked and popped. Chris blew them out a long time ago, causing a huge fight with dad, but since they were already ruined, Drew turned it up past comfortable.

They pulled into the driveway outside their home a few minutes later. Chris grabbed the pizzas and nearly ran inside. Drew hung out, finishing his cigarette and listening closely for the roar of the Gougers in the distance or the thump…scrape of their hooves…

Nothing.

Drew tossed the butt into the repurposed coffee can on the back steps and went inside. The far side of the house had lights on, but Drew first had to navigate through the dark kitchen and dining room. The house felt like mom and dad were already in bed. Chris's room glowed from around his closed bedroom door's frame and one of the pizzas sat untouched on the table.

Drew looked into the living room and saw his parents' door was closed. Dad must have gotten too high on pills and gone to bed before Chris got back with the pizza.

The pizza sat there teasing him. Drew shrugged to himself and snagged two pieces, hoping dad would blame Chris or mom in the morning. That was assuming he didn't think he ate them himself during his mid-sleep dose of pain killers.

Drew basically had the basement to himself. Half of it was still unfinished cinder blocks, but Drew had converted the other half into a decent bedroom. He got himself a waterbed, some nice carpet, some cool posters, a new TV, and the only DVD player in the house.

The cinder block half of the basement was dark, and tonight it felt scary. Who knew what other monsters might be hiding in the cinderblock corners? The sound of his feet slapping the concrete floor as he raced for his bedroom echoed on the bare walls. Pizza grease made twisting the doorknob a chore, and a feeling of panic grew in his chest while he struggled to twist it.

Drew was suddenly afraid of the dark again. Stickboy was reintroducing himself. Drew hoped the pissing his pants part was over.

Finally, the door clicked open and as soon as there was room enough for his body, Drew slid through and hit the light switch in the same motion. He ripped a paper towel off the roll on his table and set the pizza down. The remotes on the table all clicked as he hit the appropriate buttons to get a show on and get the speakers turned up.

The X Files was on. Usually, it was his favorite show, but he was already spooked, so he needed something lighter. The channels all turned up Halloween shows unsurprisingly, so Drew put on a movie from his modest collection of DVDs.

Something funny.

After starting the movie, Drew looked at his closet and furrowed his brow.

He had to look at it. It had been too long.

The pizza sat cooling on the table while Drew dug for the little black box that was locked in the closet below the steps. It was exactly where he thought it would be. In the deepest, darkest corner.

The little wooden box that was painted black was still locked with the cheap little padlock he bought at Ben Franklin's when he was a kid. Drew wondered where the key was for a split second before realizing he hadn't seen it in years. He plopped the black box on the table next to the slices of pizza and grabbed a paper clip from the catch-all bowl on his desk.

Carefully, Drew used some pliers to bend the tip into a ninety-degree angle. Satisfied with the shape, he poked the hooked end into the lock and felt for the rotating pin that would release the cheap lock. He found the small lump of metal that resisted the paperclip, and he urged it along its groove until…

CLICK.

Drew smiled.

That was way easier than it should have been.

The lid to the box opened with a weak squeak, revealing the Polaroid and what looked like the beak of an eagle. First, Drew grabbed the claw. He turned it over in his hands. The fleshy bit near the top was dried to leather, and was yellow and blistered and resembled a lizard's skin. Drew poked the tip of the black claw. Still as sharp as a needle. Now Drew sucked in a big breath of air and picked up the photograph. One of the four eyes he had seen less than an hour ago chasing him home on the highway was staring back at him. The yellow burning eye was just as imposing in his room as it was on the dark stretch of road. Drew thought back on the stupid kid setting traps for the Gougers in the woods, and he wondered if he would be brave enough to do it today as a senior in high school. The goosebumps on his arms gave him reason to believe he wouldn't be. If he couldn't face a childhood monster, was he going to be brave enough to face the new monsters? The ones who had been his friends up until that night in the tent.

Drew knew that the fight tonight on Battle Mountain wasn't the end of his trouble with them.

He had ruined their sick plan to rape and murder Stephanie, and Drew knew them well enough to know this would not be the last he heard of it.

He remembered the night they got drunk a few weeks ago and the two had told him of their plan when he found their notebook. At first, Drew thought they were just tough talking, but the longer Nick rambled on, the more Drew realized they were serious. They already had places they knew Stephanie liked to hang out and might be alone…chokepoints. Ruts in her life that she had fallen into and they had picked up on. They planned on burying her in her car, so both were missing, leading people to believe she had just gotten in her car and run away. But even if people suspected something happened to her, they would never find the spot where they were going to bury her.

It was sloppy, but it seemed like they were learning along the way as they planned it out in their notebook.

Drew remembered trying to smile and nod as Nick had talked, but he had felt like throwing up. He was acutely aware that he was sharing a tent with two guys who wanted to rape and kill a girl from school, and they thought he wanted to be a part of it.

Drew knew he had to be careful.

That night in the tent, Drew had let Nick finish bragging about the completeness and complexity of their plan, and as he explained how they were all going to get away scot-free, Drew remembered thinking of a reason to bail.

***

"Dude, that's crazy." Drew feigned excitement after Nick's revelation. "But I better get out of here before your dad decides to have another smoke." Drew tested the waters, looking at Nick for signs of distrust. "You don't wanna get in trouble while you got this with you." Drew tapped the notebook. "And you guys better hide that. Someone's gonna find it besides me and it'll screw everything up."

"OH, shit, good call, man. My dad's a dick…By the way, we always lock it up in the bottom of his tool chest. He hasn't opened that thing in years, and I've got the only keys. He'll think he just lost 'em." Nick seemed oblivious to the fact that Drew was terrified. "I'm not trying to go to jail, dude. Fuck that."

"Yeah, same." Drew was unzipping the tent, ready to sprint to Josh's house. "I'll see you guys at school."

"Hey, Drew," Nick called behind him.

Drew poked his head back into the tent.

"You better not say a fucking word to anyone." Nick was smiling while he made the indirect threat.

Drew was bigger and could beat him in a fair fight, but Nick was willing to get even with people who didn't see it coming. Like mom and her ladle. Drew now had two extra responsibilities. Pretend to be involved enough with their plan to not make these guys suspicious enough to kill him while trying to make sure at the same time that nothing actually happened to Stephanie.

***

Drew shook his head and looked back down at the photo of the Gouger eye. The claw was still in his hand. He carefully put them both back in the box and clicked the cheap lock closed again. Instead of burying it in the closet this time, he put it next to his bed.

He might need it to help build his nerve again later.

The movie was just about over now. The pizza on his table was room temp. Drew had zero interest in either. He couldn't help wondering what Stephanie was doing. He looked at the clock on his desk.

It was too late to call her now.

After his "friends" made clear their plans to rape and kill her, Drew couldn't get Stephanie out of his mind. He always thought she was cute, but she was a good girl who didn't date or drink or do anything bad really. She was innocent and naïve, and Drew couldn't help but be attracted to her.

She was his opposite in so many ways, but the two of them were turning out to be very compatible.

***

The Monday after Nick had detailed the plan, Drew found himself stalking Stephanie, not for any nefarious reason, but to protect her from Nick and Jay. He tried not to be obvious as he followed her between classes and to lunch. Stephanie was naïve, but she wasn't stupid. The third time Drew circled the block while she was walking home after school, she smiled and waved him over.

"Are you going to follow me all day or give me a ride home?" Stephanie had said sweetly as she leaned into the window of Drew's Nova.

The boldness had shocked Drew. What if he had been Nick and Jay offering a ride? Drew got goosebumps and shuddered. He awkwardly moved the crap off his passenger seat, making room for her. Any other time, this would have been so exciting to have a pretty girl in his car, but Drew's stomach was in knots. He was too nervous to be horny.

Stephanie led the conversation and seemed giddy.

It was contagious.

As Drew had pulled up to her house, she asked if he wanted to take a cruise through town because she wasn't ready to go home. Small talk came easily and soon enough, Drew was relaxed.

They cruised town until the sun went down and Stephanie said she had to go home. She thanked Drew for the ride and told him how she was glad to be out of her house because her VW bug was broken down, but it should be back on the road soon. The thought of her driving to her own grave made Drew dart his eyes around the sidewalk for the monsters, hoping they wouldn't see him protecting their prey.

Drew dropped her off and waited until she was well inside the door; he hoped she locked it behind her. On his way out of town, Drew saw Nick and Jay walking the street on the other side of town while he was stopped for gas. Drew pretended to not see them as he pulled away from the gas station and they gave chase, waving their arms wildly, trying to get his attention. He wasn't in the mood to hide how he felt about them and couldn't risk them being suspicious of him.

Drew had spent the rest of that week following a very aware Stephanie around town and school. She seemed to like it, and Drew was starting to really like her.

When Friday came around, Drew had been cruising around hoping to see her but was coming up empty. He saw some of her friends at the wall where all the teenagers gathered to watch people who had cars cruise town. They seemed to think she was at the movies with a boy, which nearly sent Drew into a rage. He already felt possessive of her. Part of him hoped it wasn't Nick or Jay and another part of him worried it was anyone else.

After buying a ticket and walking into the one-screen theatre, Drew let his eyes adjust to the dark and saw the most beautiful thing he had ever seen.

Stephanie was sitting alone with a big bucket of popcorn and two drinks. She was wearing a cute dress that was slightly more mature than she should have been wearing, and her makeup was perfect. Stephanie smiled at him in the mostly empty theater and waved him over.

"I knew you'd show up. You've been my shadow all week." She smiled a sly smile. "I got us popcorn and drinks."

Drew spent the rest of the movie falling in love. Her soft hand felt like it belonged in his. There were no words spoken, but every exchange of glances gave him butterflies. It felt so natural, Drew couldn't imagine not having it tomorrow or the next day.

The movie ended and Drew gave Stephanie a ride home. He wished he could be in the moment and just enjoy her, but after seeing Nick and Jay walking downtown, he was rattled. He took a sharp turn to avoid letting them see Stephanie in his car, but now they could surely tell he was avoiding them.

Drew had to find an answer. He had to protect Stephanie, but now they were bound to be suspicious, and he might need to protect himself.

Drew was lost in thought as he pulled up to Stephanie's house. He had to warn her. But if he warned her, she would want to know why he didn't go to the police or why he sat in the tent planning her rape and murder, nodding like an idiot in agreement instead of pummeling the other two boys to death.

"Hey, Stephanie, uh, just be careful, ok? Lock your door and don't like go for cruises with anyone else, ok?" Drew wasn't sure he was getting his point across.

"Why, are you going to get jealous if I do?" Stephanie was smiling sweetly.

"No…well, yes…but mostly I think you're too nice for your own good." Drew was tripping over his words.

"Well, look at what being nice got me." She leaned over and planted a kiss on Drew's lips. "And don't worry, I won't go for a cruise with anyone but you." She laughed and opened her door. "Plus, I should have my car back on the road in no time. Byyye."

Drew felt like saying, "I love you" but caught himself in time.

"You're perfect," was what he found instead. It sounded, possibly more stupid, but he meant it.

"You're cute." Stephanie closed the door of the Nova and ran to her front door; she turned and gave a wave as she closed it behind her.

***

The cold pizza and DVD menu screen were staring at Drew, waiting for an action from him as he zoned out. Thinking back on their first kiss made Drew feel lightheaded. He was already regretting the fact that his Nova was on the side of the road, broken down, and not sitting in the driveway.

That meant tomorrow was going to be spent towing it home and trying to fix it so he could get back into town. He had left Nick and Jay on Battle Mountain after their big fight, and now Drew was worried that they were going to act out their plans for Stephanie sooner rather than later. Before Drew could stop them.

They had shown Drew the hole on Thursday.

There was nothing stopping them except for an opportunity…a chokepoint.

***

Drew had skipped school after lunch on Thursday after another long week of protecting Stephanie, although now it was easier as they spent more and more time together.

He met a few guys out at the lake, and they spent the afternoon fishing and drinking a couple of beers. A car none of them recognized pulled up and Nick and Jay got out. The car pulled away, leaving the two monsters stranded with Drew and his other group of friends.

Drew's fishing buddies didn't like the two other boys and before long, each of them had found a reason to bail, leaving Drew alone with Nick and Jay, again.

"You want to go burn one?" Nick asked as Drew was packing his pole and tackle box into the trunk, which was crowded with an amp and speaker box.

"Uhhh, I already had a couple of beers, and I gotta drive home." Drew said.

"Don't be a pussy. We got some med-grade. We can chill for a bit until you're ready to go," Jay chimed in, already sitting in the back seat of the Nova.

"Yeah, come on, man, you've been sketchy as hell lately," Nick said.

The accusation from the monster struck Drew as being ironic and pissed him off.

"*I've* been sketchy?" Drew shot back with more anger than he intended. He looked at the tire iron in his trunk, pausing for a moment considering his options. "Fine. Where do you want to go? We can't burn one here. The game warden is always on the ridge watching people."

"Oh, we got a place. We'll show you." Nick smiled, raising the hairs on Drew's neck.

Nick directed Drew to the archery range near the outskirts of the lake's recreation areas. Nick told Drew to leave the Nova running after he pointed to a spot and told him to stop. He then leaned forward and opened the passenger door, allowing Jay to get out of the back seat. Jay ran to the boulders surrounding the small parking lot and pushed as hard as he could, obviously struggling, until the boulder finally tipped over, making a gap large enough for a car to pass through.

"Hurry up before someone comes," Nick urged from the passenger seat as he swung the door closed, leaving Jay by the boulder.

Feeling like it was a bad idea, Drew put the Nova into drive and inched through the gap.

"Ok, hold up," Nick directed after the car was clear of the gap.

Jay tipped the boulder back into its usual position and ran to jump back into the car while Nick leaned forward to make room.

"Ok, now follow the dirt, but don't hit the grass, so we don't leave a trail." Nick was being careful, and this made Drew feel uneasy.

Nick was learning fast.

About a quarter of a mile later, Nick told Drew to stop. They were in a modest clearing at the base of a hill surrounded by jack pines. Nothing out of the ordinary.

The boys got out of the car and went to the front bumper, where Jay was already sparking the joint. The silence was uncomfortable as they passed it around. Jay left after a couple of tokes, leaving Nick and Drew to finish it on their own.

Nick was right, it was pretty good weed.

Drew's mind raced and time started to stretch back and forth, giving him a stuttering feeling as he tried to navigate the situation.

Then Jay reappeared with a shovel.

"All right, let's get back to work," Nick said and started walking.

Drew followed, not knowing what was going on. The pine needles released a fresh burst of smell as the boys walked over them, and Drew tried to blink the haze from his mind. The warm air felt like it was sticking to his arms, and he flapped them to move it away. His limbs felt heavy like he was swimming, and confusion was barely being kept at bay.

Nick and Jay got to a spot in the clearing that seemed off, but Drew couldn't put his finger on it. Then the two monsters started moving the ground. At first, Drew's weed-laden brain thought it was a puddle they were playing in. Suddenly, the flapping of his own arms and the heaviness made sense and for a minute, Drew convinced himself he had somehow fallen into water.

The branches the monsters were pulling on moved in an unnaturally floaty way. Drew could feel himself getting panicky and told himself he was standing on the ground and not in water. The strong weed was a little more than he was used to, and he felt like he was hallucinating a little.

Then Nick pulled the branches back, revealing a massive hole. It was about eight feet wide and maybe ten feet long. Currently, it was about three feet deep, but Jay was in the hole already digging furiously.

"What the hell?" Drew asked, swaying on his feet in confusion.

The med-grade was making it hard to connect the dots but the reveal of the hole and not a growing pool of water was a relief. Giddiness took the place of panic, and a smile formed on Drew's lips.

"You think that's big enough for a bug?" Nick said, smiling, obviously proud of himself, pointing to the enormous hole they were digging.

"Well, that's gonna be a helluva big bug," Drew said, almost laughing.

"No shit, Sherlock, it's for a *Volkswagen* Bug, not a *bug* bug," Nick corrected.

Drew suddenly felt like he was going to puke.

He ran back to the Nova and leaned on the bumper while the couple of beers from his stomach filled in his tire tracks. The hole was for Stephanie's body and her car. Even as high as he was, this was clear enough and the dots were easy to connect now.

"You good?" Jay said from the hole.

Drew's head was spinning, and the time stuttering effect intensified.

He wanted to leave, but there was no way he could drive.

"Yeah, I think those idiots gave me a skunky beer. I feel like shit," Drew lied, still quick on his toes despite being too stoned.

"That sucks…you gonna be good while we work on this for a bit?" Nick asked, seeming genuinely concerned.

"Uhh, yeah, for now, I guess. I don't know for how long, though." Drew lied; he was only staying until his head cleared.

Nick left him alone and came back with another shovel. He jumped into the grave and dug with Jay.

For the next hour, Drew watched them dig his girlfriend's grave. His mind raced, trying to find a solution where there was none. He was thinking that the only option was to be a narc at this point. The thought of everyone thinking he was a tattle tale again was less horrible than the thought of Stephanie's dead body rotting in her car buried in the woods. He just hoped Mrs. Rockow didn't show up with a troll doll to tuck into his pants again like the last time Drew tattled on someone, in the third grade. If he couldn't find an answer to this problem on his own by the end of the weekend, Drew knew what he had to do. He would skip school on Monday and go to the police.

Stephanie would be safe until then even though her car was nearly fixed, which would give the monsters many more chokepoints. Her family was going to Rapid City for the weekend, and that gave Drew two days to find a solution.

Halloween was his last opportunity.

There was a big party planned, assuming someone found a way to get some booze. Drew was sure Nick and Jay would be there, giving him one last chance to change their minds…by force, if necessary. He could confront them publicly at the party and air their dirty secret in front of everyone before laying into them. Drew could hope for the protection of the party herd if things went sideways.

The solutions were sobering, and the time stuttering slowed.

He was going to lose Stephanie in the process of saving her, along with his friends, but it seemed to be the only answer. Once Stephanie found out he had been involved in the planning of her murder for as long as he had and the other kids found out he was a narc, his social life would be over.

Now, after watching the monsters dig Stephanie's grave for over an hour, Drew was clear-headed enough to drive. With his mind finally made up, Drew knew it was time to get the hell out of the woods with the monsters.

"You guys ready to go? I gotta get home. I feel like crap." Drew put an end to the grave digging party.

***

"Crap," Drew said to himself, alone in his bedroom, thinking back on the grave.

He tossed the stolen slices of pizza into the trash can by his door. The movie had finished for a second time a while ago, and now the title screen was playing an obnoxious animated loop again.

Drew clicked the electronics off with their corresponding remotes and hopped into the waterbed.

Drew decided he better get some sleep so he could wake up early and get started trying to fix the Nova. If it wasn't a huge fix, he figured he may be back on the road by noon.

His head was spinning while he was lying there mixed with puppy love for Stephanie and hate for the new monsters in his life. Plus, the added fear that now the Gougers were back...both of them.

Drew blindly grabbed for a familiar spine behind him. He pulled one out at random.

Werewolf of Fever Swamp.

It was his favorite *Goosebumps*. He was too old for them now, but he kept the complete collection lined up on the headboard of his bed. He was still proud of the collection. It represented the first money he made mowing lawns and the hundred trips to Pamida to collect each and every book as they were released throughout his childhood.

Half an hour and 2/3 of a book later, Drew was sleeping. It was an uneven sleep filled with sex, fights, blood, and death. It ended with him trying to dig Stephanie out of a hole in the woods while she was screaming from inside her buried car.

Drew shot up in his bed two hours later covered in sweat.

The sun was barely above the horizon and was turning his room a dull gray. It was early enough to get started. Drew grabbed his pants and slid them on, along with a work hoodie. He made his way upstairs, trying to stay quiet, so he didn't wake anyone up to ask questions.

The house was dark except for the kitchen.

"Where the hell is your car?" a voice called before he rounded the corner of the living room.

Dad was already up, and by the sound of his voice, the pills hadn't started dulling his edge yet.

Chapter 19

After dad's morning pills kicked in, and a round of questions that Drew expertly navigated without agitating him, dad agreed to help Drew tow the Nova home. But only after Drew helped him get a couple of loads of wood.

It was a never-ending chore that Drew had been doing since he was old enough to go on the suicide drives with dad. The pistol didn't come with them anymore; the pills seemed to rob dad of his desire to end things. However, the complaining and whining had increased compared to when he drank. Sometimes, Drew missed the pistol. It gave a little excitement to the otherwise monotonous task.

***

The chainsaw roared to life.

Drew squinted and turned his head away from the flying bark and chips of wood. As soon as the revving slowed and the weight of the log shifted, Drew shoved another two-foot chunk off the end of the tailgate. With dad's back hurt, he couldn't bend over to cut anymore, so Drew had to wrestle eight-foot sections onto the tailgate while dad ran the saw and cut them into pieces short enough for the wood stove.

Drew resented the fact that dad wouldn't just let him run the saw and cut the logs while they were on the ground or let him take the truck and get the wood on his own. He had dreamed of running the saw since he had watched *The Texas*

Chainsaw Massacre, but he was growing worried that by the time he had the chance to run it, he would be living in his own house with central heat.

Chris was absent, like usual. Dad didn't even bother asking for his help anymore. If it wasn't a headache Chris was whining about, it was something else. Dad just said he would be a bigger hassle than he was worth and left him at home.

Drew had tried the headache game a couple of times, only to get met with a punch to the head and his work boots being tossed in his direction.

"You want to hurry the hell up over there? My back is killing me." A branch smacked Drew in the ass to highlight dad's point.

Drew shook himself out of his own head.

"Sorry, I'm just tired from running..." Drew pushed another couple of feet off the tailgate and the chainsaw cut him off.

After the second load of wood was stacked by the back of the house, dad reappeared. He never helped stack; it was too hard on his back. It looked as if the second or third round of pills had kicked in. The beer cozy in dad's hand probably helped them along.

"Well, you wanna go grab that hunk of junk or you want to save it for the morning?" Dad said, trying to prompt Drew to let him out of their deal.

"Uhh, well, I'd like to go grab it so I can see if I can't get it fixed, so I can go to town for Halloween tomorrow night."

Drew usually would have let dad off the hook or tried to get hold of one of his fishing buddies who had a truck to help him tow the Nova home, but he couldn't miss the Halloween party. It was his last chance to fix things and confront the monsters.

Clint, one of his fishing buddies, had called him that morning before they left and said that the word in town was that someone had got hold of a ton of booze, so half the school was going to show up out at the dunes. The dunes were the party spot just far enough outside of town for the police to not show up, but not so far out that teens couldn't get there easily.

"Shit." Dad eyed his beer. "A deal's a deal, I guess. Lemme finish this one. Go grab the tow strap and throw it in the truck."

This wasn't going to be fun, but at least he would get the Nova home.

Drew ran to the shed and grabbed the bright yellow braided nylon strap, tossed it in the back of the Travelall, and hopped in to wait for dad.

They stayed quiet on the drive to where the Nova broke down. Drew watched the odometer from where Chris picked him up to where the car sat listing in the ditch. The hazard lights were no longer blinking, meaning he also had a dead battery to contend with. They pulled up in front of the Nova and dad backed up closer so the tow strap would reach. Drew looked again at the gauge: 7.9 miles.

He had run nearly eight miles in the pitch-black with the Gougers chasing him.

Drew smiled to himself.

"We might have to call a tow truck. I don't know if that's gonna roll down the road like that." Dad eyed the tilted car with hesitation.

"I think it will. We just gotta take it slow. We can take Lime Kiln on the way back so we're only on the highway for like half a mile," Drew suggested, hoping he didn't have to pay for a tow truck.

"Jesus, well, hurry up and get the strap on. This is gonna take all damned day." Dad's voice lowered, indicating his frustration..

***

The Nova screamed as dad dragged it along.

Drew was sitting in the driver's seat fighting dad's inebriated swerving from the Travelall up ahead towing him, the listing Nova pulling him toward the ditch, and the brakes that no longer had the benefit of hydraulic assistance.

Dad braked again suddenly from up ahead. The tow strap slacked between the vehicles and Drew pulled on the wheel to get extra leverage on the brake pedal as he tried to avoid letting the strap get under his tire. His palms were sweaty, and his legs were cramping. They were almost back to Point of Rocks, maybe another half a mile of this anxiety.

The cemetery broke the pines on the left of the road, the unnatural clearing bordering the road. Its tilted tombstones and unkept grass were an eyesore. To keep it out of sight and out of mind, it was on the other side of the hill that was the backdrop for the small town.

The only house on this side of the hill was an abandoned ranch house that shared a border with the cemetery. The eerie white house flew past his window. Drew thought he saw a shadowy figure running up the steps onto the abandoned porch. He tried to get a better look, but they rounded the last curve before pulling into town and the white house disappeared.

Dad almost hit the mailbox at the end of their driveway when he took the turn too sharp.

Drew swerved into the grass on the opposite side to avoid the tow strap again and slid to a stop on the wet lawn.

Dad parked and got out of the Travelall, looking pissed off.

"Look at my damned yard! What the hell are you doing, you fucking idiot?" dad accused, accepting no responsibility.

"I'll rake it out, sorry. Thanks for towing me." Drew dried his sweaty palms on his pants.

"Yeah, you will," dad said, walking inside, still muttering under his breath.

Drew didn't have time to argue with him. He slid under the back bumper of the Nova and looked at where the wheel had failed.

It didn't look good.

The hydraulic floor jack squeaked and hissed as he pumped the handle high enough to rest the frame on the fresh chunks of wood he was using as blocks. After he had it high enough, he slid the blocks into place and let the frame down slowly by turning the release valve on the jack. Once Drew had the wheel off and eyeballed the problem, he knew he wasn't going to fix it today.

The wheel bearing had exploded, and all that was left were metal shavings and part of the sheath. The wheel had worn most of the way through the spindle that attached to the hub. So, he would at least need a new spindle and a new bearing. There was no way dad would take him to town today to get one. Mom was already long gone.

Mom said she was going shopping for groceries, but they all knew she was going to be at the casino for most of the day. Dad didn't care. It allowed him to "sneak" over to the neighbor's house and sleep with the lonely local bartender who lived there. They each knew the other was sneaking around.

Well, everyone did. But neither seemed to want to rock the boat and actually talk about it.

Drew huffed audibly while he reattached the air line for the shocks. His Saturday was ruined. The only thing he wanted to do was go to town and see if anyone had heard anything from Nick and Jay after he left them on Battle Mountain. He still had a deadline that was rapidly approaching. Stephanie was going to be home on Monday, even though there was no school. This gave the monsters a prime opportunity to find one of her chokepoints. If he hadn't resolved the situation, he was going to have to go to the cops, and who knew how that was going to go with just his word against theirs?

Drew thought back to the fight and figured he had only made things worse.

***

Yesterday, before the fight and getting chased by the Gougers, Drew had ended up at a preppy kid party after school got out. They hung out and watched *Gladiator*, then spent a few hours playing foosball and drinking a couple of beers. Someone got the great idea to try to get some girls to come over. The boys started calling around. Within an hour, a few girls had shown up, including the girls Stephanie usually hung out with. As soon as the girls started getting comfortable, Nick and Jay wandered into the party, looking around anxiously like they were trying to find someone in particular.

Drew had a pretty good idea of who it was.

Instead, they saw him.

Drew looked at them like he was surprised to see them, but didn't make the first move to go over and talk to them. They spent a few minutes pretending to say hi to people before making the first move themselves and approached him.

"Hey, what are you doing here?" Nick asked.

"I've been here all day. Why are you guys here?" Drew asked, not being overly friendly.

Nick looked hurt.

Drew couldn't help feeling bad for the guy he had been friends with for a few years at this point. Then he remembered the hole in the woods, the notebook, and what they had planned for Stephanie.

His hand clenched into a fist by his side. Maybe this was his opportunity to confront them with a crowd for backup.

"Drew, come here a minute," Clint called from across the room.

Drew didn't hesitate to leave the awkward conversation behind.

"What's up, man?" Drew asked when he had weaved his way through the growing crowd to where Clint was with a few of the other guys.

"Hey, dude, we don't want to make you leave or anything, but the girls can't stand those douche bags." Clint nodded to where Nick and Jay stood by themselves now.

"I didn't bring them. I don't know where they came from," Drew said, suddenly feeling unwelcome in the group he had spent the day with.

Stickboy was officially back.

"No, we know, but if you leave, they will go with you," Clint said, now looking at the girls. "I'll call you tomorrow though, so we can figure out what we are gonna do if we can't find any beers for Halloween," he added, softening the blow.

Drew knew his place. He was the guy with the car, and the money for beers, and the older friends who would buy the beer for them. But he was still white trash, and these kids were the preppies.

"It's fine. I was prolly gonna head home anyway. I can't drink too much since I gotta drive. Plus, Stephanie would probably be pissed if she found out I was partying with a bunch of girls anyway," Drew said, trying to save some pride for himself.

"Holy shit, are you guys actually dating? I didn't think anyone would crack that nut. She's hot, but she's cold," Clint said, smiling like usual.

"Well, I don't know if we are dating, but I hope so. And don't talk about her like that. She's cool," Drew said defensively.

"No, I know. I'm just saying, everyone has tried to date her, and she always says no." Clint laughed.

"All right, later man." Drew felt better about getting kicked out, as he knew it wasn't personal. Nick and Jay were douche bags, after all.

Drew made his way back over to the monsters in the corner. They were whispering together and looking around suspiciously.

"Hey, you guys want to go burn one? They are getting ready to kick everyone out except the hot chicks."

Drew hated having to invite them anywhere. He wanted to just drive them to the police station.

"Yeah, we were just gonna ask if you wanted to bail, too," Jay said.

The three of them piled into the Nova and Drew pushed the button on the dash to start it.

Drew started driving through town and trying to come up with an excuse to just drop them off at Nick's house. He turned toward the side of town where Nick lived while his gears spun.

"Where you going?" Nick asked almost as soon as Drew had turned the wheel.

"I'm not sure. I was thinking about maybe just heading home," Drew suggested, laying the groundwork for ditching them.

"Nah, let's go up Battle Mountain and smoke that joint. I'm not going home yet," Nick said forcefully.

"Dude, I don't know if my car has enough clearance to get up there." Drew was reaching for an excuse to not take the trip up the hill.

"Then we will just go as far as the lookout. It's all serviced up to that point." Jay leaned forward insistently from the back seat.

The mood in the car was changing quickly.

Drew felt like if he pissed them off, it might get ugly.

"Ok, I guess, but I can't stay too long and I'm not smoking any of that med-grade shit before I gotta drive home," Drew relented, knowing the six miles up to the lookout was well-maintained, just like Nick had mentioned.

He turned off the main drag and weaved his way to the base of the hill they called Battle Mountain. Drew put his car in low and started the climb. The three of them stayed quiet most of the way up. Jay was fidgeting in the back seat, causing Drew to look in his mirror every few seconds. The few beers Drew had drunk earlier decided their stay was over.

Drew slowed down and put the Nova in park right in the middle of the gravel road.

Nick shot him a suspicious look.

"I gotta take a piss quick," Drew said and opened his door, then he slammed it shut behind him and walked to the side of the road.

It had started to rain lightly, and the small drops made popping sounds on his windbreaker. Drew found a jack pine and started to take a piss. Almost as soon as the flow of piss hit the ground, Drew heard something.

He pinched off the stream of piss to listen closer.

His ears strained against the popping of the raindrops.

Thump…Scrape…Thump…

Drew pushed hard, turning the stream of piss into a torrent. He was suddenly terrified. His eyes darted around, trying desperately to see into the tree line. He could hear Nick and Jay arguing about something in the car behind him.

Thump…Scrape…

Drew cut the stream short and darted back to the car, not caring how much he dripped in his shorts.

He hadn't heard that sound since he was a kid.

It sounded just like the Gougers.

But how did they find him? Drew thought he had left them far behind when the family had moved away from North Dakota. Then, Drew thought of the Black Hills that surrounded him for sixty miles in each direction.

Maybe this was the Gougers' home now.

The Black Hills were much more of a hospitable environment for a mountain monster than the flat plains of North Dakota, and Drew had never even considered it. He had hidden the memory of the Gougers away with the photo and the claw in a locked box deep in his closet years ago.

Drew slammed the door behind him and shot his eyes around nervously, looking into the tree line with the assistance of his headlights.

"Are you dating Stephanie now?" Nick asked, reminding Drew that maybe the monsters he should be worried about were the ones in his car.

"What do you mean?" Drew asked, failing to come up with something clever.

His hands were already shaking from adrenaline before the Gougers had shown up but now, little rivulets of sweat appeared and were collecting in drops at the tips of his fingers.

"What do I mean? I mean, you've been driving her around and following her all over like a lost puppy for the last two weeks. That's what the fuck I mean."

Nick suddenly sounded furious. He fidgeted anxiously with his waistband.

"Are you just trying to figure out her routine or what, cos we've already done that work. We know where she goes and when she goes there, we even know her volleyball schedule. We know her car will be out of the shop on Monday, too," Jay chimed in from the back seat, matching Nick's intensity.

"No, I just ended up at the same places as her most of the time," Drew said, obviously lying.

Nick shifted with his waistband again.

The motion reminded Drew of someone.

The Can Man.

It was the same thing he had done when he flashed the blade at him on the way out of North Dakota. Drew had some experience with monsters and with traps from his camping trips with the Gougers.

This was beginning to feel like a trap set for Drew, a chokepoint.

"I'm not so sure about that. I don't think you 'accidentally' ended up being with her for the last two weeks non-stop," Nick said with his right hand hidden beneath his jacket. "But, whatever, it don't matter, we already know when we are gonna do it, it's already been decided. Let's just burn this joint and we can tell you about it."

Drew hesitated, but not for very long.

"Yeah, ok, but we can't smoke in here in case I get pulled over. I don't want that fuckin' smell getting me in trouble." Drew's gears were turning now.

***

The overlook was just ahead now. The headlights lit it up briefly as they swept across the concrete structure that served as a lookout tower.

Drew turned hard and spun a little gravel, trying to get his car at the right angle to force the monsters to walk around to his side of the car to get to the tower.

Before they had a chance to say or do anything, Drew got out and closed his door, but not hard enough to latch it, just enough to shut the interior light off. The monsters said something to each other inside the Nova in whispered tones. After a few nervous seconds, Nick opened his door, then waited for Jay to get out before shutting it and making their way around the back of the car.

Nick was in the lead.

As soon as he was close enough, Drew cocked back his fist and blasted him in the face as hard as he could.

Nick went down hard, almost sitting down Indian-style, before bouncing his face off his own knee. His right hand was twisted up in his jacket and Drew could have sworn there was a knife clenched in his hand. Nick's eyes rolled around in their sockets, and Jay took a few steps backward.

"If you motherfuckers touch Stephanie, I will kill you. You understand that? And if anyone, I don't care if it's an old lady, a toddler, or a high school girl, if anything happens to anyone, I'm going straight to the police." Drew was yelling at the top of his lungs.

It looked like it scared Jay, who backpedaled a few more steps.

Drew could see that Nick was slowly coming around. His eyes were focusing rather than rolling around in their sockets. His left hand was furiously trying to untangle his right hand from inside his loose jacket.

Drew couldn't wait around for them to respond.

Maybe he was a coward and should have finished the job, but he knew if he stayed, this was going to escalate quickly. He jumped back into the open door and slammed it behind him. The Nova was in reverse before he was even seated. He floored it and the Nova roared. Gravel spun and spat around the car, surely peppering the monsters with rocks. Drew gave it a little too much gas and spun out into the field beside the lookout into a patch of buckbrush.

A violent hiss of air from his shocks went unnoticed at the time.

Quickly, Drew put the Nova into drive and pushed the pedal to the floor.

SMASH!

A fist-sized rock hit the windshield and a crack split it in half. A spiderweb of smaller cracks grew away from the impact site and across his field of view.

Drew was gaining some distance now that he was back on the well-maintained road. More rocks hit the back of his car as he sped away and he could hear the monsters roaring in the darkness behind him.

***

"And a new windshield," Drew said to himself after reflecting on the fight.

He added the new windshield to the list of stuff he had to fix to get the Nova back on the road.

Drew spent the rest of the day bored and stuck at home at Point of Rocks.

He took a couple of hours to hike over the hill behind town. There was an old, abandoned quarry that held a nice-sized pond at the bottom. As far as Drew could tell, he might be the only person on Earth who even knew it existed. It may or may not be on private land. Either way, it was surrounded by gates protecting the private land, and nobody in town besides him had enough motivation to hike over the hill to get to it. Drew had established a small population of fish in the pond. A few bluegills, a monster bass, an assortment of trout plus a few crawdads. All were fish that he caught in other lakes and kept in a cooler to release in his pond. Drew hoped eventually they would establish themselves and the pond could be a little eco-system that he had created, but until then, he had to hike over every once in a while, to toss in a bag of chopped smelt and a can of corn or two.

He spent the afternoon trying to spot the monster bass and feeding the bluegill one piece of corn at a time. They were practically domesticated at this point, and they took the niblets of corn right from his fingers.The sun was setting by the time he was done feeding them and the images of the Gougers' burning yellow eyes from the highway the night before came to mind.

It was time to get out of the woods.

The crazy Y2K guy in town was using the hill as a backstop for target practice, so not wanting to catch strays with his face, Drew took the long way around the hill, past the cemetery, and back to town. The guy was a looney on his best day but with the computer glitch on the horizon, he was unpredictable.

When Drew got close to the cemetery, he was too spooked to walk through it, so he cut through the yard of the solitary, creepy white house that, for as long as Drew could remember, was uninhabited. He made his way around the property, giving the house a wide berth. The corner of his eye thought it saw movement on the front porch, like he had when dad was towing him home.

It looked like a shadow had run from the steps to the window on the front porch. Drew backed up nearly to the tree line where the Gougers were probably hiding. He was stuck between a haunted house, a cemetery, and a pair of monsters in the woods.

Out of morbid curiosity and a love for anything scary, Drew looked back at the porch, but his eyes stopped short.

There, standing in the cemetery in the headlights of a running car, was one of the most beautiful women he had ever seen.

She was kneeling and looked to be digging in the dirt in front of one of the graves. Drew stopped dead in his tracks, monsters and ghosts forgotten briefly by the sight of this beautiful woman digging with her bare hands in the cemetery.

Loose fabric from what looked like a sexy nighty waved in the air as she stood back up. She was half-naked. Her breasts nearly fell out of the top of the lingerie, and the hem of the skirt ended halfway up her exposed ass.

Suddenly, she looked straight at Drew.

They locked eyes for a moment. Then the woman grabbed a handful of something in a basket on the ground and looked back at Drew. She pursed her lips and blew him a kiss. The kiss carried some dust away from her hand and blew in Drew's direction. Then she hesitated for a moment, gathered her things, and jumped into her car.

She drove away, leaving Drew confused, scared, and horny. He looked around to see if the Gougers or the shadow on the porch had seen what he had. The sun falling behind the black hill behind him reminded him that he was in a hurry.

The image of her breasts and the thin nighty blowing in the air teased him the rest of the run home. He felt guilty because he really liked Stephanie, and she was more than hot herself. But something about the beautiful woman and her blown kiss burrowed into his brain and wouldn't go away.

Drew didn't mind much.

He even fell asleep thinking about her. The thoughts of Halloween and the monsters he had to deal with in the morning were the furthest thing from his mind.

Chapter 20

Drew woke up before his alarm sounded. After a night of sexy dreams full of the woman from the cemetery, Drew was ready for a shower.

The lights in the kitchen were on, letting him know he wasn't the first one out of bed. Dad usually got up early so he could take his morning dose before the one he took in the middle of the night wore off.

As he entered the kitchen, Drew was surprised to see his mom sitting at the table.

"What are you doing up so early?" mom asked in her gravelly voice earned from the last few years of heavy smoking.

"I was gonna take a shower and get ready to hopefully go to town," Drew hinted.

"I'm going to town later, but if I drive, you've got to put gas in my car," Mom said, never missing an opportunity to save some coins for the one-armed bandit. "But I'm not leaving until nine or ten."

"Sure, I'll get ready slow. Where's dad?" Drew noticed their bedroom door was open.

"He and Chris got up early. They said they had to make a trip to pick something up?" Mom said, eyeing Drew as if to see if he knew anything more about it.

"News to me, I don't know what they're doing. They could've told me, so I could've gotten a ride with them," Drew said, irritated that dad had included Chris on a road trip but never for hauling wood.

"Well then, we wouldn't have a chance to have a lovely ride to town together," Mom said sarcastically.

"I guess." Drew walked away, not finding the humor in it.

When Drew finished his shower, mom let him know that Stephanie had called. Drew's heart sped up. He was excited to hear her voice.

"What was the number? Did she leave one?" Drew asked, ready to dial.

"She called from her house. It was on the caller ID. Are you two dating?" Mom said with a smile.

"Her house?" Confusion swirled in Drew's head.

She was supposed to be gone until tomorrow. But now Drew was going to have to deal with making sure nothing happened to her.

After an exchange of pleasantries with Stephanie's mom, Drew finally got her on the phone.

"Hey, I thought you were going to be gone until tomorrow?" Drew started without saying hi.

"Hi…we came home early because my sister wanted to go trick or treating with her friends. Why? Are you coming into town?" Stephanie sounded excited.

"Yeah…my mom's gonna bring me in. My Nova broke down on Friday, so now I'm stuck walking until I can get the parts on Monday or Tuesday," Drew explained, leaving out the part about her being hunted by monsters.

"Are you serious? That's stupid. Are we going to go out later?" Stephanie asked now, less excited.

"Yeah, I mean, I think I can get us a ride to the dunes," Drew said, knowing Stephanie was referring to the party later that night.

"Ok, call me when you get to town later. BYYY-E." Stephanie laughed and hung up.

The drive to town was just as fun as mom had predicted. They didn't have much to talk about, so mom put on the rock station and turned the volume up, the speakers cracking and popping in objection.

Drew was busy thinking of the extra work he had to deal with now that Stephanie was back in town. Only when they pulled into the gas station at the edge of town did mom turn the radio down, interrupting his thoughts.

"You gonna fill my tank?" mom asked, pulling up to the pump.

Drew eyed the gas gauge, which was reading about an eighth of a tank. The twenty-mile drive to town definitely didn't burn seven eighths.

"I guess so. Are you going to come pick me up tomorrow morning, though?" Drew said, hating to ask her for anything, knowing there were always strings attached.

"You give me another ten bucks and I will. But you'll have to wait until I leave town sometime before I have to make dinner for dad." Mom knew she couldn't miss feeding dad her hair-filled slop or there would be hell to pay.

"Fine," Drew relented.

After he paid and handed mom the change, Drew didn't bother getting back in the car. The casino was in the opposite direction from where he was headed, so he started walking. Drew didn't mind walking. In fact, he loved to walk…on a trail, on a path, or in the woods. Walking through town always made him feel like he was even more white trash than usual. Most of the people who walked through town were the poor kids who didn't have jobs or parents to buy them cars. The other walkers were the DUI idiots who had to walk or ride a bike after their licenses were revoked, and the few homeless people who wandered through town.

To avoid judgment, Drew kept his eyes to the ground as he made his way to the main drag, where he hoped to see one of his buddies with a car.

The ten minutes spent sitting on the wall waiting for anyone to wake up and start enjoying Halloween took longer than Drew thought possible. Everyone was wasting daylight. Drew regretted having to come to town so early. Just as he was getting impatient and embarrassed for loitering, Drew heard a honk. It was one of his fishing buddies, Paul.

"Hey, what are you doing on the wall, man?" Paul asked in a surprised voice.

"My Nova broke down on me and I had to walk home at midnight almost ten miles. My mom gave me a ride to town, but now I'm stuck here like an idiot, waiting for everyone to wake up," Drew explained, glossing over more than a few details.

"Dang, that sucks, dude…well, you wanna go for a cruise and see who we can find?" Paul offered like a knight in shining armor.

"Hell yeah. If you want to go out to the junction, I'll buy lunch." Drew knew the truck stop outside town had the best food and the best opportunity to run into someone they knew.

"Sweet, let's go," Paul said, jumping back into his car.

***

Drew was right about the food. He was starving and didn't remember eating yesterday at all, so it tasted even better than usual. There were also a few other kids at the junction doing the same thing. The rumblings were that the Halloween party was canceled. Apparently, the cops were looking for a few kids they thought had robbed a liquor store last night after they stole a car. That also meant the rest of the kids were going to be lying low.

Drew and Paul spent another couple of hours cruising around after lunch, but town was dead. The families and kids were watching Halloween specials and getting costumes ready and all the troublemaking teenagers were hiding. Drew kept his eyes peeled, looking everywhere they went for Nick and Jay, though he doubted he would see them—these monsters were sneaky.

Eventually, Drew and Paul found themselves back at Clint's house playing foosball. There were only the three of them, so they took turns and listened to music. Paul and Clint were busy talking about the girls from the night before, after asking him to leave. Drew could feel himself blushing from embarrassment and a little anger. He felt like telling them he spent the night fighting with monsters on Battle Mountain and then running home in the dark, all because they had kicked him out. It would only make him even more uncomfortable, so Drew just got quiet after they put in a movie.

It was getting dark out and Drew could see the porch lights in the neighborhood around Clint's house light up, letting the trick or treaters know it was time.

"Hey, can I use your phone quick?" Drew asked Clint.

"As long as you're not calling China, I don't care," Clint joked.

"Nah, I bet he's gonna call Steph," Paul added.

Drew's face turned even redder as he walked down the hall to where the phone hung on the wall.

"Hey, Steph. I'm finally in town," Drew started his lying. He didn't feel good about it, but it was what he had to do to protect her. He needed to convince her to stay at home.

"Hi, what's up?" Drew could tell by the sound of her voice she knew it was bad news.

"Well, supposedly, a bunch of people robbed a gas station or liquor store, and the cops are looking for them, so nobody wants to party or hang out," Drew started. "So, I guess I'm gonna just stay at Clint's house tonight and probably won't do much of anything but watch some movies. I'd come get you if I had a car, but we'd just be stuck walking around."

"If you want, we could take my sister out instead of my parents. We could walk her around for trick or treating. I wish my car was fixed today, but we can use it tomorrow because my dad said it will be ready," Stephanie offered hopefully.

Drew's gears turned. It was too much risk with the monsters lurking in the shadows and with the mention of her getting back on the road, the clock was ticking in his mind.

"I kinda already told these guys I'd hang out…sorry. I feel bad now." Drew attempted to talk her out of leaving her house. "You should just let your parents take your sister out and maybe I can have Paul drop me off at your place in a little bit and we could hang out over by the civic center." Drew knew he wasn't going to go over there but hoped the lie would keep her at home safe, waiting for him to show up.

"OK, I'll be waiting, but call if you can't make it, ok?" Stephanie was back to being as bubbly as ever. "BYY-E."

"Bye, love you."

The line clicked before Drew finished talking and he couldn't have been more grateful. The *love you* had just slipped out.

Drew returned to his buddies with his face burning from the lie and the *love you*. They played a few more games of foosball before Paul announced that he had to get home, leaving Drew without a ride.

After he left, Clint and Drew watched another DVD. Drew didn't hear one word of it, but Clint seemed lost in it.

Drew could feel Clint's parents getting antsy. They crossed the hallway every few minutes and shot glances into the room the boys were watching a movie in. There was no school tomorrow, but they had to work. The white trash kid hanging around was putting a kink in their evening.

As soon as the movie was over, Drew excused himself and saved himself some embarrassment of being asked to leave the same house twice in two days. He told Clint he was meeting someone downtown; Clint was aware of his parents' pissy mood and didn't ask any questions.

Halloween had lost its magic since he had become a teen. Drew's family hadn't even bothered to get the Halloween adult diaper box out of the attic in the last three years. All the happy families going house to house reminded Drew of his shortcomings. Plus, at his size, even a costume wouldn't hide his age from the porch-lighters offering free candy to kids.

The light drizzle had turned to sleet now that it was dark. The Indian summer had lasted just long enough for the kids to get their candy in relative comfort. As Drew walked, he could see the evidence of his younger classmates' activities. The smashed pumpkins with their waxy blood were showing up with an increasing frequency as he walked.

By the time Drew made it back to the wall to see if anyone was still out and about, he realized it was in vain. Town was dead for the night. There was maybe one car every five minutes that would squish past on the slush growing on the surface of the road. The sleet was freezing now, and the streetlights bounced off the crystals, reflecting in every direction. Drew looked around, searching the darker corners, thinking he would find Nick and Jay in every one.

Drew considered calling home from the gas station, but that would just be a waste of a quarter. Mom would never drive on the ice and dad was bound to be far too high by this time in the evening. Chris was useless. Drew wondered if dad and Chris were even home from their mystery trip yet.

Another car sloshed past, and Drew tried to get a look at who was driving. The windows of the passing cars had all turned dark when the streetlights came on, so seeing the occupants was impossible. This was a revelation; every car now became a threat in his mind. Every car was now a dark corner and any of them could be carrying the monsters.

Drew decided being a stationary target wasn't wise, but he couldn't look like prey, either. He had learned that on the run home last night—the Gougers were good teachers. Drew left the wall and walked. He didn't have a destination in mind. So, he wandered from bright street corner to bright street corner.

He walked until almost 11:00, from what the bank clock read. Drew's gears started to turn. Where could he sleep tonight? Less than a month ago, the answer would have been Nick's house. Tonight, that thought brought chills.

Drew tightened up his jacket and had walked some more when another car sloshed by. It was a '69 Camaro that reminded him of his Nova. He looked at the car, knowing he would win a race with it. Then, in the same thought, Drew knew where to go: Joe's.

The old vet was a notorious night owl. Drew spent many long nights in Joe's garage with the Chilton's manual and the Nova, only to go to leave at two in the morning and find Joe pacing around his house. Drew asked him once why he stayed up so late and Joe told him his buddies from the war liked to keep him up at night.

Drew made his way uptown toward Joe's house. It was a long walk, but if he took the shortcut through the park, it would be only half as long. The problem with the shortcut through the park was that the park was surrounded on one side by steep hills and the other side by the highway bypass. The thoughts of the Gougers would keep him out of the hills, but the park was pitch-black at night, providing the other monsters, his "friends," with plenty of chokepoints.

The snow was really coming down as Drew approached the park. The white on the ground made the dark seem less foreboding, but the corners were even blacker now.

Drew felt like a scared little baby again.

He popped his collar to shake the snow off and started walking through the park, trying to convince himself that he was brave enough for it. His eyes darted from void to void, expecting an ambush at any second. The wind was blowing now, carrying away with it any familiarity the park offered during the day. The few leaves left on the trees rattled in unison, sounding like skeletons walking in an old Harryhausen movie. The snow hitting the ground was providing background noise like static from the TV after a scary movie was over and the VCR finished the empty roll of magnetic tape. Drew realized the only people who were out now were him, the homeless guys downtown, and the monsters. He was alone in this enormous park…he hoped.

The tennis court was on his left, and Drew had a great idea. He ran from the path, across the frozen blades of grass, and flipped the giant switch on the pole. The timed light instantly lit the entire corner of the park. Drew breathed easier. He had thirty minutes before it switched back off automatically. He walked a little farther and reached the boundary of protection from the lemon light behind him. The baseball fields were just a bit farther.

Drew stopped and listened for footsteps or anything out of the ordinary…

Nothing.

He sprinted for the dugout on the far side. As soon as he reached the pole by the fence, Drew flipped another timer switch, and a fresh lemon light produced more protective light over the baseball field.

Feeling better now that he was most of the way through the park, Drew walked to the dugout so he could pass through it to the other side of the fence. Something was lying on the ground in the middle of the caged-in dugout…a pillowcase. Drew kicked it and some candy spilled out.

Stolen loot.

Drew poked through the bag and picked out some choice pieces. He didn't bother checking for poison. Everyone knew that was a fake story parents used to steal candy. Drew sat down on the cold bench, glad there was a cover over his head. Joe's wasn't very much farther, but his legs were tired, so he took a break and ate some candy. While he munched on a Snickers, he saw something else lying in the dirt.

It was a pack of cigarettes.

Drew had to check.

He picked it up and flipped the top. To his surprise, there were three left. Someone must have thought they were getting chased, so they dumped their stolen candy and illicit cigarettes in the dugout.

Drew lit the cigarette with the lighter he always kept in his pocket. He took a drag and coughed a bit. The cough echoed in the empty park. The static of the snow couldn't mask it.

Thump…Thump…click…click…

It was hooves on cement.

Drew was getting very familiar with the sound. His head spun just in time to see the monster coming down the path toward him.

"AAAAAAGGHHHHHH!" Drew screamed and dropped his smoke.

The monster stopped dead in its tracks for a second, then bounded across the grass in the opposite direction.

The nearly domesticated white-tail deer was as shocked at Drew's scream as he was at it.

"HAHAHAHA," Drew laughed in the dark, trying to relieve some stress from the "attack." "Oh, my God, you scared the crap out of me," he called after the deer.

Drew picked up the smoldering cigarette and gave it a puff to bring it back to life. He looked through the pillowcase and grabbed a couple more choice pieces for the road. Before he left the park, he hung the pillowcase on a fence post near the road. Maybe the kid who got it stolen from him would find it in the morning.

The Midwest in the winter at night always reminded Drew of a photo negative. The dark lawns were bright with snow. The alleyways looked dark and abandoned against the brightness of the snow. The usually friendly, welcoming houses were dark and spooky-looking. But the questionable scary houses with the lights on all night somehow seemed welcoming.

Drew could see one of the up-all-night houses a few blocks ahead. He often wondered why people like that kept the lights on all night, but tonight, his imagination was running wild. Was it schizophrenia? Was it drugs? Was it monsters? As Drew walked past the lit-up house, he tried to get a look in the windows but realized the light was coming from around tin foil, which had been haphazardly stuck to all the glass. For a minute, Drew wanted to sneak across the yard and spy through one of the cracks in the foil to see what they were scared of for himself.

By the time Drew was in Joe's driveway ten minutes later, his neck was sore from checking so many dark corners and the snow was starting to accumulate on the ground. The snow's static had softened and now the blanket of it on the ground was muffling all the sounds around him.

Joe's lights were on, though Drew doubted he was on drugs or crazy. In fact, Drew was certain Joe was just fighting monsters of his own.

Drew hesitated before he knocked. What was he going to tell Joe? But he already knew. It had to be the truth. Joe could sniff out a lie as well as Grandpa could.

KNOCK KNOCK KNOCK.

There was some shuffling inside almost instantly. The grumblings of the old man followed shortly afterward.

"God damn trick or treaters; What time is it? TOO fuckin' late, I'll tell you that much." Joe swung the door open, still fully dressed in his work bibs. But he was holding his candy pail, ready to give a handful even if he was pissed off.

"Hey, Joe," Drew said, trying his best to look happy.

"Drew…I thought you were more damned kids here to bilk some more candy from me. What the hell are you doing walking around in the snow at midnight, kid?" Joe stepped aside to let Drew in.

"Well, we were gonna have a Halloween party, but someone robbed the gas station or something, so the cops had everyone on edge," Drew said, not lying.

"Yep, yep, yep, I heard about that last night…or the night before…on the scanner while I was having some coffee on a break." The old timer still felt the need to justify listening to the scanner by saying he was taking a break.

"Mom brought me to town, cos the Nova broke down, but it's too late to call home for a ride. You think I could maybe sleep on your couch again?" Drew felt sheepish.

"Why the hell didn't I just put a house key on the ring with your Nova keys? You're always welcome to sleep on the couch. Don't bother knocking next time. You had me thinking you were the KGB or some damned thing." Joe was in his fridge now. "Here, you're old enough for one of these, aren't ya?"

"Uhh, yeah, I guess so. Unless this is a damned trap." Drew grabbed the beer hesitantly.

The ice-cold beer felt inviting in Drew's hand.

"No, no trap. I just don't like drinking alone and I don't get much cumpny anymore, so seems like as good a time as any." They both cracked their beers and sat down. "But let me tell you, this is the key to the middle class right here. You wanna get stuck in that rut, go ahead and make a habit of it. You'll find yourself up to your axle in middle class before too long." Joe held the beer out and shook it.

"Yeah, my grandpa used to say the same thing all the time. Don't worry, I don't mind having a few beers once in a while, but I'm too busy to be hung over all the time, like some guys." Drew took a big drink.

"Grandpa sounds like he was a smart feller. What else did he tell ya?" It seemed as if Joe was trying to get Drew to talk so he could listen and drink.

Drew hesitated. He didn't want to lie, and he had to get it off his chest.

"You ever hear of a Sidehill Gouger?" Drew asked.

"Oh, I'm sure 'cept we called them Procks. Why?" Joe asked curiously.

Drew told him Grandpa's story about the Gougers. He even told him the bits that Drew was slowly adding to the story himself about being stalked, setting traps when he was a kid, and getting chased home the night before.

By the time he finished, Joe was lost in four beers and a story.

"You're one helluva storyteller, Drew. Maybe you should lean on that. And as far as Gougers go, I've heard a thing or two about a thing or two and it seems like your grandpa and you know more than I ever did. I didn't know anti-clockwisers could mate with a clockwiser—that adds an extra layer of complexity to the situation since they can't be trapped on a hill." Joe seemed lost in thought.

"So, you believe me…? Just like that." Drew was stunned.

"Hell, why not? I've seen more monsters in my life than I'd like to remember. Who's to say some of them don't have scales and short sets of legs instead of uniforms? The old timers…"

Joe looked at Drew and winked. "Well, helluva lot older than me anyway, well they knew some things. We like to think they made these monsters up just to scare kids out of the hills or other dangers, but the stories started somewhere. Maybe that somewhere was the truth."

Drew felt a huge sense of relief.

Now that Joe knew the truth, the burden didn't seem so heavy. Maybe somewhere in the treasure trove that was his mind, Joe had an answer, a better trap for the Gougers.

Feeling much better about one monster, Drew pressed his luck.

"Hey, Joe, what if I told you that a couple of my used-to-be friends might be monsters?" Drew pressed. "What if I said I might have helped them plan on hurting someone really bad…well, I didn't make the plans, but I was there and I didn't say something to someone right away."

"I'd say get us another beer because I need to hear this story, too." Joe didn't even flinch.

Three more beers each, and Drew had finished the story of his new monsters. He didn't leave out any details. Even the one about how he thought he loved Stephanie already and felt responsible for humoring the monsters for so long.

"That's a lot to swallow but I s'pose there's a solution to be found somewhere." Joe blinked as Drew finished up. "You know where these monsters are right now?"

"Nope, no idea. Nobody has heard from them as far as I know but I didn't get to talk to a whole lot of people cos I didn't have my car." Drew's head was buzzing, and his lips were numb.

"Well, why don't we sleep on it and tomorrow in the daylight we deal with it?" Joe said, not making a suggestion.

He was fluffing a pillow for the couch now.

Drew lay down as soon as the blanket was ready and he was sleeping shortly afterward. The offloading of his anxiety to Joe made him sleep like a baby. There were dreams of Stephanie, of the woman in the cemetery, and bloody smashed pumpkins crying in the streets.

Drew thought he heard something pretty early…or late in the night. But his body was exhausted, and the beers kept him asleep.

The house was cold when he woke up. Joe was nowhere to be found. Drew figured he was already out in the shop, working on a solution to his problems. Drew tied his shoes and put his still-damp jacket on. Then, after he took a piss and grabbed a glass of water, he went out the back door to the shop.

The first thing he saw was feet.

Two feet with heavy work boots were sticking out of the door to the shop. The legs disappeared into the darkness of the doorway.

Drew sprinted over.

He flipped the light on in the shop and there was Joe's body. Drew pushed the overturned tool rack aside and shook his friend. The front of his bibs was covered in blood. Drew's hands grabbed the old man by the shoulders to shake harder and felt his flesh. He was ice-cold. Drew looked around the shop for answers. There was a tipped-over tool chest. Wrenches and screwdrivers and bolts scattered everywhere. The scene reminded Drew of the mess he had made in dad's shop almost ten years ago when he was stealing rope. Joe's face was twisted and looked fearful. There were bruises and cuts covering his body.

"NOOO! JOOOE, WAKE UP." Drew knew it was too late, but he had to do something.

He sprinted back into the house and dialed 911. He told the operator what he found and where he was. The tears were choking him and making it hard to talk. As soon as he hung up with the operator, his fingers dialed home instinctively.

"Hello," dad answered.

"DAD, I stayed at Joe's last night and I just found him in his shop. I'm pretty sure he's dead." Drew was panicking and the scared little kid inside him just wanted his dad to be there with him.

"WHAT? Joe who?" Dad's pill-addled brain was struggling to put the puzzle together.

"JOE, JOE the guy who helped me with the Nova. And everything else." Anger was bubbling inside Drew now. "Just come to town, please." Drew didn't wait for an answer and hung up.

Uncertain what to do, Drew ran back out to the shop.

Joe lay there unblinking and gray. Drew looked around the yard and saw hoof prints leading through the yard to the shop door.

His heart sank.

Had he killed Joe by letting him in on the Gougers' secret? Did telling the Gouger story anger them even more? Drew wondered if there were consequences from telling the story of Nick and Jay as well…was Stephanie, ok?

Gravel crunching in the driveway behind him distracted him from the guilt. It was the police, followed shortly after by the ambulance.

Drew tried his best to explain the situation, but none of them seemed to want to hear what he had to say. They were focused on the now definitely dead body. They were pointing around at the tools and the marks all over his body. At one point, Drew interrupted to show them the tracks from the Gougers, but nobody knew what a Sidehill Gouger was and besides, "Those are deer tracks," they had explained, missing the obvious claw mark in the center of the hoof prints. Drew noticed one hoofprint that seemed to be lacking the clawed digit.

Drew thought back to the claw in his locked black box.

Dad showed up much faster than Drew expected, or maybe time was stretching around him. Dad walked around with his gravelly voice; two octaves deeper than usual from the pills. He was crying as much as Drew was. Now he was busy telling nosy neighbors about how he found Joe's corpse with his son. Drew regretted calling him. He wouldn't make that mistake again.

The cops seemed to have all the answers they needed as Joe's body was loaded into the ambulance, which drove away with the lights off. The cop doing most of the talking was Paul's dad. Before he left, he stopped at the Travelall, and he and dad started talking. Drew walked up on the conversation, only to be singled out as he approached.

"I gotta tell you, Steve, you got a good kid there despite everything. I just took two of his friends to Rapid City to wait for a judge. They stole a car from near Battle Mountain and ended up putting a blade to the throat of the Indian lady who works at the gas station. They got away with a couple hundred bucks and every bottle of liquor in the place." Paul's dad looked at Drew. "You know anything about that?"

"No, sir. Was it Nick and Jay?" Drew was stunned.

"Not supposed to say, but you're not stupid, so don't tell anyone, even though gossip spreads like soft butter in this town…Yeah, it was them. When I picked them up, I gotta tell you how relieved I was to find out you weren't involved. You would have broken the heart of every old person in town, cos for some reason they all think the world of you." Drew thought of all the free lawns and hard work he had volunteered over the years. Maybe he had built up enough goodwill to escape the white trash label his family seemed to relish.

"Well, I guess I did a pretty good job," dad chuckled and stumbled as his body swayed from the pills.

Paul's dad and Drew exchanged knowing glances.

***

Dad drove Drew home after the cops were done with their reports. Drew spent the ride feeling dizzy. Joe's was the first dead body he had seen since Grandpa's, but he was having a hard time feeling sad, as he was still in shock from learning Nick and Jay had been caught. His mind was still busy wondering if Stephanie was ok.

The monsters were gone. They were in jail…at least for now. It meant Stephanie was safe. He won. Maybe he hadn't beaten the monsters directly, but he had kept Stephanie safe enough for long enough. Now he just had to make sure she never found out they were hunting her or that he was involved in the planning.

Joe's funeral was on Thursday. Dad spent the whole time trying to earn pity again. The guests all seemed like people Joe would have kept at arm's length. The potluck after the service was more wasted daylight, full of drinking and gossip just like Grandpa's had been.

One bright spot was Stephanie sitting by his side, holding his hand the whole time. Drew had taken the week off school and work, although Taco John's was closed anyway for three of the days so his boss, Joe's daughter, could attend the funeral as well.

Now that Drew could relax with the monsters being in jail and the funeral over, he could focus more attention on Stephanie. She seemed to enjoy it because by the end of the week, they had exchanged I-love-yous. It was puppy love and Drew knew it, but he had never felt so close to another human, and he didn't want to let her out of his sight.

The next month, Drew convinced Stephanie to lie to her parents so they could camp at the lake. It was in the hills, but Drew never even thought about a Gouger. He was too busy falling even more in love. He spent the weekend talking about Joe while Stephanie asked questions, being sweet and acting interested.

The last day camping, the two of them spent most of in the sleeping bag. They both felt guilty because they knew it was wrong, but also, there was no regret.

The monsters were sentenced to two years in jail that same weekend, and that gave Drew plenty of time to figure something out, or forget they existed. In the meantime, he would keep Stephanie safe from any other monsters that might show up.

***

A month and a half after the camping trip with Stephanie, Drew was at home searching for his backup set of keys for the Nova. He had finally gotten it back on the road after driving mom's hoopty around for a couple of months. But now he couldn't find his own keys.

There was a pile of clothes on the back of the couch, so Drew thought it was worth a look. He picked up a hoodie that belonged to Chris and reached into the pocket. It crinkled and felt full of trash. Drew pulled out the handful of plastic and was shocked to his core.

It was dozens of bindles of pills wrapped and sealed in plastic.

Dad's pills.

Drew felt a lump in his throat. He knew dad and Chris had been spending more and more time together, but he never imagined Chris would get into this, too. They didn't get along anymore but Drew still felt protective of his little brother. The mystery road trips the two had been taking, and all the extra money spent taking mom to Deadwood to gamble suddenly made more sense.

RIIIING.

The phone broke the silence of the house.

Drew stuffed the baggies back into the hoodie and tossed it back on the couch. He swallowed the lump in his throat.

"Hello?" Drew asked, feeling pissed off.

There was a soft crying coming from the other end of the phone.

"Drew? I'm pregnant."

Chapter 21

Drew could see the rut coming miles away. He had been warned about it since he was a kid. Grandpa and Joe had both offered warnings about the hazard, and Drew had even taken their advice and stopped drinking and smoking pot. But, as much as he tried to avoid the rut, he found himself in it now.

It was comfortable at times. Drew figured that was how it became a rut in the first place. Just drifting along with the rut, letting life come at him and dealing with the issues that arose as they came seemed almost pleasant at times. Other times, Drew wished he had the means to plan and avoid the oncoming obstacles because they came fast and hard.

Lately, Drew just found himself wondering when the rut would run out and spit him out the other end dead or wishing he was.

The first baby came on July 4th just after he had graduated from high school. He and Stephanie had an impromptu wedding the week before graduation. Stephanie was very pregnant and wishing they could wait, but her family insisted they got married before the baby came. Drew had to quit his job at Taco John's and take a job for his dad, spraying noxious weeds for the county. Neither of them regretted the baby or the wedding, as they had only grown closer. But life wasn't easy.

The rut widened in the road ahead of them, becoming almost impossible to avoid.

Within a year, Stephanie was pregnant again.

Drew had been promoted to field supervisor and was basically his own boss. The only person he had to answer to was dad, and that only became more difficult the better Drew got at his job. Dad's pill use was getting bad, and as a result, his ability to perform his job was diminishing. The easy answer for dad was to have Drew pick up his slack. And with Drew carrying the load, dad spent his workdays in the office meeting with customers who never seemed to put in any work orders for weed spraying, but were always leaving happy customers.

Mom's gambling had progressed to the point where dad had to control the purse strings and take her to Deadwood gambling every week or two to get her fix. Otherwise, she would steal and sell stuff from the house to pawn off and hit the casino in secret.

Chris was invisible. Drew hardly saw him at all anymore except on the odd late night he spent in town, when he would randomly see Chris cruising in a car full of guys Drew tended to avoid, the hard drug types.

Stephanie wanted to live in town after they had their first child and Drew couldn't have agreed more, so they had moved from Point of Rocks to town. They got a cute little apartment above a bookstore, which had the added benefit of acting as a library as long as Drew returned the books in mint condition.

It was comfortable for a while.

Drew tried to steer out, but could feel the rut grabbing his wheels, pulling him deeper, threatening to bury him up to his axle in lower middle class.

Then last summer, Drew was poisoned.

He was spraying a steep hillside that had burned out in a wildfire. His job was to prevent noxious weeds from overtaking native plants that were trying to regain a foothold. After stretching the 300-foot hose to its maximum and covering as much area as possible with herbicide, Drew hiked back up to his work truck to wind his hose on the giant reel mounted on the back of the truck. He pulled his facemask up to catch his breath while he pulled and wound the hose onto the reel. Drew's right arm pumped furiously, dragging the loose slack of the hose up the hill. The faster he wound, the more likely it was that the hose would bounce over any snags, saving him a trip back down the steep hill to free it.

His arm pushed harder as his left hand guided the hose onto the reel like a worm gear on a fishing reel. Suddenly, the line went slack in his left hand and the reel spun freely. The old, tattered hose had snapped. The broken hose sprayed wildly and Drew, with his mouth open, puffing for air, was its prime target. Before Drew could register what had happened, a stream of commercial weed killer had sprayed at 25psi directly down his throat. Drew swallowed hard, like when you get a mouthful of water at the pool, and could taste an almost pleasant smell of fresh rain. He knew the dangers of the chemicals and despite their almost pleasant taste, Drew was in the ditch with his filthy fingers down his throat, trying to get it to come up before his thirsty body could absorb it. It didn't work and at the time, Drew remembered wishing Scrooge was there with her Ipecac poison.

Dad didn't want to file an incident report because it would get him in even more trouble with the Weed and Pest Board, who never seemed happy with him. Dad knew he should have fixed the tattered hoses on the trucks—there were multiple work orders on his desk to attest to that fact—so the accident was ultimately his fault. But dad knew Drew. Drew was nothing if not loyal. Dad had talked Drew into not filing a report, a decision that Drew would regret but dad couldn't have cared less about. He wasn't the one who was going to get sick after all. Dad had to keep his job.

The rut was in control now; there was no sense fighting it.

Now, here Drew was five years after high school, on unemployment with two young boys, moving into the abandoned white house by the cemetery that he had nightmares about in high school, and throwing up ten times a day.

Dad fired Drew a few months after the poisoning.

Drew had become unreliable, dad had said, after Drew was forced to call out sick a few times because of the puking. Drew knew the real reason was that he was a liability. Dad knew why Drew was sick, but he could never admit it or would risk losing his job. It was easier to blame firing Drew on a lack of work ethic, although Drew was the only person dad ever asked for help with anything and had been working full-time since he was ten.

Stephanie was forced to be the breadwinner now. Thankfully, she was an angel about it. Drew still had some goodwill in town and one of the old-timers he had mowed for gave her a job at his used car lot as a secretary. She liked the work and made just enough money to keep them from being homeless.

The steps on the porch of the white house creaked as Drew carried the first of many boxes up to the newly installed front door. Drew had already seen the shadow from the corner of his eye race up the steps to where the front door of the house used to be. It was the same shadow he'd seen so many times driving past the cemetery and the secluded house outside of town. He tried to ignore it. He told himself he was just worried about moving and psyching himself out.

Out of habit, Drew turned his head to see if the beautiful half-naked woman was back at the cemetery in her see-through nighty. Waiting to blow him another dusty kiss.

Nope.

Drew was glad Stephanie was at work, so she couldn't ask what he was looking for. He was also glad Stephanie wasn't here because this place felt creepy. He thought that maybe if he filled it with some of their possessions, it would start to feel like home instead of the haunted house by the cemetery and she would never even have to feel the hairs stand up on her arms.

Drew reached for the knob on the new front door, and it resisted. He tried to turn it, and the knob came to life in his hand. The sensation reminded him of catching a fish. Sometimes you'd snag a patch of moss, or a branch, and your pole would bend from the weight. You could tell it was a stick right away because it felt heavy and not alive, whereas when you caught a fish, there was the same weight but also the feeling of struggle, of life. That was the same feeling the doorknob had now. His hand dropped the brass knob, and his heart raced.

The sudden excitement made his stomach roll over, so he dropped the box. There was no resisting the feeling anymore since his gag reflex was non-existent. Drew leaned over the porch railing and dry heaved until a green, foul-tasting liquid came up. Beads of sweat were dripping from his nose. He was glad mom was watching the kids while he moved boxes from town back to Point of Rocks. He hated the boys seeing him get sick.

Drew turned and peered into the window to see what was messing with the doorknob.

The room behind the front door was empty.

This wasn't a great start.

Drew backed away from the window and caught a look at his reflection before he turned away. He froze, stunned at what he looked like. He was a human skeleton now. A hundred pounds had melted from his 6'3" frame since he'd gotten sick. The scale read 124 the last time he had stepped on it a few months ago and he hadn't stepped back on it since.

Stickboy was back.

Drew's confidence in himself was as low as it had been back when the teasing was a daily ritual in elementary school.

"Crap," Drew said to the Stickboy in the window, and he turned away in disgust and shame.

Every fiber of what was left of his body was telling him to run. To put the boxes back in the truck and find another place to live. But there were no other options. At least none he and Stephanie could afford. They only found the white house by a happy accident anyway.

Drew had run into one of the Weed and Pest Board members at the gas station and he was trying to explain why dad had fired him without making dad look like a peckerhead. The board member seemed to know more than what Drew had told him, and with what felt like pity, had offered to rent him the house for $200 a month as long as Drew fixed whatever needed fixing.

Now, with the brass doorknob turning freely in his hand and no longer feeling alive, Drew wished he could have afforded to refuse the offer.

As soon as the door opened, the smell hit him. It was musty and thick with a sweet tangy smell of rotten dead mice mixed in. Drew's first steps in echoed into the other three rooms of the small house.

After he put the box next to the window, he took a ten-second tour and made the loop through the bottom floor of the house to make sure it was empty. There was nothing, at least not anything capable of holding the doorknob still and spinning it out of his grip.

As he took the tour a second time, he opened the windows as he went. Their counterbalances echoed from within the walls as they bounced on their uneven tracks and the sounds filled the house. Drew checked all the corners as he went along, his eyes doing their familiar back-and-forth dance.

A bead of sweat dripped from his nose onto the hardwood floor, making a barely audible dripping noise. If he didn't hurry, he wasn't going to have enough energy for a second trip back to town to get the last load, and he wanted to get it over with.

An hour later, most of the boxes were unloaded, and Drew did his best to scatter some of their modest belongings around to help chase away some ghosts. Drew could see the tombstones in the cemetery outside the window were growing long shadows in the slowly setting sun. He only noticed because he was looking for the beautiful woman again. If he hurried, he could make one more trip, get dad's Travelall back to his house, and grab the boys before dad even knew Drew had borrowed it.

The old motor of the Travelall jumped to life on the first turn. It was the only thing in dad's life that he took care of.

The second trip was slightly more difficult as it was mostly furniture and odd-shaped larger objects. The stacking was trickier than with the square boxes on the first trip, but with Drew's ample stacking experience from hauling wood, he had it done in no time. He plucked the last tie-down strap like a guitar string, and it let out a tone that told Drew he'd done a good job securing it.

The gas station was just down the street on the way out of town, so just in case dad found out he took his truck, Drew filled the tank as a peace offering. While he was filling up, a car Drew knew all too well crested the hill from the direction of Point of Rocks. It was mom's car, but Drew knew after mom's last DUI, it wasn't her driving. As it approached, he crossed his fingers like a little kid, hoping it wasn't dad out looking for his truck. Drew lowered his head as it approached so he could get a look through the window and possibly hide behind the Travelall, his dad's most identifiable possession.

As the car slowed at the stop sign next to him, Drew got a good look at the driver.

It was Chris.

There were two other people in the car. They were shrouded in an unnatural-looking shadow, so Drew moved his head, hoping it was a reflection of a tree that he could shift out of his focus. Before Drew could identify them, Chris was spinning the tires on mom's car and peeling away from the stop sign. He never even looked over at dad's truck. The two passengers remained a mystery and clouded Drew's mind on the drive back to Point of Rocks.

The sun was well below the tree line by the time Drew got back to unload again. The shadow man ran up the porch, racing Drew's headlights as he pulled in. Drew tried to tell himself it was just a trick of the light. He didn't have time to worry about ghosts. Dad was going to be home at any second. Drew just stacked the furniture and other stuff in the driveway for now. He could walk the mile back out to the white house and finish hauling it inside after he dropped the truck off and picked up the boys.

Stephanie had the Nova, which was their only car. Driving it had scared her at first because she said it had too much power. To help save gas and back the power off a bit, Drew had wired the four-barrels closed on the carburetor. It hurt to neuter the Nova, but it was what he had to do to keep Stephanie safe and the gas tank full. Now with her working, Drew found himself footbound and stuck at home most of the time.

Dad still wasn't home when Drew pulled the Travelall into its spot in his driveway ten minutes later. Drew hopped out and jogged up to the back door and let himself in. The keys to the truck jingled as he hung them back up on the board full of nails next to the door.

"Hey, mom, sorry it took so long. I couldn't find anyone to help so I had to haul it all myself!" Drew yelled into the house ahead of him.

"DAAAAD!" Robert ran up to Drew and wrapped his arms around Drew's leg.

Chubby little footsteps followed Robert closely as Tyler copied his older brother and grabbed Drew's other leg.

"What's up, you chuckleheads?" Drew tousled their buzz cuts with his hands.

"Nothing. Gramma wants us to stay the night, and she bought popcorn and candy for us," Robert explained, asking permission at the same time.

"Oh, she did, huh? Mom. What the heck are these crazy kids talking about? You'd never buy candy for kids, right?" Drew said.

"Yes, she did, and pop too," Tyler said, smiling.

"Hey, I'm glad you're back before dad," mom said, entering the kitchen. "He called a bit ago and said to get stuff ready for Deadwood in the morning, but I want to keep your kids for the night. He'll probably end up at the bar or the neighbor's anyway."

There was no ruse or story for why dad spent time at the neighbor lady's house. Mom knew why, but as long as dad didn't ruffle his feathers at her extracurriculars, they could keep a status quo.

"Well, let me call Steph first and make sure she doesn't care," Drew said.

Mom made a pouty face at not getting an automatic yes. Drew grabbed the phone off the table and dialed the dealership.

"West Hills Auto," Stephanie said on the other end.

"Yeah, I want to buy a Cadillac, and I want to take you for a test drive," Drew said in a deep voice.

"Shut up, Drew," Stephanie laughed. "I can see it's you on the caller ID, stupid."

"Oh, yeah, stupid caller ID. Hey, my mom wants to keep the boys. Do you care? It would give us some time to finish moving all of our crap into the house and clean it out a little bit," Drew explained.

"Well…actually, my sister called me just a little bit ago and asked if I could stay with her tonight. Our church friends from when we lived in Denver are in town and they want to watch chick flicks and order pizza. I was going to just come home because I didn't know how to get hold of you, but now that you're calling…" Stephanie left the sentence hanging, obviously hoping Drew would tell her to go.

"Oh. I guess I don't care. Maybe I'll just crash in my old room tonight with the boys." Drew didn't like the thought of staying in the white house alone.

"Ok, sweet. I better get off the phone so I don't get in trouble. Love you BYY-E." Stephanie sounded excited for some girl time.

"Love you, too." Drew hung up.

"Looks like you just got yourself some company tonight. Stephanie is staying with her sister tonight. I might just crash here too," Drew told mom.

The boys jumped around in the kitchen, excited to be staying with Grandma, who didn't have rules like dad. Plus, they could eat all the junk food and stay up as late as they wanted watching Drew's old VHS cartoons.

Dad's daily driver pulled into the parking spot outside the kitchen window.

"Grandpa's home," Mom sounded the alarm, which didn't hold the weight it had when Drew was a scared kid.

The back door opened and dad walked in still wearing his aviator sunglasses. He was already puttering his lips.

"Who the fuck moved my truck?" was the first thing he said when he walked in the door.

"I had to take it to town so I could grab the stuff that wouldn't fit in the Nova. I was going to ask but your office line just rang and rang...I filled it up with gas though and I didn't hit anything," Drew tried to soften the blow.

"Yeah, it rang and rang because I spent all goddamn day getting my ass handed to me by the board." Dad was in rare form.

"Sorry." Drew had to stifle a laugh.

He loved the fact that the Weed and Pest department had slid downhill since he was fired, and dad was catching hell for it.

"Yeah, I bet you are." He took a step toward Drew and put his finger in his face. "You touch my truck again without asking and you're gonna get your ass handed to you. You got that, pal?"

Dad's threat was falling short, and he knew it as Drew stood his ground unflinching.

"Little asshole," Dad muttered as he turned and shut the bathroom door behind him.

The shower started spraying the curtain, letting out little hollow pops as the drops hit the vinyl. Drew looked around the kitchen at his wide-eyed boys and mom, who was busy making a stiff rum and Coke for after the shower. One of dad's many bottles of pills sat near the glass of ice.

"I think I'm gonna just take the boys home. He's in a pissy mood and I don't want them to have to deal with his crabby ass all night." Drew was already ready to go.

"Nooo!" the boys both yelled out in protest.

They didn't know how bad their grandpa could be. Drew had shielded them from most of it.

"I'll keep them downstairs with me watching movies all night and eating popcorn. He won't even be home for long. After he eats something, he'll be gone. Otherwise, he wouldn't have raced into the shower. It'll be dinner, rum and Coke, pills, and the back door," Mom argued. "They'll be fine, I promise."

Drew hesitated and gave the boys a once-over.

"You promise you'll keep them downstairs and out of his hair?" Drew looked at mom, who nodded. "And you promise you'll stay downstairs and listen to Grandma and not get too crazy if Grandpa is home?"

Drew looked at the boys, who bounced around excitedly. Drew shrugged and gave them both hugs.

"Ok, I'll walk over and grab you boys in the morning before Grandpa wants to hit the road for Deadwood."

"Where are you going?" mom asked, confused, clearly thinking Drew was still staying as well.

"Home." Drew was already halfway out the back door.

The haunted house waiting for him had been forgotten in the fight.

"I'm not in the mood to deal with his BS anyway…bye, love you guys."

"Bye, love you too, dad," both boys called after him.

Drew looked back through the window and made a goofy face. The boys laughed and raced away, hopefully to the basement and out of the way.

Halfway home, Drew had to take a knee and throw up. His heart was racing, and the sweat had never stopped rolling down his face. He wiped away a fresh drop, which felt like it almost drained the last bit of his energy. The rest of the walk home took twice as long as the first half. The thoughts of the fidgety doorknob and the shadow on the porch only returned when the cemetery appeared ahead of him. Pale light from the setting sun almost obscured the gray stones standing guard. Then the white house appeared from behind the trees lining the front yard.

Drew shuddered.

There were lights on in the living room, but Drew did not remember flipping a switch.

He approached the porch with caution, making way on the right as he ascended the steps for the shadow man. Drew didn't want to occupy the same space as it did. The light from the living room was casting its own new and unfamiliar shadows, possibly hiding the one he was currently avoiding.

Before he got to the door, Drew took a hopeful glance at the cemetery for the beautiful half-naked woman.

Nothing.

Before he twisted the knob this time, Drew knocked for some reason. He gave whatever he knocked for a minute and then tried the knob. It twisted freely in his hand and the door swung open with a creak...it may need some butter.

After another ten-second tour to make sure the house was truly empty, Drew propped the door open and started hauling in the small assortment of furniture and odds and ends.

The work kept him distracted. He did his best to organize the house, but left the finishing touches for Stephanie, so she didn't feel left out of the loop. There was a broom hidden behind the fridge that was left behind by the last occupant, so Drew put it to work, hoping to chase some of the smell out with the dust.

The sweeping nearly emptied Drew's tank. He wondered what the boys had for dinner. Probably something with hair. He thought of them watching movies, and the thought of them eating candy and popcorn made his stomach growl. The sound of his stomach almost made him jump as it bounced off the empty walls. He was hungry, but there was no food in the house yet. It didn't matter; he thought if he ate, it would just end up joining the puddle of bile out in front of the porch anyway.

The couch of unknown origins in the living room looked welcoming, but the pile of empty boxes was blocking it. For now, Drew could just stack them in the tiny room at the top of the steps that was too small for a bed. They didn't have a garbage service set up yet. Maybe he and the boys could burn the boxes out back tomorrow. They'd love that.

Drew grabbed an armload of empty boxes and made his way up the creaky steps. In the corner of the small room, there was an old vanity that Drew started to stack the empty boxes on. He caught another look at Stickboy in the mirror of the vanity and regretted skipping eating today. He looked worse than he had even a couple of hours ago. The small of his back was aching, probably from dehydration. He had thrown up at least five times since this morning and hadn't taken a break to rehydrate.

Drew remembered seeing a few cups in the cupboard above the sink, and he was curious how the well water tasted. His stomach growled again at the thought of anything to fill it up, even water. The sound from his stomach didn't scare him this time.

This time, it was something else, something downstairs.

Drew stopped breathing and listened harder to the empty house.

"Hmm hmm hnnn hmm hnn hmm…" It was the sound of an old lady humming.

The hairs on Drew's arms stood up and his blood felt cold in his neck.

Thump…thump…thump…

The sounds of footsteps were at the bottom of the stairs, getting closer as the humming intensified.

There was no fight or flight. Drew simply froze in fear.

Chapter 22

The sweat continued to pour all night and Drew wondered where it kept coming from. His mouth was so dry that his tongue felt flaky. When there were lulls in the humming and footsteps from whatever was downstairs, Drew held his breath, waiting, hoping it would stop. Then footsteps would start pacing the loop of the downstairs again, starting the same humming tune. Each time, they receded; they gradually grew in volume as they returned to the bottom of the steps. Each time, the melody would start again at the bottom of the steps while Drew cowered in fear in the little room at the top like a baby.

Eventually, dehydration and exhaustion forced Drew to sit down. He wedged himself into the small space between the empty boxes and the vanity, feeling some comfort from their protection even if internally, he felt like a scared little boy again. His stomach growled every so often and each time, the humming or the footsteps would pause, letting Drew know they were aware of him, too. His mind raced for answers and courage. But there was none to be found. Part of him hoped it was the beautiful woman from the cemetery coming to see who moved in, but the hair standing on end on his arms told him otherwise.

The footsteps began another circuit below him.

Another possible answer presented itself in Drew's imagination. Maybe it was one of the old ladies, possibly senile, from the small trailer park on the edge of Point of Rocks. They were the closest people after all…living people anyway. Drew thought of the cemetery fifty feet from the front porch of the white house, and his stomach churned. Before he sprayed the floor with bile, Drew grabbed a box and heaved into it. Mid-puke, he regretted the fact that his body had to commit the act with such vigor. Deep bass tones followed each heave, sounding more like an anguished bear than a noise coming from a puking human.

The pacing downstairs stopped, listening to him vomit.

Beads of sweat dripped into the box from his eyelashes, mixing with the thick green liquid, which appeared black in the darkness of the small room.

As soon as the heaving ceased, the footsteps began again.

Drew, feeling frustrated and angry, decided he had to have a look. He duck-walked to the top of the steps from his hiding spot by the vanity and waited.

The footsteps were close now and the humming was growing louder.

They were coming through the room Drew had designated as the boys'. Just a few more steps and he would be able to get a look at whatever was walking around down there, ghost or senile old person or whatever it might be.

Thump…thump…thump…

Hmm hn hmm hm hn…

Drew briefly thought of the Gouger trap and the talcum powder, something he hadn't done since the last time he had dealt with monsters years ago in high school.

His stomach tightened, and he refocused his attention to the bottom of the steps and the monster he was currently hiding from, not hunting.

There was just enough light sneaking around the corner from the lamp above the kitchen stove to where Drew was sure that at any second, a visage would appear at the bottom of the steps.

Thump…Thump…

Hmm hn hmm hm hn…

Nothing.

Thump…thump…thump…

Still nothing.

Drew thought from the sound of the footsteps, he should have been staring into the eyes of an apparition by now. He wished he'd had the foresight to sprinkle some talcum powder on the floor so he could check for footprints if he ever made it out of this small room at the top of the steps. Again, his racing mind wandered, and he thought of the monster hunting books Mrs. Hill used to stock along with the *Goosebumps*, just for him.

The thumps stopped, and so did Drew's wandering mind.

Maybe the steps weren't in the house. Maybe they were on the porch? Maybe the roof?

Thump…Creak…Thump…Creak…

The footsteps ascended the steps, letting out the same creaks they did when Drew had climbed them hours ago.

Drew blinked hard in the darkness, looking down the empty staircase.

There was nothing.

Thump…Creak…

Drew skidded back into his hiding spot between the puke-filled box and the vanity. His heart raced so hard in his chest that a pain replaced the lump in his throat.

Thump…Creak…

There were only a few more steps until it would be in the tiny room with him.

There was nowhere to go.

Drew scanned for anything that might help. His eyes stalled on the window opposite him. It was turning gray. A minor victory. The sun was coming up. Even if he was about to die, Drew could consider this a win. He had made it through the night.

Thump…Creak…

The footsteps stopped.

Drew tried to count the steps from memory and figured there was one or two more left before it was standing in front of his hiding spot.

Huuuh…phfff…huuuh…phfff…

It was the sound of a faint, labored breathing.

Drew pulled his knees to his chest and squinted his eyes, not wanting to face it but not able to close them completely.

There were no more footsteps.

They both waited.

The sun was going from a gray to a faint yellow in the window from what Drew could make out in his periphery.

They waited.

Drew held his breath, trying to listen for signs of the oncoming assault, but all he heard was the breathing. However, the harder he listened, the fainter the sounds became. Until he couldn't tell if he could hear them at all anymore.

Drew waited.

The sun grew brighter by the minute. Eventually, a sliver of light made its way up the steps from the front door and seconds later, more rays trickled through the window. Drew's breathing was returning to normal, as well as his heartbeat. It was early, but Drew knew someone would be awake.

Dad.

Drew took a deep breath and forced himself to move. His feet tried, but they were full of pins and needles. It didn't matter how badly they hurt; Drew had to get out of this room. He stomped his feet hard one time each to wake them up, and to serve as a warning to the unknown assailant, that he was coming down the steps. A big breath of musty air filled his lungs, and Drew held it there.

His feet were flying now. Two steps in and Drew was already on the bottom step.

Nothing was there.

His feet kept pounding anyway. Three huge leaps later, he was at the front door and headed down the porch, careful to make way for the shadow ghost on his left.

Drew ran all the way to his parents' house despite his body fighting him the entire way. Every muscle was tight, and the sweat had stopped rolling off his nose, signaling to Drew that he was now very dehydrated. His feet didn't stop until he was at his parents' back door. The habit of giving a courtesy knock was forgotten and Drew burst into the kitchen, where his dad was standing.

"What are you doing? You look terrible." There was a genuine concern on his dad's face.

"There was something…someone in my house and it had me stuck upstairs all night."

Drew was filling a glass at the sink with water. It was only half full before he pulled it away and emptied it before returning it to the cool stream from the tap.

"What? Who? Where was your gun?" Dad was getting excited, and his gravelly voice was straining against it.

"All my stuff is still packed. It just snuck up on me, but I tried to get a loo…" Drew's stomach lurched, and he couldn't finish his sentence.

The pain from the top of his stomach made his eyes water.

Drew stepped into the bathroom, which he was thankful was right next to the front door, and he splashed fresh water all over the bowl. He tried to control the stream, but the violent heaving made it impossible. The center of Drew's vision lost color, and he steadied himself on the sink. His vision blurred further, and the world drifted away in front of him.

***

Drew woke up on his parents' couch feeling confused. There was nobody in the room with him. He sat up and his head spun. The pain in his stomach was excruciating. It had hurt since the puking started, but this was different. A few painful breaths and chest stretches later and Drew found enough strength to stand up.

"Hello?" Drew called out to the seemingly empty house.

"Daaaad!" the boys called out excitedly from the basement.

Little footsteps pounded the basement steps, giving Drew flashbacks of the night he'd just had.

"Hey where is everyone?"

Drew was putting the pieces together. He must have passed out in the bathroom and someone, probably dad, put him on the couch. Drew's stomach growled, exacerbating the pain in his chest.

"Gramma and Grandpa went to Deadwood," Robert said with a smile on his face.

"They left you alone?" Drew said, astounded.

"No, I'm here. They were just watching cartoons I put on for them." Chris leaned back in his chair that sat in front of the TV in his room.

"Oh. What the hell? Why did they just bail on me after I...took a nap?" Drew didn't want to scare the boys and was unaware of how much they knew.

"Dad said you were acting crazy and passed out," Chris said, not picking up the hint.

Drew flinched at the accusation.

"I wasn't acting crazy. Someone was in my...never mind. What are you doing?"

Drew knew Chris wasn't worth an explanation, and he didn't want to scare the boys about their new home. Even if Chris believed him, Drew doubted he would care. The pain in Drew's chest refused to be ignored.

"Hey, do they got any TUMS?"

"I'm busy. And I have no idea. Go check the bathroom. Am I done babysitting?" Chris gave Drew a cold look and swung the door closed to his room as he leaned his chair forward.

"Peckerhead," Drew said reflexively.

The boys both let out a gasp and widened their eyes.

"Sorry. Don't ever fight with each other like we do. You guys need to stick together, got it? And don't you ever say that word." Drew smiled at the boys with the warning.

"Got it. Where's mom?" Tyler asked, looking homesick.

"I'm not sure, but I gotta eat something. She'll be home soon, though." Drew went to the kitchen to see if they had anything to snack on, usually forbidden by dad — but he wasn't there to stop him.

Drew riffled through the cabinets and found a fresh bag of Doritos. On the counter was a bunch of bananas he swiped as well. He put together some peanut butter and jelly sandwiches and put them in a paper bag.

"You boys want to see dad's secret spot?" Drew took a bite from one of the sandwiches he kept out of the paper bag.

"Yes. What's a secret spot?" Tyler asked.

Robert wrinkled his brow at the stupid question.

"It's a secret, dude." Robert laughed.

"Let's go, chuckleheads." Drew opened the back door and led the way.

They took the short way past the Y2K neighbor, whose preparations for an apocalypse that never came were rusting in the wind and fading with time. The hill was just like he remembered. The familiar path he stomped into so many times in high school was still clear as day. He was glad for the hike, but the stomach pain was killing him.

"Slow down for your old man," Drew called out to the boys, who were racing ahead, following the trail.

As soon as they crested the hill, they could see the quarry below them. It was the one benefit of moving into the haunted house. Drew now lived just a few hundred yards from the secret pond and frequent head-clearing space he had spent so much time at in high school.

"There it is, my secret spot. Nobody else on Earth even knows it exists." Drew didn't know the veracity of the statement, but had never seen proof otherwise.

"Whoa, what is it?" Tyler asked in awe at the hole full of boulders with a pond at the bottom.

"It's an old quarry where they used to mine sandstone, I think, or granite or feldspar…maybe all of them. Rocks either way. But in high school, I filled the pond at the bottom with fish and crawdads. Let's see if any of them made it." Drew was as excited as the boys to see how it had stood the test of time over the last couple of years.

"Race ya," Robert called out and sprinted for the small pond.

They all raced.

Drew would have liked to tell himself he let the boys win, but it would have been a lie. He was exhausted.

The pond was almost boiling with bluegills. There were at least twenty of them. The boys tried to catch them with their hands. Drew would have to remember to get some cans of corn and teach them how to hand-feed them. The air was cold, but no ice had formed a crust on the pond yet, so Drew thought he would have time to show the boys before winter really showed up. Drew spotted the bass, which was now a lunker, and pointed it out to the boys. They played and chased crawdads for a while and Drew sat on a rock watching them, feeling better than he had in a while.

"Should we do a picnic before we head to the new house?"

Drew's goosebumps returned as he thought about going back, but there was no other option. All he could do was keep the monsters a secret. He had done it his whole life.

"Yes. We never even had breakfast yet," Tyler said, looking pissed.

"Nobody fed you guys?"

Drew didn't know if it was a blessing or a curse. You never knew how much hair you'd find in your food at that house.

"Nope," Robert agreed.

"Well, let's dig in." The boys sat on a rock and ate every bite of the picnic.

The fuller Drew got, the more his stomach hurt, so he gave the last half of his sandwich to Tyler, who devoured it.

"Well, you guys ready? We better get home before mom gets back. Plus, you guys gotta see your new room. We can stop at the garden behind the house on the way. Earl said he started one this spring, but we can pick whatever's left," Drew explained, remembering what his former boss at the weed board and current landlord had told him.

"Let's go check on the garden, Bob," Tyler shouted, already running away.

The string of words with the short version of Robert stirred a memory Drew had nearly forgotten. He thought back to Bob at the State School and wondered if he ever got to go outside and grow his beans. In the same thought, Drew wondered if somehow Bob from the State School had planted a seed somewhere in his mind, and without Drew knowing, maybe that seed grew and when Drew was searching for names for his first son, he had found it.

"Yeah, let's go check on your garden, Bob." Drew had never used the shorter version, but it made him smile.

***

Two shirts -full of ripe cherry tomatoes later, the three boys were marching to the back yard of their new rental. Drew kept his eye on the cemetery, ready to shield the boys' eyes from ghosts and half-naked beauties.

There was nothing except the pain in his chest.

Gravel was crunching under tires near the trailer park on the edge of town by the time they got to the front yard. Drew waited at the bottom of the porch to see who it was.

The rumbling from the 383 stroker told him before he could see her.

Stephanie was home, and the Nova.

Drew breathed a sigh of relief that made him clutch the pain in his chest. He shot his hand down as fast as it went up. Hiding how terrible he felt was just as important as hiding the monsters. Drew could never let her be home alone here. Maybe she would never even notice the extra occupants.

Drew smiled and waved with the boys as she pulled in. Stephanie smiled, but it faded quickly as she looked like she was watching something on the porch. Drew turned his head and thought he saw the shadow disappear into the old frame where the front door used to be.

"Hi, how was town?" Drew said, not acknowledging it.

"Good." Stephanie tore her eyes from the porch and looked at Drew. "What happened to you? You look terrible."

"Jeez, I must really look like shit. That's the second time I've heard that today." Drew laughed and his chest burned.

"You need to eat something." Stephanie sounded worried.

"We did. We just had a picnic in the garden, not at a secret spot." Drew winked at the boys playfully.

"Guess what. We make so little money that now that you are on unemployment, we can use state insurance for a hospital visit and they will cover the bill. Maybe they can find out something about why you got so sick and fix it." She was obviously trying to put a positive spin on the downward spiral that had become his health and their life.

"Really? That's good news, I guess. Did you make an appointment?"

Drew hated hospitals and had been putting it off, but with the new pain in his chest, the fight was out of him. Maybe they could just give him a pill and he could get back to work and out of this haunted rental.

"Tomorrow," Stephanie said, beaming, clearly proud of taking care of Drew.

"Sweet." Drew tried to feign excitement.

"It'll be fine, I promise." Stephanie seemed to sense his phoniness. "Boys, grab the pumpkins out of the back seat and put them on the porch, please."

***

Drew made pasta Trapanese for lunch. He learned to love cooking over the course of their marriage. The first few dinners from Stephanie were good tries, but when Drew found a hair and accused her of putting it there intentionally, it started the biggest fight of their young marriage. Since then, Drew had taken it upon himself to cook and actually found himself looking forward to planning out a menu and making meals. It was relaxing, and he was good at it. Plus, he never found a hair.

After dinner and a scary movie, which Drew protested, everyone was lying in bed. They were all sound asleep, except for Drew. He lay there all night wide-eyed and waiting for the humming and footsteps to start. The pain in his chest was a great aid in keeping him alert while he stood guard. When the windows started turning gray, Drew finally let himself close his eyes and got a couple of hours of sleep before the sounds of the rest of his family waking up got him out of bed.

"You should take a shower. We have to get going so we don't miss the appointment; I was just about to come wake you up, but you looked tired, so I wanted to let you get as much sleep as possible." Stephanie was busy in the kitchen and the boys were out in the yard yelling at a squirrel.

"Ugh, ok. I guess we probably better go anyway. I've had a pain in my chest since I threw up yesterday…it's not bad but it's starting to bug me," Drew lied, feeling a bit of relief at the prospect of seeing a doctor.

Two hours later, Drew was sitting alone in the waiting room.

It was taking forever.

Stephanie kept the boys out of the waiting room with all the sick people, and Drew could see them playing on the playground outside the windows.

"Drew..." A young woman in nurse's clothes appeared from behind a door.

"Yes, Ma'am." Drew stood up.

"Ok, come with me. We have to get your weight and your vitals," the young nurse said.

The scale read 120 and Drew wanted to cry.

There was a mirror in front of the scale that was too big to avoid looking back at Stickboy. The nurse left him alone with his thoughts and shame while he waited for the doctor to show up.

It didn't take long.

"Drew?" The door opened a crack, and a pretty voice called out, "Are you decent?" A giggle followed.

"Uhh, yeah." Drew adjusted the paper gown around him, suddenly self-conscious. He was expecting a guy.

Then the beautiful half-naked woman from the cemetery walked in. Except she wasn't half-naked. She was wearing a Jackie O-style dress, holding a clipboard, and had a stethoscope around her long, pretty neck. She looked even more beautiful than he remembered her from the graveyard.

"Hello, I'm Josephine." She held out her flawless hand with her red-painted nails.

"Drew." He couldn't have reached out for her hand fast enough.

"Do I know you from somewhere?" She held his hand in the air and gave it a soft squeeze.

Drew hesitated. What was he going to say? Yeah, I remember you from the time I saw you digging up a grave half-naked in high school?

"I don't think so. Maybe though," Drew lied.

Josephine smiled.

"Well, just call me Jo. What brings you to me today?" Her perfect teeth poked out from behind her painted lips.

"I, uhh, started getting sick a few months ago. It was after I swallowed some herbicide and ever since, I've been throwing up constantly." Drew looked around the room. "And yesterday, the pain in my chest started to hurt so bad, it's hard to think about anything else."

"Oh, no. How much weight have you lost? I can tell you've lost something. You look very thin," the gorgeous doctor said.

Drew couldn't help but steal glances at her exposed cleavage.

"About a hundred pounds, maybe." Drew diverted his eyes just in time to meet her gaze.

"And you're just now coming to see me? You shouldn't have waited so long." She sounded like she was flirting.

Drew's face turned red.

Guilt was starting to be the overwhelming emotion, shoving horniness out of the way. Stephanie was right outside playing with his boys, and he would never jeopardize that.

He glanced back at her cleavage.

"Ok. Let's start with a physical exam to check for a hernia or anything else obvious." She rubbed her hands together to warm them up.

Drew lay back as her warm hands guided his body to a lying position on the table. Drew tried to think of baseball stats and cards missing from his rosters, but all he could imagine was Jo half-naked in the cemetery.

Her hands probed his body.

"Does this hurt?" She pressed on his abdomen.

"Nah." Like Drew would tell her if it did.

"What about this?" She pressed higher, this time just below the stabbing pain in his chest.

Drew winced.

"Ok, no need to answer that." She stroked the spot softly, offering comfort. "Now I have to check for a hernia, so just relax."

Her hand caressed his thigh and made its way to his semi-hard dick. Her soft, warm fingers wrapped around the shaft and held firm. The blood supply to the area increased.

She had to adjust her grip.

"I take it that doesn't hurt?" She smiled at Drew, and she gave his dick two gentle squeezes as it became fully awake.

Drew had had hernia exams before for sports, but nothing like this. He wasn't going to complain, though.

"Can you cough, or will that hurt your chest?" Her grip tightened and moved to the base of his shaft.

Drew let out the most pathetic cough ever.

"Nice." Jo smiled. "Ok, I think everything is more than ok there. I think for today, we will send you home with something for the pain. We can get you something before you leave here and before you leave town, you can fill the script. In the meantime, we will put out feelers for diagnostics and get you an appointment with a specialist."

"Yeah, sounds good." Drew's heart was racing, and he was trying to hide his hard-on with his gown. Drew would do whatever she wanted; he was under her spell.

Jo pulled a packet from her pocket and handed it to him. It was an opiate he was all too familiar with. Oxycodone. It was what dad preferred and often took mystery trips with Chris to trade his own Percocets for.

"Are you sure about this? These are pretty strong, right?" Drew hated the thought of taking them.

"Yes, we will start there to manage pain so you can put some weight on while we figure out what is going on with your tummy." She handed Drew a paper cup she had filled with water and eyed him expectantly.

"Ok." Drew put the pill on his tongue but had to swallow hard to get it down past the lump in his throat.

By the time they got to the pharmacy, waves of euphoria were already washing away the anxiety from the night before, as well as the pain in his chest. It was the best he had felt, maybe ever. His head swam, and mindless babble flowed from his mouth while they waited for the script. Stephanie seemed less worried now that they had been to the doctor and suggested grabbing tacos before they left town since she had just gotten paid.

While they waited at the drive-thru for their order, Drew let his mind wander. He watched the cars pass on the road in front of them. Suddenly, he saw one he recognized. It was mom's car but with her and dad in Deadwood for the weekend, it had to be Chris. Drew leaned forward to get a better look.

What he thought he saw shocked him to his core, so he looked again.

He tried to tell himself it was just the Oxycodone making his mind wander.

"Was that Nick and Jay with your brother? When did they get out of jail?" Stephanie asked flippantly beside him from the driver's seat.

Chapter 23

The rut almost felt comfortable again with the aid of the Oxys.

The pain in his chest was still there, but it wasn't making him pass out anymore, and eating was possible again. Drew would be lying if he said that pain management was the only benefit of the pills. They also dulled the monotony of staying at home with the boys instead of going to work and having a social life.

Drew looked over at the boys, who were busily carving their pumpkins at the table. Halloween landed on Saturday this year, so the boys had been up early watching Halloween cartoons and digging through their own modest Halloween box looking for costumes. There wasn't nearly as much as the adult diaper box sitting in his parents' attic collecting dust, but he and Stephanie added to it every year and someday, it would be even better.

Drew had thought the magic of Halloween was gone forever when he was a teenager, but seeing his kids get as excited as he once did was making him feel the magic again. He was excited to take them trick or treating in town later.

The hospital still hadn't scheduled a diagnostic appointment with the GI specialist, but Jo made sure he had more than enough pills to feel better until then. Stephanie was frustrated because of the lack of progress for a diagnosis and the fact that Drew was still throwing up multiple times a day.

The scale read his weight had somewhat stabilized at 125, so as long as it wasn't going down and he was somewhat comfortable, Jo said it would be ok.

Stephanie still didn't like that answer.

Drew looked at the bottle of pills on the table and figured he may as well take another one now before they had to leave for town to take the boys door to door. He didn't want to screw up the night feeling like crap because his guts hurt too much.

The pill stuck in his throat, giving him time to reconsider this decision. Thoughts of his dad and Chris with their little bags of pills entered his mind. The thought made him feel slimy.

Drew sloshed some more water around his mouth, shook the thoughts away, and swallowed hard.

"Did you talk to your brother about getting some of that?" Stephanie asked from the kitchen, being vague intentionally. Her cat costume with ears and whiskers made her look cute.

"I left him with the money. He said he would get it back to me tonight or tomorrow," Drew said, knowing what she was talking about.

"What is his brother getting for him?" the ever-inquisitive Robert asked, looking up, his forearm dripping pumpkin guts.

"Nothing. Hurry up with those so we can get the candles in them and get to town for some trick or treating," Drew distracted him.

"Ok, hurry up, Tyler. We gotta get to town," Robert squealed.

"I'm done."

Tyler spun the sad-looking pumpkin around. He clearly wasn't done, but he was ready for candy. Robert grabbed the little orange saw from the table and quickly carved out a rudimentary triangle face. It wasn't much better than Tyler's.

"LET'S GOOOO." Robert grabbed his cape from the back of his chair and ran for the door.

"Hold on. We gotta put them outside and put the candles in them or nobody will see them," Drew lied, knowing nobody but the shadow man on the porch and the ghosts in the cemetery were going to get a good look at them.

Ten minutes later, the Nova revved in the driveway, ushering the boys to hurry themselves. Drew was ready to go. His head was swimming from the pills, and he wanted to get on the road before it got too bad and he had to let Stephanie drive. The speaker box in the trunk had long since been removed to make room for car seats and diaper bags, so the Nova's engine provided them with the only audible distraction as they started toward town.

Drew couldn't stand the silence. He felt chatty.

It might be the Oxys.

"Hey, do you guys want to hear a scary story?" Drew asked, hoping they would say yes so he could keep talking.

"YESSSSS."

The boys never let him down. They liked anything scary as much as he did.

"Ok, but not too scary," Stephanie warned.

They both knew the boys would be in their bed tonight if it got more than PG-13.

"Do you guys want to hear about the time I got attacked by monsters on Halloween one year when I was about your ages?"

Drew winced at calling the patients at the State School monsters, but he had to lie, just a little, to make it a better story. He would remember to end it on a positive note and reveal that really, they weren't monsters at all, just helpless, harmless, disabled people.

Drew went into all the gory details of Bananahead and Moonface and the attack by the monsters in the gymnasium when his class left him behind with some obnoxious ginger kid. Drew tried to recall the kid's name during the retelling but had to make one up because it was lost.

It might be the pills.

"At the end of the hall is where I thought those monsters lived and I was sure glad my dad was there, just in case I wanted to reach out and grab his hand. Even though I never would have done that because that's what a pee pants baby would do. But guess what." Drew left the question hanging.

"What?" all three of them said in unison.

Stephanie was just as into the story as the boys were. Drew was surprised he had never told it to her.

"Instead of finding monsters, I found two of the nicest adults I had ever met. Their names were Amy and…Cynthia." Drew took a second to find the latter. "They were the Moonface and Bananahead monsters. Only they weren't monsters at all. They were two ladies with a severe disability that forced their brains to hold water, and it made their lives very difficult and full of misery. I also met a kid named Bob that same night," Drew started again.

"Just like you, Bob," Tyler pointed out proudly.

"He was stuck living in that State School all day every day and hardly ever got to go outside." Drew swallowed hard, knowing the next lie was going to hurt. But he had to tell a good story, one with a happy ending. "Well, after I met him that night, I bugged and bugged my dad to take me back. And after a week of harassing him, dad relented, and we went back to the

State School to take Bob outside. He was so happy. He showed me the bean garden he had started, and we both ate wax beans until we felt sick." Drew looked around the car, hoping nobody called him out on the lie.

"Oh, my God, Drew, was that story real?" Stephanie asked with a smile on her face.

"Every word." Drew smiled back.

"That was awesome. You are so good at telling stories." Stephanie looked impressed.

It made Drew's head spin even harder than the pills were already making it.

"Thanks. What did you boys think?" Drew said, pulling into the outskirts of town now.

"Yeah, good story. But what happened to Bob after that?" Robert asked, seeming concerned.

"Well, they closed down the State School not long after that. Last I heard, Bob was living in an assisted living facility, where he got to work in a greenhouse every day." Drew hoped at least part of it was true. "Ok let's go, first stop, get your pillowcases."

Trick or treating was fun. Drew took the boys all over town to all the best neighborhoods, filling their bags quickly. He still had a bit of goodwill left with people who knew him before he got sick. They tossed in an extra handful of candy when they saw Stickboy standing there with his family.

Halfway through, Drew's stomach started growling. For the second time, he eyed the bags the boys were slowly filling with candy and remembered his mom taking her fill from his own when he was a kid. She used the pretense of checking for poison to get dibs. Drew knew the old wives' tale wasn't going to work on the boys.

Instead, he used humor.

"Dad tax." Drew reached into Tyler's bag and fished out a Twix, then to even it up, snagged a Snickers from Robert.

"DAAAD," both boys laughed and pulled their bags away.

Drew laughed to himself. He realized the "dad tax" humor approach only worked if you took a piece from a full bag of candy. If he took the first piece, with a dad tax, dad was funny. If he went back to the Halloween bag a week later and tried to take the last piece of candy, with the same dad tax, dad was an asshole.

As they finished the upper-class housing and ran into the trailer park side of town, Drew saw two familiar shadows lurking up ahead.

Nick and Jay.

They passed each other on opposite sides of the road. Drew pretended not to notice them but kept an eye on them at the same time. He did his best to keep himself between his family and the monsters as they passed.

Upon closer examination, when the monsters walked under a streetlight, Drew noticed they no longer looked dangerous. They were as sickly and gaunt as Drew was. Their skin was red and pimply, with open sores all over. Their eyes were hollow and dark.

The groups pretended not to notice each other, but when Drew looked back over his shoulder, the monsters had stopped walking. They were now standing together, whispering. Drew met their gaze for a moment and in the darkness, could have sworn they were smiling at him.

Drew packed up his family and left town after that.

***

The pills were waning, so he didn't feel as chatty as he had on the drive in. The Nova dominated the conversation on the way back to Point of Rocks, with the boys busy trading candy in the back seat.

After they pulled in, in front of the white house, Drew found his own treat stuck in his front door. Chris had apparently come through for him. As soon as Drew opened the door, he heard something drop. The flickering lights from the pumpkin's candles illuminated the baggie.

"What's that?" Stephanie asked.

"My idiot brother left me a treat in the stupidest place imaginable." The skunky smell of the weed was so strong, Drew could smell it from his pocket, where he had quickly tucked it away.

"No, I thought I saw…like a shadow run up the porch in front of me…wait, he did?" Stephanie seemed hesitant to walk up the steps where she had just seen something.

"It must have just been a trick of the light from the candles…and yes, he did," Drew answered, hating lying to her about the shadow man.

"Ok, boys, bedtime. Brush your teeth, take a shower, and get into PJs," Stephanie barked at the boys, wanting to get them asleep so Drew could smoke some pot.

The boys complained but didn't argue. They were in bed before very long, even though they were in there talking about candy and Moonface and Bananahead.

As soon as the chatter died down, Drew snuck into the back porch and spun up a joint. He was still good at it, even though it had been a few years.

Since the pills hadn't slowed the puking down, Drew decided to give pot a try. If it worked for people in chemo, it couldn't hurt him anymore than the weight loss and the puking was.

The Bic illuminated the porch for a moment before disappearing into the rolling paper as Drew toked the joint to life. The side of the joint ran, so Drew licked his finger and moistened the paper on that side to slow down the burn. He coughed like he had pneumonia on the first hit, but after a few tokes, the itching in his chest gave way to relief. His mind slowed down from a race to a trot. The knot that had been in his stomach released and it let out an audible growl.

Two thirds of a sheet pan pizza later, Drew felt amazing. The pain was gone thanks to the pills and the retching never followed his meal thanks to the pot. Now that dinner was done, *The Blair Witch Project* was blasting on the TV and Stephanie was cuddled up with his feet on the couch of unknown origins. It was the best Drew had felt in months.

He could get used to this rut.

The thought scared him.

So many times, as a kid, Drew had fallen asleep crying, thinking about dad's drinking. So many times, as an adult, his dad's pills caused stress and problems that made life miserable. Even lately, the rumors of dad and Chris using the county shop to sell pills were following him around town, sullying his hard-earned reputation.

But now here sat Drew the hypocrite enjoying a movie, high on pills and pot, never having felt better in his life.

Was that all dad was doing? Taking a break from the monotony of the rut?

Possibly, Drew thought, but dad always made it everyone else's problem and Drew was just using it to feel better.

Now feeling justified, Drew tried to finish the rest of the movie in peace.

It was no use.

Drew tossed and turned all night.

Maybe it was dad and Chris, maybe it was Nick and Jay, maybe it was the guilt from the pills and pot, maybe it was not having a job, maybe it was worrying Stephanie was going to lose faith in him and fall out of love.

The sun came up well before Drew was ready for it. His stomach, full of pizza, was still trying to empty into intestines that were no longer accustomed to that large a volume. The discomfort had Drew reaching for a pill before he even said good morning to anyone.

Stephanie left for work soon afterward, apparently sensing Drew's bad mood. The Nova growled away in a hurry. The boys woke up because of the engine noise, so now Drew had them to deal with, when all he wanted was a nap.

The boys started arguing over candy and what to have for breakfast. The screeching of their voices clawed into his head and irritated him more than it ever had before.

Drew didn't have the patience for it.

Maybe it was the pills.

Drew slammed his hand on the table, accidentally smacking his palm against the Etch A Sketch that was sitting there.

"I'm not gonna listen to you guys argue all day. I will separate you and put you in different rooms and lock the doors. Do you hear me? I'm really not in the mood for your SHIT today," Drew almost yelled.

The boys winced at the sound of his voice, but their eyes were locked on the Etch A Sketch.

"What is that?" Robert asked timidly.

Drew looked closer at the toy.

His palm had left what looked like the shape of a face, complete with dark lines for its eyes and mouth. The fingers of Drew's hand completed the face with a wild hairstyle and what looked like horns.

It looked like a demon's face.

Drew was inspired.

"It's a demon that I summoned. And he is going to let himself out of the Etch A Sketch if you guys fight even one more time today," Drew warned.

"Nooooo," Tyler protested, crying.

He pushed his chair away from the table and ran to his room.

"Why would you do that?" Robert yelled, not far behind, the fear obvious in his voice.

Their bedroom door slammed, leaving Drew alone. The slamming of their door made the back door to the porch swing open invitingly. It reminded Drew of the butter hinges. Drew accepted the invitation, walked onto the porch, and sat on the chair to finish his joint from last night.

***

After it was done and Drew was feeling more relaxed, he wandered through the kitchen in a daze and made a sandwich with the leftovers on the stove.

The boys were still in their room. The threat of a summoned demon must have worked, as there wasn't a single sound coming from behind the closed door. Drew grabbed the Etch A Sketch and propped it up on the coffee table facing their bedroom just in case they wanted to try to sneak out while he caught a quick nap. The TV popped and hissed for a second as it turned on, then the sounds of daytime TV filled the house.

Drew's head was spinning, he was exhausted, his stomach didn't hurt very bad, he was full, and he was too high to keep his eyes open.

Drew spent the day sleeping on the couch like some transvestite momster. The boys spent the day in their room, too terrified to talk…or eat candy.

By the time Stephanie pulled into the driveway that evening, Drew was scrambling trying to finish dinner, so it didn't look like he just lay around all day.

The Etch A Sketch demon got tossed into the toy box, completely forgotten about…by Drew.

The boys hardly talked during dinner. Something about the atmosphere of the house was heavy and dark. The boys' usual bedtime conversation never started. They simply snuck away to bed quietly when it was time.

"So, did that stuff from your brother help? I haven't asked. You seemed crabby," Stephanie tested the waters after the boys were in bed.

"Yeah, I feel full for the first time in months. My guts still hurt, but not as bad. The pills help, but I don't know about how they make me feel. I think they get in my head and make me feel anxious and crabby and like, little noises make me feel pissed off…Sorry," Drew told her honestly.

"No, don't be sorry. I'm just glad you're feeling better and eating something. Did you weigh yourself?" Stephanie continued.

"Not yet." Drew laughed. "It's not gonna make me get fat overnight. But this crap from my brother is expensive. I might have to try to buy in bulk if I'm gonna keep smoking. I think I can get half a pound for 400 if I can get Chris to grab it for me from his guy. We still have like eight in my old bank account, so I'll just close it out and give you what's left for bills." Drew had already made up his mind but wanted to make sure Stephanie felt included.

"Yeah, that's smart if you're saving money and it's making you feel better. As long as you don't go to jail over it," Stephanie warned.

"Oh, my God, don't worry about that."

But Drew knew it was a risk. Some states had made pot legal for medical use, but Drew doubted South Dakota would ever be one of them. Despite everything he loved about the Black Hills, the people were very set in their ways. One of their ways was to dislike pot and or potheads. Drew didn't blame them—he didn't like lazy potheads much either, but he also realized firsthand that there were benefits to be gained for some people.

"You want to take a couple of rips?" Drew offered.

"No way. I'm afraid I'll pee my pants or something." Stephanie giggled and held up the *Texas Chainsaw Massacre* for Drew's approval.

"Hell, yeah, 'the saw is family'." Drew used a tough guy voice and laughed.

He reclined with Stephanie on the couch of unknown origins and she got a little handsy, but Drew was too relaxed to notice.

***

After the movie was over, they went to bed. Stephanie put the moves on him again under the covers. The pills had robbed him of his libido, but her hands were coaxing it out of hiding.

"Your doctor's pretty cute, huh?" Stephanie asked in a dangerous flirty tone.

"Uhh, yeah, she's hot. Why?" Drew felt guilty.

Had Jo somehow got hold of Stephanie and told her about the hernia hard-on appointment?

"Nothing, just can't help but be a little jealous when you are in a closed room half-naked with a hot chick like her." Stephanie gave his dick a familiar squeeze. "I know what you're working with, and I didn't want her to get any ideas once she got a look at it."

Drew was stiff as a board, and his intoxicated brain was blurring lines. His imagination was running away. He let it run wild with fantasies that he acted out on Stephanie's body until they were both satisfied.

As Drew lay there an hour later listening to Stephanie breathe next to him, he couldn't help feeling a little guilty for not telling her about the handsy hernia exam. Maybe next time they were fooling around, he would bring it up in some dirty talk.

Then something, in what should be the silence of the sleeping house, caught his attention.

It sounded like a choir of kids singing at a Christmas pageant, only he couldn't make out any of the words. Drew thought maybe he had left the TV on, and a song was playing. He looked into the living room but saw only blackness, letting him know the TV was, in fact, turned off.

Then suddenly, there was another layer of sound.

Mrrrm Drrrr Mrr HMM...

The muffled sounds of a man with a baritone voice interrupted the sound of the singing children, yelling some unknown words in anger.

Drew stopped breathing and listened more closely.

The sound of the choir returned. It sounded almost angelic.

DRR Hmmm BRR DGNNN

More deep yelling interrupted the singing, which stopped and let the baritone voice's anger flow freely.

Drew let his breath out quietly and held another. He noticed the breathing next to him had quieted as well. A hand grabbed his thigh, and he nearly screamed.

"Do you hear something?" Stephanie whispered.

Drew wanted to lie, but it would be too obvious.

"Yeah. Why? What do you hear?" Drew prayed she would say wind.

"It sounds like a bunch of kids singing, and, like, an old man yelling at them," she whispered, holding him close now.

The monsters were back again.

This time, Drew thought it was his fault. He had let the transvestite momster attack his kids with the Etch A Sketch demon and it had opened the door for the other monsters who were in the shadows, waiting for a chokepoint.

Or maybe it was the pills.

Neither of them got a good night's sleep.

Chapter 24

Christmas was just around the corner, but there was no holiday spirit in the white house. The pipes had frozen solid three days ago. Earl, the board member/landlord, thought it was going to stay that way until spring because he seemed to remember it always being an issue the last time someone had lived there.

The water tank Drew was trying to wedge into the trunk of the Nova to haul water wouldn't fit. The amp and 6x9 speakers that were all that were left of his sound system were in the way. Drew closed his eyes and rolled his neck on his shoulders.

Ten minutes later, the tank was in, and the stereo remnants were in a box in the little room at the top of the stairs. The trunk just barely shut, but with it now secured, Drew had to make a run to the firehall to fill it so they could hurry up and flush the toilet.

The past month was as close to torture as Drew ever hoped to get. Their savings had dried up, so there were no fancy dinners to cook. The pipes had frozen solid, so they were showering at mom and dad's house, or Stephanie would stop at her parents' house before work.

Thankfully, there was an outhouse they could use in emergencies, on the recreational trail that ran through the Black Hills not very far down the road from the white house. The wood stove ran nonstop, but the lack of insulation and the age of the building kept it cold no matter how much wood he fed it. The pain in his chest was still there, though dulled from the opiates. The puking only relented when he could afford pot, which was not very often.

Last but not least was the relentless singing ghosts. Neither he nor Stephanie had slept well with the endless serenade. There was no answer, no one to talk to, no one to fix it, no exorcist like in the movies. Just relentless phantom singing coming from somewhere under their bed. They did their best to ignore it, but that just brought more restless nights of trying to sleep.

All they could do was put their heads down and trudge forward. Try to pretend everything was ok for as long as they could until the rut eventually ran out and spit them out the other side. For better or worse.

After Drew had the water tank full and the Nova back in its parking spot in front of the white house, he pumped a few five-gallon buckets full of water and hauled them into the bathroom to use for manual flushing.

He used the first bucket to flush the bubbling mess that was growing in the bowl and stinking up the house, down the drain. The boys knew not to use the toilet, but sometimes they forgot and with no way to flush, it got out of control fast. Stephanie would be so glad it was gone and that she would be able to manually flush the toilet. She hated using the outhouse down the road.

"Ok, boys, you can use it again. Just call me when you're done so I can flush it for you," Drew called into the living room.

"Ok," they both called out, the usual cheer absent from their voices.

Drew had noticed an attitude change from the boys the last few weeks but had attributed most of it to the pills. The pills took the edge off the pain in his chest but left him feeling annoyed and angry a lot of the time. He figured the boys were just giving him a wide berth, much like he had done when his dad was drinking.

Stephanie got home, and although the toilet was flushed, she still seemed irritated and edgy, a mood that was becoming more and more her norm.

"Hey, did your brother get that yet?" Stephanie asked while Drew dumped a bucket of boiling water into the bathtub.

"Not yet. He and dad went on a run to pick up more pills from their guy in Denver. He said some lady in town was sending them to meet a contact or whatever, but I don't know what to believe because he was smoking a foily while I was talking to him."

Drew casually talked about the pill business his dad and brother had been running out of the county shop. The rumors were so thick around town that almost daily, Drew was stopped by someone asking if it was true or someone else asking if Drew could get them some pills.

"Is it too late to get the money back and just get a smaller bag from that other guy in town?" Stephanie asked, almost desperately.

"Yeah, he already left, sorry…Why?" Drew instantly felt guilty about the pot he was spending the last of their savings on.

"Ugh, no reason. I guess it just would have been nice to have a couple hundred to spend on bills or groceries." Stephanie was now audibly annoyed.

"Boys, let's go, bath time," Drew called into the living room.

The water wasn't nearly as deep as the boys would have liked it, but boiling water on the wood stove and kitchen stove wasn't nearly as efficient as a water heater.

Stephanie shut the door to the bathroom while the boys jumped in and quietly scrubbed the filth off. She pushed Drew out of the kitchen into the living room, gently but forcefully.

"Drew, what have you been telling the boys about a demon from an Etch A Sketch or something?" The emotions were flipping across Stephanie's face like a Rolodex.

Anger turned up this time.

"The what?" Drew could barely remember the Etch A Sketch demon, but it stirred a memory.

It might be the pills.

"They said you summoned a demon on that thing and told them you would turn it loose on them if they were bad. They've been scared for almost two months and just yesterday told me about it because they didn't want to piss you off. I know you're sick, but that's no reason to be an asshole to our kids."

Stephanie was turning a shade of red Drew didn't see often out of the bedroom.

It was passion.

Drew knew she meant business as his gears spun.

"OH, my God. I had no idea. I got mad when they were arguing and slapped that thing like two months ago, and it looked like a scary face, so I just went with it to kinda like scare them into their bedroom so I could take a nap…I think it was the stupid pills. The sound of their voices made me feel nuts. I was so tired, and I could feel how crabby I was getting, so I just needed them out of my hair. I hate the way those stupid pills make me feel…I swear to God, I forgot all about the Etch A Sketch. I had no idea the boys were still scared."

Drew was racing, trying to smooth over his mistake. He knew at the time he had screwed up as he lay there as the transvestite momster, but life got in the way. He forgot to put the scary away for the boys once it had served its purpose.
Guilt was making his face burn as red as Stephanie's.
His was from shame.

"Well, I get it." Stephanie softened a bit. "But you better figure out a way to make it better with them. They can't stay scared all the time…I'm serious."

"I promise, I will. I'll figure something out." Drew's gears spun. "But I might be able to cheer you up a little bit."

Drew smiled and went to the back porch. He came back with his DIY white trash shower and set it on the table.

"I drilled the bottom of the bucket so I could thread a twenty-ounce bottle onto it and sealed it with silicone. Then I poked enough holes in the bottom of the bottle to give a nice steady flow, like a shower. So, now I can hang the bucket above the tub and fill it with hot water and you can stand under the bottle to get a shower. The only thing is that I'll have to come in every four or five minutes with more hot water to refill it, because that's how long it takes to empty…But I don't mind if you don't mind?" Drew raised his eyebrows suggestively at the thought of watching her take a shower.

"Pervert." Stephanie laughed and gave him a kiss.

Later, after the boys' showers and dinner and then Drew and Stephanie's four-minute shared shower (the water in the bucket ran out long before they got out), Drew lay in bed listening to the ghostly chorus from the basement. He was too busy spinning his gears to listen to them tonight. Drew was wondering how he could fix the boys' demon.

Real-life solutions to a make-believe problem were in short supply, so Drew thought of his favorite scary movies. A few ghost movie titles and bad plots played out in his mind. After some stewing and tossing and turning, Drew had figured out a pretty good idea of how they could get rid of the Etch A Sketch demon.

He slept better than he should have, as the phantom singing continued from somewhere beneath their bed. It was almost comforting at this point. At least it was consistent.

Stephanie left for work the next day and Drew got to work putting the scary away.

He dug around and found some candles in the junk drawer. Then Drew went out back by the garden, where the boys had pulled a ton of wild sage last summer that was choking out the tomatoes and was lying in a pile drying out. Drew gathered up the driest bits of leaves from the dead sage and rolled them into a few joint-shaped bundles, securing them with a bit of wire on the ends. The dreaded Etch A Sketch was hiding under the toy box, probably put there by the boys so it was out of sight. Drew knew Stephanie had brought a bible with her from home after they got married, and after a bit of digging through her nightstand, he found it.

Drew spent the rest of the day trying to cheer the boys up. The grilled cheese and homemade tomato soup from frozen cherry tomatoes went a long way toward doing that, and the old VHS cartoons Drew watched with them all day didn't hurt either.

Later that night after the boys were in a good mood and Stephanie was home from work, Drew put his plan into action. "Boys, after dinner, we have to do something very important.

Can I trust you guys to be brave and help me?" Drew asked as the plates were nearing empty on the table.

"Yeah," Robert said.

"Why? What are we doing?" Tyler asked hesitantly.

"We are going to have an exorcism to get rid of the Etch A Sketch demon once and for all." Drew smiled but stayed serious.

"We are?" Robert asked skeptically.

"Yep, all of us are going to work together and chase it out of the house, ok?" Drew encouraged.

The boys exchanged nervous glances and looked back at Drew, shrugging in tandem. Stephanie was giving Drew a look that said she didn't know how this would end, but that she would allow it.

Stephanie dumped some of the boiling water from the wood stove into the sink and got to work on the dishes. The boys got the living room ready for the exorcism. They were nervous, but Drew could also tell they were having fun with it. That was step one. If Drew could make the scary fun, it would stop being scary.

"Ok, both of you, hold out your hands," Drew instructed as Stephanie dried her hands and joined their circle. "Steph, you know the most prayers. Do you want to start one? I don't think it matters much which one."

Stephanie started in on some Hail Marys.

"Now we all need to hold hands while mom prays." Drew grabbed one clammy little hand and one of Stephanie's, completing the already forming circle.

"DEMON from the Etch A Sketch. I made a mistake summoning you to this world," Drew started while Stephanie kept the Hail Marys going. "You are not welcome in our house any longer. Any spirits that mean to harm our family are banished from our home. Our family is powerful together and together, we tell you to leave us…Steph, keep praying."

Drew grabbed the bundles of sage and handed one to each boy. He lit the ends as the boys broke the circle and held the burning bundles out in front of them, blowing the smoke away from their eyes.

"We are burning this sacred herb to banish you from our house and to clear any evil you may have left behind…Go, boys, go."

The boys took off with their smoking sage rolls, laughing and smudging the entire house.

"Don't forget the little room at the top of the steps." Drew thought back to the night he spent trapped up there by the humming lady. "…and all of the dark corners too," Drew yelled after them, hoping they were distracted for a minute.

The Etch A Sketch was concealed under the table with a close facsimile of the original demon drawn on it. Drew pulled it out now and put it on the table, hoping it would work and not scare them even worse.

"Oh, my gosh, boys, come here." Drew was sitting at the table while Stephanie continued praying.

The boys thudded across the house, back to the safety of their dad. The smell of sage was choking as it chased them.

"Look. He's back. I think we scared him out of the house and back into the Etch A Sketch again."

"NOOOOO!" Tyler screamed as he looked at it.
Robert started backpedaling with his eyes wide in fear.

"NO, don't be scared, boys. This is our house. There is only one thing we can do now that he is trapped. Give me your hands." Drew held out his hand. "Hurry."

The boys hesitated and looked at each other. But they trusted their dad, so they took Drew's hand and let him lead their clammy hands to the sliding magnetic eraser.

"Ok, boys, this is it. On the count of three, we are going to banish him forever. One, don't be scared…Two, believe he is leaving forever…Three, send him back to hell."

On the last word, Drew could feel eager little fingers push the magnetic slide hard to the other side of the board, banishing the demon in the process as the magnet erased the likeness.

"WE DID IT," Tyler squealed, smiling for the first time Drew could remember in days.

"Is that all? Is it gone?" Robert asked in disbelief.

He took the magnetic eraser and racked it back and forth a few more times for good measure.

"I promise he will never come back. And as long as we stay strong together, no other monsters will stand a chance against us either."

Drew knew the exorcism had worked for the boys, judging by the looks on their faces. And he couldn't have been happier with the results as Stephanie planted a kiss on his lips.

"Ewww," the boys teased together.

"Ok, now that that's over, you two finish your chores and you can stay up in your room for another hour watching a cartoon. Deal?" Drew asked.

"Yep," Robert called, already running to his room with a weight lifted off his shoulders.

That night, they all got a good night's sleep. There was no late-night serenade from the ghosts from somewhere beneath their bed. No footsteps. No scared boys crawling into mom's side of the bed. Drew lay awake for a little while, slightly proud of himself, hoping he had helped the boys beat their first monster. It reminded him of when dad had done the same for him at the State School.

***

The next day was straight back into the rut.

Drew had an appointment, and since the boys were out of school, they came and waited with Stephanie, though this time they waited in the Nova, not the park, because everything was covered in ice and or snow. Drew was hoping there would finally be some forward progress with a diagnosis, but that hope was slowly dying. Jo only seemed interested in making him feel better with pills and hard-ons.

"Drew," the nurse called, looking annoyed.

Drew followed her back and avoided starting any small talk. He wasn't in the mood.

After the blood draw and the weigh-in, Drew waited. This time, the wait was excruciating. The office was cold. Drew's stomach pain was terrible, and he felt like he might throw up at any minute. An hour later, just as Drew's anger was at a boiling point and he was ready to leave the office, Jo knocked and let herself in. There was no smile on her face today, no sexy flirty looks.

Jo was pissed.

"I'm sorry that took so long, but we had to wait for your blood results and actually…I'm not very sorry at all because I am glad I waited. Your blood work came back with some very concerning results…Are you smoking marijuana?" Her face was bright red.

This was just anger, not passion.

"Uhh, yeah, a little bit," Drew said and waited in an awkward silence for her to say something.

Instead, she just stared into his eyes. Out of awkwardness, Drew continued.

"I just heard it helped cancer patients with nausea, so I figured it wasn't going to hurt…I've actually put on like three or four pounds since…"

"OH…I forgot you were a doctor. Where did you go to medical school again?" Jo sneered. "If you want more of these..." Jo shook a bottle of Oxys in front of his face. "Then you better start doing exactly what I say."

Her anger was sending up hairs on Drew's neck. This felt like another chokepoint, a trap. Had he missed something? Was she a monster, too? Not one that hides in the shadows but more like a witch whose chosen brews were opiates and love potions.

Drew thought back to the cemetery and tried to forget the fact that she was beautiful and half-naked. What had she been doing there digging? Why was Drew just now asking himself these questions? Was he under her spell? He remembered the dusty kiss she had blown to him before fleeing the cemetery. Drew told himself that was impossible. Witches weren't real.
Maybe it was the pills?

"I'm going to schedule you for another appointment with a blood draw in two months. Enough time to clean out your system from that garbage and come back to me with pure blood. In the meantime, take these for pain." She pushed the opiates into his hand. "And take these to help with appetite." Another orange bottle filled his other hand. "Any questions?"
She looked at Drew and seemed to sense that she might have gone too far.

Drew could have sworn a button must have undone itself on her blouse, as now her exposed cleavage was unmissable. Jo leaned in and gave a seated Drew a hug, pressing her exposed breasts into his neck and chin.

"I'm sorry if I got mad. I'm just so worried about you." Her flirty smile was back on her beautiful face.

"It's ok," Drew said, trying to sound placated as his eyes slowly rose from her cleavage.

He didn't want Jo to know that he was aware of what she was. Not yet. "Two months, then?"

"Yep." Jo was still smiling.

Drew shook the orange bottles at her.

"Thanks for these, by the way."

"Any time. Tell your dad I said hi, by the way," Jo called after Drew as he walked down the hall and out of the building.

Jo's attempt to seem close and friendly by mentioning his dad just came off as odd. Drew wondered how the hell she knew him. Thoughts came to mind of his dad's multiple affairs and the panties from the pretty Indian lady neighbor when he was a kid. But that didn't make sense. She was classy and beautiful, and dad was a slimy pill-head and everyone knew it.

Drew hurried out of the clinic, now acutely aware that Stephanie had been waiting with the boys for an hour or longer. He tossed the pills into the glove box with disdain. The more he took them, the further under Jo's spell he became and the closer he became to being just like dad and Chris. This would be his last refill. He didn't care how much better they made him feel. It was always just brief relief, followed by feeling guilty and angry until the next dose.

"What took so long? Your brother texted and said he had something for you, but he would meet you at seven at your parents' house." Stephanie was clearly irritated but trying to be understanding.

"She's such a fucking bitch." Drew clutched the steering wheel and pushed the starter on the Nova. "The only thing she did was get upset that I smoked some pot to feel better. But honestly, if I had to pick one or the other, pills or pot, I would pick pot. It makes me puke a lot less, and it makes me hungry enough to eat. All those stupid pills do is make me not care how shitty our life is…I'm done with them…I'm not going to refill it again…I'm gonna just ween myself off with this last refill, so I don't go through withdrawals too bad."

Drew was almost yelling now. His mind was already made up. He was done with the pills and Jo.

"Really? Calm down." Stephanie seemed scared. "I didn't think doctors cared about weed like that. Are you sure you don't want to take them anymore, though, even if just on like bad days for the pain?" Stephanie suggested, almost sounding panicky herself.

"Nope, I'm over it. Those things are pure evil. Look what it did to dad and Chris," Drew said. "And what they've started doing to me."

The Nova roared and Drew left some rubber in the parking lot as he sped home. He wanted to make dinner before he had to go pick up his weed from Chris. By then, the pill that was currently coursing through his veins would have been metabolized and he would definitely need to smoke a bowl to take the edge off.

***

Just as Drew finished cooking and the boys sat down for dinner, there was a knock at the front door.

It was Chris. He was early. Drew had expected to meet him at his parents' in an hour.

He looked sickly and high and anxious.

He looked like Nick and Jay had looked on Halloween.

Chapter 25

Snow started to fall on the already-blanketed ground. A stiff wind was blowing through the pines along both sides of the road, knocking clumps of collected snow off their branches in snowball-sized clusters. The photo negative effect the snow had on the landscape was back, as well as the eerie feeling that followed it. The familiar drive down Lime Kiln Road felt like driving in an alien landscape. Gravel kicked up behind the Nova as the back tires tried to get a grip on the slightly packed snow and the unserviced road.

"You should pull over at the end by the cattle guard," Chris said sullenly from the passenger seat.

Drew could feel an odd vibe coming from him, more so than usual.

"Yeah, I was going to break up a nug and load a bowl anyway," Drew agreed.

They stayed quiet the last couple of miles of the back road until it met the highway. When they neared the end, Drew pulled past the cattle guard and then backed into the small clearing cut into the pines. From between the seats, Drew fished out the large baggie of weed that Chris had just delivered and picked out a bowl-sized bud. He pulled the stems out of the bud and broke it apart on top of a CD case until it was a sticky green pile, free of any stems. Drew poked the pile more diligently now, looking for seeds or husks that would give it an off flavor.

"There's no seeds in that stuff. We got it from our guy in Denver. It's Hydro," Chris said, not looking up from the sheet of tinfoil he was folding into a W shape, seeming to know what Drew was looking for in the pile of weed.

"Oh, nice, thanks." Drew jammed the pile of cleaned weed into the bowl of his glass pipe.

The twin flashes of flames danced from either of the front seats as Drew took a rip from his pipe and Chris started chasing a chunk of some pill around the foil sheet with the flame. An audible hiss was coming from the gutted pen Chris was sucking the pill vapors up with. Drew realized smoking pot was a crime, but looking at his brother, smoking pills like that felt dangerous and on a different level than pot.

They sat in silence, each getting his fill of their drug of choice.

Drew waited for Chris to finish as he tucked his own paraphernalia away. He looked out the windows at the photo negative landscape and his mind wandered with the hydroponic weed. He suddenly realized the tree line was a perfect hiding spot for cops or monsters. Drew lost himself in the paranoia and scanned the trees and roadside for threats or cherries from a cop car, even though they were thirty miles from any town with police.

Now with the thoughts of monsters fresh in Drew's mind, he knew he had to talk to his brother about the real monsters, and tonight had to be the night. He didn't know how much further Chris could fall before he couldn't be saved, before Nick and Jay got their claws in him. The few rips he had taken from his pipe had loosened him up enough to say what he knew he needed to.

Drew took a deep breath and let it out.

"Hey man, by the way, what the hell are you doing hanging out with Nick and Jay anyway? Those guys are not what you think they are," Drew started clumsily. He wasn't trying to start a fight, but realized his approach was abrasive. His gears weren't turning smoothly.

Maybe it was the pills and the pot.

"Oh, yeah? How so?" Chris said, seeming uninterested.

He didn't let his lighter go out, and the hissing from the pen resumed as it chased the blackening pill.

"They just are bad people, dude. Not even counting all the stupid shit they got in trouble for and all the stuff I did with them. There is some stuff they were planning with Steph that I can't tell you about, but I promise you, if you knew, you'd feel different about them. They are monsters. And not the fake kind."

Drew swallowed hard as Chris's lighter clicked off and the hissing from the pen case stopped. He still didn't look up.

"Like, I don't know if they are like real monsters, but they are as close as you can get in human skin. And just seeing you tonight...you're starting to look like them, man. Your skin is bad, your eyes are all sunken in and dark, you don't even seem like yourself anymore."

"How would you even know?" Chris looked at him coldly.

"What do you mean how would I know? You're my brother. I think I'd be able to see a change in you even if we don't spend a lot of time together." Drew felt insulted.

"No, I don't care about that. I mean, how do you know that I don't know what they were planning with Stephanie in high school?" Chris said, breaking off another piece of a pill to chase around with his pen casing and lighter.

Drew's mouth fell open and his pipe fell from his hand into his lap. He had no words, no solution. The words Chris had just spoken stuck in his gears, grinding them to a halt.

"You might as well start driving back toward town, man. And fuck you for judging me. My skin is bad, my eyes are dark? Like I even care what you think. You've been the same judgmental prick my whole life. Always better at everything, always perfect, always everyone's favorite. But that's all coming to an end…Dad doesn't like you any more than I do. Mom could give less than a shit about anything but the casino. People in town don't trust you anymore because the apple don't fall far from the tree, and you are an unemployed junkie loser just like me." Chris finished his hateful rant and resumed smoking his pill.

Drew picked the pipe up off his lap and ripped the glovebox open, tossing it inside with no regard for if he broke it. His blood was beginning to boil.

He pulled the trigger on the quick shift and slapped it into D harder than usual. The Nova slipped on the snowpack as he pulled back onto the gravel road.

"I'm not a fucking junkie like you. I haven't even taken a pill today after my creepy fucking hospital visit and I don't plan to again. Those things are changing you and I don't plan on following you and dad into that rut. And as far as mom and dad go, they may as well already be dead anyway. They stopped living when we were kids…" Drew hesitated, trying to stifle his anger. "And if you really know what Nick and Jay were planning in high school and you still hang out with them, maybe it's already too late for you, too."

BAM!

A fist-sized ball of snow hit the windshield and forced Drew to swerve out of instinct.

The Nova barely held onto the road.

The wind was howling now. The snow had stopped falling from the sky and was only coming from the branches in huge clumps as the wind knocked them around.

Drew scanned the tree line, feeling vulnerable, like he was falling into a chokepoint.

There was a clearing on the left where Drew took the boys to feed the horses that lived there. Drew noticed the horses weren't in the barn like usual. He looked farther into the clearing and could see the horses were running in circles like mad in the field of snow, as if they were being chased. The last thing Drew looked at before refocusing on the road was Chris, who was visibly angry but smiling.

"Better watch out, you don't want to crash your precious Nova." Chris crumpled the tin foil W and pushed it into his pocket, followed by the gutted pen. "I'm better friends with Nick and Jay than I ever was with you." Chris's eyes seemed to flash in the darkness of the cab. "So, I suggest you watch what you say about them when you're around me, because they aren't finished with you yet and I haven't even gotten started."

OOOOAAAAHHHHRRR...

The sound came from the field adjacent to them.

Drew saw the horses were gathered on the far side of the field, now huddling for safety. The rest of the field was empty until it met the tree line and a hill where the evergreens got thick.

Drew knew the roar.

It had haunted his nightmares for years.

The Gougers were back.

His mind reeled and flashed back to his attempts at trapping it as a kid and then to high school and running for his life on the highway and Joe and Grandpa. The highway he ran for his life on was only half a mile from them now as the gravel road ran parallel to it all the way back to Point of Rocks. Drew never considered he was living in the Gougers' back yard at the white house this whole time.

The Nova lost traction and lurched toward the ditch. Drew nearly screamed and hit the gas pedal, trying to use RPMs to get himself out of the swerve.

The Nova lurched again at the sudden boost of power and almost hit the other ditch, which was full of snow. After a brief struggle, the tires listened to the steering wheel and got most of the way back onto the road. A couple more minor corrections and Drew was safely back in the center of the lanes. However, his eyes were still on the tree line looking for the Gougers.

"Did you hear it?" Drew asked Chris, forgetting their fight momentarily.

"Yeah, so what?" Chris seemed unfazed by the roar.

Drew said nothing and hit the gas, now in a hurry to be away from the hills and this conversation.

He drove back to the edge of Point of Rocks as fast as he could without losing control again. His mind was busy fighting with his feelings about the person sitting next to him who used to be his brother. Something was different about him now, something sinister, and Drew was pretty sure there was no coming back.

Drew stopped the Nova outside of town, a few junk-strewn blocks away from his parents' house, and didn't even bother putting the Nova into P.

"You better get out here. I gotta get home," Drew said, not looking over.

"Yeah, good plan. You better go protect your family," Chris said and chuckled.

It felt like a threat.

There was no goodbye, just a slam of the car door as Drew spun out. Drew raced home, praying to God he wasn't going to find his family stomped into mush by the Gougers or worse…Nick and Jay's unfinished business came to mind.

***

Everyone was fine at home.

Except Drew.

His mind never slowed down, even after he went to bed. His eyes were going from window to window, doorway to doorway. Every creak was a monster coming for his family. It stayed like that until late in the night, or early in the morning.

At some point, Drew couldn't take it anymore and took his pistol out to sleep on the couch. The TV brought him some relief, but there was an aching in his joints, and he felt terrible.

It was the lack of pills.

His mind raced, but every solution came back to one answer.

"Take a pill and relax, get some sleep, feel better. You have to feel better to protect your family."

The voices of his dad and every person who ever gave him bad advice echoed in his mind until Drew had no choice but to relent. He had to acknowledge his own desire as well. They offered instant relief from everything.

Drew tiptoed to the bathroom, not wanting Stephanie to know what he was doing.

"Crap," he said to himself in the slowly graying house.

The rising sun felt like a deadline—Drew knew Stephanie always woke up early with it.

Standing in the bathroom looking at the open bottle of pills, Drew had two thoughts. Take them all and just be done with it. And, there are fewer pills in the bottle than there should be.

Neither mattered, as another impulse overcame him.

It was an impulse prodded along by another voice with multiple layers, yelling out a warning. A combined collection of voices and wisdom calling out from people he once respected and loved. Joe and Grandpa were the most prominent.

"Watch out for that rut, idiot."

The pills clinked on the porcelain and before he could change his mind, Drew was tipping the flush bucket up and washing away the temptation. His arms and legs were aching like he was having growing pains, his upper abdomen cried out in anger, even his inner dialog was screaming at him.

It was too late to listen to his body or his mind; it was done. The pills were gone.

Drew watched the pills disappear down the toilet drain. The gurgling of the bowl let him know it was finished.

Drew was done, at least with them. He thought about grabbing his stash of weed and doing the same, but the prospect of turning into a living skeleton from not being able to eat was unbearable. His kids needed him and maybe he needed pot, at least until they found out what was wrong with his guts.

Before he left the bathroom, Drew caught a look at himself in the mirror when he turned to shut off the light. Stickboy was there, but so was Drew. He was still mostly himself. The pills hadn't robbed him of everything yet. Somewhere, inside his boiling guts, Drew knew that if he ever wanted to get his family out of the rut, he was going to need both Stickboy and Drew. Stickboy had experience keeping his head down and trudging forward.

***

Drew sweated on the couch of unknown origins, tossing and turning, not finding any comfort anywhere, sleeping intermittently for a while.

Stephanie slept in by accident.

Her alarm never went off, she tried to explain as she rushed to get ready for work. Drew couldn't validate this since he was on the couch, but something in her voice told him it was a lie.

Her explanation came out in a gravelly voice an octave or so lower than usual. The thought of what could cause the voice change was too scary to even consider, so Drew chalked it up to a bad night's sleep. He was feeling too awful to even think about anything except how the lack of pills was making him feel. His body was aching even worse now, and he had been dry heaving since he flushed the pills.

Stephanie left, and the puking continued. Drew set the boys up with a movie and some Pop-Tarts to try to distract them, but the older they got, the more they knew something was wrong with him, and they were on edge.

By the time he was supposed to be making lunch for the boys, Drew was much worse.

There was nobody to haul water to flush with, so the bowl slowly filled with bile. There was no hot water, or cold, so there was no shower to wash the slimy sweat off his body. Drew was leaning against the wall in the bathroom, not even bothering to leave at this point. He thought about closing his eyes for a minute, but thinking about sleeping in the bathroom reminded him of the Ipecac night and Uncle Alvin. His mouth watered at the thought of the Ipecac, and he lurched forward.

The dark green bile came out red this time. Blood-red.

Drew saw the change of color in the bowl and his head started to spin. A drop of sweat fell from his nose into the horrid mess in the bowl, with a plop instead of a splash. His vision blurred, and Drew could feel the world floating back and forth like a wave. He knew he was passing out, so he tried to lean back on the…

The world went black.

Drew could hear muffled crying in his dreams. Then there was screaming that went on for longer than anyone could muster. The high-pitched screaming ended only when the bumping and rolling feeling began. There was cool air on him at one point during the bouncing session, but it ended with a warm soft feeling like a towel from a dryer was laid on him. In his dream, Drew opened his eyes and he was in the back of an ambulance. In the back with him were Jo, Nick, and Jay. Drew tried to scream, but the world was spinning away again, and he was back in blackness.

***

The sheets still felt warm on top of him, and his pillow crunched under his head in an unfamiliar way when he rolled over. Feeling confused, Drew opened his eyes and saw a tiled floor and hospital equipment.

Stephanie was in a wooden rocking chair, watching TV.

"Crap." Drew didn't need an explanation, as the memory of passing out in the bathroom was still fresh in his mind.

"Oh, my God, you scared me," Stephanie said. "The boys called me at work and said you yelled something from the bathroom and when they went in there, you were sleeping on the floor and wouldn't wake up. I had to call the ambulance, but I beat them home."

"Sorry…Where are the boys?" Drew felt their absence.

"I left them with your mom and dad," Stephanie said, furrowing her brow.

Drew shot up in bed.

"We have to go get them." Drew stood up and instantly felt dizzy.

He grabbed her purse from the chair to hand it to her so he could get his clothes that were neatly folded under it. He went to pass the purse to Stephanie and paused. Something in the side pocket caught his eye.

It was a familiar little baggie.

Drew tugged on the corner and pulled the baggie out, and the little white pills bounced around inside.

Drew had been right about her gravelly voice, but now he knew for sure. The thought of her taking the pills scared him more than any monster.

"Stephanie, what the fuck is this?" Drew asked.

A nurse walked in and seemed shocked to see Drew standing up. Drew quickly stuffed the baggie back into the purse and held it out for Stephanie to grab. The look in her eyes was full of fear and embarrassment.

"Oh, you're awake. How are you feeling? Do you need something for the pain?" the nurse said in a pleasant, caring tone.

"NO, WE HAVE TO GO NOW!" Drew yelled in an uncharacteristic flash of public anger.

***

The Nova came to a skidding halt in the gravel driveway. Snow and rocks went flying. Dad's daily driver was gone, so Drew parked in its space closest to the house. He left Stephanie in the Nova. She had tried to talk to him on the way home about the pills, but Drew was too intent on getting to the boys to pay her any attention. Also, he was mad and knew anything he would say right now would only hurt her feelings.

The back door of mom and dad's house was locked, so Drew pounded as hard as he could. He waited a few seconds and let the door have it again. Finally, the interior door to the porch opened and two silent boys answered the door.

They looked stressed out and tired, but they were alive.

A sense of relief washed over Drew. The boys snuck past him and around the other side of the Nova to have Stephanie let them slide in behind her seat.

"Mom!" Drew yelled into the house, no longer feeling welcome inside.

Nothing.

"Where is Grandma?" Drew asked, leaning back into the Nova and looking at Robert.

"She is with Grandpa. They went to Deadwood," Robert said, looking sullen.

"Jesus Christ, those people," Drew said angrily.

He knew that meant his boys had spent the night with Chris.

There was too much on his plate to get into another fight with Chris, so Drew got in the Nova and drove them back to the white house before he could change his mind and kick his ass.

The boys went straight to their room without a word. Drew wondered if maybe Stephanie hadn't told them to lie low while they talked about what Drew had found in her purse.

As soon as the boys were out of earshot, Drew started.

"Why the FU…Why would you do that to yourself and us? Who were you even getting them from?" The venom was ready to flow so he bit his tongue. Being mean was only going to hurt both of them.

"I'm so sorry. I've only been taking them for a little bit. Everything was just so bad, and I wasn't getting any sleep. When I looked at you after you got them and how good you were sleeping, I just wanted to try it to get a few nights of sleep. But they just helped with everything, so it didn't feel bad at first. I didn't even notice any singing or anything when I took them. Then something changed and when I realized I was stealing the pills that were making you feel better, I just asked Carol if she had any. She didn't even make me pay her for these."

"Yeah, well, guess what. She will charge you for the next ones and the next ones and the ones after that. Anyone who would give you those or sell them to you isn't your friend." Drew had never liked her big-mouth friend Carol anyway, and this gave him every reason to dislike her forever. "And I know shit has been awful lately, but getting stuck in that rut is even worse than the one we are in. I'm not taking them anymore, so you won't have mine to steal. So, if you're going to keep taking them at this point, you're taking money we all need to survive." Drew hesitated, sensing the elephant in the room. "I know I smoke pot that takes food from all our mouths, but without it, I'm afraid I'm going to die. And honestly, I love you too much to watch you turn into a monster like one of them because of the pills. I'll do whatever I have to do to keep you away from those fucking things." Drew wasn't lying. "I don't care if I have to chain you to our bed. I will NOT let you do that to yourself."

Drew was crying now. He felt like he would throw up at any second.

"No, I promise I will never take another pill ever again. I love you, too. I don't want to get stuck in a rut, either." Stephanie was crying, too.

Drew could tell she wasn't lying.

"OK, then we go through withdrawals together," Drew joked, trying to lighten the mood.

A rumbling interrupted the conversation. It was coming from Drew's stomach.

"You need to eat something. What do you want? Toast?" Stephanie knew Drew well.

The tension eased, and they smiled at each other.

"Yeah, I better. But honestly, I don't know how you feel about it after the pill stuff but I don't think my stomach will settle down enough to let me eat unless I smoke some pot. I don't feel hungry enough and without it, I'll prolly just puke it all up anyway." Drew felt embarrassed by the admission, but out of anything he tried, pot was the only thing that helped.

He grabbed his keys from the table, intending on going for a drive.

"No, don't leave, just smoke on the porch…Boys, do you want some lunch?" Stephanie gave him her answer about how she felt about the pot.

Drew rolled a joint while the boys sat at the table silently watching Stephanie cook. They looked exhausted, all three of them.

Drew didn't want to stink up the house with pot, so he went to the back yard. The sun was setting, so before he sparked the joint, Drew scanned the back yard and the tree line for Gougers and other monsters.

The coast was clear.

He flicked the lighter and took a toke to get the joint going.

"NOOOOOO."

A scream came from inside the house.

"Don't fire my dad," Tyler was screaming at the window and running toward the porch.

He appeared in the doorway and Drew hid the joint. Tyler's eyes were locked on the lighter in his hand.

"What? What's wrong?" Drew asked the sobbing Tyler.

"I don't want you to get fired, please. I'm sorry," Tyler pleaded.

Stephanie appeared behind Tyler and put her hands on his shoulders.

"He's not on fire, he's just smoking a cigarette," Stephanie fibbed for Drew.

"No, fired," Tyler tried to explain, obviously confused.

"It's ok. I won't get fired. Don't worry, I don't even have a job right now," Drew tried to joke.

"Just go finish that back there and I'll calm him down. Your toast is almost ready," Stephanie offered.

Drew agreed and walked back behind the garden toward his secret spot at the quarry, though the thoughts of the Gougers' yell the night before kept him off the hill and close enough to the back door for a sprint to safety if need be.

He finished his joint, trying to relax and not think of monsters, and about not taking any more pills, and Stephanie not taking any more pills, and Tyler worried about him being "fired." By the time the joint was a roach, Drew's stomach felt better, but his mind was racing. His stomach growled, letting him know it was toast time regardless of how his mind felt.

Drew walked back to the house, opened the back door, and immediately smelled burnt toast. Stephanie was in the living room crying audibly. Drew raced to the stove, flipped off the burner, and popped the toaster, exposing his charred dinner. He hurried to the living room to check on Stephanie.

"What's going on?" Drew asked, feeling confused and slightly high.

"Oh, my God, Drew, your brother molested Tyler."

Chapter 26

Usually, the motel room would have felt like a vacation from the white house, but today it felt heavy and uncomfortable. Oddly enough, since the mock exorcism, the shadow on the porch and the singing ghosts had not returned, and the white house for a minute almost felt comfortable, almost like home. Drew chalked the missing ghosts up to good luck rather than the act of exorcising the house, although there was no time to enjoy the missing spirits, because in their absence, the house itself had become a monster. The frozen pipes, the power going out any time the wind blew, that same wind blowing through the cracks in the baseboards where they kept towels rolled up to keep out the daylight and the snow. Now the toilet had stopped flushing, even with the aid of the flushing buckets.

Earl, their landlord, shined Drew on every time he called, saying he would be out the next week or next month or in the spring when things thawed. He didn't care as long as the rent check kept showing up in the mail.

Stephanie ordered the boys a pizza to cheer them up in the motel after the therapist's appointment, but it sat on the bed, mostly untouched. The mood in the motel room was sour and Nickelodeon droned on in the background.

Any other time they had a chance to stay at a motel, it was an escape from their lives, and they would be at the pool pretending they were on a beach somewhere, even if they were just in Rapid City. There was too much sadness tonight, and no one felt like going to the beach.

The therapist, provided by Social Services, confirmed what Drew and Stephanie had gathered from Tyler's confusing and infuriating retelling of the night Drew's parents left him with Chris so they could go to Deadwood. There was a lot of pointing to private parts rather than talking during his retelling. One thing Tyler did remember was that Chris told him that if he said anything about what he did to him, grandpa, grandma, mom, everyone in the family would get "fired" and the whole town would be mad at them, even his dad. The nail in the coffin, not only for Drew and Stephanie, but the state-provided therapist as well, was the detail about the white pee that Chris had put on Tyler that came from his privates.

Drew looked at Tyler now in the motel room, looking so sad, sitting on the bed, eating his pizza slowly, letting Nickelodeon take him to another place for a little bit.

The lump in Drew's throat grew, and he had to pretend to use the bathroom.

Drew stood at the sink and splashed his face to mask the tears. He looked at Stickboy in the mirror and had never hated him more. Drew thought he looked like the coward he was always afraid of being.

The night he found out what Chris did to Tyler, his first instinct was to take his own suicide pistol and use it on Chris. Stephanie only stopped him by having the keys to the Nova buried in her hand, begging him not to do it. Even then, she had to hold him in the driveway to keep from walking to town. Eventually, her logic had won, and she convinced Drew that the best way to get revenge was to go to the police.

It seemed like a good idea at the time. Unfortunately, gossip was the primary hobby of everyone in town. The police were less than helpful to the pill junkie family who were having some sort of infighting.

The police suggested Social Services, and after jumping through multiple hoops, Drew and Stephanie found themselves at a dead end. They needed the therapist to recommend an investigation, and they needed the district attorney to bring charges.

Now, standing here in the motel bathroom staring a coward in the eye, he regretted not taking action that night and shooting Chris. Drew figured with a crime of passion, he would have been out of jail in under five years or so. Now, weeks later, it would be first degree homicide with all the premeditation he had been doing. If he shot him now, he would never see his family outside of plexiglass again.

In all the confusion of the past few weeks, there was one thing Drew couldn't help but consider. A nagging but insignificant detail that wouldn't go away. Why wasn't Chris scared of the Gougers the night he revealed himself to be a monster, or ever? Even growing up, the story of the Gougers never scared Chris. Drew had turned his gears for hours, maybe days, on the detail that didn't really matter while his life was falling apart around him. But after much internal conflict, Drew came up with the only reasonable answer he could find. Maybe Chris had always been a monster. One that was too close for him to see clearly. And, maybe, Chris wasn't afraid of the Gougers because monsters don't attack other monsters.

In hindsight, Drew was becoming acutely aware that monsters were everywhere.

The DA who was supposed to bring charges against Chris was as useless as Social Services. In fact, he was just another monster in a town that seemed to be full of them. After speaking with him and after finding out who his wife was, Drew and Stephanie both knew there would never be any justice for Tyler.

***

Drew's last hospital visit with Jo hadn't gone so well.

He hadn't taken or refilled any of the Oxys and had also refused to give a blood draw or urine sample to the nurse. The wait in the small doctor's office for Jo was punishing, Drew thought intentionally so.

Jo came in red-faced almost an hour later again with no apology or explanation. She demanded to know why he wasn't filling his prescription and why he had refused labs. Drew had explained that he wasn't taking the pills anymore and anything that she wanted to know about his blood, she could just ask him.

That was when her anger started with no pretenses.

"You listen to me. If you're not going to take my advice or my pills, then why the fuck are you even coming here? You think pot is helping you but it's illegal and with my husband being the district attorney, all it would take for me to get your kids taken away from you and your bitch wife is a casual mention of your illicit habits over dinner…" Jo paused to catch her breath. "And if you don't think I know what Chris and your dad are up to with my cut from their last run to Denver, you are mistaken. Your whole family is trash. The whole town knows it and now that my husband has someone to pin the target on, if our racket goes sideways, we have a layer of immunity you can't even imagine…And guess what. There isn't a thing you can do about it. You tell your dad we need to talk or his little side business is going to end with a prison sentence."

Josephine looked terrifying.

The beauty was gone.

***

Drew thought back on the conversation in Jo's office and the storming out he did after her rant. A week later, at the district attorney's office, Drew knew this hoop was a dead end. But at this point, if he and Stephanie didn't finish jumping through the hoops set up for them by the state, they would be the criminals for neglecting to care for their children.

Drew didn't even listen as Jo's husband, the DA, as he explained the evidence was flimsy and the therapist would only go so far in court. All the while, a smug grin was plastered on his knowing face.

Drew and Stephanie had driven back to the white house feeling guilty and angry in silence that night. They felt shame for a crime they didn't commit, and Chris was smoking pills with Nick and Jay at Drew's parents' home. Sides were chosen.

That was the same night Drew went on his one and only suicide drive.

He left alone, not wanting to subject the boys to the terror of going with their dad so he could kill himself. But like his own dad, Drew had chickened out. He told himself it was because he was scared of what the rut would do to his family if he wasn't there, but he wasn't sure that was true. He was probably just a coward, Stickboy always had been.

Instead, Drew drove back home in shame and slunk into bed next to a sleeping, but sober Stephanie.

***

Now, in the motel, after the last follow-up appointment with the state-provided therapist, the last hoop, the legal portion of the molestation was over. There was no justice. Just a promise for aftercare once they got insurance figured out. That meant Drew needed a job, which in his current condition wasn't possible.

Drew knew the only option their family had was to move on. They had to forget the molestation ever happened. They, he, Tyler, couldn't relive the trauma day after day dwelling on it, living on the fumes of hatred.

It was another trap the rut had set for them.

The ultimate chokepoint.

The single best way to live in the lower portion of the middle or the upper crust of the low. To hate, to live on that hatred, to become a Midwest monster and forget who you are.

If Robert and Tyler ever had questions or needed therapy, Drew and Stephanie would be there for them. But their part in this now was to be the best parents they could be and to keep the boys as happy as possible. Maybe, if they filled their heads with so many fun new memories, there wouldn't be room left for the bad ones. But with every part of their lives falling apart at the seams, it was going to be hard.

Drew and Stickboy shook their faces at each other in the mirror and looked at the pile of folded swim clothes and towels on the bathroom rack.

The hopeful swimsuits stared back at him, wanting to be at the beach.

***

"Ok, boys, let's GOOOOO." Drew faked excitement for the boys and tossed their swimming shorts at their faces.

"Wait, what? I thought you didn't feel like swimming." Robert looked at his bare-chested dad with his Hawaiian-style shorts on, apparently ready to go swimming.

"How the heck can you go on vacation and not go swimming? I was just starving and had to eat something first." Drew clapped at Stephanie. "You, too, goofball, let's go."

Drew tossed Stephanie her bathing suit.

Stephanie smiled and pranced to the bathroom to change.

"Wait, are we on vacation?" Tyler asked, speaking for the first time since the therapist.

"Duh, did you miss the beach out there?" Drew pointed to the heated indoor pool of the Holiday Inn.

"DAAAD, that's not a beach, that's a pool." Robert dropped trou and was putting his shorts on.

Tyler ran to wait by the bathroom so he could do the same in private.

Tyler's sudden need for privacy stung Drew but he smiled through it and continued the game.

"You're crazy. I see sand and hot water and umbrella tables and waves. That's a beach as far as I'm concerned." Drew smiled.

"Oh, ok, I didn't know that was a beach." Robert seemed to almost believe Drew at this point.

"LET'S GOOO," Tyler came screaming out of the bathroom and was smiling like a madman. Stephanie was behind him looking almost as excited.

Stephanie got busy trying to put her hair up while the boys got their flip-flops on.

"We gotta wait for mom…hurry up, Steph, these guys gotta go swimming before the sun sets and the sharks come out," Drew said, waving his hands, hurrying an already rushing Stephanie.

"I'm coming." She giggled and caught up.

"Wait, there are sharks, too?" Robert was full of questions now.

"You bet. That's why we gotta stick together. Otherwise, the sharks or other monsters from the deep dark abyss could get hold of us and drag us to the bottom to live with them, forever in darkness."

Drew loved scaring them.

Being scared was fun if you could put the scary away when you were done. Scary was the spice that made a middle-class rut a little more exciting.

"OK, Robert, you stick with me. I seen a show about sharks one time that said if you punch them in the gills, they'll swim away," Tyler said, laughing as he trotted, not ran like the pool's warning sign instructed.

Tyler was joining in on the fun, acting brave and tough. Drew was glad to see his resilience. He was going to be fine, as long as he and Stephanie gave him the opportunity and the memories. Kids could be tough as hell. Drew thought back on his monster hunting days in Mountain.

They swam until midnight. The pool closed at ten, the sign also stated, but there was no one else in the pool and there was no staff who cared. They laughed and swam and Drew told scary stories until the boys' lips started to turn blue from the cooler-than-it-should-be heated pool.

***

Leaving the motel the next morning to go back to Point of Rocks and the monstrous white house was one of the hardest things Drew had ever done.

The boys wanted McDonald's for breakfast, but Drew and Stephanie were tapped out. The pizza ate the last of their cash last night. Instead, Drew made a game of driving fast in the Nova and passing safely when he could. He pretended the whole way home to be in a race so they could get home to eat before they all starved and had to eat each other like at the Donner Pass. The boys laughed and pointed out potential slow cars to pass cos mom was looking too thin and they were getting pretty hungry. It made the painful trip fun for them.

There was no shadow on the porch of the white house waiting to race them up the steps when they pulled in. Drew laughed to himself at the possibility the exorcism had worked in real life, however slim the chances were.

The house stank. It was coming from the un-flushing toilet. The boys pretended to choke on the fumes, and Drew grabbed the leftover sage rolls and lit the ends of them.

"Here, boys, I'll open windows. You chase the smell and the spirits out of here before we all choke to death on them." Drew thought another round of sage couldn't hurt as far as ghosts went and would only improve the smell.

The pain in Drew's stomach was letting him know it was time for a few rips on his pipe. He didn't want the boys to see even if he was no longer ashamed of smoking, so he grabbed his keys and rattled them at Stephanie, letting her know he was going out.

The Nova roared to life.

It was one sound Drew never got tired of. He gave it a little extra gas once he hit the main road and sent clouds of dust up in the air behind him as he flew away. The dust overtook him a mile later once he had to slow to a crawl while he drove through Point of Rocks. Smoke from the bowl curled up through the steering wheel and hit his eyes, making them water.

Out of habit, Drew drove up past mom and dad's house, not intending to stop but just circling town long enough to finish his bowl.

Mom's car was the only one in the driveway, so they were probably at Deadwood again, meaning Chris was home alone.

A perfect chokepoint.

The words ran through Drew's mind as he premeditated some more on his brother, who was home alone now. The thoughts of all the things he wanted to do to his brother swam in his mind. Drew knew he wouldn't act them out, but fantasizing felt nice. He tried not to let the darkness of his thoughts overwhelm him, but anytime he thought of his family, it was a struggle.

As Drew drove past the house, he got a shock that spun him out of his mental rut. He could see three people standing in his parents' back yard looking toward the road.

It was Chris, Nick, and Jay.

They looked like they were expecting him. The Nova probably let them know he was coming a mile away.

Every hair on Drew's arms stood up. Seeing them after expecting his brother to be alone and vulnerable made him feel like the vulnerable one. All six hollow eyes followed him as he drove past. Their graying translucent skin almost glowed with grease in the sunlight. All the sores on their faces were highlighted in bright red. Then Drew noticed something that made his skin crawl even more.

They were laughing.

Not only that, but they were pointing and laughing.

Nick and Jay had apparently gotten the last laugh by violating his son and brother in the same motion.

Drew wondered how long they had planned to attack his family to get back at him. Was it Nick's idea? Was it Jay's? Was it Chris all along? How much did Chris know, and when did he know it? Did Chris know about their plan to rape and kill Stephanie, or was it his idea to begin with? Did Chris know that Drew was involved in the beginning when they were planning in the notebook? Was it Nick and Jay who brought up the idea of molesting his son or was it Chris who took the opportunity to them?

When could Drew find their chokepoints and get revenge?

The questions ran through his mind faster than he could process them.

Drew's instincts had him getting out of the car and pummeling the three of them. He was sick and thin, but the rage in his belly wouldn't let him down.

But this was another trap, a chokepoint for Drew's entire family.

The rage inside Drew was being used against him now.

The monsters needed Drew to stoop to their level. The gossip in town already had him in bed with pill dealers and child molesters. Drew had spent a lifetime earning goodwill from a community that turned its back overnight. If he went to jail, neither he, Stephanie nor the boys would ever have a chance of clawing their way out of this white trash rut.

He punched the gas as hard as he could.

The Nova let out the roar he wished he could.

Drew knew one thing after that drive. He couldn't live like this anymore.

***

The planning started that night.

The internet was slow, but it worked. After searching marijuana laws, cost of living, healthcare, and distance from Point of Rocks and the Midwest, and the Gougers, and the other monsters…Drew found what he was looking for. Now he just had to convince Stephanie to abandon her family and the town she went to high school in.

It wasn't very difficult at all. Stephanie was on board within five minutes. She really was perfect. She would follow Drew anywhere for any reason. All Drew had to do was keep her safe, and sober, but those might be the same things.

Drew made some phone calls the next day with a doctor who did telephone appointments for green cards for medical patients. It cost $200 up front, but Stephanie got paid and Drew would make ramen noodles taste good for the next month to cut corners. The next call was to an ad on Craigslist. Drew was able to negotiate $500 a month until they left to secure the house and pay the first and last month's rent ahead of time.

There were other hoops to jump through, but for the first time in a long time, Drew felt hopeful.

They didn't tell the boys about the plan, so they wouldn't get their hopes up if the rut reared its ugly head and everything turned to shit again. Instead, Drew and Stephanie got on their computer and looked up pictures of Astoria, Oregon. They found one they both liked and copied it as the desktop wallpaper on the computer.

That picture stayed on the monitor as a motivational background for weeks.

All spring, they scrimped and saved and cut corners and ate awful food, while trying to pretend it wasn't awful. Drew threw up a thousand times. The house stank worse every day. The pipes finally unfroze, but they had burst, and the house flooded, so the landlord just shut it off completely. Nothing went smoothly, and every day, there was a new fight.

It was wonderful.

It was a way out.

They just had to keep their heads down and focus on the goal. And, once they had waded through enough misery, they would be on the other side with a fresh start.

Every day, Drew and Stephanie woke up one dollar closer to having enough money to leave, one more sunrise down in the white house, one more headache to get through. The path out of the rut was clear, and the excitement grew. They weren't telling anyone they were leaving and they sure as hell weren't going to tell anyone where they were going.

The monsters were only as scary as you let them be.

The rut could only keep you as long as you let it. You always had the choice to crank the wheel.

Chapter 27

The Nova was absolutely screaming. The roar in the cab was deafening. Drew had his foot to the floor and the dotted yellow lines were blurring into one solid yellow line.

"DREW, SLOW DOWN!" Stephanie yelled from beside him.

"NOOOO, FASTER!" Tyler yelled excitedly from the back seat.

Drew gave it all he could. If the engine was going to blow, he wanted it to blow for him.

The engine only wanted more and gave him the boost of speed Tyler wanted.

The Oral Autobahn was coming to an end. It was a four-lane highway near the small town of Oral, built in the hope of an expansion that never came. Now it was a four-mile-long superhighway in the middle of nowhere going to nowhere.

Drew was forced to back off the gas, at least until he turned around and raced himself again on the way back to town. He had a pocket full of cash from selling almost everything he owned, including the suicide pistol, so Drew felt pretty good despite the nerves in his stomach.

They took one more lap on the deserted highway before heading back to Point of Rocks.

He dropped the boys and Stephanie off at the white house and made his way to the dealership Steph had worked at since

Drew had become too sick to work. When he pulled in and turned the engine off, the clicking of the hot metal expanding made him feel sad. He gave the wheel a pat and got out before he could start crying.

Ten minutes later, he was handing over the envelope with the Nova's title in it, the one he got from Joe years ago. The envelope with "For Drew" scrawled on it. Drew hesitated but gave it to the dealer along with the Nova's keys and an unsteady handshake. In return, the keys to the used minivan dropped into Drew's palm with a naked pink slip and no personalized envelope.

"Good luck. You guys be careful wherever you're headed. Steph made it seem like a big secret." Her old boss was prying.

"Thanks." Drew wasn't feeding the gossip monster.

He walked out without another word and looked back at the Nova one last time. He tried to be a man, but by the time the U-Haul laden minivan was pulling out of the car lot, the tears were falling freely. It wasn't a fair trade. His most prized possession for a heavily used minivan and a U-Haul rental. But it was the only way out of the rut. It was a sacrifice he was willing to make because he knew it meant a fresh start for everyone.

Drew hit the gas as hard as he could on the minivan.

It struggled to accelerate up the hill out of the dealership's parking lot.

It was a slow, somber drive back to the white house, but he pulled in with a smile.

"Ok, boys, let's get to work. Every box, every bag, everything we can fit needs to go." Drew was barking orders to distract himself from feeling sad. "Steph, will you help me grab the couch of unknown origins?" Drew smiled.

"Thanks for doing that," Stephanie said, referring to the Nova.

Stephanie gave Drew a hug and followed him into the house.

"Are we really taking that thing with us?" she asked, looking shocked.

"Uhh, yeah, I don't know how furnished the house we are moving into is. I haven't even seen it, but I don't want to move in without a couch, do you? Plus, I kinda got used to it." Drew was lifting one end, waiting for Stephanie.

"Ok." She grinned at him, trying to get him to smile.

The house seemed angry that they were leaving. It felt like something was chasing Drew every time he grabbed a new load for the U-Haul. He felt himself looking over his shoulder for the shadow man on the porch and jogging between trips, though he never appeared.

The last box Drew grabbed was the little locked black box with the Gouger claw and the photo of its burning eye. He hadn't opened it in years and wasn't about to jinx himself now. He tucked the box under his arm and carried it to the only free space left in the front of the van.

Drew had to stop to throw up two times, but after he smoked a bowl, when the heavy lifting was done, he felt better. He thought about the upcoming hospital visit in Portland and the prescription for medical marijuana that would erase some stigma and save him from buying weed from the monsters that sold drugs on the street. He didn't have much confidence in the medical field after Jo, but anyone other than a witch doctor was going to be an improvement.

***

They left at midnight.

There were no goodbyes to family or friends.

There was sadness, though. Drew was thinking of leaving the Black Hills, his fishing spots, his secret spot at the quarry, the agate hunting spots, the places he and Stephanie had made so many memories, good and bad. He knew Stephanie felt the same way, judging from her equal level of silence as they pulled out of Point of Rocks for the last time.

It felt hard to get a full breath as the tiny town disappeared in the minivan's rearview mirror.

But the farther they got from home, the easier it got to breathe.

The kids were snoring in the back seat by the time they hit the South Dakota border to Wyoming. The driving was easy, as the roads were empty and wide. Hours later, when Stephanie fell asleep next to him, Drew felt alone.

The blackness swallowed every detail around him except what his headlights could catch. His guard was up, and he felt nervous and vulnerable heading into the unknown.

As the incline started, and he made his way up the east side of the Continental Divide, the van slowed to a crawl, struggling under the load of the full trailer. Headlights appeared in the mirror behind him and started to catch up to the crawling minivan. Drew chugged along in the slow lane, wishing he could be in the center lane and away from the sheer drop just past the guardrail on his right. These were real mountains, not hills, and their scale was intimidating. For maybe the only time in his life, Drew was thankful for the darkness. It turned the drop-off into a void with no discernable bottom. He glanced into the void, feeling vertigo, and a sense of impending doom hit him like a punch to the face.

HOOONKKK!

The headlights had caught up from behind him. The driver seemed to want more room to get by and was angrily voicing his opinion with his horn. Drew hugged the chasm on his right and gripped the wheel. His stomach churned and sweat was already beading up on his forehead. The sweat on his palms made the old steering wheel feel slippery in his hands as he clenched it harder than necessary out of fear.

The truck finally got around him and immediately swerved into the slow lane in front of Drew, as he hit the brakes to avoid a collision. A half-dozen beer cans bounced out of the back of the truck and went spinning in all directions across the highway. Drew looked at the rest of the cargo in the back of the truck that was now in front of him, and he got goosebumps.

Whoever or whatever it was, was hauling two wheelchairs and a huge, oversized tricycle. A cage on the back of the tricycle was overflowing with beer cans.

Images of Bananahead and Moonface and the Can Man flashed in Drew's mind. The first monsters he had overcome made the bile crawl up his throat. The truck ahead of him gained some more distance. It swerved again sharply, sending more beer cans flying. Drew's van slowed even more with the increase of the incline and the heavy load. Eventually, the taillights disappeared into the void ahead of him.

The blackness that comforted him a moment ago returned to its usual sinister feeling. The cliff on his right had ended, and heavy woods now surrounded him. His passengers slept safely, and Drew continued sweating. He thought he had to about be at the top of the divide by now, but it just kept stretching out ahead of him. The highway was desolate, since the truck carrying the monster supplies had disappeared, but the feeling of being watched was overwhelming.

OOOOOAAAAAHHHHHRRR!

The roar came from just beside Stephanie's window, but she didn't move. Drew instinctively shot the van to the center lane without checking for traffic, and for a second was glad he was the only one awake.

He scanned the tree line, sure he had just heard the roar of the Gougers.

Then Drew saw two beads of yellow burning in the darkness. They were beside him, easily matching the crawling pace of the minivan. Drew tried to floor it, but the engine disagreed, made a loud pop, and a loud rhythmic ticking started under the hood. It sounded like a lifter. Drew hoped it was just an exhaust leak.

OOOOAAAAHHHHHRRRR!

Another howl came from the other side of the road, and Drew looked in its direction. Another twin set of burning yellow eyes locked on his own. Drew felt like screaming, but the face of Tyler sleeping in his rearview mirror stopped him.

Drew's van lurched forward slowly and clicked with an increasing rhythmic intensity. The incline leveled off; Drew prayed this was the top of the divide.

The horizon behind him was graying, but the shadow of the mountains kept the future dark. He plowed forward into the darkness. Now the van was gaining some speed, despite the audible engine issue.

HHHHOOOOOOAAAAARRRRRAAAAOOOO!

The tandem howls of anger from either side of the van blended together in a horrifying duet. Drew tried to encourage the van to go faster, but the winding road was forcing him to apply the brake more than he wanted to. Out the corner of his eye, Drew saw the closer of the scaled beasts lunge at the van.

Drew turned hard to avoid the impact. It shook Stephanie in her sleep. She moaned but stayed sleeping.

The Gouger missed its mark.

Its uneven legs tripped it up on the flat road when Drew avoided the ramming, and it let out another howl as it toppled forward. The beast from the other side of the road stopped for its fallen mate and the sets of yellow eyes disappeared into the blackness in the rearview mirror.

Drew knew he had to make some distance while they collected themselves.

He gripped the slippery wheel and pushed the accelerator, now hitting the turns on the descending road faster than he was comfortable with. The U-Haul was swaying and tipping in his mirror. Drew thought briefly about their belongings being destroyed but continued to speed up. They would just have to buy more stuff.

The sky above him was catching up to the other side of the divide and the darkness was fading, revealing the huge scar in the Earth that split the nation in half. The Divide tore through the landscape as far as he could see in either direction, north or south.

Drew had a glimmer of hope to escape the Gougers as the road straightened out in front of him.

"In five miles, take Exit 114 from Denver on the right."

"CRAP!" Drew yelled and looked to make sure his family didn't hear.

They stayed sleeping.

The stupid GPS computer voice had scared him in the silence and tension.

The alert let him know he was about to exit the highway going over the divide and start heading more northwest again off the main highway. The ticking of the van went back to being the only sound Drew could hear outside of his own heart.

Drew looked in his mirror and from behind him could see four yellow burning eyes in the center of the road. They bobbed in unison. The gray light finally gave Drew a good view of them. They were leaning on each other with their short legs locked together in the middle, putting their stronger, outer legs in control. This doubling up gave them increased speed on the flat road where they normally would topple over. The bouncing eyes grew in the mirror, gaining on them easily now that they were working together.

"Take Exit 114 from Denver on the right in one mile." Drew was waiting for the GPS this time and didn't yell.

Ahead, Drew could see his exit glowing in green. He looked in his mirror again and could see the Gougers just behind him. The beasts took a couple more powerful steps and suddenly, Drew was looking directly at them through his driver window in the slowly increasing daylight.

The four yellow eyes were fixed on him, the greenish yellow scales shining bright even in the weak morning sun. The short dangling legs in the middle were kicking the wind like they were helping to propel the beasts even faster. He could hear the clicking of the clawed hooves on the pavement outside his window. There was an obvious miss in the clicks, maybe from a missing claw. The box of memorabilia rattled behind his seat, the missing claw now just feet from its owner.

Somewhere beside him, the GPS told him to take the exit, and he did.

The Gougers swerved off the main road with him. Drew looked away from the monsters to the road and could see a bridge that spanned the width of a canyon coming up fast.

OOOOAAAAHHHHRRRR!

The Gougers let out an angry howl, sensing the oncoming chokepoint.

Drew held the wheel with no other option but to aim for the center of the bridge, not leaving enough room on either side for the Gougers.

For a moment, the Gougers looked as if they were going to leave the road, but as they reached the oncoming lane, they made a tremendous lunging motion for the minivan. The head closer to him lowered and hit the driver's door of the van hard.

CRASH

HOOOOONNNNKKKKKK

The impact forced Drew to swerve, and as he looked back at the road in front of him, he could see a familiar car headed right at him.

It was dad's Travelall. Coming from the Denver direction.

In his confusion, Drew forgot about the Gougers. He looked into the cab of the Travelall and in the brief instant they approached each other, Drew swore he saw dad and Jo occupying the front seat, with Nick, Jay, and Chris in the back.

They were all laughing and pointing at him.

Their car was coming straight at the minivan.

With no chance to avoid the impact, Drew braced himself. He prayed for an instant that the boys and Stephanie would be ok because they were asleep and limber, like the drunk who always walks away from a fatal DUI crash.

From the other side of the road, there was a massive flash of yellow and green. The Gougers plowed into the side of the Travelall, missing the minivan by just an inch or two. The impact caused the Gougers to stumble, and they hit the guardrail at the start of the bridge hard. Drew locked eyes with them one more time as the hulking weight of their body carried them over the edge of the metal barrier and into the abyss.

They looked sad.

Their short legs pumped the air, their powerful legs kicked the pavement and tried to cling on, but it was too late.

OOOOOAAAAAHHHHRRRRRrrrr…

The roar disappeared into the scar in the Earth.

In shock, Drew looked into his rearview mirror and could see dad's Travelall bouncing into the ditch on his side of the road into the tree line. A cloud of dust exploded from the pines, and a tire bounced into the road, rolling into the ditch on the other side. The Travelall tumbled end over end into the tree line.

The Gougers' anger for Drew had blinded them, and in a moment of hatred had somehow saved his life. Was that really dad's Travelall? Was it really full of monsters?

Drew watched the scene unfold in his mirror while keeping his peripheral vision on the road. He finished crossing the bridge and looked back at the Midwest for the last time.

The divide stretched wide and deep behind him. Drew only hoped the chasm was large enough to hold back the Gougers and all the rest of the Midwest horrors.

***

"Is everything ok? What's that sound?" All the action had finally woken Stephanie.

She looked worried.

Drew shook his head and refocused on the road ahead of him.

"Oh, nothing. Some crazy guy swerved at me on the bridge, but I think he just caught the side of my door with his bumper. It's fine." Drew was too excited to worry about the van or the ticking that Steph was referring to. "Do you want to stop for some breakfast?"

The blue highway sign with a plate, compete with fork and spoon, as well as a pictograph of a gas pump, told him now was a good chance for a pit stop.

"Sure, I'll wake the boys up." Stephanie shook the boys, who then couldn't stop talking about the real mountains behind them.

Drew didn't turn around to look but enjoyed their excitement.

Ten minutes later, they were pulled into a diner. There was a service station that wasn't open yet but a local assured Drew the owner could fix the engine tick and wouldn't charge him an arm and a leg. Stephanie and the boys went into the diner ahead of Drew to claim a table while Drew stretched out his legs.

The van was clicking from heat like the Nova was when he dropped it off for the title swap. At the time, Drew thought it was a bad trade, but the van had made it over the divide and helped him escape from the monsters. In hindsight, he couldn't have been happier. Drew's family had a fresh start and they had the Nova to thank.

Drew examined the door where the Gougers hit them before the bridge. Something caught his eye. It was a greenish-yellow glowing scale stuck in the crease where the door met the frame. Drew picked it out and examined it. It looked like a guitar pick made from an emerald.

The scale made him sad. He thought of the look of terror on the beasts' faces as they plunged over the guard rail.

Was this how Grandpa's story was finally going to end?

He thought about the traps and the adventures in the woods. The fun of being scared. Even the attacks from the Gougers. In some ways, Drew never would have been strong enough to escape the other monsters without building himself up fighting the Gougers. The side mirror on the minivan caught Drew's eye and he was astonished to see a smile plastered on Stickboy's face. It might have been the first time Drew had ever seen him happy. They had won.

Drew thought about the Gougers crashing into his dad's Travelall that he swore was full of monsters looking to kill his family in a head-on crash.

Was it a mistake?

Or had the Gougers saved him and his family on purpose?

Drew wasn't sure and wasn't sure it mattered either way. What he did know now was that he didn't want the Gougers to die like that. He didn't want Grandpa's story to be over. There were still things from the Midwest that Drew loved, that he would always love. Things he wanted to pass on even if they were scary. The Midwest made Drew who he was, and it would always be home. However, he knew he could never visit again because the ruts ran deep.

Drew hefted the Gouger's shiny scale in his hand. His gears were spinning. He had an idea.

He fished around the messy van and found his little locked black box containing the claw and the Polaroid that he took when he was a kid. Drew pulled on the flimsy toy lock, and it popped open easily. Looking in the open box, he saw the claw and the Polaroid of the burning yellow eye for the first time since finding it in his closet in high school. The scale clicked as he dropped it into his collection, his Gouger memorabilia.

***

Drew's gears kept spinning as he joined his family at the table.

The pancakes showed up and Drew watched the boys smile and laugh. They were so excited to start a new life, they weren't even thinking about their old one.

The thought made Drew contemplate further. Some monsters could be fun and without them, you would never learn how to beat the real ones.

Maybe Drew could give people his monsters in a safe, fun way. Maybe he could be an author and keep the monsters stuck in the ultimate chokepoint—the pages of his books—giving enough scary to people to keep them alert, but safe because "it's just a story." Give them enough scary to keep their eyes open for chokepoints, but never let them get choked.

Maybe Drew could use his monsters to build a new life for his family. He would have a job again; one he could do from home while the doctors found a solution to his poisoning. One that could keep people safe.

Drew patted the box of Gouger memorabilia on the bench seat beside him. His gears turned on his first novel. Drew needed to get an opinion on the story he was going to write. He looked across the table at the boys and over at Stephanie with a sly smile on his face.

***

"Hey, did I ever tell you guys the story about the Sidehill Gougers?"

This book is dedicated to the Midwest
I miss you